CARIBBEAN CABAL

HUGH SIMPSON

HAP STONER SERIES, BOOK #2

3Span
Publications

Published by

website: 3spanpublications.com
email: hsimpson@3spanpublications.com

Cover Design: Marianne Nowicki, PremadeEbookCoverShop.com
Interior Design: Nick Zelinger, NZGraphics.com
Editors: Sarah Lovett, Cynde Christie

ISBN: 978-1-949393-04-0 (Paperback)
ISBN: 978-1-949393-03-3 (eBook)
Library of Congress Control Number: 2019907229

First Edition

Printed in the United States of America

In Memory of Lewis Jay Elgin
March 24, 1957 – March 18, 2019
We met in Kindergarten and remained friends.
What a ride. Thanks for being that friend.

A shout out to Captain Charles Berhle USN Retired.
Thanks for keeping this jarhead within the confines
of Navy jargon. Loved the "ARGGGGGGGGGH."

Cast of Characters

Operation Spanish Main: Operation for Hap Stoner
and Will Kellogg to recover
Nazi Gold in Isle de San
Andres City.

Operation Che Guevara: Operation for Nicaragua's
invasion of Isle de San Andres,
Columbia.

Operation Cross Cut: Operation for China and
Nicaragua to build "Panama
Canal" between border of
Costa Rica and Nicaragua.

William Hunter Kellogg:
Co Founder of Vector Data Communications located in
Richardson, TX. Owner of Buccaneer Casino and Resort
in Isle de San Andres, Columbia, Isle de San Andres City.
Former Enlisted Force Recon Marine. Eight years Central
Intelligence Agency (CIA). Several separate contracts
working with Defense Intelligence Agency. (DIA). Physical
stature of a 40-year-old though his face is rough around
the edges.

Hap Stoner "Kang":
CoFounder of Vector Data Communications: Chairman,
CEO, and President. Former Marine Corps Aviator. Asked
to resign due to leading the rescue of LtCol Chuck Warden
in unauthorized mission.

Richard Dewayne Garbaccio:
Born in Auschwitz. Father was shoeshine boy for SS
Colonel Hans Krueger, Auschwitz Camp Commandant

during WWII. Former Mossad agent. After his Father passed away, he continued his Father's work as a Nazi Hunter. Krueger had shown to be illusive.

Thomas Lindblad Lefler "Blad":
Retired Marine Officer. Aviator though specialized/passion was in Intelligence. Tall, maintains crew cut with widows peak. Founder of Shadow Services with Global Reach Intelligence Network.

Rodney Reimnitz "The Roach":
Former Marine Aviator. Expert in running Operations for Training Exercise or for Combat. Became bored with the profession and became successful arms dealer. National Champ wrestler in College. Called the Roach due to not having a neck. Not an ounce of politics in his physical make up. Put up or shut mentality.

Ground Element

Eddie Barlosa "Black Eddie":
Retired Army Ranger/Explosive EOD expert. Electrician by trade in civilian life. Small arms expert. Father immigrated from Cuba.

Shaun:
Friends with Hap from Marine Officers Candidate School and Officer Basic School. Infantry Officer. Thin build. Expert in small arms and tactics. Left Marine Corps to join Drug Enforcement Agency (DEA)..

K B Hill:
Former Marine Sniper. Civilian life is IT/Communications Specialist. Short in stature, slight build. Wears round, wire rimmed glasses.

Doc Perry (Ships Surgeon):
Surgeon, former Navy Seal. Upon leaving Navy entered medical school. Short, receding hairline maintained by chemistry. Kindergarten buddy of H.D. Simmons. Grew tired of orthopedic practice and the pressure Obama Care was putting on doctors.

Doc Bennie Schragel (Combat Medic):
Son of a German brick layer and built like one as well. Aspired to be proctologist but settled to be Army Special Forces combat medic. Entered civilian life and became male nurse. Full crop of combed over hair and fists like hammers.

Note: Both surgeons and medics are referred to as Doc in the military.

Leroy:
Came up in the Merchant Marine from the ground up. Graduated with Mechanical Engineering Degree from Texas A&M. Wears hair in a mullet. Tatted, heavy smoker, drinker, and womanizer. Big Lew looks past short falls due to Leroy being the best Chief Engineer in the Gulf.

Lewis Eglin "Big Lew":
Adopted. Real father west coast lumber jack. Lew got all his dad's genes and red hair. Owner/Operator of Lonibelle and Stingray. Both vessels are oilrig resupply boats harbored in Galveston, TX. Not uncommon to see Big Lew moving about in overalls with no undershirt. Bad businessman. Great sailor.

Bruce Larson "Machine Head":
Former Navy officer. Full blooded Native American. The captain of Stingray wears captain hat tilted like John Wayne. Loves muscle cars hence the nick name. Jet black close cropped hair.

Joshua Simmons "JMan":
Son of Major Harold Simmons. Became lost after father killed while serving in Iraq. Dropped out of college and joined Merchant Marine as a cook. Blue eyed, tall, long blonde hair past shoulder, and beard. Should be a male model.

Aviation Element

"Big Alabama" "Beaver":
Marine Corp Aviator dismissed after participating in rescue of LtCol Chuck Warden. Round build. Rosy round face. Full head of brown hair. Works as simulator instructor. Lives for a good fight. Talks with a Alabama drawl. Flys hard, plays hard. Loves girls and lives for Officer's Club happy hours.

"Schlonger":
Former Marine Corps Aviator dismissed after participating in rescue of LtCol Chuck Warden. Built like a Roman gladiator with an attitude to match. Close cropped haircut with large roman nose. Math teacher when he got the call to join team.

"Hollywood":
Vector Data Corporate attorney. Marine Corp Aviator dismissed after participating in rescue of LtCol Chuck Warden. Lives for the fight..... "death from above."

Terrence LD Hicks "LD":
Marine Corp Aviator dismissed after participating in rescue of LtCol Chuck Warden. General contractor in civilian life primarily in Galveston, TX. Soft spoken but carries a big stick. Hap could always count on LD in combat.

"Killer Koch":
Marine Corp Aviator dismissed after participating in rescue of LtCol Chuck Warden. Basketball coach at Jesuit High

School as a civilian. Teaches health. Soft spoken but never go to a fight without him. Steady/Dependable

"Sluggo":
Wall Street guy. Former Squadron Mate with Roach. Rugby is his hobby. Forearms like Popeye. Speaks slow with Boston accent.

Greg "Foxie" Fox:
Former Marine Corps Master Sergeant honorably discharged after participating in the rescue of LtCol Chuck Warden. Seasoned and first rate soldier who is good friends with Greg Fox.

Spanish Main Holdings

Franz von Bock (The Baron):
Founder and Chairman of Spanish Main Holdings, global business conglomerate. Known on the Isle de San Andres as the "Baron." Involved in secret, oversees a global intelligence network. Though not publicized, he could be the richest man in the world.

Colonel Hans Krueger "Hans Guderian":
Older brother to Franz. Former commandant at Auschwitz. Picked out little Rich Garbaccio's father prior to entering gas chamber to become his shoe shiner. Shorter than Franz but stockier build and he received the better looks over his twin brother. Takes the name of Hans Guderian. Assisted his brother in building Spanish Main holdings. Brought out of Germany by U-Boat prior to end of Germany's surrender in WWII.

Captain Wilhelm Raus:
Son of a son of a German Submariner. Entire life has been in and around submarines. Served in German Kriegsmarine and Captained the submarine that brought Franz's brother to Isle de San Andres just before wars end.

Operation Che Guevara

Daniel Ortega:
President of Nicaragua. Leader of Sandinista movement in late 70's in overthrow of Somoza. Has always aspired to rule Latin America. Aligned with Russia and China for military and economic support. Aspires to operate Canal connecting Caribbean to Pacific cut through Nicaragua's southern border. Chinese requires Nicaragua Treasury to come up with $20 Billion US dollars to get project started.

General Hallesleven:
Commander of all Nicaraguan Armed Forces and commander for Che Guerra. Loyal to the president to a fault, more so than the country of Nicaragua.

Colonel Santiago:
32 years old / Born in village on western Mosquito Coast/December 3, 1972/Nueva Guinea. Hallesleven's Chief of Staff. Orphaned at 10 years old after troops under Hallesleven command executed his family. Taken in by General Hallesleven. Attended military schools in Cuba.

August – 1940
Caribbean

Off the coast of Venezuela, Germany's finest toiled to tether the shark-like submersible to the Dutch-registered vessel with the dark letters S T R A A T M A L A A K A painted wide across her stern. Side by side the Kriegsmarine sailors arched their backs to pull the slack out of the heaving lines tossed down from the German auxiliary cruiser until one of the shadowy figures could wrap a cleat hitch knot to the submersible's cleats. The catalyst behind the swells gliding below both hulls churned inside a low-pressure system holding Caracas in its bullseye.

For two weeks the undersea marauder had surfaced and submerged, disgorging crates from its torpedo rooms located in its bow and stern.

Laid by Krupp shipyards years earlier, both keels would be used to locate and destroy Allied shipping. While British Men of War prowled the oceans to locate and exterminate German surface and subsurface combatants, both Captains' orders were based on "avoidance and secrecy."

Tonight, U-56 would trade its cargo for the long cigar-shaped weapon that earned the undersea boat the moniker, Neptune's Assassin.

* * *

Alone atop a 40-foot mast, the bos'n's mate 3rd class stood relaxed, halfway through a two-hour watch. It was dark, the Caribbean air gentle as he scanned across a darkened horizon. Fantasies swirled around his head about onshore leave, cold beer, and affordable women. The Straat Malaaka's well-seasoned crew knew that they would not see their Fatherland, Germany anytime soon. As the crew had never laid eyes on their destination, Master Chief Kiser continued with white lies to verify erotic stories bantered around the galley to maintain morale.

Thoughts of the virtues of shore leave vanished the moment a dot of light appeared in the distance. He slowly raised a pair of handheld observation binoculars to just below his eyes. Cocking his head to the side he was able to get a fix on the unidentified target. Within seconds, the binos fell around his neck and he reached down to flip up the voice tube cover. His head dropped and the binos clanged off the tube as both hands cupped the voice tube opening.

"Contact off the starboard bow!"

* * *

Captain Muller peered over his wire-rimmed glasses, frowning as he watched Baron von Ribbentrop, the head of Nazi subversion in the Americas, waddle past the bridge's voice tube. Short as he was pudgy, the hem of his black leather coat brushed the deck as he moved. He wore the collar flipped up to hide his creased marshmallow neck. After pushing away from the submarine, the merchant raider remained invisible plowing through the foul weather observing strict radio silence—suppressing the ship's identification motifs. Muller also knew that allied patrol craft in these waters flew without radar capability.

With each pass, the pudgy man's shuffle added to the Captain's irritation. Muller moved from the table leaving the # 2 pencil twirling atop the chart for the Archipelago Isle de San Andres.

Von Ribbentrop immediately lit a cigarette and moved to occupy the space the Captain had just vacated. He adjusted his monocle and leaned over the table, rapidly scanning the chart. Patience was not a virture of Muller and this little waste of humanity stepped beside him to stare into a dark abyss as a shadow loomed in the distance.

Watching Ribbentrop stand with an unfiltered cigarette dangling down between thick lips, Muller knew that the recent flash of blindness created from the Zippo lighter would leave the agent's night vision useless for several seconds.

Darkness hid the irritation fixed to the Captain's angular face. "Helm… all stop."

The 18-year-old, baby-faced boy from Hamburg cycled the engine order telegraph (E.O.T.) lever up and firmly down to the stop position. "All stop, Capitan." Below decks, a bell on the telegraph rang in the engine room and its pointer fell to the stop position. Engineers in the engine room responded to the bell and moved their handle to the same position to acknowledge the order. Vibrations below the feet of the crew came to a stop.

The Baron's head turned, "What is this?" he asked mockingly.

Built like a Ruhr steelworker, Muller considered the Baron's lips moving projected only noise not worth a response. Muller had already turned to speak to his executive officer pointing towards the faint outline of a volcanic land mass.

Dormant for 2000 years, it ascended out of the water 554 feet, topographically dominating the Archipelago's main island. The Exec's head turned to Muller. "Message sent Captain. Shore party responded with the prearranged signal." "Ahead one third," the Captain said softly. The responsibility of $7.5 billion in gold bullion "American" rested squarely on his shoulders until the Baron's head agent in charge on the island took custody. In an attempt to demonstrate his importance to everyone in the stateroom busily downing bottles of schnapps, the Baron said Vichy gold would be used to ship American diesel FOB Mexico to German-held ports in France and North Africa. As the Straat Malaaka churned towards Isle de San Andres, Captain Muller made a mental note to put the crew in for a naval award. Long overdue, since Straat Malaaka sailed from Hamburg eight months earlier, their endeavors had furthered the Reich's cause in the great tradition of Germany's naval service. Now it was time to offload the king's ransom and reenter the fight.

2

Present day
Stoner Residence, Richardson, TX

The close-shaven face in the mirror, just a foot away from Hap Stoner's baby blues, reflected confidence even though the ink on his discharge papers from the Marine Corps Reserve hadn't yet dried. No misgivings, no second thoughts for leading an unauthorized mission into Mexico to rescue HMLA 767's Commanding Officer, LtCol Chuck Warden. Spiritually on sound footing, LtCol Hap Stoner was honorably discharged from the Marine Corps but remained Chairman and CEO of Vector Data Communications, co-founded with Will Kellogg six years earlier. Hap was steadfast. A life already lived couldn't change, and actions taken based *on doing the right thing* eases concerns about the consequential validity of his actions. But the man looking him in the eyes had to live with the unattended consequences any leader faces, which cost friends and Marines horrendous wounds and in some instances, their lives.

Even if it were possible, standing in his master bath, there was not much Hap and the man in the mirror would change.

Life had been good. He eyed his bullet wounds—pushed his index finger against the scar on his belly. It still made him cringe.

Maybe time to change one or two things—one high, one low, he thought.

Still, Hap couldn't ignore another feeling that had begun to show itself over the past week—a restlessness, a question that was prowling internally. *God, how I loved flying towards the sound of the guns. How soon will I do it again?*

"Hey, Hap." Carla's voice saved him from confronting the answer. Moving from the bedroom sitting area to the master bath, she eased in behind him, wrapping her arms around his tapered waist, and her smile grew wider the tighter her squeeze. Carla, beautiful without a speck of makeup and with a towel wrapped around her hair, joined the man staring himself down in the mirror. She tipped her head, eyeing his reflection. "Hmmm, you've got that look."

He eased her even closer to him. "Don't know what you're talking about. I'm happy as a pig in poop."

"Yeah, you do. It's your 'g'tting' antsy and kick some butt' look."

Hap said nothing. He reached around and grabbed a handful of green tee shirt dangling over her sexy posterior.

She looked up into his blue eyes. "If you were in the U.S. Congress, I would slap you into next week." She reached for his other hand and placed it on her other butt cheek.

Damn, she could read him better than he could read himself, he thought, working to keep his expression flat. But he liked the way she was thinking.

Carla nodded and her smile was wistful. "Yep, I do know you, Hap."

Hap turned and nuzzled her in close. "Enough with the spooky mind reading, you smell good."

"Among other things," she purred in his ear. "Have I ever told you that I love you, Mister?"

She was wearing one of his tee shirts and nothing else, and her body felt warm to the touch. Her pheromone signals hadn't changed since the first evening at the Marine Corps Birthday Ball. Both had gone home with their dates, but after one text exchange, a Southwest Airlines romance officially launched. Hap sealed the deal with a bouquet of roses delivered to her office. Depending upon who told the story, it changed when it came to which of them had sent the first text.

He bent down to give her a peck on the forehead. "You don't know how much that text you sent after the ball got us together."

Without hesitation, she pulled back and the towel coiled around her hair fell to the green slate floor. She shook her flowing mane to her shoulders and issued Hap that *Say whaaaaa?* look.

Hap gave her rear end another pat. "You know you're going to wear these 'Old Corps' shirts out and there ain't going to be any more Stoner originals."

She offered him a coy smile. "Then I will just wear your white ones." She wrapped her arms around his neck to pull him down for a long kiss. Pulling away, she held his hand and led him toward the bedroom. "You can be late this morning, Mister."

Just as they hit the mattress, Merle Haggard belted, "You're Walkin' on the Fightin' Side of Me," interrupting the moment and Carla's focus.

"Darn you, Hap," Carla moaned, "you can turn off your office sometimes."

But Hap was already rolling toward his side-table where he'd tucked his phone in the drawer. "Can't ignore Vector

Data, Baby. I still have to make payroll for 350 hard chargers, and you and I have bills to pay."

Carla stretched out on the bed with hands behind her head, showing Hap what he'd be missing. "You sure?"

Hap blinked, forcing his mind to the subject of work. "You know we've got nosey Feds and regulatory bozos coming at us from all sides while we're trying to negotiate the contract." He pressed *Talk,* and then growled, "Stoner."

"Hap, Hollywood. Sorry to bother you, but we got a couple of situations at the office and Morgan Stanley has asked to move up the meeting." As Hap heard his old friend and Vector's corporate attorney give a quick summary, his smile turned to a determined grimace, and he rolled off the bed and pulled on his Levis.

Carla, familiar with her lover's "out of my way" look, stayed on the bed, tucking a sheet under her arms. As he leaned down to give her a peck, she murmured, "Do what you do best Hap…you don't need the Marines."

* * *

Hap backed his Yellow 68 Impala SS with the black convertible top-down; out of his 125-foot driveway so fast he changed the part in his close-cropped hair. He figured that if he ever missed his aim, he'd just end up temporarily trespassing in the still-vacant lot opposite his 1.5-acre home on Ridgeview Drive.

Now that he was out of the Marine Corps, silently forced to resign, he would concentrate his efforts on getting the best price for the company. It was time to cash out of Vector Data and use a portion of the proceeds to purchase a cash strapped

Inventory Control company. Between tours of duty in both Iraq and Afghanistan, the Marine Reserve consumed 75 days of Hap's year. While friends and business associates questioned why he hadn't left the Marines years earlier, they didn't understand the balance life on the edge gave him. Hap had serious doubts about how life as an executive without the Marines would turn out.

Slipping the power glide shift to drive, he settled into navigation mode—making the usual four-and-a-half minute drive to his private entrance at Vector Data Communications in three minutes flat.

Striding through ground floor reception, Hap spun around when someone bumped him from behind. He had just enough time to catch a stack of files that Maxine, manager of accounts payable, failed to keep in hand.

"Oh, thank you, Mr. Stoner." She flashed her wide smile, showing off ruby lipstick and perfectly coifed hair that curled to her shoulders.

"No problem, Max," he said, already turning toward the elevators.

"Oh!" Maxine held out a file. "I was told you needed the report for an upcoming phone meeting. Mr. Williams included the accounts receivable. I was on my way to deliver it to Peggy."

"Thanks, I'll save you the trip." With a smile, Hap took the binder prepared by Chuck Hardage, Vector Data's CFO.

He watched as Maxine took two steps and stopped at the position of attention. She conducted an about-face that would make her father, a former Marine Drill Sergeant, proud. "Peggy and I go to lunch often and she has been silent about your situation. But the incident along the border was all over cable and Dallas Morning News. Are you okay?"

Hap offered a soft smile. "It was something that had to be done."

"Mr. Stoner," Maxine said, deep concern altering her expression, "what you and your friends did... well, it leaves me speechless." She stepped up and issued a light kiss to his cheek. "We are proud of you, Sir." And with that, she turned and vanished around the corner in the direction of the accounting department.

Good kid, Hap thought, stepping into the executive elevator. He pressed six for the short ride to the executive suites in full anticipation of discussions with Morgan Stanley's Mergers & Acquisition (M&A) Group. They would originate the conference call from their offices out of the Big Apple.

But Maxine's reference to the border incident nudged the restlessness he worked to keep buried. John "Hollywood" Hancock, Vector Data's Corporate Attorney, had stayed busy those eight weeks while Hap surrendered to rest and recuperation under Carla's supervision. She made one hell of a nurse while his injuries laid him low at his ranch, tucked away at the Guadalupe River's headwaters. Too many reporters around Richardson attempting to grab a story, they had literally camped in front of his home the hour after the story broke. He allowed Hollywood to field questions or shout "No Comment!" on his behalf.

Hap shook off the memories as he marched out of the elevators and into his executive suite reception area. He rounded the open door only to come face to face with Peg's dark eyes, wide smile, and flowing dark hair. Hap's attractive thirty-six-year-old executive secretary, as usual, was dressed to the nines. He would have taken her on deployments to keep him organized with the Marines if the Corps had allowed it. Besides, she was a hell of a lot better to look at than old Gunny Milligan.

She cocked her head, her eyes focused on his cheek. "Started early, have you? Fox Business wants an interview as well as the Communist News Network."

Hap touched the spot where Maxine had gently pressed her bright red lips.

Eyes narrowed, Peg stroked the mark with the thumb and forefinger of one hand. She tapped both his cheeks. "I have to stay one step ahead of Maxine."

Hap's light brown eyebrows arched to the ceiling.

"Now you're presentable, Hap Stoner. I'll bring your coffee as soon as I get back from the restroom. John's in the conference room." She nodded her head toward his office door. "You have three FBI agents waiting."

He shrugged, stepped off into the office only to stop just inside his door at the sound of her voice. He leaned back far enough to go eyeball to eyeball.

She nodded pointedly. "Do you want John with you for this meeting?"

Hap shook his head, and then winked. "This meeting will be brief."

As he entered his office, the agents slowly rose out of their seats.

"Special Agent Jim Gordon, FBI," the older agent said clasping Hap's hand while palming off his business card. Gordon didn't introduce the two younger agents. Hap's six-foot-two-inch frame towered over Gordon as he reached out and introduced himself to both of the younger agents, judging them to be in their late twenties. The oldest of the three—a thirty-something-year-old man with dark, slicked-back hair—carried a larger waist than his shoulders. Even with his unfortunate build, Hap knew instantly that the Fed took himself too seriously.

"So we meet again, Agent Gordon. What gives me the pleasure?" Hap asked, reflecting on their meeting in his El Centro office after Chuck Gordon's disappearance. Hap gestured for all three to sit and then pointed to their half-full cups of coffee. "Refills?"

They all declined, three heads shaking in unison.

"I hope this meeting is not an inconvenience," Agent Gordon said, a notepad resting on his knee.

Hap grinned. "It is gents, but you are here. Hell, I was wondering why I was the last. My peers in the industry told me your team was making the rounds."

"We've been busy," Gordon replied.

"Can I be blunt, Agent Gordon?" The Agent nodded. His clean shaven face showed no emotion. Hap looked at all three agents in turn. "Nothing personal gents, but knowing why you're here is like a burr in my saddle. It makes me angry. From a professional standpoint, your mission is a bunch of crap."

Hap's demeanor and candor surprised the younger agents, compelling them to shift awkwardly in their seats. He watched their eyes cut to the Marine Corp memorabilia hanging on the walls. Agent Gordon sat up in his chair.

"I was a twenty-six-year-old captain once," Hap said, forcing himself to keep his tone level. "Like you I was immortal; given a mission, only God could help the man who attempted to thwart me. I would complete my mission, come hell, or high water. I know what you had to go through to become a part of the FBI, and I hope you are no different." Hap's gaze was not as harsh as his blue eyes moved to each of the agents. "That said, the bureau is being played. If you were sitting in my chair, knowing what I know, you would be very angry too."

Agent Gordon's head turned slightly to the side—a gesture Hap read as unease and flagging confidence. The agent was used to his role as Alpha dog, but Hap was refusing to defer.

"Maybe so, Mr. Stoner, but we do have a few questions we want answered."

Hap stretched back in his leather executive chair. He rested his elbows on the arms of his chair and touched his fingertips together beneath his chin. "Agent Gordon, you and your team are unknowingly working for the benefit of a telecommunications company that is attempting to save $4.5 billion on an acquisition. The Attorney General who asked the bureau for assistance is lining his pockets with the help of the suitor."

Gordon rolled his eyes.

Hap caught the Agent's attitude and transferred his elbows to the desk as his chair let out a squeak. "Know what's funny, Gordon?" Hap asked stopping midsentence as Gordon's facial muscles relaxed as if saying 'what now?'.

Gordon smiled looking past Hap. "You were saying, Mr. Stoner?"

Hap bit into his lower lip but didn't taste blood. "I'm about to jump on a conference call with a Mergers and Acquisitions group representing a bank who speaks for the Company that is in the AG's back pocket."

The younger, red-haired, freckle-faced agent seated on Gordon's right said, "Will you answer our questions?"

Hap stayed silent for a few seconds and then said, "Because I know why you're here, I'd like you to deliver my parting words to your boss. Tell him to visit with the FCC. An AG with an agenda even Ray Charles could see is guiding your boss. You ask questions of friends of mine, questions related to regulatory matters—but then you spin that line of questioning into possible criminal behavior. I expect nothing less from the prick AG." Hap rose suddenly from his chair, pointing at Agent Gordon's dark eyes. "You, Sir, scare me, because of your naiveté."

Hap punched his intercom and Peg's voice instantly rang out, "Yes, Hap."

"Our guests are leaving now. Will you see them out?"

"I will be glad to."

Hap walked out from behind his desk. When he clasped Gordon's hand, the agent maintained a firm grip for a soft man.

"We haven't begun the interview," Gordon said, as a statement, not a question.

Smiling politely, but far from genuinely, Hap said, "Of course, Agent Gordon."

Peg stepped into Hap's office, her smile lighting up the room. "Gentlemen, if you will follow me."

Turning to the attractive woman, Gordon looked back and said, "Thank you for your time, Mr. Stoner." He looked over toward the other agents, gesturing with his head to the open door.

Peg stood at the door as the agents filed by. Looking back, she motioned, a silent question—*want the door closed?*

Shaking his head, he swung around in the chair so his back was to the door, flipping the FBI agent's business card in the circular trashcan.

Hap heard her enter the office and shuffle items on the coffee bar. "What do you want me to tell the networks regarding their interviews?"

Hap chuckled. "Thanks Peg, you are the lady. Tell the sharpshooters from the networks we appreciate the opportunity but are not available. Better yet, route them to Hollywood's voicemail. I'll be damned if I'm going to give them a target. Besides, I have better things to do."

"I'll pass your message to the networks. John has more important things on his plate. The lawyers from Morgan Stanley should be on the conference bridge within the hour and Hap, Lucianna called from the casino offices to say we should expect a call in the next few hours."

"Expected the call two days ago after Will emailed me and said he wanted to talk."

She gave one nod of her head for emphasis and then she turned into the hall.

* * *

Will Kellogg had been part of the unauthorized mission across the border into Mexico. He'd answered Hap's call for backup and, for his trouble; he'd taken a bullet off the side of his head in a shootout with some very bad guys on the rooftop of a posh seaside resort. So yeah, the Co-founder of Vector Data call would take precedence over pretty much anything.

Hap rounded the corner to the conference room to find Hollywood's legs crossed, head down, perusing an open folder. Another folder extended from the one Hollywood was reading. Hollywood peered over reading glasses perched on his pronounced nose. "What in the hell took you so long?"

Hap glanced at the coffee bar and didn't see his coffee mug. Settling into his chair, he placed the report from Vector Data's CFO on the conference table. "You see any issues on today's call?"

John nodded slowly while a grin snuck out from the corner of his narrow lips. He placed the unopened file folder next to his half-filled coffee cup and an unopened can of orange juice and slid it across the marble to Hap.

Before Hollywood said another word, Peg cocked her head around the open door, touching her index finger to her mouth as if to say, "Shhhhhhh, Hap."

The aroma filled Hap's nostrils before the cup landed on the conference table next to his CFO's folder given to him by Maxine. Peg presented a pouting lip as she turned the mug so the embossed camel dangling a cigarette from its lips faced him. As an old baseball player, Hap had superstitions, and one of those was beginning each morning going eye-to-eye with the cigarette-smoking camel.

She glanced over to John as if asking "Does your cup need to be freshened?"

John shook his head and smiled. "No thanks Peg, but thank you for asking."

As she filled a glass with ice from the bar, she issued a look to both of them, gesturing with her head to the door. *Open or closed?*

Hap leaned back savoring the aroma of his brew, while Hollywood responded with an abrupt, "Closed."

Her eyebrows arched but she said nothing and gently closed the door on the way out.

Hap reacted with a slight recoil—lucky he didn't decorate the red, white, and blue tie and a starched white shirt to wear with his Levi's and boots Carla had laid out for him with his coffee.

The two executives eyed each other until Hap started the conversation. "Are the Morgan Stanley clients serious?"

"You tell me." John slid the file across the folder he had put on the coffee table earlier. It spun a half turn before stopping in front of Hap. He set the mug to the side and eased back in his chair to read. His eyes widened as they cut across the document over the words "Binding Letter of Intent," $25 million breakup fee, and "offer price of $550 million." So, if the company doesn't bury Vector Data using the Feds, they intend to buy us out?"

Hollywood said nothing.

Hap shook his head wishing he had received board approval to execute the instrument. "How long have you had this?"

"Sunday." Hollywood stood and stepped up to the bar. Seconds passed in silence except for the sound of ice dropping into his glass. "It was in my email when I came to the office yesterday. Need anything from here?"

"Does Will know about this?"

"Not the specifics," John said returning to his chair. "Check out the contents in this memo." He slid the paper across the table.

Hap traded the folder with the binding letter of intent for the paper. He laid it open across his lap and almost spit a mouthful of coffee across the tabletop. "Well, no shit," Hap said as his eyes went back and forth across the document. He looked over the open folder to Hollywood. "And to think all I had to do is buy a few next-generation switches from Vijay Adani of Far East Industries." Vijay ran Far East Industries' U.S. affiliate. "Crap doesn't work but what the hell, it would only cost Vector Data seven and a half million." He stared at Hollywood without a hint of emotion splayed across his face.

Hollywood shook his head slowly. "I would have hoped you had me in when you visited with the FBI."

Hap chuckled. "Over before it started, and Peg escorted them out of the office."

"So how much is this going to cost the shareholders?" Hollywood asked.

Hap sent the paper spiraling into the air. Miraculously, the letter size document auto-rotated safely onto the table.

Hollywood stared at the document. "The Board is on a head-hunting mission and now the FBI visits your office."

The silence that followed between the two warriors was deafening. Hap had seen the look on Hollywood's face before— on a lazy Afghanistan afternoon when Hollywood's copilot almost bled out strapped into the front cockpit.

Hollywood didn't blink. Crickets followed. "Somebody is trying to get into your pockets, Hap."

Hap pursed his lips. The Justice Department's memo questioning the deal was one thing, but Agent Gordon, who had visited his office already on another matter, was the agent in charge of the investigation.

"Did you see who was cc'd at the bottom of the memo?"

Intrigued, Hap reached for the folder. There it was. On the bottom left-hand corner, the sons of bitches cc'd the Morgan Stanley M&A team. Hap said nothing.

"You might try Blad to see if his ear is to the ground." Hollywood sat, stiff as a statue. "I do know that once again, Hap Stoner has found his way into the middle of a shit sandwich. You should have placed the P.O. for switches from Adani, you dumb fuck."

But Hap was no longer listening to Hollywood; he was watching Peg as her head appeared around the edge of the just-opened door. "The lawyers for Morgan Stanley are on the conference bridge and yes, they called early." She shook her head, looking oddly confused.

"Peg?" Hap prompted quietly.

"And Will called and said to interrupt you no matter what—"

"Put him through," Hap ordered, sitting up sharply.

"But that's just it, he only stayed on the line for a minute, and he left you this message and said to deliver it word for word. She took a breath and read from the sticky note in her hand. "Gotta call in a marker, Colonel. Danger Close."

Isle de San Andres,
Columbia Buccaneer Casino and Resort 10 days earlier

William Hunter Kellogg slumped over his desk, his brain stumbling over the previous business day's revenue report. Line one, slightly above average day on the slots. Gaming tables were in the red, same with hospitality, food, and beverage on lines three and four. A quick glance at the tourist population over the weekend was 4% higher than the previous weekend and 6% from the previous year. Line five, catering services for two weddings, the newlyweds traveled from Paris and Calais respectively. Not too bad a day so far.

Today was Hawaiian shirt day, anything to cheer him up after the results from a shitty previous business day. Will's face went numb the moment his eyes touched the number inserted on line 29. Under the liability section, it was monies in the Casino's trust account in care of Franz von Bock, founder of the von Bock business empire. The Clint Eastwood-looking fella's account swelled by another $450,000 on yesterday's book. Will's bushy brows furrowed at the number on the far end of the ledger with parentheses ($13,500,000).

Strange fact about Franz von Bock: on down days he wrote a check to the cage cashier instead of drawing on his plentiful credit. Unfortunately for the Buccaneer, down days were few and far between.

With glasses perched precariously against the small knot at the end of his nose, Will stared at the line item due the day von Bock woke up and called in his marker. When that day came, for Will Kellogg, the Buccaneer venture would become a truly expensive hobby. He drained the last of the Kaopectate bottle he'd been nursing all morning.

He allowed his glasses to drop on the open hardback binder and rotated his chair to gaze out tinted windows overlooking Isle de San Andres Bay. A freighter from VB Freight & Forwarding crawled slowly against the tide toward tugboats waiting to guide the vessel into the company's docks.

Running a hand gingerly through his thinning brown hair he was careful to avoid the scar left by a Kalashnikov at Los Americanos Resort, *I'm 62*, he reminded himself often, and building and operating the Buccaneer had long been the dream. He wanted that dream of building a successful casino enterprise to continue.

Like any business, the Buccaneer had seen more than its share of speed bumps. Canadians constituted 35% of his revenues and their itinerary took them to either Panama City or Bogota to connect with a shuttle to Isle de San Andres.

Months earlier, a Panamanian shuttle midway to Isle de San Andres exploded over water, killing all on board the ship. The Sandinista government took advantage by starting a considerable advertising campaign to reroute the business to the four- and five-star casinos operating in Nicaragua. Most of the Europeans vacation on their side of the Hemisphere. Until the fear of their plane blowing up in the sky faded, the majority of the Buccaneer's business originated from the two cruise liners that continued to dock in San Andres Bay twice a week for 24 short hours.

Weeks later, network news briefly carried a story of two Nicaraguan government officials who mysteriously died next to their prostitutes in Managua brothels two weeks apart. Rumor had it the men were responsible for giving the order to blow the shuttle—probably part of a cover-up by Managua's government.

A flash from ignited gunpowder sparked from across the bay. Will didn't have to check the time. Discharged from a single 18th-century cannon atop the old Spanish fortress ramparts, the cannon spit flames every morning at 0830.

Six months earlier during a private Texas hold'em card game, Will had asked Franz about the daily ritual. The German casually laid down a full house while explaining that the cannons' bark guided ghost ships and spirits manning them into the bay to rest, and they would continue their eternal journey at their own leisure.

Just as calmly, the business magnate then raked in the $1.3 million dollar pot, of which $550,000 had belonged to Will.

A funny thing happened later at the cage that night. The lady behind the bulletproof glass window issued the half a million owed to Franz for his night's winnings. Nobody's fool, Will knew to keep his mouth shut when he heard the German businessman slide the check back inside the cage and walk away.

His Secretary's voice via intercom interrupted his musings. "Sir, Mr. Ortega is here to see you."

Will replied casually without turning to the phone, "Lucianna, I'm considering sailing around the world. You available to keep me organized?"

"You're thirty years too late, Sir." Thanks to her lifetime of smoking, her voice grated like a garden rake dragged over concrete. "I'll send in Mr. Ortega."

Will initialed the corner of the ledger before gently tossing the bearer of bad news into the out-basket.

He heard Daniel Ortega's cousin before he saw him, "Ramie Ortega, how have you been?" Will rose slowly from his chair and sighed. Ramie Ortega's posture hunched so severly; his head entered the room before his shoulders.

Walking over to greet him, he wrapped one arm around Ramie's shoulders and guided him toward the desk.

"You look well, my friend," Will lied.

The old man said nothing, and his fragile body struggled with each step, his breath shallow. Even with Will's assistance, he moved slowly. Ravaged by cancer, his skeletal frame looked terribly diminished. The banker had shrunk four inches since Will had seen him last, five months earlier.

Will eased his old friend into one of the two high-backed chairs in front of his desk. He couldn't help but notice the new LA Dodger cap adorning Ramie's bald scalp. "Didn't know you were a fan."

Ramie fumbled with a crumpled pack of Camels. "I'm not." It was a struggle for him to work the American-made Zippo lighter. After several attempts, he finally inhaled deeply.

Will fingered his keyboard to pull up the email Ramie had sent earlier in the week. "Reading your email didn't lift my spirits."

"If you read a little bit further, Will, you know that the 50 million dollar credit facility you're seeking does not bode well with the bank's board, at least not under current terms. One of the reasons I'm here today is to do you the courtesy of informing you of their decision face-to-face."

Will didn't give the sick man time to cough. "I can't pass gas right now Ramie, and you and your fucking board know this." He leaned back, arms crossed as his face showed disgust. "You could have used the phone to tell me that and saved your body wear and tear."

The old Panamanian cupped a wobbly hand below the smoldering cigarettes ash. "Will, I remember the first hundred grand you deposited in my bank in '83. I also remember wiring funds to an unmarked Swiss bank account when you bought a piece of jungle in Costa Rica in 1990."

Will followed the banker's weary eyes as they fixed on his ashtray, currently stuffed with three Cuban stubs and ashes covering the Buccaneer's emblem. Will carefully emptied the crystal vessel into the trashcan by his desk, and then he stood and placed the ashtray on the small table next to Ramie.

Ramie carefully flicked the growing line of ash into the ashtray and puffed gently. "The board would like to know if you will sign over your Vector Data stock?"

Without missing a beat Will said, "Fuck you and your board Ramie. Though private, you know my stake is worth close to a hundred million on a bad day."

The Panamanian pointed at the new crease on the side of Will's head. "New haircut or did somebody almost take your scalp? Read about the incident in the papers and every cable news network carried the story."

"A kiss of fate, old man," Will responded with a sudden burst of energy. "As I understand, the son of a bitch that pulled the trigger was dead before my head hit the concrete."

"You were always one for a good fight Will, and a hard man to kill." Ramie Ortega's gaze dropped to the ashtray but he lit a fresh cigarette before he snuffed out the butt of his dying smoke. He shifted in his chair, meeting Will's eyes now. "That brings me to the other reason why I'm here. So, before you rip my head off and shit down my neck, I've got a story to tell you."

Will nodded slowly wearing his best poker face. "Get on with it or get out of my office, you frigging pirate."

Ramie slowly raised a hand, choking through a spasm of deep coughs that continued for several seconds. "Better," he said finally. "Prior to America's entry into World War II, my father was working with a Swiss colleague who was handling business transactions between the Nazis and one of the American Oil Companies. The name of the oil company is not important, but the Nazis established a credit facility through a bank in Geneva. As you well know, Banco De Panama always maintains a secure position."

Will rolled his eyes. "No shit, Ramie. Tell me something I don't know?"

Ramie chuckled and another coughing spell flared up then passed within seconds. "The Germans always paid and when money was involved my father never asked questions."

Will nodded. "I haven't thrown your ass through my nice window, so keep talking." He knew of the banker ties to the Nicaraguan President and outside of a banking transaction, would never trust him.

Ramie slowly shook his head as he manipulated his mouth to expel smoke rings into the air. "Mi padre always said the initial transactions came from the island of Martinique, and that I'm sure of. The gold used to pay for the transactions had been stored at the Fort de France. Other than the Martinique transactions, we never knew, nor did we ever try to breach the client's privilege."

"Thinking back," Will said slowly, "you never asked how I came upon my first deposit."

Ramie nodded, the edges of his mouth curving up into a mischievous grin. "DIA."

Will frowned and gestured with his hands for the banker to get on with it.

"The bank was making six points on each transaction and my father received a point under the table. All he had to do at the bank was to purchase American currency and pay the oil company. Gold bullion arrived on the steps of the bank within 30 days. Same old sad story of humanity. American Oil Company sells refined diesel to fuel the very same U-Boats which went on to kill U.S. merchantmen." Ramie let out a long sigh and puffed on his cigarette before continuing. "And then the Japanese attacked Pearl Harbor and Hitler declared war on the U.S." Ramie let the cigarette dangle from his mouth as he threw his hands up in mock surrender. "Shame. My father and the bank made a ton of cash."

Will had listened intently. He raised his palms and cut to the point. "What does your story have to do with you coming to my office today to decline the Buccaneer's line of credit?" He knew the crusty banker had no love for the United States. After the 1989 invasion, Will had worked closely with CIA for the better part of a year. When President Bush gave the order for Operation Just Cause, Ramie was to be the President in waiting. But Bush balked at the last second due to his close ties to Managua.

"I don't have much time anyway." Ramie nodded and grinned. "My father told me he took a call from Geneva late in 1944. He was to receive a visitor by the name of Ribbentrop. Two weeks later, this Ribbentrop walks into my father's office while my mother and I were having lunch with him. I do remember my father was anxious for us to leave and we did not disappoint him. Later, he told me the German agent notified him to prepare to receive a large shipment of gold bullion."

Will was now all ears. A storyline in step with Ian Fleming's *Goldfinger* as its main topic always grabbed his attention. But then again, Will wouldn't trust Ramie as far as he could throw the bag of bones. *Why would he be telling me stories now?*

Maybe because Ramie was a man with one foot in the grave and wanted a cut of the deal.

"Interesting story, Ramie—think I read the novel—what became of the gold?"

Ramie shook his head while gazing out of the window. Seconds passed before he looked back at his client. "The shipment never arrived, and my father never heard from Ribbentrop again."

"I guess the Swiss Banker never raised his ugly head?" Will had spent too many years in CIA; the piece of shit was hiding plenty. Then again, gold was gold. Honorably discharged following two tours in Vietnam as a Force Recon Marine, William Kellogg's salary tripled conducting the same missions as a Central Intelligence Operative. Five years passed and Will resigned to freelance and pursue business opportunities.

Ramie flicked the burnt-out butt into the polished chrome trash receptacle next to the desk. He bent down to pick up a cigarette butt that wasn't there and brushed his hand underneath the table as he slowly returned to a slumped posture. "Not that my father ever saw him, but a Swiss banker did call just after Hitler's suicide to say he was coming our way to look for Ribbentrop and the gold. According to my father, the man did not go into specifics but was sure he knew where they vaulted the gold and most likely, its final destination. My father was always sure of the month and year of the call because of the announcement of Hitler's suicide, April 30, 1945. Needless to say, the caller vanished as well. My father called his bank for a year and the only explanation the bank would give was some story of job abandonment."

Will settled back into the chair. "Son of a bitch is probably living in South America with Ribbentrop and all that gold."

"I doubt that Will, you just don't pick up 80 million ounces of gold and move to Brazil."

Will 's eyes lit up as he lost his poker face staring at his old friend in disbelief. He quickly calculated the current value of 80 million ounces and let out a long whistle. "That's more than most countries GDP."

Ramie simply nodded. "Since mi padre told me this story in 1957, and I was to keep this in trust, I have wondered what came of the King's ransom."

"So, what do you think, my old friend?"

"Now we are old friends." Ramie fumbled with his outside coat pocket while he spoke. "When the German left my father's office his first stop was to be Isle de San Andres." He held a cigarette between the tips of his forefinger and index finger before leaving it dangling between thin lips. "My father did find out the Swiss banker made it to the destination—"

Will calmly cut him short, "Isle de San Andres seems to be a common denominator."

"It gets better." The lighter shook visibly in front of the cigarette. "Does the name Lady Luck mean anything to you?" He withdrew the cigarette and blew smoke to the ceiling.

"Yeah," Will replied. "Something I haven't had much of lately. As I understand, she was the original vessel of VB Shipping. Bucket of bolts should have been sold for scrap decades past, but the old man keeps her around."

The banker's magnified eyes blinked behind shaded glasses and, for the first time since entering the room, he smiled. "The Lady Luck was the tramp steamer that brought the Swiss banker to Isle de San Andres."

Will's poker face returned, but his mind moved at the speed of light. Ramie looked away briefly, his expression troubled. Taking a deep pull, he exhaled slowly. Will knew Ramie Ortega was not a native Panamanian. Years earlier with the help of CIA records, he had pieced together Ramie's family lineage.

His father, the youngest of three boys and a Nicaraguan businessman, married his Panamanian mother, the sole heir to the Banco de Panama in Panama City. His two older brothers, Rudy and Rito, returned to Nicaragua in the thirties to fight alongside the famed Nicaraguan Revolutionary Augusto Cesar Sandino. Sandino led the movement against the U.S. military presence from 1927 until his assassination in 1934 by National Guard forces led by General Anastasio Somoza Garcia. A U.S. Marine killed Rudy in the steamy jungles north of Managua in 1932. Rito, wounded in the same firefight traded his rifle for a plow, took a wife and fathered three boys—Daniel, Humberto, and Camilo.

Will threw up his hands. "For Christ's sake Ramie, your cousin, Daniel Ortega, is a damn Communist and the last time I looked the Berlin wall is still torn down. The fucker is broke, and you want me to give the Regime the means to take the Revolution outside Nicaragua's borders."

Will knew Daniel Ortega wanted influence beyond Nicaragua—it was no secret—but Ortega's old allies, Russia and Cuba, having little financial resources, made the thought a mere pipe dream. He also knew Ramie had played both sides of the coin during the Revolution and provided a conduit for dollars in support of his nephew to overthrow the Somoza dictatorship. Even today, he knew the dying son of a bitch was in bed with the Sandinistas and his gut screamed set up.

"Money is thicker than blood, Ramie." Will frowned. "Your bank pumped millions into my telephone startup."

"Funny thing about the money, Will," Ramie said. "The wire consisting of tens of millions left from a Swiss account to the benefit of Will Kellogg. They used the same account to issue another directive to your benefit to purchase the Buccaneer. A mere partner wearing an unmarked Swiss bank account for a name. CIA shit Will."

"Hey Ramie," Will interrupted, "the monies were equity transactions and when Vector Data paid dividends to shareholders, the CFO wired funds to the account." There just hadn't been any wires for the Buccaneer investment.

Ramie shrugged and the corners of his mouth turned down. "You have never found it odd that millions appear from thin air to your benefit?"

As he touched the scar on the side of his head, Will spoke, his tone considerate. "Maybe I'm lucky."

Ramie's face was dull, his skin as pale as a three-week-old baby. His hands trembled noticeably as he fumbled to hook the crooked part of his cane on the end of the chair. "You can't be *that* lucky," he said. "Look at you now."

Will said nothing.

"The gold, Will." Ramie pulled another cigarette from the pack before tapping the end on the wooden armrest. "Do you want one for old time sake?" His lighter fell and slid under the table. Slowly he bent down to retrieve the lighter and the underside of his hand slid across the underside of the table on its way to the lighter. He reappeared from behind the desk.

Will shook his head. "Been tobacco free for 25 years."

"Even for a dying man's final request? I turned 73 last week and the Doctors have told me I will not see my 74th birthday."

Will ignored Ramie's confession and asked, "How long will you be visiting?"

The banker's dark eyes narrowed, his smile fading rapidly. "The gold has to be on this island, Will."

Will smiled and the lines around his eyes slowly compressed.

Seconds passed before Ramie asked the billion-dollar question. "Let's assume the gold is still here. Think about what this would do for your current financial situation."

"I get what's in it for me. What's in it for you?" Will rocked forward in the chair, resting both elbows below his interlocked fingers. "What are you not telling me?"

Ramie pinched the inner portion of his mouth with tobacco stained teeth, contemplating a response. He looked Will Kellogg straight in the eye, his face contorted in anger that seemed mostly artifice.

Will let his palms fall open on the desk. "My old friend, then I guess we have nothing more to discuss."

The room was quiet except for the noise of gusts of wind racing across the bay colliding against the sliding glass doors to the veranda. Will depressed his intercom. "Lucianna."

The Secretary's raspy voice rattled out of the speaker, "Yes, Sir."

Will Kellogg looked at his old friend steadily, his pitted face expressionless. "Mr. Ortega will be staying in the Executive Suite. Have a wheelchair sent to my office and assign someone to assist our guest while he is on Buccaneer property, twenty-four-seven."

The door opened and Lucianna marched in, directing her attention to the banker. She held out a hand. "Let me help you outside, Senor Ortega," she said. "Assistance is on the way, and I have the perfect chair for you." She continued talking as she ushered him out the door.

Will pressed the remote lock and heard the outer door click. He sat for most of a minute, considering his options, which were slim to none. Ramie Ortega's bank had him by the short hairs. Was it possible that a legendary treasure of gold bullion, hidden decades earlier by Nazi's, might be the way out of this trap? Though the dividend check cut by Vector Data each quarter was nice, he was paddling up river and traveling downstream. Fast.

4.

Isle de San Andres
Buccaneer; Ramie Ortega's Suite

As a quiet porter unpacked his trunk, Ramie gazed out the window of his suite, enjoying the beauty of the day and the view of the crystal clear, turquoise Caribbean waters. So peaceful compared to the heat and poverty of Nicaragua.

Was it really only four days since his meeting with his cousin?

They had embraced affectionately outside the Café Comal 7 Internet in El Jicaral, where Daniel Ortega had delivered a speech to the town about converting an old Catholic Church across the street to a public library.

"I can't believe those Yankee bastards question my power," Daniel had bellowed as if he were addressing the crowd in the square for a second time. After all, he had been *El Presidente de Nicaragua* since 2007. "My people know who controls this country!"

Ramie had nodded slowly, sliding a cigarette lighter into his coat pocket. Pulling gently from his freshly lit cigarette, he coughed softly before he spoke, emitting puffs of smoke along with his words. "Cousin, I believe you have the means to spread your reach throughout Latin America but first and most importantly, Nicaragua."

Daniel's expression shifted from restless discomfort to wary interest. Ramie also knew his dilemma with the escrow monies needed for "Crosscut."

"So, Cousin," Daniel asked. "What is this influence throughout Latin America?"

"Gold, Cousin," Ramie replied quietly, leaning against the back of a plastic chair that should have been recycled months ago. "A king's ransom within your grasp. The beauty behind my plan is that you can explain the move politically. The gold is outside Nicaragua's borders."

Ramie now filled the silence with the story of the gold, and his plan to see Latin America united. "I am your dying cousin who wants to see you rule Latin America."

As the President of Nicaragua listened to the story, his mind was on the Chinese dignitaries who had flown out of Managua 36 hours earlier without Nicaragua's $20 Billion payment. Until China received funds 'paid in full,' China's version of the Panama Canal carved out of the San Juan River along the Nicaragua/Costa Rican border was but a Sandinista pipe dream. "And how will we get this gold?" Daniel asked softly, a grin spreading across his thick lips.

"I know just the man who would unknowingly locate the king's ransom because of his capitalistic greed, but his butt is pinched." Through the years, Ramie had heard Daniel speak of Will Kellogg as 'the Yankee dog" many times, and he never failed to add, "General Hallesleven should have killed the Yankee when he had the chance."

Ramie had never told his cousin about the financial ties his bank maintained with Will Kellogg.

Now he grinned. "The Yankee Dog will find it!"

"A bait and switch," Ortega said, the smirk below his mustache spreading from one end of his jawline to the other. "I think you're on to something, cousin."

The porter let himself out the door of the suite so quietly; Ramie almost missed the man's deferential exit. Alone now, a smile crossed his face as he thought of his sleight of hand just thirty minutes earlier, a deception pulled off in plain view of the great Will Kellogg.

He knew Will was well aware Daniel Ortega wanted influence beyond Nicaragua's borders and the lack of financial wherewithal handcuffed him.

He glanced at the room phone. The confirmation call that the tiny electronic surveillance bug was working would come any minute. A small button would broadcast from Will Kellogg's office at the Buccaneer. Not only did the device he attached on the underside of the table pick up conversations, but the device could also pick up the tones from Will's touch-pad on his office and cell phone. Nicaraguan analysts would be privy to each number Will dialed. Ramie's eyes closed and he opened them again seconds later. His plan with Daniel would come together at Will Kellogg's expense. He chuckled with the thought of the unthinkable.

I will outlive Will Kellogg.

Richardson, TX
Vector Data Communications Headquarters

Hap and Hollywood each leveled eyes on the other when they heard Will Kellogg say across the conference bridge located on the coffee table, "Colonel, I'm pinched." Seated around Hap's coffee table in his Vector Data office, Hollywood gestured, throwing both palms to the air. Hap's head shook slowly side-to-side as his lips formed the words, "I don't know."

"I need this deal, this merger, to go down, Colonel."

Hap said nothing.

"Will," Hollywood interjected. "You know a deal is not a deal until documents are signed and funds deposited."

Hap was able to find words, chiming in with, "What the hell's happened?"

In the silence following Hap's question, Peg leaned past the open door, smiling. "Coffee?" she asked quietly.

Hollywood shook his head as Hap waved her back to the other side of the door. She disappeared, closing the door, just as Will said, "I don't know if there is a right way to say what I'm about to say, but I feel like somebody is pulling my strings like a puppet master. Can't explain it, and have some work to do on this end, but I'll send Jake Tyson to visit with you."

"Why not lay your cards on the table now, Will," Hap said. "We are alone."

Silence followed as Hollywood reached for a legal pad and Will whispered through the speaker. "Colonel, not sure I'm alone right now."

Both of the Vector Data executive's eyes met as Hollywood scribbled on the legal tablet turning it for Hap to read. HE MAY BE BUGGED. END THE CALL. COULD BE THE FEDS.

Hap fell back into the cushions of the leather chair. "Send Jake. We will be hanging up now."

Hollywood reached over the coffee table and dropped the call. He straightened up and moved to the coffee bar, his hands visibly shaking, placing a Nomad coffee mug under the Keurig's spout. "What are you thinking, Hap?" He turned and leaned against the bar as coffee trickled into the cup.

Silence followed as Hap nibbled his lower lip. "So, you think this could be the—" he mouthed the word *Feds*— pulling these strings?"

"Why not, these are weird times politically. It's no secret who you and Vector Data contribute to politically."

Hap gazed at the hardwood floor for several seconds, the muscles of his jawline taut. After running both hands through his close-cropped hair he said, "I don't believe it. We have too many friends who left the Corps and joined the Bureau."

Hollywood stood holding his Nomad mug. "It wouldn't be them Hap, it's somebody higher up with more to gain by mucking up yours and Will's lives." He took a sip from the cup. "And who says it's not Justice, CIA, or one of the Intelligence bureaus. You didn't make many friends within the government when we crossed into Mexico that night." He emptied the cup's contents into the sink.

"The Feds have been systematically making their way through your address book and even paid you a visit at the office. They'll be knocking at your home any day now. Agent Gordon's had it out for you since you ran him out yours and Tuna's Office at El Centro."

A visible frown fixed across Hap's narrow face as he said, "Between Will and what we're going through at Vector Data, somebody or something is pulling strings leaving us where all we can do is react."

"Whoever it is Hap, it's keeping all of us on our heels." "

Hap nodded, his brow pinched. "We are being steered towards something or someone or, worse, we're about to be crushed."

Hollywood arched his brow. "You're not supposed to understand, Hap."

Hap nodded slowly his mind racing, and then said. "I'm growing tired reacting, Hollywood."

Hollywood thought for a moment, and then said. "So then you will listen to me on how to play offense and put them on their heels.

Hap said nothing.

Seconds passed as Hap and Hollywood looked at the other, then Hollywood said, "I have a plan."

Isle de San Andres
The Buccaneer Casino

Thirty-six hours after his rancorous meeting with Ramie Ortega, and twelve hours after his most recent call to Hap and Hollywood, Will Kellogg issued a curt nod to each dealer as he strolled past a row of the Buccaneer's Blackjack tables with a cell phone glued to an ear. Fast-paced single-deck games, double-deck, and shoe-games were in action and the seats at each table were half-full. Dealers stood inside the pit, running the deck past each patron, flipping a card face atop a down card. Many of the dealers sported bulging muscles beneath their tuxedos and moved with the fluid power of a Special Forces operator.

Will took the shortcut through the game floor, jumping into a vacant shoeshine chair. A finger pointed to his shoes and the worker, a young dark-haired man named Diego sporting a stained apron, nodded and whipped out a rag to work over his black Salvatore Ferragamo dress shoes. "The regular, Mr. Kellogg?" Diego said.

Will nodded as he spoke into the phone, "I'm listening Colonel. Long distance negotiations couldn't be better and Morgan Stanley's M&A group is top notch."

"Smooth as a baby's butt?" Will listened—not even letting the thought of a fortune in gold cross his mind much less his lips. Not yet.

Will thumbed off the call as the shoe shiner initiated the last snap of the towel and removed both shoe stands. Will slipped over a twenty as he stepped down from the stand. "Thanks, Diego."

Midway across the vast lobby, Will stopped dead in his tracks to stare at the back of a male guest entering the elevator. He couldn't help but notice that thick curly gray head of hair. Standing silently, he crossed arms to wait for the guest to turn. Three other guests entered the elevator a moment before the doors slid closed. Will frowned. He knew the guy, his physique, and thick gray hair hadn't changed since he saw him two years earlier.

So Rich Garbaccio does read his email. With his CIA and Mossad connections, I wonder who else's email the former Mossad agent reads?

It didn't take Einstein to figure it out. If you are looking for Nazi gold, ask one of the world's most renowned Nazi hunter's son.

Will had sent an encrypted email to Rich the second Ramie walked out of his office. Now here he was hours after the message. *Not bad*, he thought, strolling to Reception to inquire about one of the Buccaneer's recent guests.

The woman at Reception blinked stunning hazel eyes, looking at him over the computer monitor. "Good morning, Mr. Kellogg."

Will laid his hand holding the cell phone on the counter, checked her nametag, and then looked back toward the bank of elevators. "Gina, the gentlemen with the gray hair and medium build who just checked in. What name did he register under?"

She rattled off a list of customers recently checked in and then said, "Rich Garbaccio from New York City. Took the penthouse suite for a week, Mr. Kellogg."

Will turned to walk away but stopped in his tracks without turning when he heard her say, "Mr. Garbaccio paid cash, Mr. Kellogg."

He gave a half turn and smiled. *Nothing had changed. Rich didn't want to be tracked.* "Have a bottle of champagne delivered to his room please, Gina. Compliments of the house."

She issued a polite smile and nodded as she picked up the phone to ring the kitchen. "Right away, Mr. Kellogg."

⁂

In room 2110, Rich Garbaccio slid the dresser drawer shut, having slipped a pistol beneath a stack of neatly folded T-shirts. As he turned back to the center of the room, someone rang the low buzzer on the door. He tensed. "Who is it?" he called out.

"Your dinner, Sir, compliments of the house." The voice sounded male.

Turning for the pistol, he waved the thought off, his first mistake. The Buccaneer was Will Kellogg's house. Rich felt as safe here as he ever could. He slowly opened the door without a glance through the peephole.

That was his second mistake.

Broad shoulders crashed to his exposed midsection and he hit the ground before he could get out a scream—the wind knocked from his lungs.

The attacker did not drive him through the floor nor go for his throat, which was their first mistake.

Maybe I do have a chance. His hands went for the attacker's eyes, ready to gouge them out of the man's skull when his gaze met a wide grin.

What the?

He'd seen that shit-eating grin more times than he cared to count.

Rich reached up to grasp his old friend's open hand, which snatched him to his feet the moment their fingers closed.

"What brings you to the Buccaneer, Rich?

"I read my email."

Don't get me wrong, it's good to see you but a reply email would have answered my question."

"You're paying for my massages." Rich braced his lower back with both hands as he twisted to his either side. "How is Hap Stoner?"

"You will have to excuse the lad," Will replied, with a crooked grin peeking from one side of his mouth. "Hap was lucky to live through the Borderline incident. Took two bullets and lived to take on the fight fending off JAG and the Feds for initiating the action." Will went on to describe Hap Stoner's unauthorized mission into Mexico to rescue his Squadron Commanding Officer. Hap Stoner didn't have to ask twice for Will's help.

Rich smiled. "Good to hear. By the way, I'm glad you could afford the extra padding," he said, looking down at the plush carpet while continuing to massage his lower back.

Will laughed. "I'm sorry, I just couldn't resist." Both turned towards the rattle of a serving cart in the open door to meet the wide-eyed serving attendant.

"Excuse me, Mr. Kellogg," the woman said in broken English. "I was asked to deliver service to Mr. Garbaccio's room."

Will cocked his head to the side to look back at Rich. "You've come to the right place."

Visibly taken aback, the attendant slowly rolled the cart through the path created by the two WWE wannabees. Will slipped the attendant a twenty on her way out of the room, and then closed the door securely after her.

Moments later, he filled one glass and handed it to Rich.

Rich cocked his head. "I see you're still off the sauce."

Will filled a second glass. "Cheers."

Rich tapped his champagne glass against Will's and took a long sip. "Thank you for the hospitality."

"Please." The Buccaneer's owner gestured towards the leather love seat and settled into the low back sofa directly across the glass coffee table. "So, what part of the world were you in that brings you to Isle de San Andres so soon after my shout out?"

Rich shrugged. "You know me, Will. Chasing Nazis, even old ones, hanging their hats outside Rio."

Will's lips pursed as he nodded. "Hell, where would they hide on this island? The few still alive would need a walker with an oxygen bottle dangling off the side."

Rich straightened and walked over to slide the drawn curtains to the side, which framed the Fortress in the glass double doors. "Has to be there." He posed as if a game show host gesturing to the old stone structure across the bay.

The muscles in Will's jaw tensed. "Von Bock has an open account at the Buccaneer, Rich. The old man is not your war criminal." Will left it there; not wanting to mention the Buccaneer owed the man over $13 million.

Rich reached into a pant pocket and handed over a wallet-sized photo wrapped in thick plastic. "Never said he was."

Upon peeling away the plastic, he could see two men who appeared to be brothers. They had the same facial features, though one taller than the other. The shorter wore the uniform of an SS Officer, and the other was a younger Franz in a suit. Von Bock's widow's peak looked about the same, except it was now gray. "And you're sure this hasn't been photo shopped?"

Rich shook his square jaw. "Your Franz von Bock is really Franz Krueger, and his older brother in the SS uniform is Hans Krueger."

Will's eyes narrowed. "So where did this Hans Krueger surface? Never seen the man."

Rich polished off his glass and looked back toward the cart. Will reached over palming the bottle to fill Rich's empty glass.

"Outside Rio living on a rubber plantation," Rich continued. "Just happens the plantation and estate are owned by the von Bock business conglomerate."

"Plausible," Will said with a nod. "von Bock ships raw product from South America to Isle de San Andres for processing." Will stood from the couch and moved to the suite's plush and spacious veranda to put eyes on the billows of steam coming from the processing plant's cooling towers. The plant cleansed, dried, then baled and palletized the rubber product for von Bock to distribute throughout the globe with his very own shipping line.

Rich leaned back against the rail next to him.

"Join me for dinner tonight?" Will asked. "Compliments of the Buccaneer?"

Rich shook his head. "Want to be a recluse for a while."

"A couple of girls then?"

Rich continued to shake his head but smiled at the offer.

"How about joining me for dinner in my room?"

Will shrugged then nodded. "About 7 p.m.?"

"Seven o'clock," Rich replied along with a nod.

"Compliments of the Buccaneer." Will wasn't asking.

Rich said nothing as he turned to look across the bay.

* * *

Will Kellogg closed the door and made his way down the hall, his mind processing at 10,000 miles per hour. *A Nazi SS officer holed up across the bay?*

Really?" He blurted aloud. *The Nazi officer's brother is Franz von Bock? Or is it Krueger? Apparently, Ramie Ramirez and his story of the bullion wasn't all bullshit, after all.*

Seven p.m. could not come soon enough.

7

Isle de San Andres
Buccaneer, Rich Garbaccio's Room 7 p.m.

Nightfall, close at hand, spilled the Fortress's shadow into Isle de San Andres Bay. The setting sun's orange sphere flashed between two hostesses who stood on the veranda of Rich Garbaccio's room. They stood on either side of a serving cart with their hands clasped loosely behind their backs. The ladies' shapely figures and Will Kellogg's broad shoulders came between the sun's brightness and Rich Garbaccio's hazel eyes. When any of the three shifted, the sun's glare compelled Rich to turn away. It didn't help that Will's head dipped slightly with each sip of ice water. But in less than a minute, the ocean would snuff out the sun's glory.

Will glanced over his shoulder and gestured for the shrimp cocktail, the first course of what would be seven courses.

A lone steamer with "VB Industries" inscribed across its bow trolled toward the jetty opening, which protected the bay when the Caribbean wanted to show her supremacy. As the freighter churned through the mouth of the jetty, an easterly breeze whisked smoke from her single stack past her port bow. That same breeze provided relief to an otherwise humid evening.

Rich delicately picked at his shrimp as his thoughts locked on Hans Krueger, and how he could get in pistol range to kill him. "So, how do I get into the Castle?" Rich's disillusionment with his host was progressive and, since they'd been seated across from each other, he wasn't sure at what point the doubts and agitation swirling around his gut had begun.

Will's eyebrows gathered visibly closer together as if he were warding off a painful headache. He slowly picked on a cheese-filled celery stalk and said nothing.

Rich did what any former Mossad agent would do—he continued to probe. "I understand they have two tours per day. Have you ever been on one of these?"

"Once." Will muttered something under his breath, and then said, "I was dating the daughter of a wealthy Colombian."

Rich gingerly wiped the corners of his mouth with a Buccaneer-imprinted napkin. "The Colonel can identify me, Will." Rich looked up from his salad. "We sat across from each other at a dinner and faced off with pistols hours later. Hap Stoner sat at the same table."

"That must be some story, for another time, perhaps." Will shrugged, not surprised. *Two weeks before the Borderline incident, Hap had flown to Rio for a business meeting with a von Bock exec.* He nodded slowly, the corners of his mouth turned toward the stone floor. "Hell, Rich, Wyatt Earp, and Bat Masterson combined haven't been in the number of gunfights you've experienced."

Rich wasn't blind to the fact that his old friend likely wanted to be anywhere but on this veranda. Unfortunately, at the moment Will Kellogg had an important role to play if Rich was to put eyes on the former SS Officer. "Hence, why I need to stay incognito." Rich thanked the attractive hostess after she placed the bowl of French onion soup next to his half-eaten salad. He pointed to the celery stalk Will was holding. "That looks good."

Will nodded, chewing slowly.

The taller waitress's eyes darted around the table and back to the serving cart. Moments later, she placed a plate of three cheese-filled stalks in front of the guest. "I'm sorry, Mr. Garbaccio."

With a quick smile at the server, Rich focused his words on Will. "You invited me into this story, Will, when you reached out to me about the…"

Will attempted to look past the shapely curves of the other hostess as she placed the bowl of lobster bisque next to his untouched salad. "You must be new at the Buccaneer," he said with little enthusiasm.

"Mr. Kellogg, is your salad not to your liking? The tall brunette reached out with her right hand. "Carol Rinker from Texas City, Texas, Mr. Kellogg."

"My problem is not with the food," Will said, reaching up slowly to place a couple of fifties into her palm. "Welcome to the Buccaneer, Ms. Rinker."

She didn't bother to look at the denomination before dropping the bills in Will's untouched salad. "I believe you misplaced some cabbage, Mr. Kellogg. My Mom had Hap Stoner give me some insight before getting me this job."

"Thanks, Hap," Will said as he threw his arms up.

Rich spoke without looking up from his soup. "Smart and spirited."

As Carol Rinker from Texas left the veranda, the other hostess pushed the cart around to her boss's side of the table and retrieved the bills from the salad. She removed the dressing by running the bills through her narrow lips several times from side to side. Will restrained from speaking until she completed the money laundering, then he signaled with his free hand for her to keep the cash.

A curt wink followed as she stuffed the bills down her low-cut blouse. "Should I pour the champagne, Mr. Kellogg?" Will shook his head, glancing at her name badge. "I can take it from here, Patti."

She placed his entrée in front of him without saying a word.

"His lips pursed together as he nodded discreetly, making a mental note. She sat the salad plates on the cart, leaving the two men on the veranda when she exited the hotel suite.

When the men were alone, Rich leaned forward, speaking in a barely audible tone. "Your instincts have always been good. If you want to find Nazi gold, ask a Nazi hunter."

Will made no move to taste his entree. After a long silence he said, "Until Vector Data is sold, Buccaneer has my ass wedged between a 20-ton boulder and a hard spot."

Rich smiled faintly. "I wouldn't know by the way you throw around cash."

"How do you propose we remove your Nazi from this island?"

Rich continued to smile, thinking to himself, *some things never change but, finally, Will Kellogg gets it.* "Simply stated, I will enter the Fortress, find him…, and then kill him."

Will chuckled as both eyebrows arched toward the darkening sky. "Why not kidnap him and return the turd to Israel? The Israeli court system will take care of the Nazi, ending this saga when the rope snaps his pencil neck."

The Nazi hunter shrugged. "It's personal, Will."

"Not as personal as you wanting me to confront a man who has a marker with the Buccaneer on it for $13 million. You going waltzing into the Fortress could get a man killed, Rich, *and* cause the old man to call the marker."

"Then you wouldn't be upset if my aim is off and a bullet hits the Abwehr agent between the eyes?"

Will's facial muscles visibly tightened, and he slowly reached for his glass of ice water. "Truth be told," he said, taking a sip and returning the glass, "I'm not sure if it would only complicate my and the Buccaneer's position with the von Bock family."

Rich shrugged, and then leaned back in his chair. "I'm all for minimizing risk, although I seem to remember you take more than your share on a regular basis." Rich smiled. "So that's why we can help each other."

Isle de San Andres, Colombia
Buccaneer Casino Will Kellogg's Executive Suite

Will scanned Isle de San Andres bay leaning with both hands firmly gripping the rail. "So, you are going to kill this Hans von Bock, a.k.a. Hans Krueger? Never met the man myself," he said without turning.

Standing next to Will, Rich said nothing. Instead, he simply nodded.

"So, Franz von Bock's was a…"

The Nazi Hunter helped him complete the sentence. "Abwehr agent."

Neither man looked toward the other as they spoke. "And Franz von Bock is really Krueger?"

"When you show the hand, that's what the cards say, Will. He jump-started in business and built an empire with Nazi gold stolen from the Vichy French. I suspect he snuffed out everybody associated with the operation. Hitler silenced those in Germany who knew of the operation in the last few months of the war."

Will puffed up his upper lip and nodded. "I hope you're wrong Rich, but your story does corroborate the old man arriving on the island prior to the war." He hesitated, letting out a sigh. Franz von Bock's emissary had left his office three hours earlier to deliver a message straight from the old man's lips. He would be calling the $13 million-dollar marker within three months. Good news was that the old man might give an additional three-month extension if 'things' were progressing to his liking. *Strange the emissary never defined 'things'.* Shrewd for sure but, if he were dead, maybe the Kraut couldn't collect the marker.

"Something on your mind, Will?"

Will's eyes rolled back slightly to meet Rich's questioning stare. "Between my CIA days, your Mossad days, and everything in between, I can't let you do this alone."

* * *

8:30 am splayed across the digital display of the radio clock on the nightstand. The conversation with Rich and his plan to kill Hans Krueger had carried on past 2 am, leaving Will restless. He'd spent that energy for the next couple of hours with the Sherrill Park twins vacationing from Texas.

Now, with the help of a blue star-shaped pill and the still eager twins, Will picked up where the romp previously ended, with the taller of the two on top. By the time it was 9 am, and all was heating up nicely, Will and the twins turned to look as his cell vibrated like a tiny bumper car against the twins' phones. Energized with each three-second shudder, the phone danced to the theme song for the old western series *Bonanza*.

The smaller of the two women grabbed Will's arm and purred into an ear, "Do you have to Will?" She slowly worked her lips to his neck as the phone continued to bounce until it fell to the carpet. Still, the tones continued, only muffled now.

Will's answer came from somewhere below his diaphragm. "Yeah, Baby." He half rolled, sending the bronco rider tumbling across her sister and both let out a screech just before a soft landing on the carpeted floor. He brought the phone to his ear with full knowledge the voice on the other end would be Lucianna.

It may as well have been his Mother.

"I'm not your baby and Mr. Ramirez is waiting at your table, Mr. Kellogg." Clearly, from her pinched tone, making the call made her very unhappy. "Checking your calendar, you do have him down for a breakfast meeting."

The frequency of these reminder calls did not make Lucianna happy. The twins laughingly rolled across the carpet and seductively crawled back to hit the restart button.

"Thank you, Lucianna," Will mumbled. "Tell Mr. Ramirez I will be down in thirty minutes." Returning the phone to the nightstand, he rolled back over and the smaller of the sisters jumped into the saddle.

Fifteen minutes passed as a mere blink of the eye and he was in the shower. Will combed back his close-cropped hair as he leaned over to give both sisters a gentle kiss on their foreheads. Both had the silk sheets pulled to their chins and looked up with knowing grins.

"Call room service and feel free to call down for a massage and a manicure." He issued both a wink and a smile. "I'll be back."

Thirty minutes from the time he received Luciana's call, Will slid into his private booth across from Ramie, who was fiddling nervously with a crumpled pack of cigarettes. They had removed booths from either side for privacy and the employees reserved the area strictly for Will Kellogg and his guests.

"Have you ordered breakfast, Ramie?"

Ramie reached inside the pack of non-filter cigarettes placing one between his lips and lifted a zippo lighter. "Do you mind?"

Will shook his head and said nothing.

"I hope I didn't cut your meeting short Will."

"For you Ramie, I just pulled out."

Instead of a chuckle, the dying man emitted a deep cough.

A brunette waitress rounded the corner between a line of tables and the booths. She topped off Will's cup with steaming Nicaraguan coffee. "The regular, Mr. Kellogg," she asked?

Will nodded.

Looking over to Ramie, she freshened his cup and spoke in broken English. "And you, Sir?"

Ramie glanced up with unkempt eyebrows to focus on her smiling face. "Wheat toast and a poached egg."

She nodded without bothering to write down the orders on the pad she held at her side. "Your orders will be out shortly gentlemen."

Will cupped the mug and observed his banker through percolating steam. "Anything since yesterday?"

Ramie lit another cigarette behind the glowing butt before he stubbed it out in the ashtray. "No more than I knew sixty years ago."

"Well, I have," Will said, attempting to hold a better poker face than he had when seated across from Franz von Bock.

The banker could only cough.

Will leaned across the smoldering rim of coffee.

Natilda rounded the corner table and placed their orders in front of each.

"Anything else, Mr. Kellogg?

Will watched Ramie shake his head slowly and look up at the waitress. "That will be all for now, Natilda. Thank you." Ramie picked at the food. Will's appetite was voracious, and he downed his two over-easies, three slices of bacon, and a mound of sweet potato hash browns.

It was clear to Will that his banker was a Nicaraguan operative and the Sandinistas intended to use both of them. Daniel Ortega could kiss his ass. If Franz von Bock pigeonholed the king's ransom on San Andreas, Will would find and beat the Sandinistas to the cache.

The race was on.

Will dabbed the napkin across his lips and dropped the cloth into an empty plate. "Whatever you had in mind for me, count me out."

Groaning, Ramie dropped the napkin to the plate and worked slowly out of the booth, straining to straighten. He left his meal almost untouched.

"The bank's decision to call the line of credit is final. Good day." The banker waddled slowly, stopped, and his worn-out figure issued a half turn along with a grimacing gaze. "You sure, Will?"

It made Will hurt to witness the strain it took for the banker to rotate around his hips.

He leaned back against the wall and propped a leg onto the bench. "My rules Ramie?"

Ramie nodded and slowly turned his feet to face the booth. "Depends what it is, my old friend."

Between the bank and von Bock calling in markers, Will felt the vice tightening. Would the bank buy his bullshit? He raised a finger to the ceiling. "Hold off foreclosing on the line for 150 days?"

The old man nodded, the muscles around his sagging face didn't flex. "I have the authority to give you the time. Granted."

Will knew the Ortegas would grant his next statement, but never honor it. Go high or stay home so he threw a number to the wind. Blood was thicker than water. "Once I verify the gold's location, $25 mil…in gold and secure the $50 million increase in the line."

Ramie shrugged fumbling to find the pack of cigarettes. "Sure, Will. Whatever you want. I will have the paperwork in your email to memorialize this conversation in a couple of days." He turned and waddled down the aisle and slowly pulled himself up the gold polished handrail one step at a time for three risers to enter Buccaneer's Grand Ball Room's short staircase.

Will texted Luciana, "No interruptions please, under any circumstances." He had just bought at least 120 days. Maybe. *There would be signed agreements between parties. Buccaneer's attorneys could drag out the litigation past the 120 days to give more than enough time to pull off the operation to procure the gold.* Nicaragua's Commanding General of the National Army and his plan to remove the gold from the island with a raid was a hell of a lot easier than planning a full-blown invasion. Nicaragua's Commanding General was smart and a man not to be taken lightly—even though, decades earlier, when *Colonel* Hallesleven stood with his pistol shoved between Will's eyes, he chose not to pull the trigger. Instead of splattering himself in Will's blood, Hallesleven looked from below a jet-black pinched brow, lowered the muzzle from Will's head, holstered his weapon, turned, and walked into the jungle without a word said.

Will's mind drifted back three decades to the countless friends and acquaintances killed by soldiers under Hallesleven's command. Had the combat boots been laced onto the others' feet—and the roles reversed—Will would have pulled the trigger without giving the act a second thought.

Now, by the time President Ortega and Hallesleven discovered Will duped them; the Staff Planning would take weeks to change the plan from a raid to full-blown invasion. He also knew the moment he handed over information of the gold's location as per he and Ramie's verbal agreement, the Nicaraguan treasury would route the $25 million to an offshore bank account for Ortega and his wife's needs.

And President Ortega would sign the order for a Nicaraguan agent to put a bullet between Will's eyes. Maybe Hallesleven would do it personally to make up for the time he had the chance and didn't pull the trigger.

Will pushed send and dropped a twenty next to his empty plate as he slid out from the booth to rejoin the Sherrill Park twins.

9

Richardson, Texas
Hap Stoner's Vector Data Office

Will Kellogg's bullet-sharp eyes stared out from the 54-inch monitor in Vector Data's conference room, and Hap felt pulled gravitationally toward the screen.

"It's time for you to step down from Vector, Hap."

Hap rubbed his ear. "I hear you right, Will?" From the corner of his eye, he saw Jake Tyson rock back in the executive chair, listening, but keeping quiet.

Will's steady stare answered what wasn't really a question at all.

Hap's jaw rested atop interlocked fingers in need of Carla's manicure skills, and if Will's news had not dumbfounded Hap so, he would have made a mental note to push back his overactive cuticles. Instead, he kept his eyes on the opposite wall and the mounted screen image of his old friend and business associate.

"Don't know any way to say it but plain, Hap. I'm calling in my marker."

In the telling, Will's speech dropped a couple of octaves. *Classic Will*, Hap thought, when he aimed for emphasis, he dropped his tone a couple of octaves and lowered his volume to a hoarse stage whisper. He must be coming to the "Why Hap should resign from Vector Data," part.

Will's Eagle Globe and Anchor insignia emblazoned golf shirt seemed to adhere to the right spots—upper chest, biceps, and shoulders. Two hammer like forearms extended from a toned upper body and his forehead still bore the marking from an errant 7.62 round on the rooftop of the Los Americanos. Will's demeanor seemed almost relaxed, elbows comfortably propped on the Buccaneer's executive chair's mahogany arms as he rocked back, his head framed by a view of the turquoise bay behind him.

But the steel in Will's gaze belied comfort. Will said, "We got work to do, Colonel, and my gut tells me time is not on our side."

Hap's chair emitted its audible yelp as he rocked forward. *It appears I won't have to submit a request for a new chair.* Both elbows transferred from the chair's narrow armrests and slid to the desktop. His hands separated as if asking a question.

"Forgive me for interrupting, Will. Don't you think I need a little time selecting my replacement for day-to-day and Chairman of the Board? The Company ain't sold yet, and we both have a big upside in this thing just to throw it all into the crapper."

Will responded with a big a shit-eating grin. He wore the same smile the moment he surprised Hap with the news that *he* would be handing over the reins. "You know who your replacement should be. Crash Franklin can move into your office in the morning. Peg can pack your shit while you two conduct the turnover. It's not as if you're going to vaporize into thin air. You will be available for a while, but you have to cut that umbilical cord, Colonel."

"A while," Hap interjected. "What the hell is that supposed to mean?"

Will issued a quick shrug. His brown eyes seared a hole through the back of Hap's cranium. "One month, maybe two on the outside. Mr. Hancock and Crash can handle the sale. You're an email or call away."

Peg's calming voice reverberated from the phone's intercom. "Head's up on your 4:30 meeting."

Hap's eyes cut to the picture next to the phone. He and Carla in formal attire at the last Marine Corps Ball the two attended. Gorgeous as ever, she wore a light-blue formal cut low below her neck. She'd pulled her hair back in a French braid and her presentation rivaled Scarlet O'Hara at her most beautiful.

She wouldn't be cuddling up to him much once she heard about Will's order—not only did it jeopardize the sale of Vector Data, it jeopardized their wedding conversations. Carla would never forgive him.

"Hap?" Peg's voice again. "The Senior Technical Staff are waiting in your conference room for the 4:30 meeting."

Hap's gaze shifted from the photo to Will. Through the years, he had seen Will Kellogg in his modes, from executive, all-business cool to the middle of a firefight. Hap's arms and shoulders grew heavy. He owed Chuck Warden's life to Will. His right hand slowly massaged around both cheeks and worked its way down to a chiseled jawline. His eyes remained on Will as he spoke with a raw edge into the intercom. "Cancel 'em, Peg. Crash can take the meeting."

Will winked at his old protégé. "Since I sent you Jake, I was going to invite him over to have some of Carla's chicken enchiladas, but my gut tells me maybe he waits."

Jake turned toward Hap and their eyes met in silent understanding.

Hap shook his head. "It's going to be a late night, Will. I need to call the Directors with a replacement recommendation before my resignation. Between my staff and the pending sale on the brink, tomorrow night would be better."

Though it didn't happen often, this was one of those days, and Will flashed a third grin at Hap. "Miss Carla will be head hunting the second you break the news. Jake will be at the ranch house at seven-thirty tomorrow night, Colonel. Somebody needs to protect you from the little lady when she attempts to *gut you*."

10

Pacific Ocean
Off the Coast of Colombia

Taking in a starlit night with the salt air that came along with it, Captain Johannes Raus leaned out over Graf Spee's conning tower rail. The Type XXI U-boat also went by the name "Elektroboote" and was the world's first submarine built to operate primarily submerged. In a different era, Blohm & Voss of Hamburg assembled her eight prefabricated sections made of Krupp steel. Seventy years later, she continued to prowl the seas.

Tonight, Raus and his crew were hunting on the surface off the Colombian coast in search of Colombian Cartel submersibles. Raus used the opportunity to apply a fresh charge to the vessel's batteries.

The 59-year-old Raus was the son of a U-boat ace, Wilhelm Raus, who captained the world's first submarine when her identifier carried U–1411, a U-boat which, according to historical records, did not exist.

But not only was Raus a passenger in the spring of 1945, but he and his older brother also shared the top bunk in a berthing space with Hans Guderian. The boys' mother slept crammed against the pressure hull with their father, but she made the small berthing space like home for the four-week journey to the warm waters of the southern Caribbean.

Both Johannes and his brother grew up in Argentina until middle school in 1964 when Captain Wilhelm Raus moved Johannes' mother and the two brothers back to Berlin. Johannes chose a different career path than his sibling, electing to follow his father's legacy in Germany's Deutsche Marine. Accepted into the Naval Academy, Johannes reported to the Red Castle by the Sea in 1970. The academy's beautiful unique gothic architecture was the first thing naval officer cadets saw to begin what would be at least a thirteen-year career.

After years as an officer in Germany's small submarine force, Johannes left the service to join his father aboard the Graf Spee in 1984. His education in submarines continued as he served as his father's executive officer for a short year. His father returned to Berlin to be with his wife, Johnannes' mother, for their twilight years and made himself available to answer any question Johannes might have as he took command of the Graf Spee.

Crewmember training for the Graf Spee and the machinists who manned lathes to machine spare parts inside the bowels of the fortress never ended. Located in a large room adjacent to the submarine pen below a hundred feet of rock, the machine shop hummed for two shifts, a total of 16 hours per day, six days per week. U-1411's secret, 70 years after she submerged to evade Allied sub hunters, miraculously remained secure. As if Captain Nemo came back to life, wharf rats bantered stories in bars adjacent to ports across the globe, of ships vanishing without a trace.

The moon had settled below the horizon hours earlier and Johannes positioned Graf Spee to silhouette potential targets against light radiated from the coast. Their target's pilothouses, air intakes, and exhaust made for a difficult hunt. Propelled by diesel-electric with Kevlar or fiberglass skin, these boats had the ability to submerge to a depth of 100 feet. Capable of long-range underwater operation, the vessels could transport five tons of cocaine fetching $100 million wholesale for trips north, and million dollar bundles encased in plastic for transport south.

Johannes was aware of up to 40 semi-submersibles departing Colombia in 2007 for U.S. shores. Four years later, the waters were target rich with several hundred narco semi and fully-submersible round-trip sorties annually. The Graf Spee honed her skill set and was responsible for contributing $425 million annually to the von Bock business empire as an off-balance sheet line item. Like privateers centuries earlier, prize money paid to Captains made Johannes tens of millions and each crew member a millionaire many times over.

For Johannes, the money was fine, but he lived for the hunt. The follow-on execution of the four to six-man crews was never easy. If crews never reappeared for another mission, the assumption was they went down with the vessel, captured by the authorities, or found another way to make a living. Unfortunately, families of the crew paid the ultimate sacrifice if the cartel found the crew had absconded with either the contraband or cash.

Graf Spee submerged before sun up and moved further south in hope of finding greener pastures. Still, the horizon remained stubbornly empty even after sunset the next evening. Poor visibility followed with a low-pressure system and Johannes set the boat on the bottom to wait out the foul weather. Patrolling north two nights later the soundman pushed back from his station just forward of the control room and craned his head from the middle of the passageway.

"Commander of the watch, sonar. Surface contact three four five, heading one seven five, range one seven thousand yards. Contact is pulling a torpedo. I have confirmed there is a shadow vessel."

The executive officer leaned over a dimly lit chart to speak into a voice tube connected to the bridge. "Captain, surface contact bearing three four five range one seven thousand yards. There is a shadow vessel. Sonar suspects target is pulling a torpedo heading one seven five."

Johannes smiled hearing the contact was southbound and spoke down through the open conning tower hatch. "Take her down to periscope depth. Clear the bridge." Three crewmembers of the watch jumped from their perches and vanished into the boat counting off: "one down, two down, three down." Johannes gave one last look about the bridge to ensure he was last to leave and secured the hatch behind him.

He passed through the small confines of the conning tower and by the time his steel-toed boots touched the control room floor, Graf Spee had vanished into the sea. The claxon horn reverberated through the ship. "Officer of the watch. Full speed ahead, come left to three five five degrees."

The executive officer repeated the order. "Aye Aye Captain," and repeated the order to members of the watch.

Johannes ducked out of the front hatch and leaned into the sonar shack to look over the technician's shoulder at the blip on the scope. "Can we catch him?" he asked.

"Yes, Captain. The vessel is making six knots and we suspect it's towing a torpedo. The shadow vessel is six-miles in trail. Same course and speed."

A submersible cargo container, the torpedo contained a ballast tank for submersion control and could maintain a depth of 98 feet below the surface. Typically towed by a fishing trawler, the torpedo was difficult to spot by air below 90 feet. On chance the authorities became suspicious and approached the trawler, they released the torpedo to dissuade company.

Left to their own devices, the crew within the cramped confines of the torpedo would release a buoy with a location transmitter inside. Shaped like a piece of wood, a trailing vessel would retrieve the towline and the delivery would continue.

"Let's go active, give me one ping, Felix."

The technician nodded and opened the cover to depress the active component to their sonar system. The screen lit up with a return now and confirmed the second target directly behind and below the surface contact. "There is your torpedo Captain."

Johannes patted Felix on the shoulder and ducked back into the control room. "Plot, time to intercept."

The Executive Officer looked up from the chart. "Will be in range to shoot within 45 minutes."

"Very well," Raus said, delivering a glance towards the clock fixed above the chart table. "Alarm at the top of the hour Number One. I will be in my quarters."

Johannes flopped down in his bed with his shoes on and privacy curtain open. Located across the passageway from the sonar shack, he rested his head into cupped hands to take in the song of the boat. Music to his ears as the equipment responded to the valves opening and closing allowing pumps to push ballast throughout the boat.

"Passing one five zero feet," the diving officer announced in a deliberate tone.

The executive officer voice replied, "Very well, level off at two zero zero feet."

"Captain, it's time," the exec said, gently patting his leg. Johanne's eyes opened slowly. "Range, Number One"

"1700 yards, Captain. We are parallel to the target's course."

Johannes' legs swung out of bed gingerly, straightening his stiff back. "Call the crew to general quarters."

Alone, he splashed water on his face from the sink next to his bed as the claxon reverberated throughout the Graf Spee. He ducked into the control room. "Recommended heading?"

"Two six five, Captain," the exec said.

"Bring the vessel to periscope depth, come left to two six five degrees," Johannes ordered as he clambered into the conning tower.

Graf Spee's bow pitched toward the surface as its single propeller pushed the submarine into a climbing left turn. Minutes later, he felt the aluminum deck fall out from under his feet as the boat leveled off.

"Periscope depth Captain, heading two six five. Angle off the bow two seven zero degrees. Shadow vessel bearing is two two zero."

"Up scope," Johannes ordered. Clutching the grips, he adjusted the handles focusing in on the target bathed in the moon's weak glow. "Does sonar have the torpedo?" The cross hairs on Raus' scope focused on the port side of the vessel and moved left and away from their position.

The exec cut his eyes forward to see Felix in the passageway nodding his head. "Second target still in tow, Captain."

"Open outer doors one through four. Set the safety for one thousand meters. Active on guidance." Now the torpedo's sonar would go active 1000 meters from Graf Spee's bow. The exec spoke into a voice tube relaying the order to the vessel's only torpedo room. Moments later the petty officer's muffled voice traveled through the voice tube. "Tubes one through four outer doors open, tubes pressurized, safety set for 1000 meter with active homing."

The exec spoke up, "Fish are spun up. We are ready to fire Captain."

"Fire one," Johannes said calmly, and a kick followed as the torpedo whooshed from the tube. Seconds passed.

"Fire two," Johannes repeated. Another kick and the second torpedo left the tube.

"Fire three '…fire four." Two kicks followed as both torpedoes, one then the other whooshed out of its tube.

"Fish running hot and true, Captain," the exec said.

Johannes peered into the scope, the only person on the boat with the view for a kill as Graf Spee's torpedoes sped away at 40 miles per hour.

"Ten seconds to impact on the primary target, Captain. Twenty seconds for shadow vessel."

Almost to the second, the first torpedo exploded underneath the unsuspecting vessel's hull. Framed in the explosion's yellow flash, human bodies and ships parts spewed out of the light and into the night sky. The second torpedo explosion ensured any of the crew who survived the initial explosion, were DOA. He swung the scope to the left as the exec counted down the seconds for the torpedo to make contact. The initial explosion mirrored what had happened moments before and the second torpedo issued the coup de grace.

"Down scope," Johannes slapped the handles of the periscope into place. "Down scope. Close outer doors, full speed ahead. Extend spar. Sonar you have the conn." As the periscope sucked into Graf Spee's bowels, the outer doors sealed tubes one through four. Graf Spee would make its run on the torpedo under control of the sonar operator.

Four explosions all passed through the hull seconds from the other.

Johannes could hear Felix's voice from the passageway. "Come left to two six three degrees and dive to nine zero feet."

"Left two-six-three, take her down to nine zero feet diving officer," the Exec parroted. "Time to impact: 4 minutes and 35 seconds. Spar extended, Captain."

Johannes said nothing, instead focused on the crew coordination as the Graf Spee zeroed in for the kill. At 200 meters, Johannes would order the propeller into reverse attempting to ram the torpedo as close to 5 knots of forward speed as possible, to prevent the torpedo from splitting in half and scattering the booty over a vast expanse of seabed.

"Target maintaining nine zero feet, Captain, come left to two six three degrees,"

The exec repeated sounds instructions in a low tone, "Helm, come left to two six three 263 degrees, maintain nine zero feet,"

"Reverse in 30 seconds," Felix said, his voice growing anxious.

"Mark," Johannes said.

The exec started the stopwatch palmed in his right hand. He reached over to depress the claxon warning the crew of the pending collision. They could hear the watertight doors closing throughout Graf Spee.

"Ten seconds Captain," the exec said staring down at the watch.

Gripping the periscope housing to brace for the impact, Johannes said nothing.

The exec began counting down the seconds. "Five, four, three, two, one…" he spoke into the voice tube connected to the maneuvering room. "Full reverse."

The Graf Spee vibrated brutally as the hunter slowed to ensure the bundles of U.S. currency remained inside the confines of the torpedo. Seconds later, the familiar noise passed through Graf Spee's hull—the scraping sound of the 51-foot spar punching a six-inch hole on either side of the torpedo. Toggles on the end of the 51-foot spear deployed, gigging the torpedo as if it were a flounder. In seconds, the vessel would fill with seawater. Graf Spee would punch the spar off after removing the bundles of cash. The early years of "gigging" properly named "Happy Times," as the environment was rich with unsuspecting targets.

As more torpedo crews vanished without a trace, the cartels adapted. They added contingency breathing apparatuses for each of the crew in case of a breach of their fiberglass hulls with the spar. In those instances, sonar would hear crewmembers struggling to free themselves from inside their tomb. If any of the crew were so fortunate to make it to the surface, Johannes would personally issue a coup de grace to the head and leave the bodies for shark bait.

Once there was no more movement inside the hull, Graf Spee would blow its ballast and surface. They would then attach the cable to a winch to pull it to the surface. Once they transferred the cargo into Graf Spee's torpedo room, they would release the cable and the hulk, with spar still embedded, sank into the abyss.

"On course, on depth, Captain," Felix stated.

* * *

Johannes rested with his back against the conning tower rail adjusting the satellite phone out of the small of his back as the phone beeped. An email had arrived.

The last million-dollar bundle of cash had vanished inside the Graf Spee and the exec signaled the senior crewmember topside with a quick slash across his throat. An officer barked an order and a bolt cutter sliced through the cable and the drug runner became a tomb as it slowly vanished into the depths.

"38 bundles, Captain," the exec said.

Johannes nodded, opened his email, which read, "Wilhelmshaven," the prearranged code to return to Isle de San Andres immediately. He leaned over the rail and barked out an order. "Clear the decks, prepare to get underway." He turned to lean over the open hatch. "Watch to the bridge. Prepare to make way."

Johannes dropped into the control room landing on both feet with a clunk. "Come left to 180 full speed ahead. We are going home."

Smiles broke out amongst the control room. The Graf Spee was going home, and the 30-man crew would split $10 million of the $38 million in prize money.

11

Richardson, Texas
Vector Data Communications

Bob Holder, founder of NanoTech, headquartered in Richardson, interrupted Hap via conference call in the only way the man spoke-bluntly.

"Hap," Holder said, "it would be best for the company and its shareholders if you make a clean break from day-to-day management and remain as Vector Data's Chair."

The weight of each of his old friends' words pulled Hap's jaw closer toward the desk. Holder served as a Force Recon Marine before attending Texas A&M to study computer science. Will made the introduction over a single malt in this office during Vector Data's early years.

Hap shook his head. "Bob, did I hear you correctly?"

"Have you ever known me to stutter, Hap?"

Hap gave a sympathetic gaze to his office since much of his life outside the Marine Corps had taken place in what he always referred to as his bunker. A blessed life and career, yet at the moment he was fit to be tied. His fingers hovered inches over the phone-a punch with one finger would terminate the call.

"Let me be clear, if you're asking me to give up the day-to-day as the company's CEO, the board doesn't need me as its chair."

Another voice came through the speaker: "Think before you do something rash."

Hap recognized Jimmie Don Grafton, founder of Advanced Technologies, the world leader in amphibian drones. Hap had nominated Jimmie Don two meetings before he and John "Hollywood" Hancock went wheels in well on their flight to El Centro California.

Jimmie Don said, "Your net worth is tied up in the company. It would be foolish for you to throw it in the shitter over spilled milk."

Jimmie Don's words felt like a high voltage transmission passing down his spine.

"Excuse me, gentlemen. Do you mind if the woman on this call gets a word in?" MC Simmons, the widow of Major Harold D. Simmons, had joined the board after the Borderline incident. "Colonel, you have the full support of the board to remain as chairman. Get off your damn high horse." Her tenor matched the tone she'd used when she stood in front of her husband's casket and delivered his eulogy. Hap still remembered the long flight to Dover to escort Major Simmons' casket home, before acting as officer in charge of his mentor's burial detail.

"So, you too?" Hap chided. "Let's get this killing over with. Is there a motion to have Hap Stoner removed as Vector Data's CEO and replaced by Crash Ferguson?"

Bob Holder didn't hesitate, "I move Hap Stoner be removed as CEO of Vector Data, but remain as Chairman."

Hap's heart rate quickened similar to the times tracer fire raced past the cockpit of his Cobra.

"I second the motion," Don Reynolds said.

Hap could picture Don seated in his study looking out over Charleston Harbor where Fort Sumter and the World

War II aircraft carrier turned museum, USS Yorktown, lived.

John Hancock spoke abruptly. "Hap, I want to make a note for the record that you will recuse yourself from this vote."

What could he do but roll his eyes at Hollywood? "Please make a note for the record that I have recused myself from this vote."

A six-two vote for Hap to step down followed. Only Jimmie Don and MC dissented. Hap was confident MC dissented only because her vote didn't matter. If her vote had been a swing vote, her vote would have been to throw his ass to the curb. Maybe it had to do with how Jonathan, her oldest got shot up in Chuck Warden's rescue. The entire meeting felt staged, teed up like a golf ball on a golf tee. There could be only one man responsible… Will Kellogg. Trapped in a box, Hap pushed the meeting to get it over with.

"Now that I'm removed from the day-to-day, do I hear a motion to remove Hap Stoner as Chairman?"

You could have heard crickets on the conference bridge if any would have been on the line.

Jimmie Don broke the ice. "So, you will remain as Vector Data's Chair?"

Hap took in a deep breath and let his head fall back to gaze at the slow-moving ceiling fan. Carla had been right all along. Will Kellogg wanted him on the mission.

12

Richard, Texas
Stoner Residence Dining Room

The phone slipped into its cradle ending the board meeting and his role as chief executive office at Vector Data. He contemplated a phone call to break the news to Peg, but knew her mind had touched REM hours earlier.

His jawline tightened thinking about Pop and his endless one-liners. "Hap, it can always be worse."

Crash Ferguson would do a great job as Vector Data's CEO. He was instrumental in strategizing sales, marketing, product development, and streamlining operations to shore up the company's income statement, and Hap could think of no other executive more qualified.

Meeting adjourned, Hap sipped on a scotch with the realization that as bad as the call had gone, in a couple of hours the sun would rise in the east. It was time to go home. His private line flashed, and the caller ID made him dread the browbeating that was about to take place.

"Hey Babe," he said, glad Carla was not sitting across the desk to see his grimace. "How was your day?"

The thought of a reprieve vanished a half minute later when she unloaded on him with both barrels. "What in the hell have you done, Hap Stoner?" she chided. "Have you fallen off your rocker—?"

Holding the phone slightly away from his ears so her rant didn't break his eardrums, he interrupted. "They fired me, babe."

"You deserved it, Hap. Peggy filled me in at 5:30 but then covered for you saying you were out of the office. What lunacy is this? Tell me you're not preparing to leave the country. What about the wedding?"

There was no getting around it—events would cause a delay to their wedding discussions. A sure indicator the love of Hap Stoner's life had taken matrimony off the table was when she snapped out, *what have you done, Hap Stoner?* Before the line went dead.

Even at four in the morning, when Hap entered the door to the Ranch house, his three-year-old miniature Yorkie met him at the door pawing at his ankles. Hap's pup matched him stair by stair up the circular staircase staying a step ahead as both entered an empty bedroom. It was no surprise Carla's side of the closet and all her drawers were empty. There was no note, and Hap felt relieved she hadn't stuffed Maggie under an arm on her way out of the door. He wondered what Carla knew about Will's mission and what it meant for them.

13

Richardson, Texas
Stoner Residence

16 hours later, Hap lounged in his customary place at the end
of twelve-foot long dining room remembering the phone
slipping into its cradle ending the board meeting, and his role
as chief executive officer at Vector Data. His jawline tightened
thinking about Pop and his endless one-liners.

If Carla had been sitting in her empty seat to his right, she
would have stared at him accusingly, then say, "Listen to your
father, Hap Stoner."

Jake Tyson sat at the opposite end of the table, and peering
over the rim of the brown paper bag, he quipped as he unpacked
dinner. "Sorry, I'm missing Carla's legendary enchiladas." A
former Marine Corp's F-18 driver, Jake's build was between a
bodybuilder and surfer with blonde hair kept in a crew cut
to go with deep blue eyes. The man could have played the
leading role in 'Beach Blanket Bingo'.

Hap didn't bother to respond. No way could Jake understand the full meaning of her absence.

Jake pursed his lips around a straw to take a long draw
from one of Hap's insulated workout mugs before he settled
into the high back chair. "Did Will ever discuss an old colleague
of his who made a fortune writing WWII history?"

From the other end of the table, Hap picked at the last of
an enchilada like a kid pushing around the cabbage on his

plate. Even before rolling in the sack for the first time, Carla won him over by satiating his palate with a homemade chicken enchiladas recipe. "No, Jake," he said between chews in a less than enthusiastic tone.

Jake sipped from a crystal scotch glass and leaned around Carla's favorite homegrown flower arrangement centered on the table. "Rich Garbaccio traveled the world in search of the old goose-stepping sons of bitches. He used writing as a cover."

Hap spoke from behind the arrangement. "Met Rich on a plane from Stockholm to Rio months ago. Sat at a dinner table briefly with an executive discussing contract deal points and I'll be damn if he didn't join us, uninvited. The situation spun out of control from there."

"Apparently he's been on the trail of a particular SS Colonel for decades and found the son of a bitch in Rio."

"I was there, Jake, and that explains some of the night's events. But we haven't spoken since then." Hap rested both elbows on the cherry wood table and slowly massaged his forehead. "Would have never thought the man sitting across from me that night was old enough to serve in the Reich. If Hans Guderian is the Nazi he was looking for, the old fucker aged like a fine wine."

Jake peered around the other side of the arrangement.

Hap continued. "Explains why the minute Rich joined Mr. Guderian the situation went to hell in a handbasket. So, what does a Nazi war criminal pissing Rich off in Rio have to do with a king's ransom?"

Jake's response was to begin pulling the tablecloth hand over hand toward his end of the table.

Hap leaned over the table and his strapping forearms corralled the take-out, a Styrofoam container holding luke-warm enchiladas, as the cloth moved caddy corner toward Jake.

The arrangement the size of a large raccoon veered towards the side of the table. Jake didn't stop pulling until the men could look at each other without straining their necks.

"Better," Jake said smiling. "Apparently, the bastard took the name of an SS Officer killed during the Ardennes offensive."

Hap leaned across his empty paper plate to reach for the humidor. "Thousands of Krauts took another name to escape the gallows. Want a stogie?" Hap looked at Jake over the opened lid. Made of cherry wood the arched lid carried a Marine Corps Eagle Globe and Anchor carved into the top.

Jake returned a nod but remained silent.

Hap stuffed a cigar into his mouth. "There are a lot of coves with plenty of natural caverns snaking all through the island, so that gold could be anywhere. But let me guess, the gold is in the Buccaneer's vault?"

Jake frowned. "Not exactly, Colonel."

Hap said nothing as he reached into the humidor for a cigar.

Jake's fingers manipulated the crystal glass now void of scotch. "Across the bay from the Buccaneer."

Thin lines sneaking from the corners of Hap's eyes tightened closer together. How many times had he heard Will speak of the Fortress guarding the bay?

"When you refill my glass and hand me a cigar, I will tell you a little story, Colonel." He held up the empty glass as if issuing a toast until Hap took it from him.

Hap stepped behind the high back chair to the 1900 French Renaissance buffet cabinet. Made of walnut, Carla just had to have it when the two of them shopped in Fredericksburg, Texas after a several hour visit to the Nimitz museum. Jake bit off the end of the cigar and spit the tobacco remnants into the empty take-out container while he flicked his lighter into action. He brought the cigar to life with each draw then picked up on the story as Hap dropped the first cube of ice into the empty glass. "Han's brother was the number two Nazi for subversion in the Americas. He worked for an agent named Ribbentrop based out of Mexico City."

Hap returned double-fisted holding out his right hand. "Cut to the chase, Jake."

Jake smiled and relieved Hap of one of the glasses. He resumed his conversation as Hap retook his seat. "The brother was responsible to ensure gold made it to a Panamanian Bank before each transaction with the U.S. oil company. From there, it converted to American greenbacks with banks friendly to the Nazis. America enters the war and the U.S. and British governments threaten certain oil executives, leaving the two Nazis with a lot of loose change and nothing to spend it on."

Hap bit the inside of his lips, savoring the taste of the 18-year-old single malt. "I have heard these stories. U.S. Merchantmen and U.S. Sailors killed by U-boats whose fuel bunkers were full of U.S. refined diesel. "

"Had Germany not declared war on the U.S., the oilies would have continued to do business with the Nazis." Jake raised his glass to his lips and polished off its contents. "Come on, Colonel, under similar circumstances you wouldn't have cut similar deals with the Nazis?"

"Bullshit, Jake. Cutting deals at the expense of American lives - so many innocent civilians, is unbecoming." Hap shook his head around a stiff lower jaw. "It would compel me to pass. If my board would have insisted, I would have resigned, but not before challenging each one to a fist fight."

"Luckily I didn't come here tonight to debate the morals of business."

Hap leaned back, paused, and finally allowed himself to muster a half-smile.

Jake stretched his arms overhead, letting out a drawn-out belch. "That's a compliment to the chef, whoever that is," Jake said. "How about we move on to the reason I'm here."

After a moment, Hap leaned forward, unable to repress a deep sigh. "Jake, Carla has left me." He removed a couple of cigar aficionadi from the lacquered walnut humidor. Offering one as if gripping an exclamation mark, he flipped it end over end in a low arc across the table. "Take it with you."

Hands clasped behind his head, Jake slowly nodded,—the cigar wedged between big teeth in a mouth turned down at the corners. Reaching out with his right hand, he snagged the second cigar and tucked it into his pocket. "Based on credible information from Rich, the gold is sitting in the old Spanish fortress across from the Buccaneer."

"Jake," Hap said rolling the cigar back and forth between his fingers. "What makes everybody believe the gold is in the Fortress?"

"Gold has a big footprint Hap. Besides, they removed the gold from Fort Saint Louis on Martinique and only makes sense the Germans would use another Fortress to create the second cache.

Hap flipped open a Zippo with the Marine Corp emblem on one side and, on the other side, the figure of the Camel in sunglasses smoking a cig. Hap wedged the cigar between the fingers of his left hand and spoke behind a cloud of smoke. "And we are simply going to take it?"

"All seven billion Hap . . . and that's in 1945 dollars."

14

Bogota, Columbia
Cafe

It had been two days since Ramie left the Buccaneer and Will sat across from Jamie Ross in a small café in Bogota, Columbia. Situated halfway up a long incline wedged between a pharmacy and liquor store, neither man spent time on small talk as they sipped from their coffee mugs.

"I have your confirmation of identity," Jamie said, his gaze slowly but constantly shifting to assess their surroundings.

Both men had shared combat missions in the jungles of Vietnam, where they first met, and another ten years in the Central Intelligence Agency. Will resigned to go independent while Jamie stayed on, spending time between stations throughout Latin America. Will noticed Jamie had picked up a few more lines on a face that was already as lined as a topo-map. The sandy-haired crew cut he kept while in Vietnam had since grown shoulder length and gray. Upon retiring, Jamie never left Latin America.

Since Ramie's departure from the Buccaneer, Will had reached out to every resource within CIA and DIA, attempting to find any information obtainable relative to Vichy gold on the island of Martinique and the owners of the von Bock Empire. Dead ends followed, except one email Will had sent to Jamie that led them both to the café on the poor side of

Bogota Street. Just cross the street, the windows and doors had bars like on the poor side, but they'd maintained their structures, surrounded by walls with a layer of jagged glass along the rim. On the poor side, some of the windows had broken glass and they'd constructed the roofs with rusted tin.

Jake Tyson had been in Richardson for two days now.

Will felt his blood pressure rise with Jamie's last comment, "You sure, Jamie boy?"

"I have confirmed Franz von Bock along with his brother, Hans own Von Bock holdings. Split neatly down the middle, but you'd never know it by Googling them. Remember Will, he who controls the past controls the future. These Krauts aren't stupid."

Will said nothing thinking about the $13 million dollar marker Franz carried. He called this meeting to listen.

"Langley reported one anomaly." Jamie used a small napkin to dab sweat beading on his forehead. "There was a Colonel Hans Guderian killed during the Battle of the Bulge."

"Hell, Jamie, there could be more than one Hans Guderian in the world."

Jamie shrugged, his facial muscles relaxed. "Or maybe Franz's Kraut partner took the Guderian name to get out of Germany and at some point in time both took the name von Bock."

"The obvious answer," Will said. "Colonel Han Krueger was SS—did a lot of bad shit that he wanted to leave behind in someone else's grave."

"Then let's verify," Jamie said. "I have the section, row, and number for the grave marker for Colonel Guderian. Supposedly he is buried at the Lommel German war cemetery."

Will reached over the table and shook hands with his old colleague. "Don't be a stranger, Jamie. You know there is an open invitation to the Buccaneer."

"You know I don't gamble," Jamie said with a broad smile. "I'll call my contact in Belgium and don't worry about the tab."

Will stepped out of the small café onto a narrow sidewalk, where he stood looking casually in both directions. Situated halfway up an incline in the old downtown part of La Candelaria, the street looked empty. *Best time to move while inconspicuously placing eyes on a tail, because a crowd would be easier for the one who is doing the tailing to hide.* In less than an hour, the sidewalks would be laden with eager street vendors and shoppers. He walked downhill, careful to make a wide berth of the liquor store proprietor who worked head down, sweeping the straw broom across the sidewalk.

Dirt and wooden sidewalks lined the poor side of the narrow street and the other side of the street was concrete. Framed in the background, lay the city of Bogota; neat but shanty-like homes and businesses lined the streets.

He picked up the pace and turned onto a narrow walkway half the width of the sidewalk he just walked down. One literally had to step around thick concrete power poles centered in the narrow paths. The closer to the city center, the more bustle on the sidewalks and streets with cars parked here and there on one side of the road.

When he'd left the table, Jamie had been placing a call to a CIA field Operative near the Lommel German war cemetery in Belgium. The cemetery held 39,102 German graves, and most dated around World War II. Jamie would send a photo of the grave marker.

Will flagged a cab at the first major intersection and jumped into the empty backseat.

"*El Dorado Internationale*," he rattled off in rapid Spanish. With any luck, he might get a photo of the marker over Colonel Hans Guderian grave before the Citation landed at Love Field. He looked forward to seeing Hap Stoner but questioned whether a right jab was to be his greeting or a firm handshake and man hug. Though they hadn't seen each other since shaking hands goodbye at Columbus, New Mexico, Will knew Hap had been blindsided by his forced retirement out as Vector Data's CEO.

Will shrugged as if he'd answered a silent question. Hap Stoner had bigger and better things to do, he just didn't know it.

*   *   *

Back at the Vector Data Communication in Texas, Peggy Smith perused her unread email and noticed one from Will Kellogg sent at 2:30 a.m. As late into the night as the message was sent, she was surprised the subject line wasn't marked urgent or confidential nor was Hap copied. She double clicked the message.

Peg – Through the years, I have always wanted to tell you of my appreciation for all you have done for me, the organization, and especially Hap, always keeping his shit straight. Your loyalty, especially during the tough times has not gone unnoticed. You have always had our back and your laughter and caring for us as if we are the children you never had, will always be embedded in my

mind. Hap and I have gone through so much together, but he and I have a calling. I know that calling Peg, but Hap doesn't. I will always remember you and whatever happens in the future, be there for Hap, for so many who surround him will not be able to understand the why. And Peg – please keep this message confidential.
God Bless and Semper Fi.
William Hunter Kellogg

She spoke deliberately to herself while her brown eyes flicked back and forth across the message. She turned slowly toward the door; her mind contemplated the meaning of "a calling." News was about to break on the street about Hap being asked to step down. Tears puddled below her dark eyes and mixed with her mascara. She raised both hands to massage both eyes. A glance at her fingertips made it clear she needed to clean up. She moved quickly to close the door connecting the executive suite to the hallway.

As she slowly pushed the solid core door around its hinges, out of nowhere the door stopped. Then a man's head appeared, and he held a finger to his lips.

Peg let out a muffled gasp and seconds passed before she could take in a breath, she looked down at the carpet to mask her appearance. "How...how long have you been standing there, Mr. Kellogg?"

Will kissed the startled secretary on each cheek and pushed back maintaining a firm grip on each of her narrow shoulders "Who died?"

"Shame on you Will Kellogg," she said. Both hands covered her striking features as she let an anticlimactic laugh radiate between her manicured fingers. She fell into his arms.

Will had a nice coat of dark mascara stamped on his thick lips. "Something is up with the acquisition. Hollywood's at Hap's house."

Will gently eased her away so he could wipe his lips. His attempt to tidy up left the markings of a centerfielder on a sunny afternoon under both her eyes.

"I'm just glad the board allowed Hap to stay on as the chair instead of throwing his ass onto the street like a dog."

Peg scowled as she retreated to her desk and dabbed a fistful of tissue from the box Billie Joe had left earlier. She opened her top drawer and flipped open a pocket mirror.

"Something about outside influences attempting to squash the deal currently on the table." Will gazed around the old digs. "Who designed the executive suites? "

"I wouldn't know anything about outside influences, Will." She stared at the creature in the mirror and took in a deep breath. Her hand holding the tissue danced around both sides of her narrow face. "As for the suite, Hap let Carla and I design it."

Will rocked his head towards the old office. "I see Crash already moved into my old office."

Peggy shook her head while she blew her nose into the soiled tissue. "You know how sentimental Hap is. He would never let anybody move in, in case you wanted to come back. Crash will be taking Hap's office. I'll call Hap and let him know you're on the way to the house."

15

Richardson, Texas
Hap's Study at the Stoner Residence

Parked in their customary places around a coffee table milled from a slab of mesquite, Hollywood sat across from Hap, who relaxed in his favorite low back leather chair. Identical custom loveseats with Texas's Lone Star burned center mass into the leather, sat positioned across from the one another in line with the table's long axis.

Burning the Texas Star into each piece of furniture had been Carla's idea. She'd convinced Hap as he hovered over her while relaxing in the hot tub. Several glasses into the second bottle of wine, her epiphany of the butler's pantry outside the study's double doors came into being. In addition to a stove, the room had a dishwasher, an overabundance of cabinets, a sink, a microwave, and a double oven. He begged Carla to change the name of the room during but the remodel that followed, but the name stuck. The room screamed "toity" especially when there was a 900-square-foot kitchen around the corner.

Hap was many things, but not an ounce of toity ran through his veins.

Like clockwork, Hollywood peered over reading glasses perched on the end of a Roman nose. "Talk is all over Richardson that you were thrown out of Vector Data like a dog."

Hap said nothing, and the room went silent except the humming sounds of the ceiling fan and computer equipment. Larger than life, Will Kellogg's stout frame suddenly entered the study's open double doors. Hap straightened and approached the old man, contemplating a left hook, but the scar on Will's forehead compelled him to initiate a firm handshake instead, asking, "Coffee?"

Will shook his head and reached over to greet Hollywood.

"Good to see you, John," Will said, his voice packed with insincerity. He seated himself on the couch facing windows on the other side of the expansive desk. Hap and Hollywood returned to their seats.

"Great office, Hap."

Hap replied with an unassuming nod.

"Haven't seen the place since Carla's remodel. So, who is sticking their dick into the middle of this deal?"

Hollywood removed his glasses and cleaned the lenses with the paper napkin his coffee cup had rested on. "Clueless at this point. You know something we don't?" Hollywood complained.

"Two things. Though I'm not sure if the two are related."

Hap and Hollywood's eyes met somewhere over the coffee table and Vector Data's Legal Officer's head moved slowly back and forth. "We are all ears, Will," Hap said peering Will's direction.

Will eased back into the couch with crossed legs; his body language suggesting he didn't have a tense bone in his body. "I received two messages on the flight over from Mexico City to Dallas. The first confirms Hans Guderian's real name is probably Colonel Hans Krueger. The real Hans Guderian died during the Battle of the Bulge. Someone replaced Colonel

Guderian's headstone with a stone carved with Colonel Hans Krueger's name. Krueger was an SS Officer and assistant Commandant at Auschwitz.. You don't have to look hard to see how ruthless the man was. On a mere bet, the son of a bitch actually put two inmates back-to-back and ensured the back of their heads were touching. He shot one in the forehead to see if the bullet would go through one skull and then kill the other. He killed both and won the bet." Will reached into a coat pocket and leaned over to hand Hap a folded piece of paper.

Hap slowly unfolded the letter size sheet of paper, which revealed a grainy black and white photo print. Two males in their early teens had arms around the other's shoulder. They appeared to be brothers posing for the photo on a cobblestone street. The shorter of the two, wearing the SS uniform, could have easily been the man he sat across from Rio in the Von Bock contract negotiations.

"Three questions. Where did you get the photo? Who is the taller fella with the widow's peak, and why now?" Hap leaned over the table to meet Hollywood's extended hand with the photo. Hollywood returned the glasses to perch on the end of his nose and settled back into the chair.

Will softly ran his hand over the crease on his forehead and locked his eyes on Hap. "It's been a busy few days. I had an old Mossad contact from when I was CIA visit the Buccaneer. The taller brother is Franz Krueger, but goes by Franz Von Bock. He was a known Abwehr Military Intelligence agent responsible for operations in the Caribbean region during World War II. He is also somebody the Buccaneer owes $13 million."

Hap's head tilted to the side hearing the debt Will owed the man, but now understood why Rich was on the plane to Rio and joined their table at the meeting in the Rio Hilton. All along, Hans and Rich knew who the other was, and Hap just sat with his dick in his hand trying to score a large contract.

Will's eyes went cold, and then he said, "You know the female at the table that night died of a bullet wound fired from Hans' pistol."

For several seconds, time stood still in the room. Hap's brow furrowed closer together. "I didn't know."

"She died in Rich's arms outside that son of a bitch's front door." Will looked out the two windows, which framed the construction site. "What can you tell me about what's going on across the street?"

Hap shrugged. "A builder was specking a home. Rumor on the street somebody purchased the project outright and not much has happened since."

"How long ago did the purchase take place?" Will's eyes scoured the lot.

"Recent," Hap answered. "Within the last couple of weeks for sure.

Hollywood held up a finger from the same hand with which he palmed the photo. "Why now? The board's timing to fire Hap couldn't have been worse. Now outside influences are trying to block the sale of the company. Why?"

"Reading between tea leaves somebody wants to ensure all of us are occupied with the sale," Will said, his face splayed with conviction. "At this point, all hands point to Managua."

Hap settled back in his chair as Hollywood removed his glasses and leaned over a knee to speak.

"Say, what?"

Hap propped a cowboy boot on the coffee table. "I know there is no love lost between the higher-ups in Nicaragua and you, but I must be missing something."

"Hap, my CIA friends tell me Nicaragua and China want to build a canal. Tensions along the Costa Rican and Nicaraguan border are high, as Nicaragua needs Costa Rican dirt to pull this off and a hell of a lot of money for China to pony up finances. Currently, they have neither."

Hollywood settled back into his chair as Hap bit on the inside of his lower lip. He knew Isle de San Andres mirrored the Falkland Islands squabble over ownership. Closer to Nicaragua than Colombia, Colombia's flag fluttered above Isle de San Andres government buildings. "It's the perfect storm," Hap muttered.

"Excuse me, Hap?" Hollywood chimed.

"If the Nicaraguans believe Nazi gold is on the island, they will invade. The land dispute provides diplomatic cover so, if I'm in Daniel Ortega's shoes, I use the ongoing land dispute to hide the real purpose of the invasion. Colombian officials have no clue of the existence of the gold, and if the Nicaraguan military can pull off the raid, they gain possession of the gold and withdraw back inside their borders."

"All the more reason we go," Will announced. Seconds of silence followed as the three looked to the other. Will pressed a finger to his lips.

Hap saw it after Hollywood's jaw seemed to sag to the polished oak floor. Will got up from the couch, walked over to the stereo amplifier and punched up the power button. Hank Thompson singing "Six Pack to Go" poured out from the surround sound and he cranked the volume to a point where the next quarter turn would break glass.

He gestured with his head to leave the room. Hap and Hollywood followed Will through the butler's pantry, around the corner through the breakfast nook, and into the cavernous kitchen. Will continued through the kitchen doors on the house's west side to the outdoor living area, stopping in front of the jacuzzi, which spilled into the pool.

Will watched Maggie chase a pair of squirrels across one of Hap's golf greens yapping passionately. "Somebody is listening to your conversations, Hap."

"No way, Will," Hap replied as Maggie circled the plum tree to the side of the green. Every few steps all four feet left the ground as she leaped at the cackling animals safely secure fifteen feet above the outstretched paws of Hap's killer Yorkie.

"Do you have a gun close?" Will asked.

"In the study," Hap replied.

"Meet Hollywood and me out front, we are going to take a little walk. And Colonel, bring a crowbar."

* * *

Minutes later, Hap joined them on the driveway with the Belgium Browning holstered beneath a pulled out long sleeve shirt. "Thought you might want this."

Stopping in his tracks, Will turned and Hap palmed a Beretta 380 into his hand. A smile appeared the moment stainless steel touched flesh. The pistol vanished into Will's back pocket of his Levis. "Shall we?" he said, grabbing the crowbar.

With Will in the lead, Hap stayed close on his heels since nobody knew their destination except for the man on point. Being a school day, the neighborhood was void of children, and parents were at work. He crossed the street without looking, then bee-lined towards the construction trailer. Will stopped, peeked around the corner before continuing to the steps and up to the door. Hap watched as Will turned the knob. It didn't budge an inch.

Hap remained on the first step and noticed the Cat 6 line coming from the bedroom. Somebody had simply drilled a hole and snaked the line up the exterior wall to a small antenna fixed above the roof. It had been two weeks since Maggie bolted from the door and he found her sniffing around the back of the trailer. As before, the trailer was vacant, but the wire was surely a new addition.

Will slid the flat end of the crowbar between the jamb and strike pad. A quick tug later and the door popped open. Hap went for the Belgium Browning as Will's right hand reached for the 380, both men stepping into the trailer.

"Take the left half of the trailer, Colonel." Hap followed a narrow hall and did a quick check of the small bathroom. He moved around the corner and stopped. That same someone apparently locked the door. Will joined him at the door and, without a word, inserted the crowbar to repeat steps used to pry the front door open. As the door swung open, Will put his finger to his lips. The room was empty except for a foldout table pushed against the wall, where the Cat 6 poked through the wall. A piece of electronic equipment with a small antenna poking from its top sat next to a computer, powered up. He noticed the Cat 6 he saw outside connected to the back of the electronics with the single antenna. A Cat 6 cable ran from the electronic equipment to the computer with a dual ear headset rested next to the computer's mouse. Will and Hollywood vanished down the hall as Hap slid the mouse back and forth to bring it to life. He clicked on the Wi-Fi network the system was using and shook his head.

The sons of bitches had cracked into his Wi-Fi network across the street.

Will returned and slipped on the headphones as he slid the pistol back into his jeans. His index finger touched the right headphone and seconds later, he grimaced. He removed his cell phone and texted a message to Hollywood. Removing the headphones, he handed them to Hap and exited down the hall. Hap covered both ears to avoid Hollywood's rendition of "Build me up Buttercup." He was wrapping up the third verse, then silence.

"You really have outdone yourself on this one, Hap," Hollywood announced.

16

Managua Nicaragua
Military Headquarters

President Ortega's deep-throated berating seemed like it would never end. "We have traveled many jungle trails together, Omar, and it all began in our guerrilla training in Cuba."

"Yes, Mr. President. I remember."

"Do you remember my final order to begin the operation to take Managua?"

General Omar Hallesleven said nothing. The thought of issuing a resounding "Yes, Sir" crossed his mind, but decades of serving with the man, an outburst such as this had become commonplace. Managua maintained an attitude that generals were mere throwaways, as a line of colonels were in line waiting for a star.

"Because of me General, nationalization, land reform, wealth redistribution, and literacy programs began for all Nicaraguans."

Commander in Chief Armed Forces Nicaragua remained quiet. Since Ortega became the leader of the ruling multi-partisan Junta of Nation Reconstruction in 1979, he had always provided the muscle. Communism had replaced a dictatorship submerging Nicaragua's people deeper into despair.

"I have got to get my hands on the money to begin digging the much-needed canal connecting the Caribbean to the

Pacific. The order to begin preparation for the invasion with my signature will be in your hands in 24 hours."

Hallesleven would lead the invasion of the Isle de San Andres and with that responsibility, carried the future of the Revolution. "Will that be all, Mr. President?" Silence followed and the click of the President disconnecting issued the opportunity for the oversized phone to slide into its metal cradle. He swung his legs, which supported his solid six-foot frame from the desk and walked to the door.

No turning back now.

After a quick breath, Hallesleven proceeded to swing the polished mahogany door open and peer into the anteroom.

Seated behind a small desk shuffling papers, his chief of staff kept his head shaved and carried three stars on each lapel signifying the rank of colonel. On his desk, his small name placard spelled "Colonel Santiago."

"Colonel Santiago, call the chiefs into my office in three hours. No excuses. Mandatory attendance."

The shaved head turned and looked over his dark-rimmed glasses. "Sir?"

General Hallesleven's eyebrows crimped in, his jawline taut.

"All branches, General?"

"Did I stutter, Colonel?"

Santiago said nothing and issued a curt nod.

Hallesleven slowly swung the door closed and walked behind his desk to the map of Latin America hanging on the wall. His mind began to formulate directives to the chiefs putting wheels in motion to carry out the invasion. Nicaragua's fledgling Army, Navy, and Air Force would carry out a brigade-size operation equivalent to the U.S. invasion of Normandy in 1944. His square jaw shook slowly as he flopped into his chair and picked up the telephone.

His wife of 25 years answered on the third ring. "I will not be home for a few days." He knew she wouldn't question him.

"Be careful, Omar," she replied softly. "I will see you when you get home."

Inside 120 days, H-Hour and the future of Nicaragua rested on his shoulders.

17

Richardson, Texas
Stoner Residence

Eddie Barlosa stooped his muscular frame to comb the extended-stay hotel refrigerator, only to find the thirty-pack of Budweiser empty. A half-eaten can of bean and bacon soup and a plate with a half-brick of cheddar encircled in musty crackers bookended the red, white, and blue carton. He let the door swing shut.

No need to peek as the alarm sounded on his cell phone—he was on the clock, and he had twenty minutes to be on the steps of the Stoner residence. In Richardson for less than a week, he had only spoken to Hap Stoner once after Blad's introduction.

He fumbled with the bottom button of the weathered Hawaiian shirt until the brooch pinged to the tile floor and scooted under the refrigerator. "Fuck it," he grumbled. The jet-red t-shirt he wore underneath snugged up to every cut in his waist and upper body throwing off a nice reflection on the stainless refrigerator door.

As Eddie high stepped down the fire escape, the lower portion of the Hawaiian shirt billowed to either side of his waist. His socked feet raced across the parking lot in full stride while holding his cowboy boots in either hand. There was nothing hard about jumping from the fourth step of an outdoor stairwell wearing socks. The retired Airborne Sergeant

Major had executed jumps into Panama and Grenada, an eight-month stint in the sandbox for Operation Desert Storm and 2 additional tours in Iraqi Freedom. Eddie Barlosa would have changed one thing in his life if God would give him the opportunity, he would have join Shadow Operations years earlier. Shadow pay was better and never a dull moment when on the clock and something Stoner could never learn.

Since retiring from the Army, he had turned his Army 89D MOS into a handy civilian master electrician for his day job. The transition from explosive expert to electrician was second nature. Unless one is shooting into a can of tannerite laced with ball bearings to eradicate a herd of hogs, one would need some type of electrical current to set off the charge.

He slid on the worn Tony Llamas and spun into the driver's seat and turned the key giving life to 350 cubic inches tucked underneath the hood of the restored banana yellow 1971 Monte Carlo. The engine rumbled to life, muscle cars were second only to a fast woman.

Knuckles molded by continued years of karate gripped the steering wheel. His assignment was to stay close to Stoner, act as a personal bodyguard, and report back to Operations re: ongoing plans. He pulled into the half-moon circular drive and stopped in front of the twelve-foot tall mahogany front doors. "Nice digs," he said, as he peered through the open passenger window at small lone star insignias burned into the double doors beveled glass panels.

Exiting the car his sixth sense kicked in. He peered over a muscular shoulder to eye the other side of the street and a vacant lot with a construction trailer on site.

Stoner's door lock clicked just as he raised a fist to knock. The latch released, and Hap didn't allow Eddie to express his concerns, instead, he shoved a long neck Shiner Premium into his palm.

"Great seeing you, too," Eddie said as Hap ushered him through the remarkable foyer. He couldn't help but notice the painting of the Alamo tucked to the left of the stairwell landing before its oak steps spiraled tightly around the early 19th-century chandelier. With the country's political climate, some would throw the rendering and Sam Houston's 67-foot-statue overlooking I-45 south of Huntsville Texas, into a concrete grinder.

A man the size of a lumberjack straightened as Eddie walked through the cased opening to enter the living room.

Thick as he was wide, Lew Eglin, at six-foot-six, wore a close-cropped beard as red as the wavy hair touching his shoulders, giving him the appearance of being ready for the WWE. Shifting a bottle between the knuckles of his left hand, Lew extended his bear paw.

"Lew Eglin," he said with a crooked smile.

Eddie offered his right hand. "Eddie Barlosa."

Hap escorted Eddie over to a wiry figure seated in the corner of the room next to a bronze of Lady Justice, blindfolded clutching the scales of justice. "Eddie," Hap said gesturing with a half-empty long neck, "I would like you to meet Shaun O'Hare." Hap's eyes cut to Eddie. "Shaun, Eddie Barlosa."

Eddie sized Shaun to be a shade over six feet and 160 pounds coming out of a shower. Shaun issued a curt nod and said nothing. He extended a hand without standing or a word said between the two men.

Hap walked over to the Wi-Fi booster to the left of the Austin stone fireplace and casually unplugged the device just as his cell phone vibrated in his pocket.

"Good call," Eddie said.

Hap glanced at the caller id, narrowed his eyes, and then looked around the room.

"Gotta take this one, guys." Hap turned toward the large bay window looking into the back yard, then said, "Stoner." Hap listened intently. Scratched the crown of his head and coughed up a belly laugh. "You're kidding me," A large smile crossed his face from one end to the other. "So, she is okay?"

"Yes Sir, Mr. Stoner. Miss Carla seems to be on a mission. She is jumping Dixie hard Mr. Stoner, and your Arabian looks like he is about to run out of gas." He didn't worry about Carla on the back of a horse. She loved to ride and hurting Dixie would be the last thing on her mind. The love of his life was venting, and Dixie could jump all day. Just when you wanted that break, the Arabian would nudge you towards the saddle without an apple slice even on offer.

With the news, he worked his way towards the bar in the sunroom and hung up the phone. *Carla hadn't left town, after all.* Like an electrical current, her presence issued his zest for life. Hap reappeared with beers in hand. He handed a Shiner to Shaun, leaving a whisk of condensation on the Turkish rug, which covered two-thirds of the large living room. The others offered up empty bottles. Long necks spiraled lazily in Eddie and Lew's direction.

The first sound from Shaun's mouth was a chuckle. "Having only met her couple of times Hap, I'd say she was one hell of a lady."

"Still is," Hap said as he looked at his old TBS roommate with a smile. "I'm in feet first, Shaun. Shall we?"

By the expressions on their faces, all present were ready to listen. "You will not have much time. You will be in…or out. I will admit during a negotiation where I have been across the conference table and heard this crap, I normally very politely excused myself. In no way will I hold ill will if you politely excuse yourself."

Shaun spoke to his character. "Cut to the chase, Hap. It's hard to blow off something we know nothing about."

Hap passed by the game table and scooped a stack of photos. As he slowly moved around the room, he began to drop black and whites in each lap. Every face carried a don't bullshit a bullshitter expression.

They passed the photos amongst themselves in silence. An occasional photo drifted to the floor. A hand would reach down, and the photo would continue its path around the room. Eddie paid little attention to the photos focusing more on his beer.

Lew asked quizzically, "Hap, I'm a man with a large boat and no military experience. What do you want with me?"

Hap flipped a photo depicting a seaward approach. "It's an island, Lew, and we need a boat with a good crew and better Skipper. We need transport for a vertical assault, then dock to move goods off the island."

"Vertical assault?" Lew replied.

"Goods?" Eddie chuckled. "What goods?"

Hap sensed Eddie was attempting to steer the conversation. Why? He wondered. Hap walked in front of the fireplace and turned away from the TV mounted above the Austin stone façade to face his audience. "Within the walls of the Fortress could be as much as $150 billion in gold bullion. Air is out of the question. This mission needs a boat, a small air force, and ground assets second to none in the world."

Shaun coughed on the number. "What's in it for the grunts, Hap?"

A grin peeked out between Hap's salt and pepper Fu Manchu, which he'd grown since his discharge from the Corps. "A piece of the action for each man, but I am not going to bullshit any of you. There is a hell of a lot of risk. Eddie, Blad tells me you are expert with explosives, Shaun, heavy weapons and small unit tactics. The keepers of the king's ransom are not going to allow us to waltz in and fill Lew's boat and just sail away."

"Are you sure, Hap?" Eddie said. "What makes you think we just can't walk into the Fortress and take it?"

Hap said nothing. Shaun raised his beer over his head and pointed the open-end in Hap's direction.

Eddie glanced over an aerial picture taken at an angle looking down into the fortress. "This doesn't look that tough, Hap. When do we go?"

"I'm getting tired of the Peruvian jungles. I can take a leave of absence from the agency," Shaun said. "I'm in."

Hap knew Shaun was growing bored with the DEA, as Shaun referred to the Agency to fight drugs, "It's like masturbation, Hap. Feels good, just don't brag about it."

Seconds passed as Hap was still thinking about Eddie. The man seemed to know more about the opportunity than he did, but wasn't advertising. Hap cocked his head to the side as if to ask, *you in, Lew?*

Lew shifted in the couch, a bit uncomfortably like a man that just cut a fart in front of future in-laws on their first meeting. "You know my second wife left me when my company went into the crapper. I have two vessels left and, unless something changes, Stingray is months from being repossessed. I'm in."

More personnel with specific skill sets would be required.

He also knew Will Kellogg was tapping his fingers of both hands on the steering wheel of his rental car parked across the street.

Will's left thumb engaged the blue tooth before the first ring was completed. "Kellogg,"

"We're ready."

Peering from the door, Hap couldn't see Will reach into the glove box for his 9 mm. He did see Will pause to allow a car with tinted windows, a shade rare for the neighborhood, to pass. The red tint of the Cadillac's brake lights appeared as the vehicle slowed. Will continued across the street without paying mind to the vehicle.

Entering through the double doors, he stopped to greet with a firm handshake and a head gesture in the car's direction. "What brings that ghetto wagon to the community? Friends of yours?"

Hap shook his head slowly and smiled. "I unplugged the Wi-Fi."

18

The Fortress; Isle de San Andres
Flashback to 1939

Franz stood hands on hips with a flashlight sticking out of his back pocket still mesmerized by the 17th-century relic. Emil Prufart, breathing hard from the one-hundred-yard walk from the car, joined him in front of the moat.

"I still can't get over the engineering accomplishment, Emil." Franz looked over the arrow-shaped outwork constructed to protect the Fortress's main entrance from ground assault.

"Herr Baron," Emil said, "notice the firing ports on both sides of the drawbridge cut through the walls to allow musketeers to mow down invaders attempting to storm the main entrance in deadly crossfires.

"How about the walls, Emil?"

"11 to 19-feet thick at the base and the 17th-century walls tapered to the ramparts to a 9-foot width at the firing ports for the cannoneers."

The driver of the 32 Ford joined them and rattled off in rapid Spanish. "Legend has it not a single invader's boot touched the Fortress ramparts."

Emil translated Hector's response in German as Franz gingerly worked the heel of the German military leather dress shoe across the stationary bridge. "You trust this thing?"

"Careful Franz," Emil in a matter of fact tone. "Maybe we should wait until we can get sturdier planks in place."

On the third step, Franz's leg punched through a plank to his thigh.

Wooden remnants fell harmlessly into the dry moat six feet below. Without hesitation, Franz worked his leg loose and ran his eyes up and down his leg. *No bloodstains and I escaped with only a tear in my pants.* "Dodged a bullet, Emil, I have a job to do and you're three days late to the island, so I'm behind schedule." Successive steps were more vigilant as if crossing a British minefield. Thirty feet later, his patent leather shoes crossed the threshold where the stationary bridge connected to the 20-foot drawbridge. The 4 x 6 planks sagged slightly, and emitted a groan each time the weight of his 6-foot, 4-inch frame landed on a plank.

"We are behind you, Franz," Emil said.

Franz didn't look back but could hear the planks groan as they moved across the bridge. The fortress's last line of defense to separate defenders inside the walls from attackers clearly sat unused for decades.

Inside the Fortress, Hector's small frame led the inspection through narrow passageways and expansive chambers situated off the main square. Throughout the inspection, it felt as though he counted each of the 400,000 coquina shell bricks that made up Germany's lone outpost in the Caribbean.

Regular polygon—four equal sides, and four bastions resembling a star shape—wasn't unique to the times. The design allowed for no blind spots and multiple cannon or muskets could fire on any one target.

Their flashlights lit up a staircase to their left and they came to a stop in front of a pair of partially open doors. Franz tugged one of the circular cast iron ornaments and the arched door casing was frozen on its hinges. His hand followed the beam across the 18-inch opening to the other ornament, tugged with the same result.

"How long has the Fortress been vacant?" Franz twisted around to look past two beams and the dark outline of Emil Prufurt's small frame behind one of the flashlights.

Emil spoke in a heavy Latin accent. "Since the last person crossed the bridge. I say at least five decades Herr von Bock."

The man behind the second flashlight rattled off in rapid Spanish. "Eso es correcto, Emil."

Franz bent at the waist to wedge his wiry frame through a maze of cobwebs. He straightened exiting the silk tunnel, and wiped away strips of white from his shoulders and pronounced widow's peak.

Beams from his flashlight bounced around the chamber's empty space lighting up a fireplace large enough for a man to stand in at the far end of the chamber. He watched Emil Prufurt's flashlight beam dance off the chamber's 20-foot ceiling before dropping to the floor and back up a wall to the arched ceiling. The Colombian businessman had been loyal to the Nazi cause for five years and was offering the Fortress as a gift with business strings to support Abwehr operations in Latin and South America.

Hector worked his arms as if swimming and plowed through the cobwebs. He began to swipe away sheets of cobwebs from his shoulders and head as he approached the fireplace. He came to a stop next to Franz. "This is going to take a lot of work, senor."

"You up for the job?" Franz asked in a quizzical tone.

"Que"?

Their voices echoed off the walls and ceiling of the chamber, and overhearing their conversation, Emil jumped into the conversation. "Estas listo para el trabajo, *you are ready for work, Hector?*

Franz looked down over a shoulder at the top of Hector's head and could see he was nodding.

"Si, Senor."

Franz padded Hector's shoulder and turned to Emil who had placed a shoe on the fireplace's rock hearth.

Gesturing with the flashlight towards the arched ceiling Emil said, "Franz, being German you probably marvel at the engineering and architecture more so than I."

* * *

Franz rocked back in his executive chair, admiring decades of continual transformation. Centuries-old coquina floors and walls were resurfaced smooth. Chambers walls now covered with flowing drapes and European art. Sections of the fortress not open to the public contained paintings from Nazi plunder of occupied Europe and Asia, still unaccounted for after the war ended.

Floor-to-ceiling bookshelves made from tropical hardwoods lined the walls. The far side of the room still contained the rock fireplace and the chamber's centerpiece. An 8-foot tall portrait hung above the mantel displaying a figure standing erect, eyes impenetrable, and wore the same outfit as the figure gazing up at the portrait except for the red sash wrapped around a narrow waist.

Hector pulled the room's 10-foot mahogany double doors until they latched, leaving the two brothers alone. Franz's facial expression softened and he walked toward his brother to exchange warm greetings, a strong handshake, a rapid patting of the man's shoulder with a left hand, combined with a glad to see you smile.

Hans peeled off his mustache and goatee, rubbing his face to soothe the itch of the adhesive and joined his brother on the couch. He dropped the dark glasses and hairpiece to his lap revealing blue eyes and thin silver hair combed straight back.

"I will need to get off the island as soon as possible, brother. I'm growing tired of walking the streets like some kind of Hollywood imposter," Hans said. "I was thinking about Graf Spee."

Franz said nothing. His thoughts were on Will Kellogg's call. His warning Rich Garbaccio would be part of a Fortress tour to find and kill the man sitting across the couch signaled all was going to plan.

Hans' blue eyes had grown tired over the years but still could burn a hole into a man during moments like these. His brother's facial muscles were relaxed and the three circles below his eyes depicted a man searching for sympathy. "Rich Garbaccio will come to this island, I know it. My tracks were covered changing planes in Panama but brother, he knows. Besides, it seems we both had feelings for the same woman and during our shootout at the Plantation, I accidentally shot her."

Franz's face angled to the side and his stare dropped to the desktop. He said nothing.

It was ten minutes past noon and Franz had people expecting him for lunch in the sunroom in fifteen minutes. Gaining his feet, he tapped a pencil on a chart marking assets held by the Spanish Main Holdings Corporation.

"The question, brother, is where to go?" Franz spoke looking through glasses perched on the end of his pronounced muzzle.

Hans leaned in and tapped a finger on a marker with small crossed picks denoting a diamond mine asset located in the heart of South Africa.

Franz reached his arm around his brother's shoulder. "We have traveled a long and winding path, brother. Some things shouldn't be discussed."

Hans turned to embrace his brother around the neck. "We mustn't let anyone come between us, brother."

Franz stood and wiped away the moisture collecting below his eyes. "The Graf Spee is not scheduled to be back for three weeks. I advise you to take a Company plane tomorrow afternoon."

"Planes are easier to track than a submarine that doesn't exist."

Franz nodded. "True. Graf Spee will take a week if I recall her immediately."

Hans' head angled up his silver brows pinched. "Rich Garbaccio's father was my shoeshine boy at Auschwitz. He witnessed many of bad things I did,"

Franz maintained a poker face staring down at his brother. "You did, or were you simply a Nazi officer following orders?

Hans' head moved side to side and the corners of his narrow mouth turned down. "Guilty as charged brother. Much of what I did was in front of Rich's father and it is another reason why he fully intends to kill me."

Franz proffered a sympathetic smile. "I'm not proud of the things I did during the war."

"So what do we do, little brother?"

Franz paused steering his gaze toward the fireplace. "Let this Rich Garbaccio follow you to Isle de San Andres." Eyes closed, Franz's head tipped back thinking back to Will Kellogg's call. "We will let this Nazi hunter come to you."

The wrinkles around Hans' eyes straightened. "And once Rich is inside the Fortress?"

"Kill him."

19

Fortress Tour
Isle de San Andres

Rich moved through the empty corridor as a tourist separated from his tour group. *After passing the fifteenth door to my right and the fourteenth to my left, the corridor would begin a slight bend to the right. Fifty feet and there should be a stairwell. Thirteen right, twelve left. Don't lose count now. Fourteen right, thirteen left, fifteen right and as advertised the fourteenth door left, and the bend to the right began.*

The stone monolith 'as built' plans had been put to memory after countless hours of study made available by a Mossad agent who Rich knew was assigned to Madrid Spain. Over beers a few months past, the pretty boy let on about an ongoing affair with the Director over the National Archives of Spain.

Piece of cake.

As if by divine intervention, the plans arrived through a network tunneled through Mossad's private network and used by former agents who left the agency in good standing. Active agents never complained as they would become former agents and need access to information.

A quick glance at the watch said 6:30. The tour would end in less than 30 minutes. *Hope my tour guide, Michael, failed math, and security enjoys their happy hour.* If he had picked the right corridor, the only turn available at the bottom would be right. Good to go. He moved swiftly to cover the 100 feet to the next set of stairs only to find a vault door closer to the next stairwell 25 feet on the other side of the door. Heavy-duty, high-tech, and secure with an electronic lock and key backup. *To protect what?* A small foyer peeled off to the right and darkness. If "X" marked the spot, a door was fifteen feet away and where he wanted to be.

One click resonated from the other side followed by five subsequent pad entries. Movement of locking bolts followed, and the three-prong handle slowly turned counter clockwise. He pulled the .22 caliber LRS from the small of his back as he hugged the wall and backed into the darkness of the foyer. Fortunately, the door swung opened towards the foyer and a jumpsuit-clad figure passed, eyes straight, his walk brisk. Rich's free hand snagged the edge of the door when the figure had passed. Immediately, hydraulics began to tug against his hand. He knew the system and, in four seconds, an alarm would sound. He whirled around and through the door as it slowly shut, hearing the lock bolts sliding into place.

The corridor well lit, and lights and the sound of a TV resonated from a room at the base of the stairs. A closet door was to his right and the fortress key room was down the hall. As he returned his pistol to the holster, it was time to play the role of a new IT contractor. Rounding the corner at the base of the stairwell he entered a well-lit room and another figure behind a desk lowered the Playboy magazine he was reading and went wide-eyed.

"How did you get in here?"

Rich's eyes began to wander glancing to his shoulder and both arms. *It's better to be lucky than good.* His left thumb pointed over the shoulder. "The guy let me in to take care of some networking issues he had reported." He was definitely in the old dungeon, although they had modernized the room. An elevator was to his left and over the shoulder of the avid reader was a vault door ten foot across and at least the same in height.

"He didn't tell me," the guard said.

Rich said nothing and shrugged. The man carried no visible sidearm and wore a jumpsuit, which meant if he had a gun it was inside the desk. "It's been a couple of days," Rich answered reaching into his pant pockets as if searching for something. "I have the work order somewhere."

The sides of the guard mouth twisted up. He slid the magazine into the top left drawer and straightened. "Are you new?"

Rich nodded but said nothing still fumbling with his pockets, then said. "I can come back."

The guard gestured a hand toward the corridor. "I will let you out the way you came in,"

As they approached the keypad, Rich angled against the wall to allow the guard access to the keypad. Standing in front of the keypad the locking bolts retracted and the door slowly opened from the outside. Somebody was entering from the outside.

Rich grasped the pistol grip with his right hand and cracked the unsuspecting guard over the back of the head. The limp figure collapsed to both knees below the keypad. Rich pressed himself to the door as the hydraulics slowly pushed the door open. The guard he passed earlier angled through the partially open door and Rich slammed the butt to the temple dropping him next to his partner. It would be seconds before the hydraulic actuator began to pull the door closed.

Rich opened the closest door to find an oversized janitor's closet. Inside were three brooms and a couple of mops resting inside a mop bucket. On the top shelf were some loose tools, gallon size containers of cleaning solvents, loose rags, and a roll of electrical tape.

Rich grabbed the tape and made a half dozen passes around each of their mouths. He moved the second guard into the closet as the actuators to close the vault door energized. Rich whisked him up by the back of the shoulders and let him fall over the first guard. As much as he wanted to bind their hands, time didn't allow for it, so he swung the door closed and dropped the tape into his pocket.

Ten minutes later, Rich was at the top of stairs looking down at the Commissar's offices closed doors. A voice spoke in broken English. "Are you lost, Sir?"

Rich froze and half turned to meet his tour guide, Michael, standing in an open door.

"Seem to have lost the group," he lied.

"I should say so," speaking in between shallow breaths as he drew close. "They left fifteen minutes ago."

Rich spoke behind a poker face. "I had to visit the restroom."

Michael started to pull a small handheld walkie-talkie from his belt, but was unconscious before the back of his head whiplashed into the stone floor. Rich could only hope security was doing anything other than monitoring their screens. He wasted no time grabbing Michael's collar and dragging his unmoving body toward the door the guide just had entered. The office was vacant and had the appearance of an administration office with two desks with computers and 10-key machines on top and a few filing cabinets. *Thank God, it was Saturday.* The crimson trail left from the blood pouring from the shattered nose would not allow much time. Rich closed the door behind them and slapped Michael's limp body back to life. The guide slowly came to a knee and wiped the blood from his nose. "For an old fucker, you sure deliver a punch." Rich filled one hand with the .22 caliber. The man built as a linebacker slowly shook his head to clear the cobwebs with one eye struggling just to remain half-open. Rich grabbed his throat with the free hand. Decades of pent-up emotion exacted as he spoke. "Where did von Bock and his brother go?"

Michael's head wobbled side to side with a question mark stamped across his face. "Sir, I don't understand. Mr. von Bock doesn't have a brother."

"Maybe you understand this." Rich thumbed the hammer back on his pistol, and then pointed it at the man's face.

He blinked slowly, staring at the barrel, and then smiled and moved to both knees. "Look, take some paintings."

Rich whipped the pistol across the chin spinning him to the floor. He grabbed the bloodied collar and lifted Michael to his knees talking under his breath. "You are trying my patience, Michael."

"There is a business colleague visiting from Rio," he spewed with blood and a tooth.

The barrel of the pistol touched the half-conscious victim's sawed-off chin. "His name wouldn't be Guderian or maybe von Bock, would it?"

Rich allowed Michael's hand to move the barrel to the side. "I left them in the study."

"What's so special about the vaulted door that it needs armed guards?" Rich knew he was reaching.

"It's a dungeon, you fool."

"The guards?"

Michael's head moved slowly side to side, his gaze drifted around the room.

Rich shoved the barrel of the pistol into his mouth prepared to blow the back of his head across the desk behind him.

The man's gag reflex kicked in, he motioned with his right hand to remove the pistol and spoke the moment the barrel cleared his quivering lips. "Gold," he blurted with spittles of blood.

Rich released the collar and stepped to the side to allow his tour guide to collapse face down on the floor. *Michael was more than just a tour guide.* His hands and arms moved slowly to cover his head in anticipation of the hammer dropping.

20

Fortress
Isle de San Andres

With no regard for security cameras, Rich took the stairs two at a time leaving a bloody shoe imprint each time his leather soles touched carpet on the way down. His breathing and heart rate seemed to be in rhythm as he stood in front of von Bock's doors. Both were close and one of the mahogany doors at the main entrance opened. His hand found the pistol grip as he half turned to see a female employee in her early thirty's enter head down.

"Uh ummm," Rich grunted.

She looked up and stopped in her tracks. She attempted a scream, but nothing came from her wide-open mouth. Rich had the silencer tapping his upper lip. He knew he was a sight for sore eyes and her dark eyes were as wide as her mouth that formed an "O." He reached back to the handle and moved without a sound. *Good sign*, he thought, as he pirouetted through the small opening. The same two men seen earlier stood near a desk situated on the left side of the room. Oblivious of his presence he eased the door closed without looking. The two continued their discussion, the taller seated on the corner of the desk. As much as he wanted to sprint and finish the job, he regulated his breathing and walked slowly concealing the pistol behind his right side. Rich knew it was only a matter of time before the employee reported him to security. Fifteen feet separated the assailants before the taller of the two looked up. By the old black and white photos, this was Franz von Bock. Instead of a scream or movement to run away, a smile appeared below the prominent widow's peak. Rich stood with his hands by his side, the LRS in clear view.

"May I help you?" Franz's his upper and lower torso blocked his right hand.

Rich gestured with the pistol to raise his hands. Franz already had pulled the drawer exposing a pistol. Hans turned slowly to face Rich. Rich said nothing because there was nothing more to say. Decades of work would be complete with two pulls of the .22 caliber semi-automatic LRS.

Rich worked the pistol's open sight and stopped on Hans Krueger's forehead.

Franz spoke, his tone as if in a business meeting. "I believe you have a mistaken me for somebody else. "My name is Franz von Bock."

Without hesitation, but with extreme malice spread over his facial feature, the pistol barrel settled on Franz's forehead. Rich was amazed at how composed both were. The pistol swung back to Hans and the moment the sights lined up on the old man's forehead, the doors he entered moments before, slammed open.

Will watched as Rich's head turned to the side pulling his eyes and barrel off the target, "Pull the trigger."

Franz pointed a strange looking pistol and pulled the trigger. A muffled report followed. As much as he wanted the former SS Colonel to sink to the floor, he returned a wide-eyed smile as Rich grabbed his neck and sank to both knees. The pistol dropped from his right hand, and then seconds later fell face first onto the rug. No visible signs of blood spilled out on the antique rug, but Rich lay motionless.

Will and Rich's target darted simultaneously toward the pistol as Franz swung the strange looking gun his direction. Will's life didn't matter now; he had killed Rich with the phone call to Franz.

As Hans got closer to Rich's lifeless form by 10 feet, his hand touched the pistol grip and Will's body moved parallel to the ground. Twirling right, for the split second his back was to his target, he wasn't sure which would come first—a bullet from Franz's weapon or the 22 caliber from Rich's pistol. As his back came around, followed by his head, he picked up the target. With his right leg coiled like a snake ready to strike, the shot from Franz never came.

Will's brown eyes peered into Hans' lifeless gawk as the .22 caliber came to bear the moment his right leg shot out. The blow struck just below the German's chin crushing the larynx and propelling him back, his hands clasping at his throat spitting blood. With both feet settled on the ground, Will watched the murderer thrash for the breath that would never come. He still waited for the bullet from Franz's strange looking pistol. As the SS officer lay motionless gurgling up his own blood, Will said nothing.

Franz spoke sternly without looking over to his brother's lifeless figure. "I'm sure you have what you came for, Will Kellogg."

Their eyes locked on one another as Will bent down to pick up the .22 caliber. "SS Colonel Hans Krueger is dead. But so is my friend."

"Can we call this an eye-for-eye then?"

Will smiled. He knew Franz von Bock was a cool customer at the poker table, but now? With the pistol hidden, the German gestured with a hand to one of the two chairs and with the other to his own chair behind the desk. "May I?"

A quick nod followed, and Will said nothing. Both were seated, Franz with hands on the desk while Will sat with legs crossed and the cocked pistol draped across a leg.

"I didn't say," Will replied.

"Mr. Garbaccio's reputation makes what few Nazis like my brother who still walk this earth, tremble at the mention of his name."

"You mean used to make. And you…?"

Franz smiled like he did before laying down a winning hand at the Buccaneer. "You know I'm not a Nazi, so I never was concerned. My brother, on the other hand, always looked over his shoulder. Hans did bad things, but then, it was a bad war."

Will barely gave him time to utter the last word before responding. "And why don't I lay you out next to your brother and put a bullet to your face?"

A narrow grin, almost a smirk, appeared across the German's angular features. "And this is why I'm allowing you to walk out of this fortress with your life. You can take Mr. Garbaccio with you. He will be conscious in 30 minutes, but punch drunk for hours. The dart I put into his neck saw to that. He was out like a light before his face hit the floor."

Will's eyes flicked back and forth between Rich and Franz. One of Rich's hands pressed against his own neck with dart fins protruded between his fingers. Rich's chest heaved, then slowly fell then heaved again, and then thinking to himself, *what the hell, Rich was sleeping like a baby?* Will's head slowly turned back to the man he owed $13 million dollars with a question mark stamped to his face. "Why?"

Franz's angular facial expression remained stoic. "I think the question should be why did you warn me Rich would be coming to kill my brother?"

21

Richardson, Texas
Stoner Residence

A Richardson's patrol car eased to a stop on the vacant lot's side of the street. From his first-floor study, Hap peered over shrubs cut below the home's window seals while a white SUV eased curbside between the circular drives on his side of the street. He could only hope they would not be questioning him about breaking and entering but was more interested in how to get his hands on $25 million. Roach's encrypted email was true to his every fiber, they needed to discuss payment of the invoices forwarded nine days earlier before aircraft delivery.

It was hard to miss Officer Jimmy Holliday's shaved mug exit the white Tahoe accompanied by of all people, Agent Gordon. Holliday circled behind the unmarked unit and he and Gordon joined two officers conversing by their patrol car's rear bumper. Holliday handed the Corporal a document, which both officers reviewed and handed back.

Holliday handed the folded the document to Agent Gordon who slid it inside his coat pocket. All three officers drew pistols and Gordon followed before vanishing around the corner of the trailer.

Hap glanced back to his desk to see his cell phone dance across the top of the desk splaying Roach's caller ID. "Roach looking for money," he said out loud. *He could hear it now, cash to begin filling the order.*

Roach didn't give him a chance to answer. "Hey Mofo," Roach snapped. "Did you read my email?"

Hap said nothing as his Marine Corps buddy turned arms dealer smacked on a sandwich.

"Hap, I read your pie in the sky order for aircraft and ordnance."

Hap could only nod as the blinds in the trailer across the street, opened. "Working with my banker to hedge my stock in Vector Data."

"I don't run a Goodwill Hap."

Hap said nothing. He knew the next line.

"Good funds deposited up front Mofo, and only then I will source specifics in the order." Roach continued to smack in Hap's ear.

"Double-decker ham and cheese?"

"How did *smack…smack…smack* ya know."

"If it was tuna, your oversized tongue would be stuck to the bridge of your big Mofo mouth!"

"Speaking of eyes bigger than one's stomach, what is this crap about reworking a vessel at Todd Shipyard and then arming her? How in the hell will you pay that invoice?"

Holliday appeared around the corner with arms corralled around a pair of PCs. *Cleaning out the trailer. Crap in the trailer must have been hot. My fingerprints are all over the place.*

"You have a sugar daddy, Half Boner? Tell me you haven't gone queer since Carla punched, showers on Lonibelle are small."

Hap said nothing. Holliday looked back over a shoulder as Agent Gordon rounded the corner grappling with a pair of desktop boxes. The patrolman appeared clutching a foldout table the PC's had resided on. "Sorry, Roach. What was that about a sugar daddy?" His face contorted. "No, I'm not a gay blade and, yes, I'm concerned about Carla's whereabouts."

"With the little lady's absence, didn't wanna be hanging around the Lonibelle's shower if you were in the area."

"Who invited you to the show?"

Roach chuckled. "Listen, you prick, you're going to need a damn good Ops O after I deliver an air force and arsenal package most third world dictators would envy."

"So, you're a mind reader. Okay, you have the job, but what's this crap about a sugar daddy?"

Roach laughed for a second and let out a roaring belch. "Half Boner, you ain't gonna believe this shit. My banker called yesterday to apprise me of a credit facility I can draw upon. Just have to send invoices to an email address and money is deposited the same day."

Hap's hands massaged both temples. *How many lives did this cat have?* Another table appeared in front of the trailer'and it filled as quickly as the first table as the officer's daisy chained in and out of the trailer. Chief Jones, Richardson's Police Chief exited an unmarked SUV parked behind the patrol car and walked towards the trailer.

"Hope it was enough to get you in the game," Hap said in an easy voice.

Roach ripped another bite from what Hap pictured was a mauled double-decker ham and cheese the size of a small football. "Hey, Mofo, my banker assured me there are at least 35 million pieces of cake available. From a table of equipment (T/E) standpoint, this mission is a go."

22

Richardson, Texas
Stoner Residence

Ten minutes after Roach dropped the bombshell; a panel van
eased into the circular drive and tucked perpendicular behind
Holliday's SUV, as Holliday and the Richardson Police Chief
chatted standing next to Hap's stone column mailbox.

The patrolman first on the scene, stood like a motorcycle
cop with a boot on the van's bumper scribbling on a notepad
as officers carried hardware to the van's rear doors.

Hap swiveled back to check his computer, which faced
away from the street, and opened Will's email. Will's parting
words in the encrypted email. Don't look a gift horse in the
mouth Colonel. *The old adage good news travels fast remains
in good standing.*

Richardson's top law enforcement officer slapped Holliday
on the shoulder and angled past to his SUV. Without looking
back to the action across the street, Agent Gordon joined
Holliday as they walked up the driveway. *Not Gordon again.*

Both angled towards the sidewalk and passed the study
towards the front doors. Arms crossed, Hap leaned against
the doorjamb before swinging one boot over the other as
Holliday rounded the corner.

Gordon began to move his coattail to the side and expose
his badge.

"Don't bother, Agent Gordon."

Holliday cut his eyes to Hap with a slight head movement over his right shoulder and issued a slight shrug.

Hap said nothing and nodded as Gordon returned the badge to his belt inside his coat.

Both law enforcement officials gave a firm handshake as they passed Hap and entered the foyer. Holliday cleared his throat as Hap closed the door behind them.

"You won't mind answering a few questions?"

Hap said nothing, nodded, and gestured with his hand to enter the living room. Holliday and Gordon led Hap into his own living room where the whole scene seemed undeniably odd. On several occasions, Carla held fundraisers at the house for the City's Police Scholarship fund. The fifty or so thousand raised each year went to continued education for the officers and children of fallen and injured officers and first responders for the city.

He and Gordon eased into the half-moon couch right of the fireplace while Hap settled into his chair and glanced toward Carla's vacant chair. Holliday reached into his coat pocket and pulled two folded letter size photos. Hap leaned forward to retrieve the prints. Two Latinos and both appeared photogenic, photographed standing near the trailer across the street. He shook his head and passed the photos back to Holliday. "Why are you asking me?"

"We got a tip on the police website claiming these two had been spotted around the trailer." Holliday gestured with an extended thumb over his shoulder across the street. Chief had the photos sent to Quantico and is the reason Agent Gordon joined the conversation."

Hap continued to shake his head. "Not me."

"How about Carla?"

Hap used a finger to massage the bridge of his nose. "Funny you ask, detective. I haven't seen her in a week."

Jimmy's head turned to the side and he fought to keep a poker face. "I'm surprised Hap," he said. "Lynn told me you were at the stable at the same time Carla was the day before yesterday."

"Hmm." Hap's lower lip pushed against his upper lip. "I didn't see her."

"So, you were there."

Hap nodded, but said nothing.

The detective's eyes cut over to Gordon.

Gordon took his cue and placed both elbows on his knees. He wore the same suit and tie he had worn when visiting Hap's office. "The FBI has confirmed the spics in the photos are known foreign intelligence freelancers." Gordon's dark eyes looked straight into Hap's baby blues." Beside the Venezuelan, Colombian, and Mexican Cartels, they have known contacts with the Russians and MS13. While you were caught on the stable's security cameras canvassing the premises."

Stoner's jaws clenched and the space between his eyebrows pinched. "So where is Carla?"

Holliday leaned back into the couch. His hazel eyes burned a hole through the back of Hap's skull. "I was hoping you could answer that question. The Fed's advised me both were Operatives of the Scorpion's Black Stone. Sound familiar?"

As Hap's heart pumped the flow of blood through his body, a wretched feeling settled below his empty stomach. "You think her disappearance has something to do with the Border incident against Black Stone?"

Gordon glanced over to Hap. "Stoner, whoever set up across the street was surveilling somebody. It is all stolen hardware traced to a fencing operation on the southeast side of Dallas. My 18 years in the FBI tell me it was these two. Why?"

Hap glanced over to the agent in hopes of finding understanding. "I was just a Marine officer doing my job."

Gordon swallowed as Holliday straightened, and then stepped over Gordon to lean his shoulder into the fireplace mantle. "Did you never think you might possibly piss off a few folks south of the border when the mission was launched?"

Hap fought to maintain a poker face. *How could he tell these two that his house was being surveilled because he was about to be part of an invasion of an island where the flag of Colombia flew from government office's rooftops?*

23

Somewhere in South Texas
Lonesome Dove

Greg Fox's flat top haircut complemented a flight deck of an Amphib Carrier. Foxie, as we called him, didn't reach Hap's shoulder, even with the help of his old Marine Corps issued flight boots. After 14 years of service, the Marine Corps and former Staff Sgt Fox parted ways.

Always first to the bar after a flight was one thing, but the Marine Corps had drawn a line in the sand with his unfortunate habit of throwing the first punch in defense of a fellow Marine. On base or off, coming to the defense of a Marine, didn't.

Foxie's dark eyes softened as he gazed across his rounded shoulder towards Hap. "Sir, I heard about you going to bat for me," he said in a southern Louisiana drawl. "Above and beyond, Sir, I cannot thank you enough."

"You know something, Foxie," Hap chimed back, chuckling. "When Colonel Shank said, LtCol Stoner, focus on your own career, it's on a little bit better standing than Staff Sergeant Fox's. Now get the hell out of my office."

Foxie chuckling kicking the ground with his boot, looked up, then said, "Well Sir, what did you say?"

Hap shrugged. "Did my best about face movement in my career and didn't say a thing." Foxie's short legs took three strides to Hap's one as they entered through vintage hanger doors installed during WWII. Hap stopped and turned, the sound of a low flying jet aircraft resonated from the Northwest. His gaze drifted down to Foxie. "Expecting someone?"

Foxie poked out a lower lip and shook his head. They angled past two plastic crates marked *Transmission AH* in black spray paint. A pair of AH1-W's airframes waited their turn to have a transmission lowered into the aircraft's main mounts. A 10-ton cherry picker maneuvered between the work stands with a built-up rotor head coupled to a pair of 24-foot rotor blades. Four-line personnel clad in blue overalls were doing the last checks with torque wrenches.

On the far side of the Cobra's, a pair of egg-shaped Hughes 500's panels lay on the hangar floor to allow mechs clad in the same blue coveralls to screw down and safety wire avionics boxes, radios, and black boxes for ordnance.

"So, when can we fly to Mother?" Hap questioned.

Even in a sweat-drenched jumpsuit zipped down to just above his protruding stomach, Foxie carried a John Wayne swagger. "Fully combat ready Sir, we are talking one week." He pointed towards a pair of screen doors, which led to an old maintenance space from a previous era. "Kellogg is waiting for you in our conference room."

Hap acknowledged with a nod and half smile. "Outstanding, Foxie," As he walked through the double doors, which had more space between the wood frames than just the screen. The doors slammed together behind him.

Will looked up from a planner to allow one side of his mouth to curl up and form a lopsided grin. He leaned back in the worn-out secretary's chair and a hand snuck back to feel for the wall.

"Grab a seat, Hap, we have competition."

Hap gave Will an incredulous look and placed the briefcase on a ¾-inch piece of plywood Will used as a desk propped up by sawhorses cut from 2 x 4's. "The Sandinistas know about the gold."

"Good guess, Colonel." Will stuffed a dried-up cigar into his mouth and offered a mischievous smile. "Daniel Ortega found out the same way I did. Communist son of a bitch is not stupid."

"Rule Latin America?" Hap replied.

"Before that car salesman is finished, he will make Colombia's military look like a Boy Scout troop."

Hap shrugged. "U.S. will never let the commie get away with this."

Will shook his head. "Country is broke Colonel, and POTUS doesn't have the stomach for war except ordering an occasional drone strike and bragging about it on CNN. Besides, the President and his Secretary of State do not believe in the Monroe Doctrine. POTUS would never think about hurting the New York City's mayor's feelings fucking around with the country the mayor was married in."

Hap eased back gingerly in an office chair that was ready for the dumpster years past, along with Will's chair. He rocked back in full anticipation of falling back on his ass. "Where did you get this shit?"

Will laughed. "It came with the property lease Joe D gave me. All 250 thousand acres included with the stipulation we have to be gone by fall dove season. Hell, we don't even have to pick up the spent brass."

Hap smiled, then said, "Okay big guy. We ride into the Alamo, what follows if we just happen to survive?"

Will was a statue. "Wouldn't that be something Colonel, if pulling off this operation incubates an organization which would assist in world peace?"

"Star Chamber shit, Will." Hap nodded once followed by a speedy blink and a chuckle. "Maybe this is what Pop always referred to growing up without my dumb ass knowing what he truly meant."

"Maybe so, Colonel, but is it worth dying for?" Will asked.

Slowly a wide grin spread across Hap's face. "A man can't live forever,"

"That's my line, Colonel," Will pushed an operations order in front of Hap. In turn, Hap reached into his briefcase and flipped an Air Order in Will's direction. Hap spoke as he flipped through the pages of the Op Order. "Roach will allow Trixie to conduct a HALO jump for Team A and B's insert."

"You read my mind. I want the Roach to run operations." Will replied. "He did a hell of a job on the border. How are we looking for pilots and aircrew?"

"Who do you think wrote the Air Order? 100 % table of organization (T/O). All aircrew and pilots to included replacement crew are due at Lonesome Dove in five days."

Will acknowledged with a nod and tapped a finger on the map splayed out under his planner. "The bridges comprise intermediate objectives A and B, and Shaun's teams have to be prepared to blow on order. Once confirmed destroyed," Will's stubby finger traced down the map and began to tap on a small knoll denoted by three concentric circles. "I want two drones for surveillance. Just have a queasy feeling in my gut about my old rival Daniel Ortega and will want an extra eye to monitor his chess moves."

Hap let out a grunt making a mental note on the drones. "You know I have to acquire hardware and software for Lonibelle to conduct drone operations. A monitor and controls for the pilot, launcher, capture net, and maintenance personnel and then find a pilot."

"Call Roach," Will shot back sarcastically. "Feed the man a double ham and cheese and he could get you the space shuttle."

"I'm on it…" Hap stopped in midsentence hearing the screen door bang against the wall behind him, then creaked as the spring slammed the door shut. He continued to speak without turning. "Any consideration given for resupply and medical considerations?"

"Roach can figure it out," Will answered displaying a look as if he had facial paralysis.

Hap stood and turned to see Hollywood clad in a blue flight suit and polished flight boots with an overstuffed drab green sea bag thrown across a shoulder. "What the hell you doing here?"

Hollywood's light brown mane arrangement appeared tossed into a mullet by a dust devil crossing the tarmac to the hanger. Hollywood didn't flinch as he let the bag fall on its end next to his flight boot. "BW needed a check ride so I gave a check ride flying down from Dallas. BW is a signer now."

The corners of Haps mouth twisted to the ground as if he really cared that BW could now sign as pilot in command of Vector Data's corporate jet. "Who is going to lead the negotiations on the sale?'

Hollywood chuckled. "Because of the gold, I was inclined to table the negotiations for a couple of weeks. If I'm not back, Crash will pick up the baton."

Hap nodded slowly, his lower jaw locked in place.

"Besides, there is flying and shooting going on," Hollywood said. "How could you expect me to miss this? Look, if we pull off this mission we can make an offer to buy Vector Data's suiter."

"Welcome aboard Hollywood," Will said. "Go store your shit. Pilot's hooch is behind the hanger and there are a couple of empty cots."

Hollywood smiled as the bag landed back on his shoulder. Hap stepped around him and pulled open one of the screen doors for Hollywood to angle through with the bag. Hap slammed the screen door closed as Hollywood vanished around the corner.

"Impressive Hap," Will said using the number two pencil as a pointer moving it in a deliberate manner to points on the map. "As much as I want the Company to be purchased, I'm glad Hollywood joined the fight."

Hap stuffed a stick of gum as he stepped up to the table, then said, "Get on with it." Hap didn't bother to sit, instead stood with arms crossed looking down at the map slowly grinding the gum between his molars.

Will moved to the Commander's intent. "I'm expecting Barlosa to blow the vault, so he need not bother to die on the initial objective."

Hap knew Teams A and B's initial objective was the knoll located between the bridge and the fortress. Will ran the pencil traced from the two bridges, labeled intermediate objectives A and B to the fortress.

"Upon confirmation the bridges are wired, on order, Shaun will lead A and B to the knoll. Eddie and one man retrograde to link up with Team C inside the fortress walls, and blow the vault doors. If Eddie goes down, KB Hill will be the backup EOD."

The thought of what was just said actually happening made Hap Stoner's stomach turn. Hap interrupted. "KB will be located on Lonibelle."

Will pulled a personnel file from the corner of table with KB Hill written diagnolly across the front. After opening the file, his darted back and forth perusing the file. "Sniper?"

Hap nodded and tapped the eraser end of the pencil he picked up from the plywood table before tucking it behind his ear.

"For being a geek, the man has some unique talents."

"Not to change the subject, but, how far in front of D-Day do we put Shaun's teams ashore?"

Will closed the file and returned it to the corner of the desk. "As early as we can get Roach on board and teams trained up for the HALO jump."

Will's thick lips shaped a grin and gaze wandered from the wobbly ceiling fan above the table to his second in command.

Hap's expression asked the question, "What?"

"Damn it, Colonel, get Roach on board."

Hap nodded and pushed back from the table, straightened and walked into the empty office behind Will's chair. He punched the "Roach's" speed dial on his mobile phone. Two rings later, Roach's raspy voice was in his ear.

"What the hell, Hap? You miss me already?"

"Just need more dipshit. Ready to copy."

"Sure," was the reply in a go to hell tone.

"Need one AAI RQ-7 drone and all accessories and one Operations Officer." Hap rattled off his order as calm as a #7 with cheese and jalapeno at Whataburger, cut the onions.

Hap could hear Roach's fingers dance across a keyboard.

"OK, I found one drone," Roach said. "The RQ-7 is located in Puerto Rico controlled by a local anti-drug detail. I copied Air Freight personnel on my payroll to dispatch immediately to pick up the gear and deliver to Lonesome Dove. I just wired $700,000 into a Swiss account. You will have the gear required for Lonibelle delivered to Galveston within 8 hours. Looking at one hour to offload and fuel up and will be in Lonesome Dove two and a half hours later.

"What about the pilot?'

"I will reach out to Sluggo," Roach replied.

Hap responded without hesitation. "Good choice." Sluggo had left flying real aircraft to command one of the Marine Corps early drone units when he left the Corps to become a successful financial analyst on Wall Street. "You know how to contact him?"

"Of course, I do," Roach said after a long belch. "Sluggo handles my investment portfolio."

"Get him to Galveston and on the Lonibelle in a week."

"No prob. For the record," Roach answered, "I will be at Lonesome Dove in 24 hours to take over Operations."

"Hey, Roach," Hap said.

"Hap, I got shit to do to."

Hap pulled the phone away from his ear. Roach had hung up on him. The man was already on the job.

Lonesome Dove
Conference Room D – 40

Despite protest from the secretarial chair's worn out spring, Hap examined the table legs to admire Roach's creativity since his arrival 75 days earlier. Never short of adapting to any situation, he replaced Will's hand-made sawhorses with worn-out folding tables. Roach had stuffed corks from the wine bottles consumed during the previous 24 hours to various depths into the bottom of the table legs to bring the table to level. KB had mounted the 65-inch TV he had thrown into the Merlin's cargo hold before leaving Galveston on the wall behind his chair.

"Never saw wine corks used to level tables before," Hap said.

Roach spoke without looking up from the newly revised Op order. "Improvise and adapt Mofo. It agitated the crap out me working maps and flow charts left wing low. Besides, my pencils kept rolling off the table. Came to me around 0400 the first week I reported on board."

"When did putting the gorilla tape around the laminate come into play?"

"Amazon's delivery truck's dust cloud didn't have time to settle before Foxie and I wrapped the table top as if it were a mummy. The laminate was curling up and creasing my maps."

Similar to his approach to life, Roach leaped into mission planning feet first and declared a personal war on sleep. Gravity tugged on the dark circles below his bloodshot eyes settling above his rounded cheeks. It didn't matter how sad the Roach appeared, nobody had the balls to tell the man to shut it down. In the back of every man's mind was fear that "he who spoke" would find himself in a pretzel by the Roach's infamous figure-four leg lock. A line of binders spread across the taped tabletop accumulated after God knew how many hours of brainpower, research, and little to no sleep.

"Has Will seen any of this?" Will was training the ground element in a small portion of jungle in Northern Costa Rica labeled X-Ray.

Roach said nothing responding with a shake of his oversized head.

"We ready with the Air Tasking Order (ATO)?" Hap asked.

Roach nodded clamping down on a soggy cigar. "All here, Mofo. Sorties, call signs, aircraft type, and mission for the 24 hours to take down the Fortress and retrograde." His finger tapped another binder to the side. "This is your Air support plan. I have designated a number of aircraft for troop insert, resupply, as well as close in air support to include contingencies if we lose aircraft due to maintenance or combat loss."

Hap grabbed the third binder in the middle of the table. He flipped through to the index to see weather outlooks and moon phases, which would set H-Hour.

Roach flipped another binder like a wobbly frisbee, which banged the table as it came to rest in front of Hap. "This is my first pass for a Fire Support plan for the Ground Element as well as ordnance loads for air. And just for you, Hap, Trixie has been upgraded since the Borderline incident and now capable of mounting two M-134 six-barrel 7.62 chain guns and will arrive at Lonesome Dove at D - 15. It's all there if we need it. Hopefully we don't. A lot of people would die."

Hap reeled back, careful not to flip back in the chair. The M-134 was capable of firing 2000 to 4000 rounds per minute. Within seconds Trixie could blanket a football field with a full metal jacket in every square inch of the field and with the night sensors, the enemy had no place to hide.

Roach leaned over to his right for a pink binder marked INTEL in black magic marker down the spine. "This will grow as Blad's Shadow organization feeds human intelligence (HUMINT) and signal intelligence (SIGINT) to the Command Group."

Roach reached back, tapped the blank screen, and reached for his opened laptop on the other side of the wall of binders as the screen came to life.

Hap watched as a topographical map of Isle de San Andres appeared on the screen. Numerous photos of the fortress, bay, downtown, airfields loaded into the software showed vertically aligned on the left side of the screen.

KB eased his five-foot, eight-inch frame into the chair to Hap's right. KB had spent the last two months between Lonibelle and Lonesome Dove working closely with the Roach on the vessel's IT and Communication requirements. Hap had pulled KB from the Silicon Valley to head up IT and Communications for Vector Data a couple of years before. KB immediately resigned after Hap's departure from CEO and joined the mission before Hap finished his first cup of coffee at an II Creeks coffee shop in Richardson. Though he didn't carry the physical stature, KB's other skill set from a previous life was learned while a Force Recon Marine. Though KB didn't talk about it, he had 24 confirmed kills as a sniper with two tours each in Iraq and Afghanistan.

For being an arms dealer, Roach proved he was light years ahead of Hap in hands-on technology. Standing in front of the screen he drew, punched index squares, and like a magician whisked the drawing to the side with his hand moving on to the next slide. Occasionally he would use his finger to press on the screen to insert an unseen photo.

Roach's head pivoted. "I don't like the idea of using Lonibelle as the forward arming and refueling point (FARP). Keep thinking of those damn Japanese carriers at Midway with the decks loaded with fuel hoses, armaments, and that damn ship is headquarters and the bus ride home."

Hap continued to rock in the chair whose squeak drowned out the out of balance ceiling fan attempting to wiggle out of its mounts.

"I'm not going to argue the point, but where are we going to rearm and fuel?"

"I hear you, Hap, I just don't like it." Roach scratched the top of his shaved head mulling the problem, snapped his fingers before pointing at a point three miles northeast of the Fortress. "Add another vessel and anchor her here."

"Shit, Roach, people in hell want ice water; we can't afford the delay for the refit."

Roach shook his head. "Wouldn't have to do anything to the boat. Refuel and rearm, that's all she has to do—two birds at a time. Maybe use her as a hospital ship as well."

Hap smiled as he pulled out his cell phone. The Roach had done it again. Hap spoke as he waited for the cell signal to connect. "Still would like to add a few heavy weapon mounts. I have a feeling we are going to stir up a hornet's nest."

Roach drew a circle with his finger northeast of Isle de San Andres.

Lew's deep voice answered on the fourth ring. He sounded tired. "What's up, Hap?"

"Need another boat for arming and fueling the birds. She will also be a hospital boat for casualties."

"You know where to go." Lew replied.

"Slip available at the shipyard?" Hap asked.

"Will have the vessel in dry dock tomorrow afternoon."

"I will fly to Galveston sometime tonight to go over details." Hanging up the phone, he dialed Foxie.

"Yes, Colonel?"

"Ensure the Merlin is ready for a 1 a.m. launch."

"Destination?"

"Galveston, no aircrew required. KB will accompany me."

"Aye-aye. I will have the tanks top offed," Foxie replied. With Carla still absent, Hap positioned the phone on the table to keep it in eyeshot to read incoming email.

"I'm sold on the HALO idea," Roach said. Placing the palm of his hand on the screen, he pulled out a map of the Caribbean somewhere within the TV. Roach half turned to Hap and KB.

Hap leaned back in his chair and emitted sounds from between his lips. Baby blue eyes went from Roach's ominous brown eyes to the screen and back. Biting his lower lip, he leaned forward onto the table.

"You got a burr up your ass?" Roach questioned.

Hap twirled the cell phone on the table, his right ear resting in the hand propped on the table. As he twirled, Hap spoke, "My gut is telling me Will wants us retrograding to the southwest when we need to point our bow northwest."

Roach's mind activated by a problem began working towards a solution, neither even flinched as a Cobra fired up one of its turboshaft engines on the tarmac.

"Have you expressed these concerns to Will because it sure has got my attention? Hell, between the Nicaraguans, and not knowing if, and how fast the frigging Colombians will react, we need to be hauling our happy asses to Belize."

Hap considered how foolish to think for one moment the Colombians do not have agents inside Nicaragua and vice versa. He made the mental note to talk to Will on the satellite phone and add Blad to his call list to check on any news about Carla.

25

Somewhere in South Texas,
Lonesome Dove, Training Range D – 30

Hap's phone rattled across the metal cruise box settling up against Carla's photo resting in a small plastic frame beside his wallet. The moment the phone's vibrations ceased, the Marine Corps Hymn sounded. Both eyes blinked open to meet a scene resembling a gypsy camp. Hap's space inside the WWII Quonset hut was similar to the makeup of the other eight pilots spaces spread out across the half-moon looking structure.

What was not in the cruise box, which served as his personal dresser, rested on hangers. Two blue flight suits, a Hawaiian shirt with wrinkles mirroring his freshman year in college, three pairs of skivvies, and faded orange Texas City Stingaree golf shirt weighed down the rope causing the bottom of the flight suits to touch the dirt.

Big Alabama's round cheeks appeared inches above Hap's head. "0530 Hap. Drop your cock and put on your socks."

Hap sighed and slowly rubbed both eyes with the palms of his hands. "Sorry I missed the poker game. The stench of your breath makes me believe you had a great time."

"With this morning's brief, the game was shut down at midnight. How was the flight from Galveston?"

Hap rolled to place bare feet to his prayer rug purchased at an Iraqi market on his first tour. A stomach-turning aroma of sweat and alcohol filled the area around BA like Pigpen from Charlie Brown fame. "One takeoff and one landing."

"Best kind I know of," BA replied with a chuckle. "Get a move on. Goose made up a batch of egg sandwiches on wheat at the flight line grill and I need coffee. We can eat while we brief." BA turned and pushed aside the poncho liner covering the entrance closest to Hap's rack. It was anybody's guess how long the half-moon tin structure's door had been missing from its hinges.

After a stop at the one-holer outhouse constructed from plywood and a few 2x4's Hap angled through the maze of seating which made up the makeshift ready room. Located just outside the conference room Hap couldn't help but see Goose Helm's grin touch either side of his narrow jawline. "Do you always smile, Goose?"

Goose reached into a grease-stained paper bag and over-handed an aluminum foil package in Hap's direction as if the sandwich was a grenade.

"Put something to cover those bags, Hap." The Yankee would be referring to the very pronounced bags drooping under both Hap's eyes. He left KB in Galveston to oversee the installation of the new communication package for Stingray. *Thank God for autopilot.*

* * *

Behind the controls of the lead AH-1W Cobra, the section of snakes escorted Big Alabama and Goose's flight of two Hughes 500s. Big Alabama went by BA, or as the round mound of irrelevant sound would say "Bad Ass."

Hap lowered the dark visor over his eyes as BA turned the flight into a sun low on the eastern horizon. *Perfect day to fly.*

Wind calm and not a cloud occupied a South Texas sky. The cobras flew loose on BA's section at the five and seven o'clock position. Racing beneath their skids, a checkerboard of bright yellow sunflower fields and millet stretched as far as the eye could see.

"Hey LD, what are those other fields planted wi..." Hap didn't finish the sentence.

BA's booming Alabama drawl came over the flight's common frequency.

"Ground fire, ten o'clock. Break right!"

BA's little bird stood on its rotor disc in a descending right turn. Goose traded airspeed for altitude to give BA room to turn and avoid a midair collision. As BA's bird passed beneath Goose's skids, he wrapped in full cyclic and right rudder to race down the chute to rejoin BA.

Hap kept the beaks of both Cobras straight ahead as LD's head dropped into the bucket toggling the joystick with the fingertips of his right hand and clutching the trigger grip with his left pointing finger.

"Kang flight, target 12 o'clock, infantry on road," Hap spoke through the aircraft's intercom. "Cleared hot, LD."

A burst of 20mm rounds peppered the imaginary target of tires deployed in an infantry column. Hap pulled off while LD kept the "X" on the middle of the column manipulating the joystick so the 20-millimeter chain gun raked the tires through 120 degrees of turn.

Killer Koch, piloting Hap's dash two, crossed behind Hap's six o'clock, three barrels spinning as Love Doctor, who joined the mission as a replacement pilot in the event a pilot was wounded or killed, sat in the front seat. 20mm high explosive rounds flipped tires into the air like quarters, to cover Hap's break. Killer pulled the cyclic against his right thigh and collective into his armpit feeding right pedal to maintain a stable gun platform for Love Doctor to shoot accurately during the turn.

Hap looked over his shoulder to see Killer's Cobra pounding the simulated troop movement covering Hap's turn off target.

Rejoining the flight at the 5 o'clock position, Killer clicked twice over the inter-flight frequency signaling dash 2 was in position.

Minutes later, Hap called out, "Taking fire at 12 o'clock. Beaver flight, break!"

"Beaver flight, split turn," BA transmitted over the inter-flight frequency.

The little birds initiated a split turn, climbing turns pulling away from each other for one hundred and eighty degrees, and then diving towards fields of sunflowers, sorghum, and millet to become part of the South Texas landscape.

Hap and Killer closed in on three rusted out truck hulks lined up on a dirt road separating broomcorn and a cornfield.

Killer broke hard to starboard to allow his bird to engage the target at a 45-degree angle. Hap bore in with 2.75 rockets while LD raked the convoy with small adjustments front to back with the 20 mm gun. Hap broke hard left and dove leveling off just above the sunflower pods as Killer covered Hap's turn popping flares off either side of the tail boom to guard against a simulated infrared shoulder-fired surface-to-air missile threat.

Two minutes later the flight reconstituted with the sun to their 6 o'clock when Killer called out an air threat at 3 o'clock low. The imaginary threat was to their right and low.

"Tally ho," BA called out. "Beaver flight, break left." BA turned the little birds away from the make-believe threat to make room for the Cobras to streak in for the kill.

Hap hesitated in taking control of the situation wanting Killer to gain situational awareness (SA), and react like a former Marine Attack Helo pilot. With Killer's Cobra closest to the threat, Hap expected Killer to demand lead for the initial run in on the target. (TAC lead). He didn't have to wait long.

"Kang flight break right," Killer barked. "Killer has TAC lead. Bandit in site."

Two miles north, the mission's drone—call sign Magellan— towed a streamer 25-foot long, and 8-foot tall, 150 feet behind it to simulate an air threat. Hap knew data flowed up and down Lonibell's satellite dish peeking out from under the tarp to give Sluggo feedback required to pilot the drone while he sat on board Lonibelle in a cushioned chair Captain Kirk would have envied. Three MFD screens appeared inside a sixty-two-inch TV screen mounted just above eye level displaying the aircraft's view, moving map, engine, and flight instruments.

Killer pulled collective to close on the simulated bandit. After a hard, diving turn at military power, Hap pulled online in a spread formation.

"Clear to fire," Killer announced.

"Don't hit Magellan, boys," Sluggo added in a New York twang.

20-millimeter tracer ripped the white streamer to shreds. Hap couldn't help but notice the proverbial middle finger someone on Lonibelle had spray-painted in black across the streamer. After 15 seconds, Killer called out, "Cease-fire, cease-fire. Kang, you have the lead."

"Kang has lead," Hap replied. "BA, take us home." Hap's Cobra slashed across the South Texas sky breaking away from Killer's Cobra as it tipped the twirling rotors into the sky to stay inside Hap's turn. BA clicked the trigger switch on his cyclic twice communicating to the flight he understood and would comply. The little birds broke left while Hap and Killer completed a climbing scissor that maneuvered the Cobras beak-like noses pointed to the sky and airframes across the other's flight path to descend in a max power dive to rejoin Beaver flight for the return flight to Lonesome Dove. Hap looked back through the rotor disc to see the underside of Killer's fuselage whip across toward his 9 o'clock before cranking in full right cyclic and pedal, whipping the snout 180 degrees into a max power dive.

Within two minutes, Kang Flight had rejoined at Beaver flight's five and 7 o'clock for the return flight to Lonesome Dove to debrief with Roach's full attention. This evening the moon would settle below the eastern horizon at 2100 hours where a man couldn't see the hand in front of his face. The same pilots would brief at 2030 for a 2200 hundred takeoff to conduct another training mission with night vision goggles. Tonight's schedule, BA and Goose would have door guns on board to give aircrew air to ground gunnery training with Cobra's occupying the same airspace. Roach's aggressive training schedule would hone the edge on this knife to razor sharp before the fly away to Lonibelle.

26

Galveston, Texas
Lonibelle D - 23

While lights from Galveston's skyline filled the Merlin's windscreen, Hap Stoner shifted in his seat side to side as the feint sign of light appeared below the eastern horizons gentle wakening. Besides the little body aches, his heavy eyelids telegraphed it was time for uninterrupted sleep. But not yet, first, he had to land the twin turbo aircraft configured to hold ten passengers. The aircraft radios, for the most part, had been quiet rotating into the air at 0300.

"Houston Approach," Hap said in a stoic voice. "421 Delta Victor."

"Go ahead, 421 Delta Victor. Houston Approach, over."

Hap shifted in his seat and let out a wide yawn with both arms spread out to his side. "421 Delta Victor request 2000."

"Roger, 421 Delta Victor. Cleared from two five thousand to two thousand. Come left zero two zero. Altimeter two-niner-niner two."

"Four two one Delta Victor leaving flight level two five to two thousand. Altimeter setting niner-niner-two four two one, Delta Victor." With approach issuing the green light to descend from twenty-five thousand to two thousand feet, Hap lowered the nose to begin the descent but kept power up to put wheels on the ground that much faster. He adjusted the altimeter setting to two-niner-niner two. Once in Galveston airspace, Hap steered the Merlin over Todd's shipyards. Its line of drydocks was lit up like a traveling carnival except for a blob of darkness on the northern two docks. Lonibelle and Stingray rested under camouflage netting to conceal both vessel's transformations from supply vessels to ships of war.

"Four two one Delta Victor, at your discretion cleared for a straight in runway 18, winds calm altimeter niner-niner-two. Be advised field is closed and you will land at your own risk. Clear to switch Scholes tower…good morning."

* * *

Hap passed underneath the netting to look up at Lonibelle through pinpricks for pupils and an olive drab sea bag slung over a shoulder with Stoner stenciled across the bottom. The sentimental man he was, Hap still lay claim to the bag issued day one of Marine Officer Candidate School. Also called a duffel bag, with S T O N E R spray painted black across its bottom, and after all the years and travels still remained legible. First meeting at 0700, less than two hours after he closed his eyes, and then the shipyard would come to life, its cranes, diesels, and winches, hoisting steel from pier side to each vessel wedged into its dry docks. The sounds of hammers against steel would reverberate through Lonibelle's hull and bulkheads where only the deaf or dead could sleep.

With one arm balancing the sea bag across his shoulder, his free hand clutched the piped handrail to muscle up the steep walkway. Less than an hour earlier, he greased the Merlin squeaking the main mounts on the numbers, which would make any naval aviator worth their salt proud. His closed field landing almost met with disaster, narrowly avoiding colliding with a small plane landing on three six. Fortunately, the pilot waved off banking hard toward the gulf as Hap eased the throttles into beta throwing out a waffling sound across the airfield as the props reversed pitch. The irate pilot whipped a quick 360 to set up an extended right base. The Cessna whipped to a stop in the tie-down spot next to the Merlin. Hap had already tied down and chocked both main mounts inserting pillows into the engines intakes as the pilot walked up to initiate the berating.

Hap took the deserved browbeating and did not offer up an excuse. Attentive as a first grader with his teacher the heated one-way conversation settled into conversation after the wide-eyed pilot finished venting. The 29-year-old entrepreneur had flown in from Amarillo for a business meeting and had enough time to find transportation, to drop his bags…shit shower, and shave before a 7 a.m. meeting kicked off.

The face behind the Pancho Villa mustache standing on the quarterdeck was familiar.

Hap issued a firm grip and it was no surprise when Doc Perry returned the gesture with a tighter squeeze. "How in the hell did a Doctor win the prize?"

Doc Perry held a steaming cup of joe to the side to keep the spillage from burning exposed flesh. "Truth be known Hap, Captain Lew welcomed me to the team yesterday. Son of a bitch issued a handshake and announced I had the third watch, which ends in an hour. You up for a couple of drinks afterward?"

Hap said nothing and returned a *you got to be shitting me* look.

Doc's lower jaw extended to create an overbite while he slowly moved his head side to side. "I only called you because of Carla."

Hap said nothing.

"I never told you, but she reached out after you guys broke off the marriage."

Hap shifted the sea bag to remove the hot spot to another part of his shoulder. "Who said we broke off our marriage?"

Doc raised an empty hand and coffee cup to chin height. "Hey, Hap- she did, and let me tell you, she was one upset lady." He took a long swig from his coffee mug and pursed his lips to take in the flavor. "Hey fucker, don't shoot the messenger."

Hap said nothing.

"She explained her involvement in that Borderline thing you led. Hey, dipshit, you know what pissed me off about that?"

Again, Hap said nothing.

Doc yanked an extended thumb into his chest. "See what being junior on Lonibelle gets you? And, to think you never reached out for my help. My God, Hap, I would have given my right nut for that mission. That is why I didn't hesitate to come on board now. Besides, you bought all the drinks that night."

Hap's bloodshot eyes shifted back around to the pier as ship workers began to mingle around the equipment holding cups of coffee and smoking cigarettes. "The new guy always gets screwed, Doc. You aware of the change?"

"Stingray," Doc Perry said behind a sleepy nod. "Name is close to the heart, Hap."

Anxious to cut the conversation short and grab a fighter nap, Hap quickly injected, "We need a 15-bed medical facility in two weeks."

Doc's head arched back for a widespread yawn. "Sounds exciting. You really think we need 15 beds."

"Will wanted more," Hap replied. "Roach and I thought it would be bad for morale. You having regrets for taking a leave of absence from the surgical center?"

"Get some sleep," Doc said. "Didn't spend six years killing bad guys and patching up good guys on most of the continents around the world to pass up this opportunity. "

"Very well," Hap said vanishing into the superstructure without as much as a good night.

Hap lay in his bunk, eyelids pasted to his brow. Except for the strip of light creeping in under the door, the room was dark. He mentally revisited the conversation with Blad as he strapped the Merlin to his back for the flight to Scholes Field.

"So, Ortega is going to do it?"

"Looks that way, Hap."

As usual, his old friend didn't pull a punch.

"Aircraft, light armor, and infantry are on the move staging at ports and airfields on the Caribbean coastline. I recommend you stand down."

Hap killed the starter sequence on number one when the bastard told him to stand down. Faced with stiff odds on the Warden rescue, Blad made the same recommendation.

Minutes later at the hold short waiting for the engine oil to heat, he spoke with Will. KB had wired the aircraft to allow Hap to jack a Sat phone into the planes communication system. The old buzzard's response, "damn the torpedoes, Colonel."

The harder he fought to sleep, the more his brain continued to fire on six of eight cylinders even after twenty-two hours with little to no sleep. Stripped down to only P.T. shorts, he had hung his soiled light blue flight suit two day past a necessary washing on the corner of the wall locker. Electing to go with the moment, he clasped fingers around his close-cropped haircut and crossed both ankles as his eyes meandered around the room's abyss.

He owed Will and couldn't have pulled off Warden's rescue without him. Carla would never understand the bond and with her absence, he was looking for a reason to abort.

Blad commenting to abort reminded him about a night at the O'Club in Atsugi Japan during another time. *Two lovelies were throwing back shooters at the other end of the bar. The stripes on their Navy Blues indicated both were senior to the junior Captains. Both Marine aviators were drunker than a pair of hoot owls.*

Blad had said back then, "Hap, you go for the blonde and I will go for her wing." Been there and done that Hap said under his breath. The blonde could have played offensive guard for the Green Bay Packers and her wing was a knockout. He helped a friend that night, walked over to the blonde and threw out a polite, "Ma'am."

She looked up from her drink and peered through vodka goggles. "Yes, Captain?"

Hap leaned over with his elbow on the bar rattling an empty scotch glass. "I just happened to notice you staring at my small hands."

The Lt Commander turned to lean against the hand-carved bar with a blank as her facial expression. "Excuse me, Captain?"

Hap was sure if he could pull the bar out from her she would have fallen flat on her pudgy ass.

Like that night in Atsugi, he was all in for a friend, even if it meant a Butch Cassidy and Sundance Kid type ending.

What was certain was that Operation Spanish Main was going against more than a company minus of untrained Colombian infantry. If all went to plan, the world wouldn't know the Nicaraguan military had come into play, or why the Sandinista's invaded. Spanish Main would sail away with the cache. In fact, the incident wouldn't make Cable News. His eyelids slowly closed shut as he mumbled under his breath, "game on."

27

Galveston, Texas
Lonibelle D-22

Hap Stoner's Naval Aviation career gave birth to a relationship comparable to a Texas hillside of bluebonnets after a spring shower. There was no gender, didn't have a dark side, nor carry a call sign like Mullet, Cloud Runner, Satan, or Thumper. His soul mate never slept nor took days off.

Once Hap made the decision to pursue a business interest outside the Marine Corps, Hap made a point to carry the sixth sense that kept him alive in the cockpit to the boardroom. The "gut feel" pulled his head out of his ass on more than one occasion to grab situational awareness.

He sensed someone leaning over him and the foul breath shocked both eyelids back.

"Time on deck is 0700," Lew Eglin announced.

Hap's head lolled to the side and the back of his hand provided an additional barrier to the overhead light that came on seconds later. "Hey sailor, were you about to give this big old bad Marine a smack on the lips?"

Lew leaned against the steel doorjamb with arms and ankles crossed. "Drop your cock and put on your socks, fly boy. Hot joe and breakfast waiting in the galley."

Hap groaned, sucked both knees into his chest, then rolled until both feet touched steel and let out a wide yawn. "We may have to fight the whole Nicaraguan military to get off that island."

Lonibelle's Captain's large frame had turned to leave, but stopped midstep, then slowly turned. Both hands went deep into both of his baggy overall pockets while the corner of his narrow mouth curled toward the steel deck. "So?"

Hap's elbows rested on either knee and both hands raked across his close-cropped hair. "This was never going to be a cakewalk, but I'm afraid we could be running up against a brick wall on this one. Thought you would want to know ahead of time."

Lew pursed his lips, his mind lost in thought. Then, as if someone pushed a four finger single malt scotch into one of his bear paws, the edges of his mouth turned toward the ceiling and he said, "You know Hap, over the years I have made money, and lost even more. Bankers try to throw me boatloads of cash only to chase me around the Gulf of Mexico to get it back along with both vessels. You have given me the opportunity to join a venture that would make all "good and bad" worthwhile."

The room went still except the air whirring through the rooms lone vent, Lew's eyes fixed on Hap's like a hungry tiger.

"So, I take it you are all in?" Hap replied.

"Yes, and to the man, I can speak for my crew. I will jump onto the plank and say Machine Head and Stingray's crew are all in."

Hap straightened and quickly slid on his blue flight suit. He didn't bother with laces.

"Let me buy you breakfast," Lew countered.

Hap swept his hand toward the open hatch. "Lead the way."

Hap followed close behind his old friend through the passageway toward the aroma of percolating coffee and frying bacon. From Hap's vantage point, Spanish Main had dodged its first bullet. At this juncture, he had to take Lew at his word; there were no second thoughts about sailing into harm's way. If wrong, it would compromise the entire operation.

28

Somewhere in the Jungles of Costa Rica
D-22

Will's hands moved across the rabbit ears draped around his neck as he felt for the whistle while moving along the berm behind a line of ten commandoes making up the first relay. Seated with jungle boots crossed and green camouflaged bush hats pulled low in anticipation of the order to commence firing, the shooters smeared in black and green patterns on their faces, unifying their black fatigues bloused over jungle boots against black tee shirts pockmarked in sweat.

"Lock and load," Will called out belting out the order from somewhere below his diaphragm and placed the hearing protection over his ears. Sounds of metal on metal resonated up and down the line as shooters inserted 30-round magazines and pulled the M4 bolts back against the weapons buffer spring before slamming a 5.56 round into the rifle's chamber. He worked the bill of the old 8-point field cover low over his brow then blew the whistle alerting all relays that the firing line was hot. The floppy cover was sentimental, still carried its faded Marine Corps emblem, and was the same cover though starched the day he left the Marine Corps to join the CIA. "You are clear to fire when your target comes to bear."

Up and down the line, cracking sounds of members on the firing line squeezing off single fire filled the air, sending spent brass tumbling past the shooter's shoulder. Will watched the targets drop below the berm a heartbeat after the round thumped through the target.

Local teenagers worked their butts off for $20 American, from a sun up to sun down lowering their assigned target after each pull of the trigger. They covered the bullet holes in white or black pasties before running the target back up to the steel frames. They raised a cylinder with white on one side, and black on the other to the area where the target was last marked. To a man, each conducting the training had years of Special Operations experience in hostile territory.

Hard for some to transition from the hostile life and death world of Spec Ops to civilian life, for many it would be easier to climb Mt Everest.

Each man on the firing line wore a Spec Ops DELTA ballistic helmet with a plug crammed into each ear for hearing protection. Five minutes from the first round going down range, each of the relays rocked forward to assume the prone position. Five minutes later the relay quickly exchanged magazines as they straightened to assume an off-hand firing position.

Binocular straps dangled from one of Will's hands, while the other hand fingered a chewed-up cigar. His shoulders flexed with each squeeze of the M4's trigger from the range 100-yard line. The range was nothing more than a narrow alley carved into the Costa Rican rainforest, 50 yards wide by 300 yards in length. Created with the help of DIA dollars to train Contras in the late '80s, Will purchased 150 acres from the Costa Rican Government before leaving for Desert Shield as a CIA contractor in the summer of 1990.

It was just another chapter in the life of Will Kellogg.

An old breed, Will came from the one-shot, one-kill ilk. Occasionally, he stopped by a shooter and leaned down, offering such encouragement as, "Shit man, you shoot like my Grandma, but at least she had an excuse."

The shooter looked back over his stock. "What was the excuse Will?"

Will couldn't hear the question but knew he said. "She was old and blind," Will barked. "Now cowboy up and blow out the center ring or pack your shit."

Without as much as a flinch from the tongue-lashing, the Hispanic shooter ejected a mag and before it touched the ground, he inserted a fresh one. During the rapid-fire sequence, fifteen seconds after the frontal silhouette of a figure lying prone appeared, 10 pulls of the trigger erased where the head and shoulders had been emptying their 30 round magazines.

Down the line, Will stopped, pulled the Beretta from its shoulder holster, and thumbed off the safety. Without notice, he cocked the trigger and banged 16 rounds to the sky. The shooter didn't flinch and continued to fire.

"Fuck you, Will," Jim Moore said rolling onto his left elbow baring a muscular physique wrapped around a six-foot frame. The retired Gunny's eyebrows needed trimming weeks past, but the salt and pepper crew cut always remained in perfect form. White walls and a short widows peak over large ears. "It's been a pretty fun ride, Will; can I please hang onto what little fucking hearing I have left?"

Will's finger tapped his rabbit ears and shook his head while mouthing the words, Can't hear you. He cracked a smile back to Jim Moore who had just returned from Sudan and had been on the Warden rescue. Moore would be in charge of the indirect weapons made up of two 81mm mortars.

"Advance," Will shouted and gestured down range.

Moore rolled onto his belly, cradled his M4 to low crawl down the berm with the rest of the relay. The second relay scampered up the berm and assumed the sitting position while the first relay's asses and upper bodies moved through the native grasses and flowers to the next rise 100 yards to their front. M-240 machine gunners positioned on either end of each relay with a barrel cut half its normal length. Will expected accurate fire from each squad's heavy weaponry in the form of six to eight round burst with the anticipated fight in close quarters clearing the fortress room-to-room.

"Get some," Will called out as the line of tired, filthy Buccaneers of the second relay belly-flopped with a crunching sound and "grunts" for the long low crawl to the 300-yard line. He waited for the third relay to flop in front of him and with a quick check left and right, Will blew the whistle and the burst of three rounds whizzed overhead.

One who would never ask any man in his command to go where he would not—*Leaders lead from the front*, he was fond of saying—Will rolled onto his belly and snaked up the berm with the sound of rounds cracking inches overhead. He covered the 30 feet in seconds and crawled down the berm towards the right side of the 300-yard firing line, which served as the entry point to the agility course. He joined Jim Moore standing by the side of two metal stakes, which would be the course's starting point and finish line. Jim held up the weapon to show that the breech was open, no magazine, and the weapon was on safe. He had rabbit ears down around his neck.

"So, did you talk them into retrograde to Belize?"

Will brushed a layer of sweat from his suntanned forehead and replaced his old Marine Corp hat around the top of his sunburned ears.

"Lonibelle and Stingray will retrograde north to a point on the map, then would assume a westerly heading for Belize if so lucky.

"Hate to go into this one without my team," Moore said. Beads of sweat clung to his eyebrows.

Will listened as he looked down the trail that quickly vanished with a sharp turn into the rainforest to the left. "They have had two in a row and need a break. You, on the other hand, live for this shit."

"No different than you," Moore shot back.

A chuckle snuck out of the side of Will's mouth. "Like me and Stoner."

"Any concerns with Stoner?" Moore said looking back as each man worked on a canteen or readied weapons for the next phase of their training. "I know you bailed his ass out rescuing his CO, but this is a whole different ball game."

Will's eyes turned to meet Moore's dark eyes. "If it's any consolation, the man would give his life for me, and you."

"Not doubting you Will, just asked a question. My team is at Camp Magsai Sai awaiting further orders."

Each time he thought about the 15 acres on the Caribbean side of Belize, which made up Camp Magsai Sai, he thought about the time he had a better day than Franz did at the poker table the year before. Even with the Buccaneer owing him millions, to Will's surprise the old bastard signed over the property for reasons he could never justify in his mind. The 8000-foot plantation home overlooked a private channel that spilled into the Caribbean and was deep enough for Lonibelle and Stingray to navigate.

"Odds?" Moore asked, cinching up his gear.

Will followed with a quick jerk of his head towards the squad lining up for an equipment check. "Equipment check, Jim." When he first laid out the plan, the odds surviving in one piece were better than average. Today, if Vegas were setting the odds and possible confrontation with components of Nicaragua's army, navy, and airforce, the odds against the operation's success increased by three-fold.

Will gave the whistle a long blast, and each member of the relay doubled-timed weapons down the line at the port. Even with the professionalism "the Buccaneers" maintained, Will personally had each man stop and inspect every weapon to ensure safety. A tap on the shoulder sent the team member down the steep trail, vanishing around the sharp turn to begin the excruciating experience of the obstacle course. After the last man passed, the next relay would take their position to go into action as the third relay began their firing sequence.

Each team would meet a dozen obstacles spread over three miles of undulating terrain and swamp. The course required endurance, strength, self-confidence and the most important trait that Will demanded from everyone: mental toughness. As if that wasn't enough, each team member sported full combat gear consisting of two full canteens, a vest, and ruck dangling six canteens. Each man also added an additional 15 pounds of large rocks, tucked away inside their gear.

The course offered ropes to scale bluffs manufactured by Mother Nature fifteen feet in height, while man-made wooden planked walls of eight feet required upper body strength to surmount. Further down the course and a chance to catch a breather, the course presented a gorge forty-foot-wide with cliffs one hundred seventy-five foot requiring rappelling technique. Slogging along the meadow floor in waist-high water was a struggle only to arrive at barbwire barriers the moment their boots touched the sand. Each man dropped and rolled to their back and inched along on using assault rifles to keep the razor wire from slicing uniforms and flesh.

Next came rope ladders used to scramble fifty foot to a landing, and then transfer to a cargo net for the remaining fifty feet. The last mile consisted of a pull-up, a push-up station, and finally yet importantly a sit-up station where the individual hung like a bat by his combat boots from parallel bars.

Not for the meek, they were to repeat the hell before completing the morning's training sequence. Not to be one left out of the fun, Will joined the third team on their second pass through the course.

* * *

Will stood in his skivvies as soiled fatigues began to form a pile, while a second stack consisted of the team member's web gear. Stripped Buccaneers' staggered to the open sun showers while Mestizo women armed with forked sticks and paddles stirred their muddy clothing in a boiling pot large enough for two wild hogs. Other women toiled with brushes to clean web gear and vests to prepare for the next day's training schedule.

He had to laugh each time the gal's round face and triple chin formed a scowl when she worked nature's pitchfork carved from a tree limb. Instead of magic ingredients to add to her witch's brew, she stuck the wooden tool into the stack of soiled dungarees and heaved them into the boiling cauldron as she had done in the '80s fighting the Sandinista. Another woman, decades younger, grimaced as she stirred the brew with a wooden paddle normally used to feed pizza in and out of a brick oven.

The women functioned around parachute cord clotheslines straining from the weight of drying sheets, pillowcases, tee shirts, underwear, and fatigues. Web gear and vests hung from tree limbs and would be married with the owner's folded fatigues, tee shirts, socks, and polished boots.

Will walked over from the shower area to his CP tent, donned a clean set of woodland fatigue bottoms and black tee shirt before blousing a polished pair of jungle boots. He walked over to the general-purpose tent with all four sides rolled up serving as the camp's chow hall. Stacks of ham and cheese sandwiches, chips, fruit, and loaves of bread next to jars of peanut butter greeted the men as they ducked into the hastily prepared eatery. A dozen four-man tables with small wooden stools sat evenly placed within the perimeter of the tent. Ladies manning the kitchen crew would peek on the serving table to ensure the table remained stocked.

Moore settled across from Will and threw back a long pull from his canteen while his free hand clutched a ham and cheese. He leaned after ripping into the sandwich and slowly chewed. "I heard we may be taking on the entire Sandinista army?"

Will polished off a banana and looked his old friend in the eye. "That's what I'm hearing."

"Outstanding," Moore barked. "It's my firm conviction when called by God, I go. If it were easy, everybody would do it!" He tore another swath from the sandwich and began to peel back a banana peel. "You know I really hate to hear it, but you know how I feel about whiners."

*   *   *

After lunch was free time until 1400. Most of the men would grab a ten to fifteen-minute nap commonly referred to as a "fighter nap"; some would read while others cleaned their weapons. Just before 1400, the Buccaneers would find an opening in the rows of benches to go through planning scenarios.

Each man knew plans were useless, but planning was crucial. To the man, they expected the moment the first shot went down range, everything they learned would change. After the initial "oh shit" moment, actions at the team leader level and their seconds made or didn't make would make or break the mission.

29

Galveston, Texas
Lonibelle D-15

KB and Sluggo dropped into their seats in front of their respective consoles. Both slid headsets over their ears as KB leaned forward and punched in the VHF frequency for Lonnibele's prifly into one of the vessel's four radios. Voices came across the frequency from speakers mounted around the Ops Center.

"Bridge, Operations. Have comm with both helos," KB said informing personnel on Lonibelle's bridge, he had positive comm with the helos. His eyes darted left to the radar console where two blips flashed. Other targets popped as the dish completed its initial 360 degrees track inside the safe confines of the radome fixed atop the superstructure.

Hap pulled the hatch close dogging the hatch behind him.

Big Alabama chimed in with his slow, deliberate southern drawl. "Mother, Sierra Hotel zero-zero with two chick's starboard delta for landing."

"Sierra Hotel zero-zero," KB replied. "Clear to break downwind for landing Spot 1. Call abeam Spot 1."

⁕ ⁂ ⁜

Hap observed Big Alabama from Vultures' Row stand his little bird on its rotor disc to pick up a left downwind.

Communications between the ship and helos blared from the speaker mounted on the superstructure behind and above his right shoulder. "V" trotted into view to take position midway between Spot 1 and the superstructure.

Spots 1 and 3 brought the rotor disc closest to the superstructure. Spots 2 and 4 aft and with the additional flight deck added in dry dock, both Cobras and the little birds could land on any of the four Spots.

"Mother, Sierra Hotel 00 abeam Spot 1. One pack drop-off."

KB's voice immediately rang out across Lonibelle's flight deck. "Roger, Sierra Hotel. Cleared to land Spot 1 and disembark one pax."

Hearing the call through the wireless headset fixed inside his cranial earlobes, V's hands immediately went into action. It had been just a year since the boys flew off the boat as Marines, but a year is a year.

As expected in anticipation of the little birds rounded snout crossing Lonibelle's port side, BA eased in left peddle to kick the tale boom parallel to the direction of the ship's heading. Simultaneous with V's hands coming together to form a "V" he motioned towards the deck for the aircraft to land.

BA gloved right hand extended from the small window holding up one finger.

V answered with one hand behind his cranial and pointed to the passenger with the other, it was clear to pass under the rotor disk. Flipping his fingers in a rapid manner, as if waving him on, V pointed to the center of the flight deck.

Bent at the waist to clear the little bird's low-slung rotor arc, Roach carried the overstuffed seabag as it if were a loaf of bread. Clearing the rotor disc V motioned for Jim Bob to come to a hover. Sliding him clear of the deck, he motioned both hands forward in advance of dealing a sharp salute.

Simultaneous with receiving the salute, BA dropped his chin in acknowledgment. Dipping the nose of the aircraft, the helo accelerated rapidly just above the water before commencing a steep climbing left-hand turn.

"V" turned his attention to Schlonger piloting dash two currently in a sharp left-hand turn to gain final. Extending his right arm above the cranial, Schlonger flashed his landing light acknowledging "V's" signal.

∗ ∗ ∗

Hap leaned against a fifty-caliber mount as Roach bounded up the ladder pulling with both arms. Reaching out with a firm shake Hap asked, "Ops O, what's the pleasure."

Roach leaned into Hap's ear to talk over the whining turboshaft engine and turning rotors.

"Situation is fluid, Hap. Want to run something by you and thought it important enough to do in person. Decided to thumb a ride since BA was coming your way."

Hap could see it in his eyes, something had changed and maybe the night would not see them in a bar drinking to excess.

Hap gestured with his head toward the hatch to the Operations Center. "Let's take it inside," Hap replied.

Roach shook his head, "Not yet, want you to see something."

Lonibelle's diesel came to life and weighed anchor.

∗ ∗ ∗

On Lonibelle's bridge, Lew propped a leg over one of the armrests of his Captain's chair. He listened through his headset akin to a head football coach. Able to switch channels by turning a knob on the switch box hanging around his waist, he listened to all elements on board and by toggling, could break into any conversation. Pleased when the sounds of the radios filled his headset minutes before, he raised a fist as Schlonger broke across the bow. Leaning back, he issued orders to the helmsman as if Captain Kirk issuing orders to Sulu.

"Mr. Hoffman, come right to two-three-zero degrees," Lew eased back in the Captain's chair feeling upright with his commands. Lonibelle's Captain continued, "throttles to full Melvin," his voice sounded, more commanding than it sounded in twenty years.

"Coming right two three zero and engines to max throttle, aye, Sir," Melvin Hoffman, the skinny freckle faced helmsman from Texas City replied trying to hide the satisfaction that came with the order.

Bringing the helm hard to starboard hand over hand the teenager's shoulder length hair flowed magnificently in the crosswind rushing through the bridge's open windows.

Lonibelle had become LZ Hollywood to fishermen working the sand flats and those observing from beach houses dotting Salvation Cove's coastline. He could picture Little Leroy steadying himself between the howling turbo diesel laughing incessantly as if a supporting actor in "It's a Mad Mad World."

The flagship of the Spanish Main Operation answered the helm magnificently. Her angled stern came around spewing spray at hovering seagulls compelling the birds to toil in an effort to claw for altitude to remain dry. V's hand and knee went to the deck while Roach and Hap grabbed handrails to prevent from tumbling on their asses.

"Steady on two three zero Mr. Hoffman," Lew bade while switching up Magellan's frequency. "Sluggo, do we have an ETA for the trap?"

Sluggo waved to KB who ducked out of the hatch to Vultures' Row.

"Fifteen minutes," Sluggo replied switching over to prifly. "Have a passenger that needs to get over to Stingray."

Big Alabama broke in, "I got this one Schlonger, pick up a port delta on Stingray and anchor."

Sluggo switched over to ships intercom. "Captain, BA will be coming in to Spot 2 for a passenger pickup. Set the trap for Magellan the moment BA's skids break ground."

V nodded raising an arm above his cranial while toggling with the volume switch with the other.

"Spot 2 BA," Sluggo said playing the role of tower operator.

"Cleared to land Spot 2," BA replied flashing his landing light to V as if saying *understand buddy?*

Hap called out to KB leading him as he underhanded a cranial. Catching the head protection in stride, he slid down the rail using both hands. Within seconds of the skids settling on Spot 2, KB leaped aboard as BA pulled collective to depart for the short ride to Stingray.

V cut a salute to the departing helo as two deckhands began to drag a net across the flight deck.

Lonibelle's snare utilized three inertial reels secured to steel poles with an end of a bay shrimping net tied to either side. Placed two thirds down the flight deck, the net became Magellan's last chance if Sluggo botched the landing. In a perfect world, the net would capture the drone before breaking into pieces against the superstructure.

Hap issued Roach a quizzical question mark expression as if saying. "Is the Slug ready for this?"

Leaning on the rail using his fireplug forearms for support, Roach's rounded jaws ground on a piece of Hallettsville beef jerky "Sure."

Working towards thirty-five-knot approach speed, Sluggo eased back on the throttle using thumb and forefinger as if in a video game. Holding the flaps until final approach, Sluggo steered the lumbering drone toward the sprinting Lonibelle.

Sluggo knew Magellan would cross Lonibelle's threshold with five knots of forward motion give or take a knot. His insurance was the assumed headwind provided by Lonibelle's power plant and Mother Nature's breezes working together would provide thirty knots of wind across the deck.

"Lew, maintain course and keep the speed up," Sluggo requested.

"No problem, Sluggo," Lew replied turning to the helm. "Mr. Hoffman, maintain course and speed. And don't fuck this up."

Melvin responded with an ear-to-ear smile, "Maintain course, and speed aye, Sir. And don't fuck it up – Aye Sir!"

It was all over in seconds. Sluggo had Magellan's main gear touchdown 10 feet after crossing Lonibelle's threshold. Two deckhands raced across the flight deck to lash the drone to the tie-downs between the superstructure and Spot 1.

Hap and Roach looked to the other with a smile ecstatic and each gave Sluggo a resounding slap on the back as they made their way forward to their shared stateroom. Entering their small space, Hap pulled out the bottom drawer of his desk revealing a bottle of Texas made single malt whiskey.

Roach waved him off. "Boys will be doing NVG work and I want Sluggo to get a landing in with no moon as well."

Hap let the bottle settle back to the bottom of the drawer before guiding the drawer closed with the heel of his boot. "So, what's so important you had to come all the way from Lonesome Dove to tell me?"

Silence followed, except for the hum of Lonibelle's twin Wartsila diesels.

Roach leaned into Hap and shouted over the diesels and the whistling wind. Hap's jaw could have hit the flight deck when he did.

30

Fortress Study
Isle de San Andres

"Thank you, Hector," Franz Krueger said settling back in the high back chair twirling the brandy around in his glass. "Can you give me some time alone?"

Hector gestured with his eyes and head toward the bottle next to a glass turned on its end. *Leave it?*

Franz cracked a smile and pointed toward his desk.

Hector turned over the glass and poured a generous pour. "If you don't mind, Franz, let's sit together.

Franz's mind raced as if a lithograph as diskettes of imaginative slides passed in and quickly out of view.

"What are you thinking, Sir?" Hector said.

Franz chuckled and looked into his old friend's penetrating eyes. "My childhood in Germany, undergrad and law school in the States during the prewar years, and Judith. Have I told you about the true love of my life and mother of our son?"

"Little Wilhelm," Hector replied. "I still remember traveling with you to attend both funerals."

Franz nodded slowly as the brandy swirled around in his glass. "To think millions of other good Germans gave everything for that Corporal."

Hector polished off the glass and leaned over with the glass out. "I still remember the night we met."

Frames of history appeared clearly into his mind's view as Franz poured. Hector waved his palm as the liquid approached the rim. A pause, as quick as the lithograph shuttered, it spooled, the journey continued up until the site of Hans' lifeless body sprawled face down appeared. The third glass empty now, the lithograph at a standstill, Franz tapped the crystal glass with manicured fingers.

"Have you considered your legacy?"

His mind fogged with brandy, Franz's life's journey continued and the transition of the business through its next generations of leaders would require more, much more than the proverbial magic wand or pixie dust. "Maybe I'm becoming sentimental with age, but it's as if a puppet master tugged on the strings and I'm the puppet."

Hector sat comfortably in a chair to the side of the desk, legs crossed, resting the glass on a knee. "Mother earth is a dangerous place Franz, but nothing the old lady hasn't seen before."

Franz offered a soft smile. "Man and his governments, good and bad, sometimes require a small push for the betterment of mankind."

"Is this why the Graf Spee spends so much time at sea?" Hector's tenor was soft and non-threatening. "All we do when you order one of the drug runners submarines to be sunk is raise the retail price for the cocaine or heroin the second they touch US soil."

"Don't forget the innocence, Hector." Franz refreshed his glass, emptying the bottle. "I have had analyst inside the organization tell me we save three lives on the average for each vessel we take down."

"The millions that come with them are just a consolation prize?" Hector raised his empty glass to his front as if offering up a toast.

Franz let out a sigh. "My old friend, the closer I draw to the end of my life I am prodded to be that gravitational pull to do good for mankind."

"Why?" Hector replied.

"I owe it to mankind and the German people to make up for the misery we brought over two World Wars."

31

Galveston, Texas
Lonibelle D-15

Roach turned sideways to get his sea bag through the open hatch, then stopped and pointing to the rack on the right asked. "Mine?"

Hap nodded, entering the cracker box size room.

The sea bag left his shoulder as if shot out by a mortar, bouncing off the bulkhead left of the small reading lamp fixed to the wall. "And this is what Captain Lew calls a stateroom?"

"Apparently on the Lonibelle it is," Hap echoed as his old friend's slept-out mattress seemed to swallow his butt. "What the hell, Hap? He wiggled his butt into the bed like a D.C. 14th Street hooker with a frown prominently fixed above his squared chin. "The least the big guy could have done is bought new mattresses. With the money being spent on this ship-wreck, mattresses would have been nothing."

Hap leaned crossways in his rack with his knees tucked up under his chin. There was something amiss with the Roach. Normally every other word in this type situation would contain an F-bomb.

"Say again, Ops O, you're mumbling".

Sitting up now on the edge of the rack with boots firmly planted on the deck, Roach leaned back against the metal bulkhead hands clasped behind his shaved head.

"Hap, this Sandinista concern has grown legs to such a point we should consider aborting Spanish Main."

Quiet followed except for the hum of Lonibelle's diesel and the Roach removing the wrapper off a Cuban cigar.

"What did Blad have to say, asshole?"

Roach stuffed the cigar into his mouth and looked over his brow. "The Sandinista are invading Isle de San Andres as sure as we are, Hap. If there is any good news, it's that we are a few days ahead of them."

"Put yourself in my boots. If the word was go, what would you recommend?"

Roach squirmed in his rack in an attempt to get comfortable scratching the underside of his chin still chewing the cigar as if it were a piece of jerked venison. "Create a diversion."

Hap nodded and fought back a smile. "Not bad, but stop with the prick tease, bitch."

"Come on, Hap. Whatever the diversion is, the Sandinista will not abort their H-Hour, it'll just delay them. Either way," Roach shrugged his broad shoulders, "a monkey wrench might be thrown into "Che Guevara."

"Wait one second," Hap interrupted. "Che Guevara?"

"Blad outdid himself on this one, Hap. Do not know how, but he picked up the name of the Sandinista Operation to invade Isle de San Andres."

Hap shook his head. "How does he do this shit?"

Roach interrupted, "Let's be clear, the primary objective would simply create a cushion of time between Spanish Main and Che Guevara. If Ortega hits the lotto and with political objectives coming together the commie will never look past Che Guevara and the power that it will yield. That being said, not sure his military leadership would advise to stop an insurgency and initiate Che Guevara simultaneously"

Hap broke in, "Make no mistake; his generals will do whatever necessary to safeguard their pension and live to see another sunrise. Confronted with an either-or decision would be either avoiding the lonely walk to meet a firing squad or languishing in a prison cell for the rest of their lives."

Hap rolled out of the bed and slid into the chair behind the metal desk on his side of their shared locker. Fingers raced across the keys as he typed an email to Will with the turn of events. He closed with a note of suggestions to overcome the problem.

Let me suggest you plan one hell of a diversion.

Roach leaned against the wall with arms crossed, his square jaw firm. "Since I know you're not going to puss out on the mission, Stingray needs to put to sea tomorrow."

Hap nodded slowly as he typed an email to Carla. "Assets on board?"

Roach thumbed the back of his head with both shoulders burrowed against the steel bulkhead. "One little bird with crew and maintenance assets. As planned, we conduct a HALO for the insert with Trixie as the delivery platform. The little bird can provide logistical support for Tom's team until H Hour. We have to create as much space between us and the Sandinista as we can."

Hap reached for the black phone receiver hanging between the bed and the desk punching the button labeled "Bridge."

The helmsman's voice answered on the other end.

"Is Lew at the conn?" Hap asked.

"Yes, Sir, Mr. Stoner."

"Would you have him come to my quarters?"

Hap heard, "Captain, Mr. Stoner would like your presence in his quarters." He could hear Lew groan slightly as he pushed himself out of the chair,

"You have the conn, Mr. Hoffman."

"Aye-aye, Captain," came the reply.

Hap heard his door open, broke away from reading Will's response, and spotted Lew's red beard peering around the partially open cabin door.

"You rang, Hap?" he asked.

"Wait one, Lew. Let me finish Will's email." As expected, Will had maintained his *damn-the-torpedoes* attitude, electing not to abort and give him some time to come up with the proper diversion for his old nemesis Daniel Ortega. Hap tapped, "enter" to continue and put the Stingray to sea. It would be a two-week journey to international waters off the coast of Costa Rica. He spoke with his back to Lew.

"We have a change of plans."

Hap rotated slowly in his chair while Roach outlined the recent changes to the Operation on a legal pad he'd picked up off his metal desk. Lew stuffed both hands deep into his overall pockets. A pronounced slump of his broad shoulders appeared, and hands pressed deeper into the denim pockets.

Roach spoke as he continued to scribble notes across the pad. "We have to launch Stingray tomorrow."

Lew nodded. "You still feel pretty good about this thing?"

Hap cut a glance over to Roach who was looking down at the floor massaging both temples.

"I'm not going to bullshit you, Lew, the situation is fluid, and one would be foolish to think otherwise. We have to keep our wits about us and adapt to the situation, improvising as the situation changes."

Lonibelle's Captain's narrow lips tightened while he slowly began to nod. "I would like to tell Machine Head face-to-face. Can I get a lift to Stingray?"

Hap reached around for his receiver punching the button for PriFly. Schlonger and Big Alabama were going back and forth, over who would have priority for fueling.

"Break, break, break, need a lift from Lonibelle to Stingray, one pax," said Hap, notifying the helos in the pattern that they needed one bird to lift a passenger from Lonibelle to Stingray

"I got it," Schlonger broke in.

"Roger," Big Alabama squawked, banking hard left to give way to Schlonger.

Lew turned to leave the cabin stopping at the sound of Hap calling his name.

"Tell Machine Head to ensure KB gets another look at the communications systems."

"Will do. I will take him with me," Lew said before closing the door behind him.

"Hap, can I make a suggestion?"

Replacing the receiver, Hap responded. "I'm all ears, Ops O."

"Send V, Magellan, and both little birds."

"I'm not going to argue with that call."

"I'll have Stingray steer off the coast of Corpus Christi but remain in international waters to pick up maintenance personnel, weapons, and ordnance."

Hap nodded. "Besides, the additional lift capability will expedite the vert rep evolution if we have to extract the team before Lonibelle enters the Op area." Hap raised his forefinger. "One more thing, Roach."

Roach had one hand on the doorknob and stopped, cutting his eyes over a shoulder towards Hap, who was no longer facing the computer screen.

Hap leaned back in his chair with a shit-eating grin. "Let's light this roman candle."

Roach's answer consisted of a headshake and a chuckle. "Stop it, Hap…I'm beginning to become accustomed to hanging around with your dead ass."

Hap's eyes cut to Roach's baby browns and nodded in agreement. "Indeed, Roach. Yes, indeed."

32

Isle de San Andres
OP-I-D-10

Fixed on Isle de San Andres 3,500-foot perch, OP One delivered all the characteristics for a good observation point. Located on the dormant volcano's forward slope, the position was neither obvious nor conspicuous from the ground or air. Shaun was the first to dive off Trixie's ramp a little after 0300. Descending out at 25,000 like a human bullet, the chute, along with the seven others, deployed automatically at 10,000 feet and he steered the chute to a mesa on the mountain's southwest side.

Soundlessly setting in their position, each of the four-man team cut tree limbs with their Treeman Combat Guard knives to lace in ponchos. Each of their faces, streaked with green and black face paint, blending in with the volcanic rock and vegetation. Shaun's narrow brow rested against the rubber eyecup of a tripod scope set atop a piece of lava with the outline of Isle de San Andres harbor in the foreground. Lights from the capital city of Isle de San Andres Providencia and Santa Catalina City cast an aura over the island's largest municipality of more than 60,000.

A pair of headlights turned onto the island's major highway from an Isle de San Andres City side street. The island's only highway circled the island traveling through the heart of the city. Other than this vehicle, the roads were void of vehicular traffic at 0415. *Did anybody party after 4 a.m.?* He reached for the push to talk switch taped above his right breast to speak through a MICH headset system.

"OP Two, comm check. Over."

"Loud and clear."

"How is the view?"

"Cat bird's seat. The city and airport are in clear view along with the western two-thirds of the island."

"On my way to your position."

"Roger," Eddie replied just above a whisper.

Shaun stepped off, carefully covering the 100 meters in less than 5 minutes. Eddie and his team continued around the north sides of the mountain. That left Shaun's team to set in OP One, dropping a trail of IR sticks along the way. If one was wearing night vision, the trail lit up like the duty runway at O'Hare International.

"OP Two," Shaun whispered through his headset, "entering your position from the east."

"Continue," Eddie said.

Like any good leader, Eddie stood watch with his M4 over a shoulder, barrel down, to allow his team time for shut-eye before sunup. He was finishing off the slipknot to secure a corner of the camouflaged poncho that would be the roof to his hooch until Stoner arrived.

"Nice choice."

Eddie turned his head and smiled, illuminating a white streak of teeth to an otherwise black and green façade. "Wish I could have brought my surfboard."

"Maybe next time," Shaun said, chortling. He offered a can of Copenhagen.

"You know better than that."

Shaun shrugged and removed a generous pinch and tucked the tobacco between cheek and gum. He could make out a coconut palm plantation and the island's native trees 20 meters in height all the way to the airport.

Eddie dropped to a knee and removed the charges that he would attach to the bridges wooden structure after midnight. He carefully placed the last charge into the ruck laying open in front of him. He slid his bush hat on top of the charges and hands raked his close-cropped curly hair.

Shaun had sat with his back resting against a native tree reaching 60 feet into the sky, a loaded M4 across his lap.

"What's up?"

Eddie's eyes slashed across to Shaun. "What do you think the chances are we go face-to-face with the Sandinista?"

"You okay?" Shaun replied offering a shrug. "It doesn't matter if the Sandinista shows up for the party. Cowboy up and get some rest. The next few nights are going to be a bitch."

33

Lonibelle

Magellan's snout rotated above the horizon to begin a gentle climb away from Puerto Cabezas airspace. The Wankel rotary engine delivered its rated 38 horsepower to push the three hundred seventy-five-pound airframe through partly cloudy skies to its 15,000-foot service ceiling.

Hap cocked his head to look over Sluggo's shoulder at the drone's current feed. "Can you put up the archived feed of Puerto Cabezas on Roach's screen?"

KB nodded, and his fingers danced across the console. Hap turned to Roach's interactive screen on the opposite bulkhead.

"Thanks, KB," Hap said.

Sluggo scraped Magellan's wing tips through broken cumulus weaving along Nicaragua's eastern coastline. "Great call allowing Magellan to leave with Stingray," Sluggo said in more of an announcement.

Hap watched the archived feed for the Puerto Cabezas area while sipping on a mug of coffee. Lonibelle's diesel delivered a steady vibration through the steel deck and up through his flight boots. "We are not watching a naval exercise." He finished off the cup and let it drop to his side. "Look at the rust on the Tapir's deck," Hap said referring to one of two Russian amphibious transport docks given to the Nicaraguan

Navy three years earlier. Similar to the landing ships used by the US Marine Corps, the vessel was beachable, 370 feet long, and could carry up to 425 troops, 20 tanks, or 40 armored vehicles.

"Like father, like son," Roach chirped.

Hap retreated to the table acknowledging Sluggo with a smile before placing the cup next to a pile of plastic figurines. The Russian navy was notorious for rust on their naval vessels and apparently, passed on the tradition to the Nicaraguan navy, who wouldn't know any better.

Sluggo shrugged.

"Surprised?" Roach asked. "The Sandinista intend to invade Isle de San Andres using these rust buckets. Mark my words, we will contribute to the preservation of the ocean's reefs."

Sluggo chuckled. "Punch a few holes in the corroded hull and a big part of their ground combat element becomes an artificial reef."

"The Cousteau Society will be diving on the wreck by the end of the year for National Geo." KB injected speaking over a shoulder.

"Where is our intel on the Sandinista threat?" Roach said, cutting a glance to Hap. "Shouldn't we be hearing about the head fake?"

Hap loathed the thought of not knowing the makeup of the Sandinista threat. The silence on the diversion didn't help calm his growing angst. He said nothing.

"Stingray is on station," KB announced. .

Roach reached over to the corner of the table and pulled a small plastic burnt orange Stingray from the pile of figurines. "Very well. Ensure Lew knows."

"He is the one that told me," KB replied.

Roach placed the plastic Stingray on a point of the map that represented 20 miles off the northeastern coast of Isle de San Andres. "When I want to hear a smart ass remark, I'll ask you for it. Eat shit, KB."

Hap eyed the chart while Roach leaned on the table propped up by both arms. "I will be speaking with Will after we get our feed from Blue Fields and El Bluff."

Roach looked across the table towards Hap, "I want to be part of the call."

Hap's baby blues looked over his brow. "Of course," he responded, just as Lew's voice came across Roach's handheld. "Plot us on the map. Dead center between the Caymans and Chetumal, speed—eighteen knots, heading one six two."

Roach clicked the transmitter on his belt twice, placing a plastic figurine of a dirty blonde sporting a bikini and enormous breasts onto the chart. "If these favorable seas continue, we are going to make good time."

"Nice touch, Roach," Sluggo said.

"Least I could do for Lew, since we *are* using his frigging dining room table."

KB appeared with a smile stretched from ear to ear cleaning his wire-rimmed glasses with a napkin.

Roach looked up and spoke like the gentlemen he wasn't, "You want something digit head?"

Without turning away from the monitor, KB's head shook side to side.

Hap reached down and flipped to bridge on his control box. "You ready, Lew? Lonibelle is going into harm's way."

It was if crickets manned the bridge. There was no answer.

34

Gulf of Mexico
Lonibelle

Yellow cheese oozed from the Philly cheesesteak compressed by Sluggo's stubby fingers before taking a bite of the manwich. A brown paper bag of sweet potato fries puddled grease next to Magellan's joystick. He punched the autopilot to trace his navigation route to lazily circle between El Bluff and Blue Fields airfield at 5,000 feet. Splayed back in the Captain's chair as if in a theatre, he watched video feed while dropping fries as if the oily treats were popcorn.

Hap reached over Sluggo's shoulder into the bag of fries as another Tapir class landing ship came into view.

"You over El Bluff?" Hap questioned.

"You bet," Sluggo responded in between smacks. "Those white beaches look as good as the ones we chased pussy at on Okinawa."

Hap didn't catch his last comment as he thought about Blad's intelligence reports. Based on the two amphibious ships between Puerto Cabezas and El Bluff, they planned to deploy the entire armored complement within Managua's standing army if each of the vessels were only half filled. It was clear between the two amphibious vessels and the helos lined up at Blue Fields airfield; they would base their attack on three assault groups and intended to use an amphibian operation in their overall scheme of maneuver.

As Blue Fields came into view Sluggo licked the cheese from between his empty fingers then zoomed Magellan's lens to catch a unit boarding a Mi8 turning on the tarmac. Roach's hand replaced Hap's in the grease-saturated bag.

"Hap, I thought Roberto Duran was Panamanian?"

"He is, Sluggo, but damned if that Nicaraguan doesn't project a mirror image of the tuff bastard in his prime."

Roach never missed an opportunity to make a person feel like a goat and this moment was no different. "A Roberto Duran look-alike takes full metal jackets to the body just like any other Sandinista." Reaching into the bag for another handful of fries, he returned to the map table.

Hap tapped Sluggo on the shoulder and leaned into his ear. "Follow that bird. I want to know if this flight has anything to do with Isle de San Andres. Add the Ready Room TV to the feed."

Sluggo finished taking a long pull of diet coke. "KB?"

"I'm on it," KB answered tapping the keyboard.

Hap joined the Roach mulling over Lew's dining room table studying the map.

"So, what do you think?"

Roach leaned over the table with both hands holding up his weight. He spoke without looking up. "It's all bullshit, Hap."

"You going to be able to work through this?" Hap asked.

"What the fuck. I was worried when my wife left me years past not understanding why. The obstacles we face I consider a mere nuisance. No biggie."

Hap peeked at his old friend. "Having an ex-wife causes worry and the Sandinista army a mere nuisance. Are you out of your frigging gourd?"

"Hap, you know what Trixie meant to me."

"Hell Roach, I told you don't marry a stripper the night you meet her. How many trips to ATM did you make that night to feed her tips? Hell, her friend I hooked up with was Psycho!"

Roach shook his head. "You got me there, Hap; I should have taken 30 days leave to ensure she was the one instead of a long weekend. At least you didn't marry your stripper."

"That was then, and this is now, big guy," Hap retorted.

"Don't worry. I'm working on my issues. If you don't mind, I want Lew to take Lonibelle to max sustainable speed. Order Stingray to divert to X Ray and get Will's assault teams on board."

Hap rubbed his chin as if studying the next move on a chessboard.

Roach eyed his old friend as if asking and?

"Ohhhhhh, boys," Sluggo spouted.

Both turned from the table as KB leaned over from his station to watch the Sandinista helo skim over the water westward.

"If I didn't know better, this bird's mission is going to Isle de San Andres."

Hap turned his head towards Roach. "Ok," he said, "do it."

Roach chimed a quick response as he reached for his handheld radio. "Suggest you get good comm with Will and let him in on the change of plans. Shaun will be updated on recent events."

Holding the handheld to his lips he waited to key the transmit button until Hap acknowledged with a nod and he spoke to KB. "KB, I need comm with Shaun. Stat!" Keying the mike, he said, "Lew, you up?"

Twenty seconds later Lew replied, "I'm here."

"Need you to take Lonibelle to max sustainable speed."

"Will do," Lew replied. "Turns for max speed, Mr. Hoffman."

Melvin's right hand had already begun easing the throttles forward before Lew uttered his last name.

After the throttles bumped up against the stops, the young helmsman responded, "Full throttle, Captain."

Lew switched to intercom. "Leroy, we are going to push the engines for about 30 hours."

Wearing wireless ear protection snug around each ear the vessel's chief engineer replied immediately, his high-pitched voice shouting over the whining engines, "Only 30 hours? She will take it, Captain, no problem." Having moved to the instrument board the moment the engines replied to Melvin's throttle inputs, he eyed the gauges, which remained steady on the high side of the green. He ambled around the massive contraptions driving Lonibelle's screw with the same scrutiny as George Patton inspecting troops. Satisfied, he keyed the intercom. "Go with it, Lew. Lonibelle is good in engineering."

Lew waited nervously for engineering to report while he nibbled on the end of a soggy sweet potato fry. The moment he heard Little Leroy give a thumbs up he dropped the soggy fry into the trash, then eased over to the coffee pot. Pouring with one hand, he pressed the trigger with the other. "Leroy, the second your gut says enough, bring them back. Otherwise, use bubble gum and duct tape to keep the engines from coming apart."

"Will do, Captain," Leroy replied continuing to pace between the racing power plants all the while hoping like hell he wouldn't *actually* need to use bubblegum and duct tape to hold the massive motors together.

35

Caribbean
Lonibelle D-7

Tucked away on the opposite end of the Operations Center, eight high back leather ready room style chairs were screwed to the deck with two rows of four split down the middle by a three-foot aisle. There was an interactive TV bolted into the bulkhead center mass to the seating area. A small podium sat off the side of the TV. Magellan's current digital feed filled the screen.

Silent, Hap and Roach sat in the front row, without a word uttered between them. KB had communications between BA's flight and Lonibelle piped into the Operations Center overhead speakers as they prepared to land.

"About fucking time," Roach replied.

Hap's head lolled toward the Roach. "Blad thinks we might have a three day lead on Ortega."

Roach's eyes narrowed as his round face splayed a crooked smile. "Bullshit, Hap. The Nicaraguan invasion has begun."

Hap's gazed turned to the screen and said nothing.

"Diversion?" Roach slid his laptop off the small table into the adjacent seat, stored the small table to the side, and then pushed up from his chair.

"Killer eggs safe on deck," KB called out.

"We heard," Roach said, pushing himself out of the chair.

Hap reached up, grabbed Roach's arm, and looked into his old friend's eyes. "Let's keep our wits. We have been in tougher scrapes."

Roach shrugged off Hap's hold. "If you don't mind me saying, I will not bullshit the guys."

The sounds of flight boots pounding up the steel steps from the flight deck echoed in the room as Hollywood entered the Operations Center followed by LD Hicks. "Excuse me, boys," Hollywood said. "What the hell is going on here?"

Hap's eyes went from Roach to the rest of the aircrew gathering in front of the TV. "The Sandinista's have begun their invasion."

Killer Koch joined the gaggle congregated in front of Roach and Hap. "Are we late?"

Hap slowly pushed himself out of his chair. "At this moment I would say yes."

"So, let's kick some Sandinista ass," Hollywood replied.

Hap didn't give Roach the chance to tell Hollywood politely to go to hell. He said, "This operation ends the moment either Colombia or Nicaragua's military enters the fray in advance of Spanish Main's L Hour. Assuming Lonibelle's power plant doesn't go into the shitter between then and now, we will begin vertical replenishment in 24 hours to get the heavy weapons and ordnance from Stingray onboard."

Roach moved off to a chair at the end of the row, his laptop underarm.

Hollywood looked at Killer and LD, and then shrugged. "Let's go play poker." All three exited from the Operations Center through the front hatch.

Hap eased over behind Sluggo's Captain Chair.

"Still tracking east, Hap," Sluggo said without looking back.

"How long can Magellan remain on station," Hap asked?

Having already worked through time on station and the intercept of Stingray, Sluggo's reply was instantaneous, "45 minutes on the outside before breaking off to rendezvous with Stingray.

"As much as I would like to know where the Sandinista chopper offloads the cargo, can't afford to lose Magellan. So, don't screw this up."

Sluggo acknowledged with a reassuring nod as Hap ducked through the hatch to Vultures' Row. He clambered down the ladder well leading to the flight deck wanting to conduct a walk-through of the maintenance effort and check morale.

* * *

Outside of Puerto Limon Costa Rica

One hundred and fifty species of orchids flourished in Hotel Westfalia's garden, radiating beautiful colors along with rich aromas. Will Kellogg's elbows rested on the steel rail wrapped around his fourth-floor penthouse suite patio. A satellite phone rested on the side table next to the suite's outdoor living area ensemble.

A howler monkey ran for its life chased by an irate housekeeper with a broom raised over her head. The incident began because of an unattended fruit plate pulled from a table where a sign in English off to the side hung from an awning, "PLEASE do not leave food UNATTENDED." By the girl's expletives in Espanol, the teenage girl made it clear to the black haired creature she intended to brain it if she could catch it. After a couple of laps around the garden, the monkey climbed an awning and vanished onto the roof.

Even all the comic relief could not make Will smile because of the text he received before stepping through the French doors, announcing that Diana Olvera, the Westfalia's Manager had met Costa Rica's Vice President at the food service loading dock. The satellite phone buzzed. He reached over and scooped up the phone to glance at the phone's screen. Hap Stoner was on the end of the digital link.

"Yes, Colonel?"

"We have eight hours before the ground assault element will embark onto Stingray."

Will nodded slowly and turned away from the rail. "I will be ready for extraction from the hotel helo pad in twelve hours."

"Worried?" Hap asked.

Will said nothing, knowing full well that the diversion failure was inconceivable. Diana had taken the call directly from the second most powerful politician in Costa Rica, and she would be visiting the Hotel. As the Hotel's Manager, she knew she had a reservation for the Master Suite under the name Bill Randolph Barber. The Vice President was going to rendezvous with Will Kellogg just as they had done off and on for 30 years.

Will recognized the light tap at the door. "I have to go, Colonel." He entered the room, and then set the phone on top of the nightstand on his side of the bed. She would do the same on the right nightstand. He didn't bother to look through the peephole. He swung open the door and she fell into his arms without a word said. Another monkey's howl echoed through the balcony doors as Will lifted Costa Rica's Vice President, Maria Venezuela, in his arms. He used his knee to swing the door shut. Pinned against the wall in a passionate embrace her hand felt around the door and found the latch, then dropped to throw the lock.

Will knew what he had to do, but he made a point for at least a while, to keep his mind off what Hap really wanted out of the rendezvous.

36

Caribbean
Stingray D-6

Captain Machine Head Larson's facial features reflected in silhouette off the Stingray's radar and the sonar console's faint green glow. Radar reflected numerous targets working the calm waters around Stingray, none closer than two miles. *Most likely fishing vessels and a possible drug runner, no threat to Stingray.* There was one airborne target to the southwest. Slow moving, it flew at only 2500 feet and 50 miles out. Except for the five-man watch, the crew had the evening off.

He reached for the night vision goggles swinging above the sat phone resting on the chart table. With the moon in its last quarter floating high over the seascape, he thought of his adopted mother's one-liners.

"Never worry about darkness for that is when the stars shine brightest. Or, when you have a goal and the path is wrought in darkness, to be a star sometimes you must shine your own light. Her best line however, was, "what're you doing running with the likes of Hap Stoner? Trouble seems to be attracted to that boy."

"Captain, you worried about the order to leave Isle de San Andres?"

Larson turned his head. Cedric Ray stood as tall as the wheel taken from an old riverboat. "Not yet anyway. Spent too many years in Navy submarines not to know situations change."

Cedric said nothing.

The sun had set hours earlier and the assigned coordinate had Stingray's angular bow pointed to the northeastern coast of Costa Rica.

Looking straight out over the bow, Cedric asked, "How did the guys on the island take the news?"

Larson had waited to make the call to Shaun 30 minutes after Stingray turned her bow leaving Isle de San Andres in her wake. He mumbled a reply. "Son of a bitch said now I know how the Marines at Guadalcanal felt when the Navy pulled out."

Cedric's head turned revealing large round eyes and large teeth bearing a slight smile. "Say what?"

"Told him, I shall return."

A tap on the door from the rear passageway, and light from the partially open door, splashed across the left side of the bridge. He recognized Doc's voice.

"Mind some company, Machine Head?"

"How was the sausage and sauerkraut?" Larson asked.

V, Foxie, Schlonger, and BA filed in behind Doc reflecting faces analogous to queasy stomachs. Doc eased back in the chair opposite Larson's, the four aviators continued towards the compass platform, but stopped with Larson's next words.

Stingray's captain pointed his finger in the direction of a very old friend. "Hey, all Susan talked about on prom night was why I didn't drive a Mustang. I was at the door when she went inside."

"I drove a Mustang," Doc said leaning back with his legs crossed gesturing with his hands. "Hey man, did you kiss her goodnight?"

Larson said nothing and lay the goggles next to the Sat phone.

"Figured as much," Doc replied. "What can I say; Susan went straight from shaking your hand goodnight, to sneaking out of her window to my car waiting in the alley. Couldn't drive fast enough to the levee and her prom gown was hiked above her waist before your shoes stepped over the threshold of your home."

KB's voice came across the bridge's squawk box.

"Stingray, Magellan fifteen minutes north and west inbound for landing. Give as much wind over the deck as you can. Sluggo is requesting vectors."

Larson eased over to the helm and slowly eased the throttles to the max. "Engine room, bridge. We are going to flank speed to land the drone." He glanced at the radar showing a lone blip northwest as V, Foxie, BA, and Schlonger shot by to prepare the flight deck for landing. He leaned over the chart table and plotted Stingray to Magellan's position, once the turn into the wind was completed.

"Helm, come right to one-three-five."

"Coming right to one-three-five, aye-aye, Captain." Cedric spun the riverboat wheel. Larson intended to put Stingray's bow 15 degrees off the wind direction to keep the superstructure from obstructing the wind line. Stingray's deck plates shook as her engines put out as much horsepower as her worn O-rings would allow. Larson wasn't sure what would give first, the engine mounts or the welds on Stingray's hull.

"Magellan, Stingray. Come left to one five zero degrees." He said.

"Left one-five-zero for Magellan," Sluggo replied.

Within five minutes, Stingray completed her turn to its desired heading and made ready to capture the drone.

Schlonger had followed V and Foxie out of the bridge but suddenly reappeared, "Doc, you coming," he queried?

Doc looked around. "Hell, Schlonger I'm the ship's surgeon."

Larson's voice sounded over the 1MC, "Prepare for flight operations. We will be landing the drone. Watch return to the bridge and bring the captain a plate of chow. Out."

Schlonger smiled and threw him an inflatable jacket. "Put this on. You might be the ships surgeon, but tonight, you're just a deck ape like the rest of us."

37

Isle de San Andres
OP-1

For the past two hours, Shaun used rapid blinks to shield his eyes from sheets of unrelenting rain. An hour earlier, his hooch gave way and now it draped over his head and shoulders. He wedged his wiry frame between two mangrove stumps to prevent the small streams that ran past either butt cheek to wash him down the slope. Black Eddie and his team of sappers had been running wire and setting C-4 for the better part of three hours. If they hadn't completed the mission by 0500, they would return the following night.

A flash of lightning danced across the top of the old fortress, skylighting Tommy Kelso's solid build and short frame approach with the barrel of his M4 poking out from the poncho liner draped like a burka. "Mind if I join you?" Tommy said in a southern drawl.

"Yours, too?" Shaun replied without looking up.

"Didn't have a chance in this shit storm. Not a hooch standing amongst the team."

Shaun laughed as a crack of thunder shook the entire mountain. Neither man flinched as Tommy settled down against the stump to his right. "Will need you to take your team to OP Two before sunup. Black Eddie's sappers need to sleep."

"Aye-aye," Tommy answered cynically. "That'll give us a reason to stretch our legs. Not as young as I used to be."

Tommy nudged his back against the stump. "Motherfucker, Shaun, I might have to tie myself off to the stump to keep from being washed away. Thought I heard a helo circling overhead."

Shaun looked straight ahead, into what could have been the abyss. "Thought so, but blew it off thinking who in the hell would be flying in this crap?"

"You trust this Hap Stoner guy?"

"Why do you ask?" Shaun shot back.

"Look around, mofo. Our OP is washed out beneath us and we have no support within 400 miles."

"Tommy, you don't know me, nor I you. But Hap Stoner, well, I know the man. We were TBS roommates and years later he was in the flight that saved the lives of my Marines in Fallujah."

"You were there in '06?"

"I was. My Company was taking down the last building which would have been my HQ when we ran into a shit storm." Shaun pulled out an aluminum package of Beechnut and offered it to Tommy who shook his head. After stuffing a wad of gummy tobacco into his cheek, he continued with the story. "Jethro flight, it was always Jethro flight when the air was handed off to my air officer. The son of a bitch was Hap Stoner's mentor and the two happened to be combat crew. I had three WIA on the third floor wedged between floors of bad guys. The flight was close to Winchester and Bingo fuel but Jethro kept the flight on station in support of our attack. Hap usually doesn't talk about it, but when we crossed paths at the Bahrain O'Club, he talked."

Tommy didn't move and his eyes focused on Shaun's every word.

Shaun's head lolled toward Tommy as he spoke. "As Hap tells it, a jihadi with an AK had a better day than Jethro. Major Harold D Simmons took it in the neck. A shot from nowhere. Before his air passage filled with blood, he ordered Hap to stay on station."

Tommy remained silent for the blast of thunder to follow the bolt of lightning that zapped a building somewhere on Isle de San Andres harbor. "So, what did this Stoner guy do?"

"He continued to direct the fight until we were able to get our Marines out of that building. Then they blew the building to hell with their last TOW and Hellfire. Hap landed on a hard surface road outside of town and had to wait for an ambulance and fuel trucks. Simmons had already died."

"Shhhh." Tommy raised a finger in front of Shaun's face. "There it is again."

The poncho liner draped over Shaun's head looked like an old Granny moving forward, then back. "Who in the hell would be circling our position? Bravo Echo six, you hear the chopper?" Shaun said elbowing Tommy. "Get the team into a 360."

Tommy moved from a tree stump and the ground went out from both waterlogged combat boots. "Mother fucker," he howled traveling down a river of mud flat on his back for 20 feet before rolling into a large rock. The sound is west of my position and moving slowly south around the western side of the mountain," Black Eddie replied. "Whoever is the pilot has cast iron balls flying in this crap."

"If the bird gets any closer, the pilot will scrape the bird off the side of the mountain."

Shaun leaned against a stump and raised the sat phone to his ear. He checked his watch and was time for his 2230 situation report anyway. "OP One SitRep over." Several seconds passed as the sound of rotors faded.

"Go ahead OP One," Roach replied.

"Low flying helicopter circling position a second time. Departed southwest."

"It's the Sandinista," Roach answered. "Pilot must be good, flying in this weather. The weather is our friend tonight."

A clap of thunder cracked over his head. "Speak for yourself. OP One out," Shaun replied. Though miserable, the next couple of hours he didn't seem as tired.

Shaun moved guardedly to OP Two and found Eddie moving slowly, hanging a damp poncho liner on a lava rock to dry. He stretched his muscled arms to the sky and let out a long yawn.

"How did it go?" Shaun asked.

Eddie turned revealing deep red bloodshot eyes. "About as well as wet conditions would allow. We have one twisted knee and another separated shoulder caused by the slippery conditions. I popped in the man's shoulder and neither will be out of the fight."

Shaun tossed Eddie an MRE from a waterlogged rucksack and slung the M-4 over an aching shoulder. He moved passed elements of Eddie's team to sit next to Tommy leaning against a lava rock grimacing in pain.

"Fall that bad?"

Tommy grimaced and said nothing.

"Grab your team and patrol the back side of the volcano and set in an OP. Don't want any surprises from the backside of the mountain. Move it."

38

Lonibelle 0100 D- 11 hours

With a sudden onset of achy feet and wanting to take Lew's temperature, Hap quietly eased into the unoccupied pilot's chair because Roach had become agitated with his presence. He knew you could not take spots from a leopard and if allowed, history always repeats itself. Roach telegraphed when on the dot, and his decision would put lives on the line. It was times like this when Roach actually shut up, then retreated to contemplate last hour deviations to his operation, which would kick off in 24 hours.

Shaun's SitRep, which included mention of the chopper overhead, disturbed his Operations Officer. Magellan successfully trapped on Stingray and Mr. reliable V, ramrodded the improvised deck crew to turn the drone around for an immediate launch. Sluggo steered the drone southeast of the island in search of the helo but didn't know their adversary had fast-roped onto a tossing stern of a pre-positioned fishing trawler.

Spanish Main's naval flotilla closed the distance to allow mutual support prior to L – Hour. Lonibelle's rounded bow slapped against the three-foot swells as the diesel continued to maintain Little Leroy's assurance of "22 knots guaranteed."

Since coming to the bridge, Lew was aware of the latest SitRep from OP One. Lonibelle's helmsman slept like a baby on a cot set up behind both Captain chairs. Sporadically, Lew would work his way behind the pilot's chairs, careful to avoid the cot, to peruse the chart table or freshen his coffee. Hap watched Lew retrieve a blanket from a closet near the coffee mess to cover the young helmsman as if he were his own.

The next thing he knew, Lew woke him from a deep slumber. Slowly sitting up, he stretched both arms over his head then followed with a bear-like yawn. "Time on deck?" Hap asked both eyelids blinking rapidly.

Lew answered, pouring a cup of coffee. "0230," he said extending the cup."

Hap eagerly reached out for the cup of brew.

"You're wanted in the Ops Center. Magellan has spotted the Sandinista and Machine Head has reported Will on board Stingray."

Hap nodded as his ass slid from the chair. "Thanks, Lew. You ok?

"Locked and loaded Hap. Don't worry about me."

Except for the dim instrument lights, the bridge was dark waving off Lew's facial expression.

Hap ducked out of the bridge and moved rapidly to the Ops Center. Clutching his cup of joe, Hap watched the recorded video feed streamed on both interactive screens. Roach strolled over to the dining room table to place a small boat east of the island.

Roach gestured with his head for Hap to join him by the interactive screen in the makeshift ready room. He ran the video back then tapped the screen with a fingertip for the video to begin. After only a few frames he tapped the screen to freeze the picture, tapped a small button in the toolbar to place the frame in the software. His fingers danced across the screen coming to a stop on the stern of an old trawler and opened his fingers similar to flower blooming, thus maximizing the size of the vessel on the screen. He circled the trawler's stern with a fingernail leaving a trail of red behind.

Hap could see the Sandinista soldiers. What intrigued him were the soldiers who wore a different camouflage on their utilities, were smaller in stature and struggling over the side from a rubber boat to clamber into the trawler with a pack strap over one shoulder.

Hap spoke without taking his gaze from the screen, "You thinking what I'm thinking?"

Roach nodded. "Bet a dime to donuts they are."

"Then how in the hell did these Chinamen-looking goofballs appear from nowhere?"

"Then you didn't see it before exploding the frame"? He placed an open palm on the screen and made the blossom close by bringing his fingers together.

"See what?"

Hollywood entered from Vultures' Row hatch. He secured the hatch then removed his cranial cutting his eyes toward the screen. "The wake behind the periscope off the port side of the boat. In the distance something seems to be hovering around the surface like a whale or something big," he said. "By the way, snakes fueled and armed."

"Armed with what," Hap asked looking around the room for an answer knowing Lonibelle had not received live ordnance.

Roach intervened. "Took the liberty to have some of the inert ordnance embarked for additional training. Never thought we would use blue death for an actual mission."

Scratching the nubs on the back of his head he continued with the toe-tapping explanation, "I had the inert ordnance loaded Hap, the moment Sluggo reported his findings. Your flight will have to turn the boat into Swiss cheese. "

Handing Hollywood his coffee, he could see KB and Sluggo observing the conversation. "Crews alerted?" Hap asked.

Hollywood choked down the last of the coffee. We are in preflight. Birds will be positioned with the noses pointed to the two and 10 o'clock for arming."

"Enlighten me with the ordnance load," Hap inquired

"Both birds, 600 rounds and four 19 shot pods. All blue death."

Cutting his eyes over Hollywood, Hap queried Sluggo. "Time to target?"

"Calculating 1 + 15 Hap, assuming you launch in 45 minutes," Sluggo replied. Throwing a map of the Caribbean onto the interactive screen, he punched up the software and with his finger placed a red X east of Isle de San Andres. "Boat should be about 35 miles from the island heading east when you initiate the attack. And the good news is there's not much going as it relates to boat activity except for a periscope and a whale. Long story short, there is funky shit going on with the sub but all in all, it's quiet."

Roach jumped in. "Stingray can be used for a low fuel divert. If need be, we can launch the little birds from Stingray to begin delivering the live ordnance to Lonibelle and clear deck space."

Nodding slowly, Hap replied, "The more the merrier."

"Hell, Hap," Roach answered, "Snakes trained with the little birds, they should go into the fight together. Besides, they will have live ordnance." He turned to Sluggo, "Magellan will coordinate the attack?"

Sluggo nodded. "Magellan will be in the fight, Hap. Next time give Magellan the means to shoot Hellfire."

Roach chimed in, "You will have to take out the antennas and bridge on the first pass. We can't afford a transmission from the trawler."

39

Lonibelle Ready Room

"At ease gentlemen," Hap called out as he arranged an iPad tablet and briefing guide atop the small metal podium fixed to the ready room deck by four bolts. At six-feet, two-inches inches tall, he slumped over the podium and the tip of the bowie knife scabbard under his left armpit tapped metal each time he shifted his weight from one side to the other.

Hap dressed in a blue flight suit and jungle boots like the others, with his trusty 9 mm Belgium Browning High Power dangled loosely below his right shoulder. LD, Killer, and Hollywood sat with their kneeboards resting on the small writing surface. Their faces were taut, and pistols dangled from shoulder holsters, they were going back into harm's way. As back up crew, Chewie and Ambassador nestled in the back row taking in the brief as if they were going to launch with the crew. Should any crewmember be killed in action, either pilot would immediately jump in the seat and continue the mission. KB and Sluggo manned their stations. Magellan's video feed splayed on all three interactive screens.

"Last night at approximately 2230 a helicopter was reported in the vicinity of OP 1." Hap pulled up a jogair on the interactive screen as well as his tablet. Using his forefinger Hap circled the position of OP One on his tablet. The same markings appeared on the interactive screen. "The aircraft departed to the southwest and Shaun reported the incident. Based on the report, it appears this bird was Sandinista attempting to offload its cargo in the general vicinity of the volcano. Weather prevented the insert.

"Magellan tracked an MI8 Hip from Blue Fields after sundown. The helo tracked east towards Isle de San Andres. Magellan broke off surveillance to divert to Stingray for a gas and go.

"Kudos to Sluggo for finding the Sandinista combat team."

"So, where are they?" LD asked.

Hap punched the small keypad on the podium and half turned towards the screen. A trawler was nestled near a sail of a submarine with rubber boats pushing away from the submarine. "Yes, it's a trawler, and yes, it's parked next to a sail of a Kilo Class submarine." He turned around to face the ready room. "Video is two hours old."

"Country of origin?" Ambassador asked as if asking for a cup of coffee at a donut shop.

Hap shrugged giving a facial expression showing that he was clueless. "Seven countries outside Russia use the boat and not one is in this hemisphere."

"So, the men in the rubber boats pushing away from the submarine have to be commandoes of some sort," Roach said. Should cut down the list by a few notches."

Killer Koch said nothing seated beside Hollywood.

"Gotta be Chinese, Hap," LD said, "Outside Russia they are the only country with a stake in Nicaragua and has Kilos in their submarine fleet."

Hap's brow pinched closer together glancing over at Roach and back to the Cobra crews.

Killer's broad shoulder shifted in his seat. "Hap, why China, and why the Southern Caribbean?"

Hap's eyes cut toward Killer. "Gotta be Crosscut."

Killer looked over his brow. "So, this is how China gets her Panama Canal?"

"I'm speaking out loud on this one, but China wins in two ways," Hap replied. "Money to build the facility and possible control of Latin America, and the Chinamen know the U.S. administration doesn't believe in the Monroe doctrine."

Hollywood interrupted. "So, we going to take out the trawler tonight?"

LD raised his hand nibbling on the eraser of his pencil. "How about the sub? I would have thought taking on Nicaragua would be tough enough, but China too?"

Roach didn't give Hap a chance to answer and blurted out from behind the high back leather chairs, "Chinamen included LD."

Hap issued a reluctant nod. "We want to throw off the Sandinista command element. If nothing else for a day or so, as they try to figure out what happened to their recon element.

"The Chinese can go to hell," Roach blurted.

Hollywood cut in. "Tough mission to accomplish with inert ordnance Hap." All the pilots slowly nodded but said nothing.

"Can't use Kabars, Hollywood," Roach replied sarcastically. There wasn't a chuckle in the room.

Hap looked about, "Questions?"

Roach handed out kneeboard cards and maps to each of the aircrews. The kneeboard cards depicted turn up times, frequencies, route, and proposed attack configuration.

Hap continued when Ambassador and Chewie received their package. "Turn up will be at 0320 with check-in at 0327 with aircraft status. Arming will commence at 0335. Go no go is one aircraft. Schlonger and BA will loiter north of the target and join the flight at 0450 hours. The Killer Eggs will be carrying two seven-shot pods of 2.75 HE and 7.62. Sluggo will be Tactical Air Control (TACAir) call sign Magellan. I have the flight and my section call sign Kang. BA's section of Killer Egg's call sign Beaver. Divert to Stingray on your own cognizance. The little birds will act as on-site SAR. Ingressing to the target will be to the south. Magellan will be fine-tuning our course en route. The flights will ingress into AO sections in the trail. Beaver's section will depart to the south and east to set up for the L attack at 0450."

Hap punched up a blank white slide and using his finger drew a sorry excuse for a trawler. To the east and north, he again butchered depictions of attack helos. Satisfied he continued.

"Each Snake will have 600 rounds and 4 nineteen shot pods, all inert. We will conduct an L attack in sections. First shots down range at 0500 and the antennas have to go down on the first pass. Weather is clear, visibility unrestricted (CAVU) and the moon will be in its last quarter low on the horizon to the northwest, no factor. Weapons will be safe until Beaver's flight joins and conditions go to weapons tight. Magellan will make the call if additional passes are required. On each run in, call in blind, please. Magellan will act as Forward Air Controller – Airborne (FAC-A) and clear hot. If communication fails with Magellan, and you see me shoot, you are clear to fire. Right turns. Questions?" Hap looked around the room while Roach joined him at the podium.

"One change, I would like the little birds to return to Stingray to prepare for the vert rep of ordnance for Lonibelle."

Turning to Hap, he cocked his head to the side, "Problems with this Hap?"

Hap's head shook as he checked his watch. "Time hack, in 30 seconds." Counting down the last five seconds, Hap called out "five, four, three, two, one, and hack. Time on deck is 0300. Conduct your own cockpit briefs and see you on check in."

* * *

Kang flight tracked beneath star-packed skies to deliver Spanish Main's opening shots. Hap scanned the distance through the goggles' forty-degree field of view. Except for blinking lights at three o'clock, the sea was vacant.

Two General Electric turboshaft engines powered the Cobra 145 knots 500 feet above the water. Very little was said inter-cockpit between Hap and LD but then again, going into combat they rarely spoke inter cockpit, but then this mission was different than the others.

"Hey Hap," LD said from the rear cockpit. "Good, bad, or indifferent- good men will die tonight."

Hap said nothing knowing LD was right. Looking across his right shoulder Hap could see Hollywood displaced 250 feet at his four o'clock position, and then answered. "Looks that way, LD."

"Kang Flight, weapons check," Hap said over the squadron common push.

"You're armed," LD said.

Hap spit out a short burst of 20 mm. Splashes into the water from Hollywood's 20 mm kicked up water at two o'clock.

"Weapons safe, Hap."

Hap transmitted inter-flight. "Kang flight, Safe weapons." Clicks on the radio acknowledged the directive.

"Sure going to miss the tracer rounds," LD said.

"That's what the splashes are for," Hap answered. "I never asked if you regretted flying to rescue Warden."

"Gave up a promising career on that one," LD replied. "Hell, it was kinda cool getting kicked out of the Marine Corps the same day you were asked to pack your shit and leave."

Hap said nothing and only the sounds of whirling rotors and high-pitched turbines passed through the cockpit.

"Hap, I never told you, but if I had to do it all over again, I would. It was the right thing to do and glad you tracked me down flying those DOD missions in Uganda for this one."

Hap knew one email had LD on a plane to share beers and swap sea stories at Hap's local haunt. Minutes after landing in Houston, LD allowed a buxom blonde flight attendant he met on the flight across the pond to take him home. LD didn't surface for a week having fallen in love again."

"Kang flight. Sluggo."

"Go ahead, Sluggo," Hap replied.

"Beaver flight is at your twelve o'clock, three miles right-hand turns. On his next turn to the north, you will pick him up. He is twenty miles north of the target. Target is heading two six seven at six knots."

* * *

Captain Hernandez leaned back against the wooden bulkhead next to LtCol Dmitry Konstantin. The Russian Spetsnaz officer had been on Top Secret orders from the Russian GRU since Moscow received an alert about the upcoming mission to invade Isle de San Andres. Hernandez received his briefing; the Russian was the interface between the Chinese commandoes and his Command. Both kept their heads below the wind line taking long drags from American cigarettes. The Spetznaz Officer had leaped onto the ramp seconds before the ramp raised prior to take off.

"How long were you in Syria, Colonel?" Hernandez asked in rapid Spanish.

"Dos anos," Konstantin replied. "Muslim bastards were tough to find, but once engaged, we cut through them like a hot knife through butter."

"When I bumped into you on the ramp to go down the rope, General Hallesleven told me the Russians wanted an advisor on this mission. Truth be known, if it had to be, I'm glad it was you."

"My Government is not happy the Chinks are part of this operation."

Hernandez flipped his butt over the side and pulled the pack of Camels from an open breast pocket. Shaking the pack, the Russian nodded and greedily fingered inside the pack to retrieve another smoke. Hernandez flipped out a Zippo with its distinctive clink cupping the flame to allow the Russian to light his smoke as he tossed his butt overboard.

"So, what brings the Chinese to the game?"

The Russian's AKS-74U carbine's stock rested between his legs, the barrel snugged into his right shoulder. "Looks like our President wants to ensure Russia has closer relations with Nicaragua than the Chinese. It's no secret Captain, that Russia's Navy wants a warm water port on the Caribbean. On the other hand, the Chinese want to build a canal through Nicaragua and parts of Costa Rica. With all the attention in the Ukraine, Syria, Iran, Libya, Egypt to name a few, Russia believes the Americana Presidente is feckless. The big question, who carries the most influence over Managua and Latin America, the Chinese or Russians?"

Hernandez lolled his head to the side to exhale a trail of smoke away from the Russian. "Colonel, do you truly believe the Americans will allow Russia to build that port and the Chinese to build a canal?"

The Russian laughed, "The Americana doesn't have the stomach to stop it." Taking in a long draw, he cut eyes to the night sky. "Do you hear that Captain?"

Hernandez turned an ear to the sky but only could hear the chug of the vessel's diesel and seawater slapping against the hull.

Dmitry hopped to his feet clutching the rifle scanning the star-filled sky to the north. "We have company Captain."

The Nicaraguan officer was already on his, but only could see a star-filled horizon.

"Do you hear it, Captain? Dimitri turned, but Hernandez was scurrying around the deck using his boot to nudge a slumbering Sergeant Martinez to his feet. Each of the Chinese had taken to a knee seemingly aiming their weapons at stars.

"We have company, get to your feet," he yelled.

The Spetnatz officer powered up a set of Cobra Fury Night Vision Goggles pulled from his ruck. The IR searchlights of the birds were in plain view suddenly going dark.

"Captain Hernandez, call in a SPOTREP."

Hernandez turned to his radio operator bent over Russian made communications gear. "Torrez, get this SPOTREP out immediately. Unidentified aircraft approaching with lights off."

The young radio operator powered up the communications gear. "Sir, it will be a couple of minutes before we can transmit."

Dumbfounded with the response, Hernandez's jaw felt as if it could touch the deck.

40

Kang Flight

Hap eased the trigger to the first détente of the cyclic fixed to front cockpit's right side to transmit over ICS. He raised his gloved hand, with the fingertips cut off, on either side of his head. Cobra pilots were notorious for cutting the fingertips off their flight gloves to make it easier to pull circuit breaker and throw switches.

"You have the controls LD, BA is at our 2 long."

"Tally 2 little birds," LD replied as he flashed the Cobra's IR searchlight flying from the rear seat.

BA's IR searchlight blinked in response.

Hap eased his left boot on the foot transmission switch passed the first détente. "Beaver, join and go sections in trail." Hollywood closed the gap as BA's flight began their turn to port to gain a very loose trail at Hap's six.

Minutes later two klicks passed across squadron common. BA's flight had joined.

Sluggo's northeastern drawl broke the silence. "Magellan will put a light on the target in five, four, three, two, and you should have your target at 12."

"You have the trawler?" LD said.

From the front seat with its panoramic view, through the goggles, Hap could see the trawler bow to stern within the radius of Magellan's IR light. "Target in sight. Flight Arm,"

Hap directed. "Kang will anchor, right-hand turns. Good hunting, Beaver."

Standing the little bird on its side, BA made a hard turn as Schlonger in full anticipation crossed over to settle in at the eight o'clock position as LD steered the section of Cobras in a gentle right-hand turn.

LD spoke over the intercom. "Commence attack in 5 minutes Hap."

Sluggo's frantic voice came across the net. "Kang flight, initiate attack immediately. They have goggles!"

"Get some LD," Hap barked.

LD clicked twice rolling the Cobra onto its side. Surprised by the maneuver Hollywood worked hard to regain position as LD began the run into the target. "Kang inbound," LD reported. He lowered the helo's nose to begin the attack 250 feet above the water and 125 knots.

"Beaver flight inbound," BA reported.

"Rockets at 1500 meters," Hap said over the intercom. "I will engage with the gun at 1200 meters." Hap raised his goggles and settled behind the scope. In full view, the trawlers occupants gathered on the starboard side of the vessel. The range ticks down on the scope.

"They are onto us," Hap transmitted.

"Range?" LD asked.

"2000 meters," Hap replied.

Not daring to drop the Cobra's nose to accelerate LD gave himself a stable platform to launch the rockets.

"1700 meters LD."

"Kang is in hot," Hap called out over the radio.

"Beaver flight is in hot," BA reported.

"Cleared hot Kang flight," Sluggo said.

Each time LD depressed the trigger button, two rockets swooshed from their tubes. The fourth salvo of 2.75 rockets punched holes below the vessel's main cabin.

"You're on it, LD. Fire for effect and going hot with the gun." Hap let go with the 20 mm as LD punched the trigger switch as fast as he could move his thumb. The 20's initial burst kicked up tiny splashes 100 meters short but was easily adjustable with small movements of the joystick until the sea around the trawler exploded in large and small white geysers as the rockets and 20mm merged at the cabin. Three seconds later, Beaver flight's rocket and machine-gun fire plunged into the damaged vessel raking the stern and appeared both the 20mm and 7.62 crossed at the pilothouse ripping it and all on the bridge into Swiss cheese. The stern was sprayed with chunks of transom as fires began to spread across several areas of the ship.

As the stern exploded, its flash lighting the night sky bounced Hernandez's head off the bulkhead. As his eyes fluttered back into focus, Torrez's upper torso slumped as if in slow motion over the radio. Dazed and bleeding from wounds to the hip and abdomen, he fought unconsciousness. Painfully crawling towards Torrez, blood poured from a mortal wound the size of a fist punched into his back. "SPOTREP," he mumbled spitting up blood. He grimaced and screamed to the heavens as exposed parts of his body blistered in the heat. Slowly, he crawled over Dimitri's body. A river of blood flowed from where his head disconnected from the neck. Pools of Chinese and Sandinista blood flowing across the steel deck bubbled from the heat. He covered the last three feet to the radio in a painful roll. He gripped the superheated handset screaming into the receiver allowing it to fall from his fingers as he saw a softball size hole punched through the radio's metal skin. The sound of rockets and automatic cannon fire continued to rake the stricken vessel as he rolled to his back to glare into the heavens with full knowledge only God could hear his cries of warning.

* * *

Hap kept the gun on the trawler spewing death as LD pulled off target. The trawler exploded, scattering human corpses and chunks of the burning craft to the sea. Orbiting above, Magellan continued to stream live video until the last flickers of flame slipped beneath the waves.

"Target destroyed," Sluggo reported. "I have a periscope to your six. No factor."

"Request vectors to Mother and Father," Hap said racking his brain over the submarine's ownership waiting for a heading to rendezvous with Lonibelle or Stingray.

Seconds later, Sluggo complied with Hap's earlier request for vectors. "Mother is zero-zero-five and 115 miles. Father is two-two-six at 50 miles." *Hap knew by using the axiom mother and father, Sluggo had identified Lonibelle and Stingray without announcing the ship's name over the airwaves.*

"Beaver flight, divert to Father," Hap instructed. "Hollywood, fuel state?"

BA gave two clicks over the common frequency and rolled away with Schlonger in loose formation.

"Eleven-fifty," came the reply from Hollywood.

"Kang flight, push to Mother."

Hollywood replied with two clicks telegraphing he understood and would comply.

Hap couldn't wait to view the Caribbean sunrise through a shaded visor as he took the controls from LD to settle in for the remaining 45 minutes to Spanish Main's flagship. Hollywood slid out to a more comfortable spread position before padlocking to Hap's wing.

He couldn't take his mind off the men who died tonight. All had mothers, fathers, wives, children—and the thought that his order killed them weighed heavily. The moment Will heard of the success of the mission, Hap could picture him beating a war drum, pissed, missing the party.

Hap knew his Mother would ask, Why go against the Ten Commandments, Hap? He didn't think twice. The action tonight will save countless lives of different nationalities. Jettisoned politics drove the mission. She would have to trust my path is as clear as my conscience. Love you mom.

LD's voice startled him out of his thoughts, "What are you thinking about Hap?"

Hap let the whine of the turbines and the dull thud of the gunships massive rotors soothe his nerves. Seconds passed before electing to be forthright with his brother in arms. "If you promise not to tell anyone, I was thinking of my Mom and what she would say if she knew what we were doing."

"Knowing your Mom like I do, Hap, she would be up your ass. Hell, I still remember the look on her face when she hit the principal's office to pull your ass out of high school for mooning classmates returning from lunch

Hap smiled, remembering the event. "You were busted along with the rest of us, LD."

"Yeah, but my parents only laughed." And then midway through college we both told our parents our intentions on joining the Corps. You, on the other hand, were following a path she just couldn't comprehend." LD paused, and then continued to speak. "We killed a lot of people tonight, Hap."

We could hear only the whine of the Cobra engines and rotors cutting air, for several seconds. "You sorry?" Hap inquired.

He couldn't see LD reach underneath his visor flicking away tears. "Never lost a minute of sleep killing in Iraq and Afganistan. I felt bad about the Borderline incident and shed tears like this morning, but I have no regrets now, and I sure as hell am not going to tell my Mother what the hell I'm doing."

"Thanks, I needed that," Hap said flicking away tears trickling past his high set cheekbones. Tonight's sortie was the bottom of the first inning. The good guys drew first blood incurring no casualties and aircraft incurred no battle damage. Hap lowered his head for a brief moment knowing he would do what he could to limit casualties on both sides. But he also knew that at the end of the day, he would do what it took to get the job done.

41

Lonibelle

Hap ducked through the Vultures' Row hatch leaving the door open behind him, and then pushed the helmet bag over the back of one of the ready room seats without breaking stride. With a sweep of the hand, the sweat-drenched bandana left his head and slapped across Sluggo's broad shoulders. "Good job tonight."

Sluggo lolled his head over his left shoulder. "No rest for the weary until we trap this bad boy."

"How far out?" Hap questioned as he strode to join Roach around the Ops table revealing two CD disks out of his right breast pocket. "Heads up KB." He flipped the first like a Frisbee followed by the second.

Hearing his name, KB turned in his chair just in time to snag the first disk with his left hand followed by the second with his right. "I will get the data in the Library under the "W" drive."

Roach reached out with a bear like a paw and grabbed Hap's hand. "Great job, Hap," he said followed by a brief man hug and rock-solid slap on the back.

Hap returned a firmer grip and harder slap to Roach's back. "This doesn't mean we will be taking showers in wee hours of the morning?"

Roach pulled away to casually lift an index finger in front of his round face momentarily then the suggestive hand signal dropped to the side. "Schlonger is thirty minutes out with a sling load of ordnance. Magellan will trap behind Schlonger."

"What about BA?"

"Half hour behind," Roach said massaging both eyes. Lonibelle is putting distance between us and the crash site?"

Hap nodded standing with his trusty bowie knife and Belgium Browning under either arm. "Surely the Sandinista will put some kind of SAR effort together," he said, referring to a Search and Rescue operation.

Though Roach's face was relaxed, the bags under both eyes were the size of silver dollars similar to his look at Lonesome Dove. "Lew is keeping the pedal to the metal maintaining a direct course to Stingray to shorten the little bird's legs during the vert rep."

Hap said nothing as his head lolled down toward the map.

Roach's stubby finger landed on the chart for the rendezvous with Stingray and placed the index finger of his other hand on the crash site. Satisfied, he looked up over his brow. "I think 250 miles will keep us from meddling eyes. Russian and Chinese satellites are another matter."

The space between Hap's eyebrows moved closer together without a smile. "We have to go tomorrow night."

"You don't say. Planning is already taking place."

Hap nodded, and said nothing. He wasn't going to allow himself to step into this bear trap.

"I don't give a fuck what country these turds come from," Roach answered behind a coy smile. "If you're asking me, kind of cool killing these guys." The same smile Hap had witnessed for years, it was Roach's way of telegraphing *I really don't give a shit about what you think about my last comment.* "I didn't ask," Hap replied looking over to KB deflecting any further conversation with an agitated Roach.

KB's fingers tapped across his keyboard, his hand dancing off the end like a concert pianist. "Both gun CDs loaded and in the 'W" drive."

"Thanks, KB," Hap said. "I will ask Blad to have his contacts in Nicaragua put the word in the right places that the missing soldiers defected."

KB scratched around the area of his headset. "Wouldn't the submarine already have reported the incident to Managua? One would think so since we just blew their soldiers to hell."

Hap's lips pursed. "Maybe KB, but, maybe whatever country the sub's captain answers to is communicating with their HQ, to allow politicians to make the decision on how to handle the situation. Remember, they are probably not supposed to be there. Totally covert, I bet." He made his way toward the forward hatch, stopped and turned. "Any whereabouts on Will's POS?"

"Schlonger's bird," Roach said.

"Have him join me in the galley. I'm going for a quick bite after speaking with Blad." Hap vanished, nauseous from the days killing.

"I will walk him down," Roach said to an empty door opening. "I'm hungry," he said tapping his belly. "This shit builds a man's appetite."

Hollywood followed by LD and Killer entered through Vultures' Row dropping their flight bags on tops of Haps before flopping silently down in the front row chairs.

KB spoke over his shoulder. "The first tape will be Hollywood's, and Hap's will follow." He returned to his station and pulled up the Library in "W" drive directing the video to stream to the Ready Room.

Hollywood picked up the GameBoy hand controller to manipulate the video. By working the coolie hat, he could direct the feed forward or back and as deliberate as one frame at a time.

"Action," he demanded, settling back into his seat. "I'm hoping we have video of the sub."

"Who brought the popcorn," Sluggo said.

Roach spoke continuing to gaze down at the map. "Don't be so anxious to put eyes on the sub. It just means there is a larger player in the game."

Blue Fields Nicaragua

General Hallesleven's swiveled his six-feet-three-inch frame around to a rickety table arrangement holding a plate of three over easy eggs, ham slices, and flour torts. More deserving of a fireplace in most settings for the well to do in Nicaraguan government, the Executive chair and field desk would have to do for the general. It seemed to take forever to chew the over-cooked pork to allow him to choke it down.

Santiago ducked through the flap extending a red folder marked on top with 'ultra secreto' over the crate size desk. "General, I didn't think you would wait, Sir."

"Thank you Santiago," he said still chewing on the last piece of ham. He laid the folder on the desk without opening and returned a gaze with a large question mark stamped across his forehead. "Cliff note version, Colonel? "

Santiago's dark eyes locked on Hallesleven's gaze with an all-knowing stare. He had seen this look too many times since the general fostered him as a child.

Hallesleven picked up the top sheet to peruse slowly flipping it over to the folder's left side. "I'm waiting, Santiago," he said without raising his head.

"General," Santiago said timidly. "Captain Hernandez, along with his command are missing, Sir."

Hallesleven peered over his bushy brows. "I thought they diverted? Besides, there are Russian and Chinese on board."

Santiago nodded. "Yes General. After the helo diverted to the alternate insertion method, a contingent of People's Liberation Army special operations forces boarded from a Chinese sub.

His eyes dropped down to a section highlighted in yellow and continued to read when his salt and pepper brows stretched for the tents patched ceiling. The fork slipped from his hand into a pool of yellow egg yolk.

Captain Hernandez's missed two reporting sequences. Intelligence reports though not confirmed suspect a possible defection of all team members. Suspect Hernandez's team terminated the Russian and Chinese actors. Reconnaissance aircraft ordered airborne at 0700 hours to investigate. In Department 14, Costa Rican Politicians are threatening to intervene in the disputed territory on the San Juan River.

He swatted away his coffee tin banging it against a tent pole. Teary-eyed, Hallesleven slowly raised his head replying softly. "It's OK Santiago. Need time alone."

"General, I forgot to inform you the President is on the line. He sounded anxious."

The General spoke not bothering to wipe away the tears. "Thank you, Santiago; I will take the call at my desk."

Santiago saluted, conducted a crisp facing movement, and then ducked through the flap.

He removed the receiver from its phone cradle. "Yes, Mr. President."

* * *

President Ortega's morning started at 4 a.m. taking a call from his Secretary of State. He settled in behind a small desk in his bedroom, an inauguration gift from his wife. Hand carved, the three-piece Pont Lafayette office group arrived only last week. Smoking his second Cuban cigar since waking, he anxiously sent smoke rings drifting into the haze from an earlier ring. Days after guaranteeing his and his wife Rosario Murillo's rule until death, the phone rang regarding Costa Rican's hasty action. Hallesleven's voice came across the speakerphone snapped the President back into the now and picked up his handset. "General Hallesleven, I'm having a little problem with our Costa Rican neighbor."

"I just read the report. Costa Rica does not wield a military arm. Their small Special Forces component and a police force are comparable to our basic infantry soldier. "

Ortega interrupted. "General, we are going to have to move troops and armor to the San Juan District." He glanced at the easel off to the side holding up the chart of Nicaragua's Table of Organization.

"El Presidente, our military can't be in two places at one time. I would have to pull assets from Che Guevara. A semblance of a territorial dispute will have the area crawling with the likes of Fox News which could be problematic."

Ortega slammed his fist clutching the cigar on the desk throwing up a cloud of cigar ash. "Nicaragua will not lose a foot of territory that would jeopardize 'Crosscut' General."

"I understand the importance of Crosscut, but El Presidente, I beg you to reconsider."

Ortega removed the cigar to blow a smoke ring through the building cloud of cigar smoke collecting below the ceiling of the room. "Do what you have to do, General," he said then paused. "I'm sorry to hear about your nephew." He didn't bother discussing the possibilities of a possible defection.

"Thank you, El Presidente," the General replied. "I will call my sister and deliver the news Captain Hernandez is MIA, Sir."

"Always admired Maria, General. She is quite the lady, and a good mother. Give her my prayers."

"I will El Presidente. Will that be all?"

Ortega didn't hear the general's last sentence, having already hung up the phone.

43

Isle de San Andres
Op-1

Propped against a lava rock formation, Shaun slowly drew in both knees as another Boeing 737 disappeared into a puff of billowing cumulus and glanced at his watch. It was 11a.m. A distinct whine from the plane's turbofans was audible moments before the airliner popped out to descend over the city.

Tommy Kelso's voice came through his earpiece perched on OP Three. "You catching all this, Shaun?"

Shaun squirmed the area of irritation on his shoulder attempting to pacify the itch inside the right shoulder blade. He leaned back to scrape the area of irritation lightly against one of many pointed pieces of lava. Seconds later he whipped out, "Got it!"

A moment passed, "Got what," Tommy answered, sounding perplexed.

"Forget it," Shaun answered. "Same marking as the previous three," he said under his breath. "I thought Evergreen had closed its doors."

"They did back in 2014," Tommy answered. "Chapter seven."

"Seems to be similar markings as the Evergreen DC-8's I took back and forth to WestPac." The main mounts trailed a puff of smoke as the pilot squeaked them to the runway. For everything the air facility lacked, notably a working control tower, a large fuel farm had been constructed 600 feet left of a magnificent hangar large enough to house two 737's.

Mystified at best, worse an out and out evacuation before a Nicaraguan invasion was taking place. He used a thumb to kick back the bush hat's 360-degree brim to make room for the eyewear's dark plastic frames to rest above his forehead. Slowly he raised the binoculars in front of his eyes focusing in on the passengers. In military order, dogs, cats, men, women, and children gathered to the side of the remaining three aircraft aligned nose to tail across an expansive tarmac.

The binoculars came to rest across his knee. "OP One. OP Two."

"737 – 800's with Evergreen markings," Eddie answered. "Someone is writing a big ass check."

Shaun's boot pawed the ground in frustration. "And I thought only the Nicaraguan high command and elements of Spanish Main knew anything about Nicaraguan intentions."

"They act as if they are going to Disneyland," Eddie replied." Kids running around with leashed dogs, and cats. Adults are in casual conversations with others like it's a picnic."

"You've seen the two fix wing aircraft conducting a search in the direction of last night's light show?"

"I have," Eddie said.

Shaun was well aware Hap was probably not sitting well with the early morning attack. The taking of lives is something Hap Stoner didn't take lightly.

"OK, the first bird is buttoned up and turning up."

"It's noon. Two hours turn to include fuel with two fuel trucks," Eddie answered. "Not bad."

Upon crossing the hold short, the 737 pilot pointed the nose down the runway firewalling both turbofans coming out of the turn. As the pilot rotated the nose, the 737 lumbered clear of the runaway sucking landing gear into the fuselage as the plane eased into a gentle climbing turn vanishing into a wall of cumulus building to the northwest.

* * *

KB flipped the incoming transmissions to the speakers in each corner of the Ops Center that made up the ships 1MC. Schlonger's voice bounced off the room's steel bulkheads. "One down," he said.

"Not bad after the third pass," Roach said. "Still not bad flying on three hours sleep for the past 39 hours. At least the ordnance is beginning to show, we can't throw inert ordnance at the Sandinista forever."

Prepositioned in front of the interactive screen in anticipation of the report from OP One, he eyed the fruit basket centered on the Ops table. Shaun's voice sounded out. "Fourth aircraft landing as we have the first aircraft is departing to the northwest." His finger drew a stick airframe behind the other with a number noting arrival interval and erased the initial aircraft with his finger.

Roach snapped his fingers to gain KB's attention using fingers as if speaking on a telly.

KB turned, flipped a switch, and nodded. "You're good to go."

He reached for the black handset and keyed the mike. "OP One Mother. Any sense of urgency going on by the passengers?"

"None," came the reply.

"Full flights?" Roach asked forcing the thought of Schlonger dropping a load into the sea out of his head. It was Sluggo's turn to trap Magellan. BA would follow as the killer eggs daisy chained between Stingray and Lonibelle.

"Chock-full, mother goose."

Roach scanned the room jutting out his dimpled chin. "Understood. Mother out."

After returning the handset to its cradle, Roach grabbed two banana from the fruit basket and tossed the shorter of the fruit morsels to Sluggo entering through the forward hatch.

"Sluggo, let's get Magellan turned and back into the air." Roach tossed a piece from his banana into the air leaving his mouth wide open as if the fruit were an M&M, pausing for gravity to take effect.

Sluggo nodded. "I will preflight her as soon as she traps." He settled into his Captain's chair.

Roach gave out a bark on his way out of the forward hatch, "KB, I will be in with Hap. You have the conn."

A wide grin appeared across KB's air as he turned and jacked his cellular phone into the intercom. Flipping through his downloads he stopped at Jimi Hendrix's "Purple Haze" cranking the volume in the process. The last thing Roach witnessed ducking through the hatch was KB leaning back in his chair with hands resting behind his head while Sluggo worked the controls to trap the drone.

❊ ❊ ❊

Roach found his stateroom door open, with Hap standing over the sink. Will leaned back precariously balancing the chair to Roach's desk on its back two legs as Hap rigorously brushed his teeth. His locker door was open, and his Belgium Browning's holster hung over the Bowie knife's scabbard.

"Careful there, Hap, you may lose a couple of caps if you keep that up."

Hap spit out a mouth full of toothpaste suds, then turned his head. "What is on your mind?"

"That obvious, huh?" Roach replied settling his rump into his mattress leaning back against the steel bulkhead. Will entered into the conversation, "Can't be that bad."

Roach ground the heels of his palms into both eyes giving out a wide yawn and crossed his Popeye-sized forearms. "Resupply effort is going as smooth as could be expected with exhausted aircrews."

Hap could see bewilderment in his friend's demeanor, his thoughts elsewhere. Although Roach may have lacked polish, history proved he constantly demonstrated a refreshing ability to listen and learn to adapt to the situation despite its fluidity. He might stumble, he might grumble, but Hap could count on the Roach to operate effectively in a complex combat situation.

"What's on your mind?"

Sucking his knees below his chin like an insecure child, Roach rested his palms on either knee. Lonibelle's air conditioning whizzed through the vents and the vibrations of the engine pulsed up through the steel deck. "Somebody has initiated some sort of evacuation."

"From where?" Will rocked forward slamming the front two legs to the steel deck.

"The private airfield next to the fortress." Roach replied. "Four 737 800's with Evergreen markings loaded to their capacity with Men, women, children, and their pets with luggage complements. No sense of urgency noted from the passengers. It's as if they are going on an all expense trip to

Disneyland. The first aircraft has launched and departed northwest."

Will came to his feet and scratched the small bald spot on the back of his head. "Old CIA contractor taking on passengers on a Isle de San Andres private airfield. Damn, I thought Evergreen was defunct"

"They are," Hap cut in with a question mark stamped across his forehead, "I will reach out to Blad...Magellan?"

"Airborne shortly," Roach said. "Your section is being uploaded as ordnance arrives. Will's assault group will launch from Stingray."

Will spoke without emotion, "To trodden tyranny across the globe gentlemen, we must take down the fortress tonight. Despite the obstacles, I know no man on this operation will turn their faces away from the foe and undoubtedly will press forward. It starts tonight." He rocked the chair forward allowing the front legs to slam against the steel deck. Straightening, he left the room without closing the door.

Roach looked up at Hap. "Do you want to call this thing off?"

Hap worked the top of his hand to scrub his chin as he pondered Roach's query. "Good men died earlier this morning on my order."

"Fuck 'em. Just a few Sandinista and whoever the hell boarded from the sub."

"They had families, but most importantly, they were soldiers who died following orders."

"Enough philosophy, dickhead," Roach answered casually. "These fuckers would have done the same to us. But they aren't as good as we are, so they died. By the way, something tells me there will be plenty of opportunities to send more Sandinista to hell."

Hap slowly lowered his head to look Roach into his eyes. His upper teeth work slowly, massaged his lower lip. "Waving off now, American lives, and lives from other nations would die in the near future, as sure as we are standing here. I remember Simmons telling me that years after the fact, when the U.S. President announced "cease fire" putting the skids to Desert Storm. A First Louie who was there told the story Simmons' announced to the ready room that there are children playing in America playgrounds that would die in that God forsaken desert sometime in the future."

"So, what are you going to do Hap Stoner? You're not POTUS, but you are in the hot seat – good, bad, or indifferent."

In hindsight, with a full understanding of the circumstances in 1990, he wished the U.S. had not intervened. Look at the mess now. Although, Hap knew that had he been in the desert in 1991 when POTUS issued the order initiating Desert Storm, he would have followed orders, as he done in Operation Iraqi Freedom, which he also knew was a mistake.

Fly to the sound of the guns.

"We go, Roach," he said solemnly. "You have a problem with that?"

Roach shook his head puffing out a lower lip. "I would have had a problem if you said to turn the boats back to the Texas coast." He stretched both arms to the side as if posing for the west coast big boy contest as he gained his feet. He stopped as he ducked through the hatch and turned. "Let's save the world, Devil Dog!"

44

Border of Nicaragua and Costa Rica

For the villagers living another day of life on Nicaraguan southern border, the distinctive whine of turbine engines and rotor blades cutting the morning sky caused pause and demanded their attention. As a pair of MI 8's padlocked on leads 5 and 7 o'clock whizzed overhead visible for a second or two before roaring out of sight somewhere between the top of the trees and low puffy clouds.

Hallesleven sat up, adjusted his cranial twisting his torso to peer through a side window as the MI 8 Hip nosed towards the lush jungle canopy leveling 50 feet above the San Juan River delta. Sandinista youth toiled in waist-high water moving mud between Harbor Head and Costa Rica using the air show as an excuse to take a trifling break. Arms waving vigorously above mud-caked heads, the children belonged to members of the Sandinista Youth Brigade. The unit was Ortega's way to secure free labor while building a nationalistic fervor. "With any luck, I may live to command some of these boys," he said to himself.

The children traveled unaccompanied by foot, donkey, bus, and boat from all corners of Nicaragua to spend one week to preserve Nicaragua's geographical integrity. According to Daniel Ortega, as long as the San Juan flowed south around the island, Nicaragua laid claim and would do battle to keep it. Weekly the Youth Brigade rotated in and out of

Harbor Head to dredge a channel by hand to ensure the river flowed between the island and Costa Rica.

Their mission precludes the channel from silting to become an extension of Costa Rica. Prior to the Youth Brigade's arrival 8 months earlier, Harbor Island had been the tip of a peninsula claimed by Costa Rica.

The Costa Rican government took the position that the camp was nothing more than a Sandinista military training facility. Dug in along the southern shore of the Los Portillos Lagoon, a company of Costa Rican police lounged around fighting holes and sandbagging bunkers with orders to observe only.

Along the coast highway a half-dozen Costa Rican armored vehicles came into view parked on either side of a two-lane leading out of Punta de Castilla to the south. Soldier's laundry dangled from a rope tied between each vehicle. "So, they have been in the field for a few days," Hallesleven made a note of the troop strength passing it to Colonel Santiago sitting by his side.

His thoughts flashed back to the fate of Captain Hernandez. The Hernandez name and the legacy of the commander of Nicaragua's armed forces were in play. Search and rescue efforts had come up empty. The Elysian winds this time of year helped create stronger than usual currents to the southeast. Ocean flows aside, the overabundant tiger, and hammerhead shark population would scarf any human bobbing around the surface lifejacket and all.

He felt a tap on the knee and Santiago leaned in, his hand pointed at a sizable force of Costa Rican Police. "Company strength at least digging in to defend the San Juan."

"Defensive in nature," Hallesleven replied through the

ICS. No attempts to camouflage their positions. How many positions have we passed similar to this?"

"Provinces of Heredia and Alajuela in Central Costa Rica for sure," Santiago said using the ICS. "It's as if they are on a training exercise."

Santiago hunched over a plotting board listening to Hallesleven call out position, size of the unit, and any rolling stock. He plotted the positions although not really sure why, too many volleyball games on the Costa Rican side of the San Juan.

"Colonel Santiago," the General's finger touched the plastic window bubble. "Uniformed Police are playing local villagers and now they are waving at Nicaragua's version of the Blue Angels."

They both saw policemen sunbathing on beach towels beside the U.S. built M-114 armored personnel carrier which had one side of the net tied off to it.

"Do you smell what I do?" Hallesleven asked.

Santiago adjusted the microphone to his lips. "A ruse, General?"

Hallesleven nodded as he turned to Santiago. "Will Kellogg can't be far away. My instincts tell me otherwise, but we'll wait before calling off Southern Wall."

Earlier in the day, Santiago issued orders disembarking armor vehicles and infantry assigned to Che Guevara's southern assault group. These same units would take position along the San Juan to initiate Operation Southern Wall. Columns of armor vehicles, buses, military, and civilian trucks moved south and west along paved roads. They would wave a column on to roads slightly worse than an East Texas firebreak to snake slowly to the northern banks of the San Juan.

They passed a Nicaraguan Engineering unit with bridging rolling stock anchored north of the San Juan. "The Russian NCO is on it," Hallesleven said.

"Probably telling our Engineers to shelter the vehicles in place with camouflaged netting." Santiago hesitated. "How far you willing to take Southern Wall General?"

Hallesleven stared at the flurry of triple canopy whizzing beneath them, "as much Costa Rican territory as President Ortega deems necessary."

, As the flight approached the eastern banks of Lago de Nicaragua, they had a clear view of a Costa Rican Police officer startled in the act of urinating beside his cruiser.

Hallesleven and Santiago joined the pilots in laughter at the sight of one of the Costa Rican police officers, scrambling around the cruiser with his pants draped around both ankles.

As the northern outcrop of Costa Rican territory came into view. "Shall we go around General?" The pilot's head was twisted back to put eyes on the general.

Hallesleven shook his head as the side of his thick lips turned down. He gestured as if wielding a hatchet to blow through Costa Rican airspace.

Costa Rican Police lounging around their positions waved while a few dropped their trousers around their ankles to expose their buttocks.

"General, LZ Rivas is five minutes out," the pilot said.

"Thank you, Major," Hallesleven sighed and shook his head at the sideshow they were witnessing. The location of Rivas was south of the resort town of San Juan Del Sur and the Costa Rican border that was over the next ridge. As the pilot angled to the LZ he could see a plume of white smoke float above the waist-high elephant grass. He watched both escorts break off to the south, no doubt to put eyes on the border-crossing village of Penas Blancas.

The emboldened pilots crossed on either side of the border checkpoint at treetop level performing a high-speed 180-degree crossing maneuver and rejoined the flight north of town for the short retrograde to LZ Rivas.

＊ ＊ ＊

Seated across from the head of the Rivas Department's military complement, Hallesleven slowly sipped from a steaming coffee tin. The deep lines above his eyebrow tightened as he perused the commanding officer's appearance not hearing a damn word the officer said. The LtCol used flailing arm gestures to point out known Costa Rican positions noted in red on the map. His midriff weighed down a tucked in camouflaged blouse below an unseen beltline.

Hallesleven considered the Officer's personal appearance a disgrace. A young soldier with a Russian made 9mm strapped to his side stood by the easel to ensure the Department map taped to a scrap of wood withstood the LtCol's stubby fingers.

Hallesleven lit the cigar clenched between his jaws as he contemplated the next moves. Then there was President Ortega's berating that would follow. Costa Rica's deception had thrown a monkey wrench at the Operation Che Guevara. He passed a note to Santiago.

Santiago unfolded the yellow paper and his eyes passed back and forth across the lines. *"Will speak to the President and be prepared to issue an order to recall forces. Relieve the LtCol by the end of the day."*

The why associated with their southern neighbor's action at such an inopportune time intrigued Hallesleven. He would sort out the details associated with the Costa Rican exploits after Che Guevara. In time, Nicaragua's President would punish Costa Rica's ill-timed behavior with a Nicaraguan expedition. The latest ruse would be the second time Costa Rican politicians poked the Sandinista Government in the proverbial eye. The first time, Costa Rican politicians offered safe haven to the likes of Will Kellogg.

45

Lonibelle D-1

Haps fingers danced across the keyboard ending the message with, "You're always on my mind," the finishing touches to the body of the email hastily jumping up to enter Carla's private email address. A quick peek towards the 'wedge' prominent in their six-year relationship, a filled shoulder holster, and bowie knife dangling from a small hook outside his wall locker door. Both she and these instruments, even after the Marine Corps, unfortunately, continued to be a big part of his and by proxy her life. He tried to think past the half dozen calls tapping 'send,' which ended with the same result. "Voice mailbox is full."

No looking back, Hap made peace with his maker a half hour earlier kneeling over his rack terminating with a small prayer. Would their relationship be 'collateral damage'? Carla's mistake, falling for a knucklehead and his mistake was never saying goodbye. The sound of little feet was her music the "Stoners" as a family would dance to; instead, Hap gave her the sound of her pacing the living room floor…alone.

Stripped to his orange puma underwear, dog tags, and socks—he removed a fresh blue flight suit from the locker. He slipped on the fire-retardant ensemble, stopping halfway between abdomen and chest. The shoulder holster followed, slipping the military issue holster over his flight suit where the holster covered his right breast. He removed the 9 mm from his holster and depressed the magazine release button with his left pinkie allowing the mag to bounce off the made-up bed. A quick slide to the rear using his right palm and glance into the chamber ensured it was clear. His left pointer finger released the slide and quickly replaced the 13-round mag, snapping the piece into the holster.

The sheathed knife Jim Bowie would have begrudged came to rest below his left armpit. As menacing as the look of a pistol and large knife appeared, the knife was a tool. If the Cobra flipped onto its side either on water or on hard surface, he would pull the canopy blow handles located between his legs. A circular strand of det-cord mere inches from the pilot's head would blow a hole in the canopy. If the pilots weren't decapitated in the blast, the thought was they could simply release their harness and crawl out of the cockpit. If, by chance, the det-cord failed to explode—the knife came into play. The only option between the grim reaper and, as BA would magnificently articulate, "another happy hour."

A last look around the small room confirmed he was leaving nothing required for the mission and closed the metal door behind him. On the way to the bridge, he cinched a fresh black bandana snugly over his close-cropped hairline. He ducked into the bridge through the rear hatch and came onto a scene where only John Candy could have been the star.

Big Lew hovered over the chart table, palms resting on the nickel plated 45's holstered on either hip. Lonibelle's Captain's overalls had no undershirt, white high-top tennis shoes topped off with the most recent Texas City High School's baseball hat.

Across the ships 5MC, Petula Clark's original version of "Downtown" played across the ship's intercom. Little Leroy sat slumped in the second Captain's chair with grease-stained fingers running over plans of the ship's heavy weapon displacements. The ship's engineer packed a nickel-plated 357 dangling under his left armpit. Melvin Hoffman's six-foot frame stood over the helm with an AR-15 slung across the shoulder, the barrel angled towards the steel deck with a 9 mm holstered snug to his right hip.

Hap gave Melvin a slap on the shoulder and stuffed one of his black bandanas into his hand. "This will bring you luck."

Without hesitation, Melvin tied down the bandana over his shoulder-length hair giving out a distinct "Argh!"

Little Leroy and Lew turned with the out of character outburst and both had the same bandanas shoved into their palms.

"All set?" Hap asked.

Lew stuffed the bandanna into the back pocket of his overalls. "Born ready. Hap."

Hap cut his eyes to the Lonibelle's Engineer. "How about you, Leroy? Wouldn't you rather be drinking beers on Clear Lake on your cigarette boat impressing ladies?"

Leroy scratched the back of his head with the hand holding the bandanna. His blue eyes went to Lonibelle's steel deck, then angled into Haps questioning gaze. "Lonibelle's power plant and I will be top notch." Patting his pistol, he flinched his eyelids. "Remember this one?" he asked.

"Coolie let you borrow it," Hap replied.

Nodding, Leroy held back most of his grin. "Told him I was going to your ranch to shoot. You know Coolie didn't bat an eye. The little fucker said, 'bring it back clean.'"

Hap grasped the back of their necks to bring their foreheads against his. "Let's ride like the wind, gentlemen. See you at the Fortress."

He worked his way to the Ops Center and Roach stood with a handset glued to his ear, wide stance, the free fist on his hip, elbow wide. In passing, Roach issued a distant, unfocused smile. KB and Sluggo sat at their consoles. He smiled hearing Shaun acknowledge Roach's order to hold as he picked his helmet bag from the same seat he'd dropped it after the early morning mission. Not a word uttered between them as he ducked out of the rear hatch.

* * *

Shaun admired the sheer power of Mother Nature as a line of cumulonimbus clouds east of the island billowed towards a darkening horizon.

Eddie flopped down beside him. "Any change?"

He gestured his narrow head to the east using a sawed-off chin as the exclamation point. "Have about a half hour before the dump." He tilted a canteen inches from his lips savoring the plastic containers last drops of water. "Have your team top off their canteens with the water running off their poncho liners."

"Will do," Eddie replied removing his bush hat to scratch the top of his head. "Do you think we will have to fight to take the bridge?"

Shaun winced at the words. "I have prayed like hell when we cross the line of departure the security vacates their position. Rules of engagement, as long as the explosive remained intact…we will not engage."

"I like that," Eddie replied.

"If an attempt was made to remove the blocks of C4, each member would go down by sniper fire or we blow the bridge." Without hesitation, Eddie replied. "Really hate to see either happen."

Shaun couldn't smile about the situation. "I'm not on this island to kill anyone, but push comes to shove, it's us or them."

Eddie fielded the response. "You know, I always wrestled with the thought of taking lives for the Grand old U.S.A. or Operation Spanish Main." Eddie didn't look at Shaun as his voice lost its power. "Funny thing, I'm not concerned about dying for the same."

"These guys aren't Nazis. They just happen to work for a former National Socialist operative. Let me get in the 2100 report." Shaun raised the sat phone to his ear. "OP One 2100 report. Bridge manned, airfield vacant."

Roach dispensed a decisive directive, "Hold position. If threat remains, do not push until landing confirmed and on Mother's orders. Acknowledge."

Shaun let his head fall back and slowly let out a long breath of air.

"OP One, acknowledge."

"OP One…understood. Hold position until advised."

Eddie checked the illuminated dials on his watch. "What's up with that?"

"I don't know," Shaun replied. "But those dozen men standing between us and our objective have just been issued a reprieve. He let the phone fall to the side with the earpiece still in his ear.

46

Dallas, Texas
Law Offices of Wallace, Smith, McCreery, and Leach

The woman's cowboy boots trod across the parking garage's concrete floor towards the elevator leading to the building's bottom floor. Like she had done thousands of times before, she navigated the corner directly to the security station guarding the elevators used to access the class-A's upper floors of the building. The top of Jackson Smith's bald head appeared behind the half-moon station. He looked up from his cellular phone as if he saw a ghost.

"Yes, ma'am, may I help you?"

She fumbled with her purse and fished out an access card tethered to a USMC key ring. *Do I look so bad even Jackson doesn't recognize me?*

His round eyes went from the picture card to her face, back to the card and quickly gained his feet. "Sorry, miss, I didn't recognize you." He moved from behind the desk escorting her to the bank of elevators that accessed the 30th floor and above. He ducked in an open elevator and pulled an access card dangling from a reel attached to his belt. "33rd floor, Miss?"

She smiled. "Working late, Jackson."

He returned the smile and let the card reel back to the key ring. "We were worried about you, Missy. Lots of rumors running around the building. The custodians said you haven't been at the office in days."

He used a shoulder to hold the door open as she stepped past and turned. "Vacationing," she lied.

Jackson Smith's smiling face vanished behind the polished doors. Now she understood why Jackson asked for her badge. Unkempt hair rested below her shoulders and those half-moon bags below her eyes belonged in a facial cream commercial.

"Good evening," the lady facing the doors said.

The haggard woman facing her said nothing.

"You look like I feel."

The lady in the reflection remained quiet.

Seconds after the ding sounding the car's arrival on the 33rd floor, the polished gold doors opened and, in the blink of an eye, Carla was alone.

After the right turn, thirty feet later, she came to a stop in front of a pair of double glass doors. She pulled on both doors, only to find them locked. Her hand dove into her purse and reappeared with keys.

Two custodians working the Law Firm's reception area stopped in their tracks. By the looks on their faces, they had to be thinking 'how the woman dressed like a street person and weathered jeans would believe her key would match the doors lower base locking mechanism.'

"Loco," the young Hispanic man holding the vacuum handle said.

A short woman who had been dusting the reception area nodded in agreement. Engraved into the glass the names, Wallace, Smith, McCreery and Leach, P.C., centered below the line of the founders, 'Attorneys at Law.' Both faces flashed surprise when the tumbler on the left door tripped and the small knob inside of door rotated. As she straightened, her shoulder and legs pushed open the 10-foot piece of one-inch thick glass.

Both custodians twisted back to the four-by-four portrait of the founding partners etched into the glass. The man behind the vacuum pointed to the picture and looked back to the doors with raised eyebrows. "Sorry, Miss, I didn't recognize you."

Carla glanced to the portrait, back to the custodians, and knelt to relock the door. She stood third from the right wearing a Marine Corps green business suit, and heels, which happened to be Hap's fav.

The vacuum zoomed to life, the custodian whipped the machinery around a leather couch, and the other returned moving the duster rapidly across mahogany.

Business as usual, the door between the reception area and lawyer's corridor was closed. As casually as walking her niece inside an ice cream parlor, she passed to the left of the reception station and stopped in front of the door. Without turning she held her breath and rapidly punched in her personal five-digit access code hoping the Firm's Security Officer was not in front of his computer. The moment she entered the fifth digit, a signal went through the internet to the Firm's hard drive, accessible to the Firm's Security Officer who doubled as their chief investigator. She questioned if they'd deactivated her code, but either way the Firm would know she had surfaced.

"Click." She let out a long sigh, opened the solid core door, and quickly pushed it close behind her. Twenty offices on the east wing corridor were between where she stood allowing her eyes to adjust to the low light. Partner's offices took up the south side of the Firm's office spaces at the end of the hall.

A rectangular stream of light lit up the hallway halfway down the hall. Of all the lawyers to be working tonight, it had to be Luther Williams. Since walking out on Hap, she had driven her Tahoe in no particular direction with no particular destination in mind. How bad she wanted simply to turn around, but the answers to Hap's latest crusade resided in the letter sized manila envelope stored in her safe. How could she have been so naïve to think the writing in sharpie across the front of the envelope, "Do not open dickhead" should have telegraphed the seriousness of the material inside? Maybe a script for a James Bond movie, not in real life in Richardson, Texas. The picture of Blad shoving the envelope into Hap's hand and then Hap saluting Jeff Sharver sitting behind the controls of the yellow helo remains forever fixed in her mind.

As if walking across a minefield she carefully placed each step of her bulldogging boot, heel to toe, across the hardwood floors to pass undetected. Two doors remained between where the light intersected her path ... so far so good. Now only one door then Luther's shaved head peered around the corner.

"Carla," Luther said looking as if he had seen a ghost. "I thought that was you. Saw you enter the front door on my computer screen."

She froze in place putting eyes on Luther's shaved head. How could she forget the Firm's security system pinged all attorney's computers? Her hands crossed over to toss back a patch of matted hair across both shoulders. "That's great, Luther."

"You are my Supervising Partner," he said shaking his head. "I have pressing questions on the West Texas Frackers matter."

Carla nodded. "You're right, Luther. We will revisit this topic."

"Everybody at the firm has been worried sick," he said.

"I'm fine Luther…but if you don't mind, I need to get into my office to catch up on my schedule. Been absent way too long."

Still wide-eyed, Luther reached over and clutched her wrist to slowly bring her into the light. Now in full light, she thought back to her high school play with lights and the entire audience's eyes on her. He placed both bear paw-like hands on her shoulders, which she found repulsive. Luther was an up and comer and would be a partner within 12 months. The real problem was he knew it.

"So, have you finally left Hap Stoner?"

She knew the lug pined for her attention always throwing grenades at Hap. She said nothing.

His broad lips parted and formed a devious smile. "Never knew why you hung with that baby killer. Dummy could have never made it through law school. You deserve better Carla."

She said nothing, only nodding, and then moved her head side to side.

"We had a breach, and somebody gained access to your office three nights back."

She clutched both of his wrists and slowly removed them to the side. "Didn't hear about that one. I really have to go to my office Luther."

"I think the partners may have had the locks changed," he said. "You know, with the breach and all"

"The partners only acted in the best interest of the firm, Luther."

Luther leaned against the casing of his open door both arms crossed. "Somebody has been looking for you for two days Carla. Probably a detective. Partners aren't talking."

She grimaced at the thought and stepped around to continue to her office. The heels of her boots banged against the floor as the door to Luther's office closed behind her. As if Security had not caught on, she was inside the office, the brown nose bastard was calling one of the partners, she thought. She moved fast, coming to a stop in front of her office. She lifted the keypad cover and punched in her four-digit code with no result. Reaching into her purse, she fumbled with her keyring. Fortunately, Hap had sprayed painted the key green and for moments like this placed a green plastic cover on the wide end so she could find the key by feel. She felt a breath of relief as the key went easily into the lock. Anxiety set in when the lock didn't turn and leaned against the door as pent-up feelings appeared as tears tumbling down her cheeks. Her head gently tapped the door in an attempt to come up with the "next step."

She heard the latch before the door lever turned against her hip. A light appeared from beneath the door. Her boots dug in fighting the urge to run as both doors opened slowly. A man slightly taller than her with a waist broader than his shoulders shoved a badge in front of her dazed face.

"Agent Jim Gordon, FBI. My gut told me you would come to the office tonight."

Hap had told her about their meeting in El Centro and Peg mentioned the same agent had visited Hap at his office. She already didn't like the man. "By the size of your gut Agent Gordon, you had a good inclination for sure."

Gordon issued a flat look below his jet-black hair slicked back to reflect muscle the man didn't possess physically. Wide-eyed, Carla stepped into her office and gave a quick glance toward the wall-mounted picture to her right. She eased in behind the desk and shook her head.

Gordon stood by the corner of the desk and screwed the cap on his thermos. Carla declined his head gesture for a cup. "Hank Leach called me the day I interviewed Hap Stoner." His brow furrowed as he cut his eyes towards the same photo she glanced at moments earlier.

Carla glanced over to where the detective looked. With the stables at the Ranch in the background, she rested on her Appaloosa, "Wiggles," while Hap looked down to the ground to their front sitting on top of his Arabian. Hap's little Yorkie sat on her haunches in front of the two horses supporting a recent "teddy bear" style grooming gazing toward the camera. A cowboy hat rested back on the crown of Carla's head and a boot was propped over her saddle horn. Hap was standing in the stirrups and wore an Astros baseball cap tucked low over his brow.

"Recent?" he said.

Without a moment of hesitation, she replied, "Why do you ask?" She looked back to attempt to get a read on his facial expression.

Gordon shrugged and looked her in the eyes. "That's how I make my living. Observation and asking questions."

Carla liked his answer. This one was better than your average agent was. "Why are you talking to Hap? Wouldn't be politics?"

His gaze returned to the photo.

Both forearms rested on the edge of the desk as she leaned into Gordon. "We took it while Hap recovered from his wounds and he resigned from the Marine Corps."

"Resigned or dishonorably discharged," he replied. He smirked. "I have spoken to several attorneys and their opinion of Hap is that he is a dumb ass 'jarhead.'"

She returned a smile that screamed a polite 'F U'. "You talk as if you have military experience Detective."

"A little bit," he answered. "Left the National Guard after graduating from college to join the Bureau. I was discharged honorably a sergeant. I was in Admin."

Her narrow chin slowly moved up and down. "First of all, let me thank you for your service. Hap did resign and was able to maintain his rank of LtCol. Unfortunately, the Marine Corps needed a fall guy. Hap was never one to back away from a face shot for friends or fellow Marines. It wasn't advertised by the Cable Networks, but all the living Marines or dependents of the dead were able to maintain hard earned benefits because Hap gave up all of his."

"Honorable of the Lt. Colonel. Did he leave you in this condition before falling off the face of the earth?" His eyes slowly traced everything exposed above her desk.

She remained silent knowing to what he was referring.

Gordon eased back into one of the two client chairs. A small end table wedged between the chairs had a half-eaten pepperoni pizza and an empty quart of coke resting on top. Other signs Agent Gordon had settled into her office became obvious. Pillows wedged against the couch's armrest and empty sacks of Whataburger and Dunkin donuts spilling out of a small trashcan. Apparently searching her office, he moved the small receptacle from under her desk to the couch placed against the opposite wall from the safe. If her intuition were exact, Gordon had been waiting in the office for possibly days telegraphing one, if not all of the partners including security so they were aware he had camped inside her office. At this point, she didn't give a shit.

Carla fell back into her chair…nodded, then cut her eyes to the picture. "The answer is in the safe."

"You wouldn't be referring to the safe behind the picture?"

She turned back and their eyes fixed on the other. "I didn't say that," she replied.

His response was swift. "I did."

She straightened in her chair as if a bolt of electricity ran through her spine. "You rummaged through my office because of Hap. What is the beef?" After a brief lull, her head pitched to the side.

He said nothing turning his head back to the photo.

She cringed with the realization of what she was about to do swinging the chair to the side, then stepping to the photo. Her hand swung the frame open. He knew the safe was behind the photo. Rapidly spinning the dial, she ran through the combination, left 20, right 36, two full turns clockwise then stopping at 18. A discernible click followed. Her hand lowered the small lever sending out a distinct clap as the locking bar extracted. On first glance, everything appeared to be in place. Their wills, Hap's mom's will, several deeds and an envelope containing their passwords. She continued working her way to the bottom searching for the manila envelope with Blad's writing across the front. Slowly turning, an expression of trepidation flashed across her face.

"Don't tell me," Gordon said craning to glimpse at the contents of the safe. "Whoever broke into your office was able to breach the firm's security and crack your safe?"

Her body tightened as she tapped a finger against the wall, "And they took the file."

47

Arlen Siu

In 1975, Somoza's Nicaraguan National Guard conducted the perfect ambush making Arlen Siu—the talented singer and songwriter, a national celebrity before joining the Sandinista resistance—a martyr. By her 18th birthday, she befriended the future wife of the current President and was dead at the fledgling age of 20. Not surprising, President Ortega named the Russian vessel carrying General Hallesleven's flag for Operation Che Guevara, Arlen Siu.

Hallesleven's jaw clenched a Cuban cigar as he leaned into the LST's rail scanning the horizon for the armored columns returning to their nest. Hours earlier, he called President Ortega to apprise him of the ruse. He pictured the President's chin tilting back emitting smoke rings in short puffs like a steam locomotive. "Recall all forces," he screamed.

He pulled the phone from his ear in anticipation as Ortega initiated another rant slamming the phone into its cradle. Within minutes, Halleslevan issued the recall order and assets dedicated to Che Guevara began to flock back to El Bluff like birds to their nests.

Except for the stars, the heavens over Nicaragua were clear. The last of the thunderstorms had passed and the Russian weather guessers stationed in Managua called 48 hours of favorable weather.

Nicaragua's Commanding General's forearms rested on Arlen Siu's top rail as a polished combat boot slipped onto the rail below. Years of work on the family farm in his youth chiseled his frame and even after 60, he stayed committed to a rigorous workout regimen in the ousted President's private gym.

"General," Colonel Santiago eased in beside him clutching a crumpled-up memo. "You told me your gut screamed the trawler perished by foul play."

Hallesleven spoke looking over the bow. "Then we have news. I… I… don't know whether my nephew is alive and well, or if he's a traitor to his country."

"Do you want to read the memo? The message was delivered to the President personally by the Chinese ambassador."

The General's chin swung around toward Santiago almost touching his shoulder. "I smell Will Kellogg's stench."

Santiago extended the paper to Hallesleven.

Hallesleven's fireplug sized forearm pushed away from the document. "Is there really any reason to read it, Colonel?"

His Chief of Staff shook his head. "A Chinese submarine on scene reported to Beijing the trawler was attacked by slow moving aircraft. Most likely helicopters."

"This operation is being plagued by diversions from a cunning foe," Hallesleven said his head tilted to the heavens. "Somebody is pulling the strings. Santiago, we have a bad apple inside Headquarters."

Santiago's head leaned into the General's ear, "A spy?"

Hallesleven nodded slowly. "I could have killed Will Kellogg decades past."

"No, General."

Hallesleven spat into the water, "I was leading a relief column into eviscerated villages along the Costa Rican border vacated by the Contras. Kellogg was picking up Russian communications gear and funneling it to the Yankee Defense Intelligence Agency. We cornered the bastard in an ambush north of the San Juan. An RPG knocked the piece of shit out cold." Hallesleven's fist clenched. "And to think I put my Colt 1911 to Will's temple and didn't pull the trigger. You know what the son of a bitch said to me?"

Santiago only nodded.

"Let me quote the infamous Will Kellogg, 'Would you mind placing the barrel to my forehead and get mighty close so my blood spews all over your commie face.'"

"What did you do General, since the hammer never dropped?"

I honored the request. No doubt, Will Kellogg wasn't afraid to die. After guiding the hammer home, I holstered my weapon, conducted a facing movement to the right, and walked into the jungle without a word said."

Santiago's brows furred closer together. "So, if you didn't shoot him, General, how did he get away?"

"The Contras came back to the village and raided the police station. We believe the operation was CIA."

"Makes sense," Santiago replied. "He has ties into the Yankee Intelligence agency."

Hallesleven interrupted, his voice trembling. "Thinking back and able to do it over again, I would have stepped back several steps and then shot the bastard. My way of saying 'fuck you, too.'"

The distinctive lights of a BTR 60PB four wheeled Soviet bloc era armor personnel carrier's slit headlight arrangement appeared, followed by another. A narrow grin replaced a look of trepidation.

"Finally," Santiago said with a heavy sigh. "Are we ready?"

"After each of the President's rants, I advise El Jefe that Nicaragua's military is able and willing." Hallesleven pushed back from the rail. "You know Santiago, through the years the President's rants have become the norm."

"The man has ousted Somoza. Killed Contras by the thousands. Maybe he is tired, General."

"The trails the President and I have traveled together are long and bloodstained. Friends who gave their lives in the name of the Revolution were many." Now it was time to pull off the biggest raid of his career. His thoughts migrated back to Will Kellogg.

He seemed always to be thinking of Kellogg lately.

The man had many distinguishable traits as a leader and chief of warriors. If their paths crossed in this operation, one of them would die.

D-Day
Stingray

Stingray's darkened bridge flushed from the dull-green console lights and overhead, casting off shades of blue over Larson's Captain's chair. Larson's six-foot frame paced past Doc Perry, the ship's surgeon who was sitting cross-legged in his chair. He glanced overhead to the digital display, painting heading, and speed like a banner at a retail outlet. Full blood Choctaw, Larson's high cheekbones and squared off jaw appeared sketched from the backlight's green glow. The bow was pointed south by southwest as she had been for the past four hours. His pace quickened each time his mind drifted leading men in combat for the first time. *His decisions good and bad, could cost the lives of Stingray's crew.* His pace quickened at the thought like a nervous father at the birth of his first child.

Quietly sitting crossed legged in Larson's Captain's chair, Doc perused a fifteen-year-old Playboy magazine. "Anything more current?"

Larson stopped and looked over his shoulder. "You get off on Kaitlyn Jenner? That's what you get with the newer mags."

The headlamp above the chair highlighted the contortion fixed across Doc's angular face. Larson went back to stalking the bridge.

"Doc, the thought of the injuries that could enter your home-built infirmary makes me cringe."

Doc returned a grunt flipping through dog-eared pages. "Let me worry about the wounded. Make sure you Captain Stingray." He extended his arm to allow gravity to pull the trifold open.

Larson stopped behind his occupied chair. "Now that ain't Kaitlyn Jenner."

"How in the hell would you know?" Doc lowered the mag to his lap and both hands gingerly gathered the trifold into place. "I have had surgeries easier than trying to keep this gem in one piece."

Larson said nothing as the sound of turbines spooled slowly to life from the flight deck. Doc reached up and turned off the light, pushed out of the chair gingerly replacing the magazine into the chair.

"All ahead, flank Pablo!" Larson barked. "Come to two seven zero."

"Heading two seven zero. All ahead flank."

"Very well," Larson answered as pulsations up through his tennis shoes telegraphed the engines responding. "After launch, make turns for one zero knots and come back to two three zero."

"Understood, Captain. Aye-aye," came the reply. "Standing by."

* * *

Doc Perry eased in next to Stingray's cook though curved over the rail at the waist and took in the flurry of activity across Stingray's flight deck. Uniformed in black fatigue bottoms and short sleeve V cut tee shirts, three sticks of 6 comprising Will Kellogg's assault force completed final equipment checks. Each stick stood in line, arms at the order while Will did a once over occasionally stopping to point out loose or out of place gear. He then reached into the ruck's cargo pouches.

"Are you watching?" Doc said.

"Uh huh," the ship's cook responded, his head moving back and forth across the small formations.

"All men have their gear in the same spot as the next in case of wounds or death. They know where to go to get what they need regardless of the corpse being fleeced."

Will faced off to inspect the next man in line. The previously inspected member worked deliberately to correct discrepancies. In some instances, a couple of wraps of electrical tape secured a loose item or moving an item like spare ammo or grenades from one pouch to another.

Doc nudged Harold Simmons' wide-eyed son's ribs, looking up his 6ft 5in frame. "To a man, these men see no sight of pageantry in human conflict."

JMan lowered his gaze to Doc's. "Then why do it?"

Chuckling, Doc gazed over the stern of the ship. "Purpose. Let's go downstairs."

A half-moon, school circle quickly formed around Will and each member knelt to a pad-covered knee. Steady eyes stared from behind darkened faces, Will donned a dark shaded watch cap, and the others followed suit as he spoke over the idling Killer Egg's engines.

"Tonight, we impose our will with the tools learned in training." His gaze traveled to each set of blinking eyes as he spoke. "I hope like hell the same number who go on this raid come out. Let there be no illusions about tonight. We have a tradition as a group with scores of separate skirmishes in far off places." His voice slowly elevated. "That abstract thing called mission over self-preservation has its place when triggered by enemy contact. We overcome fear by falling back on experience and training. Now let's go."

Simmons had honed in on Will's speech and stood mesmerized.

Doc eased in beside Harold Simmons' baby boy. "This ain't no NFL game, JMan," he said placing his hand on a shoulder. "I'm not telling you something you don't know already."

JMan swept his hand below both eyes and said nothing.

Doc slapped his back and said nothing.

"Thanks, Doc." He gestured his head toward Will. "Who is this guy?"

Doc shook his head sniggering. "Your old man would have loved to been on this mission."

JMan's head turned slowly looking down at Doc. "You're not the first person to tell me this. Many a story is floating around about the old man."

Doc nodded. "Most of them are true."

JMan spoke looking out towards the killer eggs idling rotors. "I wish he could have been my father."

Doc's head turned in amazement, "Harold Simmons is your father, and don't think otherwise. If alive, no doubt your old man would be flying into harm's way tonight. Your Pop may have been a shitty golfer, but never knew him to turn from a good fight, much less a worthy cause. Can I make a suggestion?"

JMan stood in silence not bothering to wipe away the tears reappearing down both high set cheeks. "I was 12 when he died."

Doc nodded and choked down what little saliva his dry mouth could muster. "Stoner told me the story. They were on their third rearm and fueling for the day during the battle for Fallujah. An Iraqi 7.62 round from nowhere left a small hole in the canopy before striking your dad in the neck. He got out a quick call to Hap to take the controls before his airway filled with blood and died quietly minutes later without a whimper of regret."

A stick moved assertively to board the second bird.

Schlonger rolled the killer eggs throttle to fly as V stood beside the bird with goggles flipped back over the crown of his helmet. Foxie stood outside Big Alabama's rotor arc waving Will's stick in, like a traffic cop in a school zone. With M4 dangling from his right hand, Will pumped his left hand then pointed to the first bird.

Big Alabama side taxied clearing the deck then lowered the nose as the drooping rotors clawed sky.

V moved deliberately around the rounded off nose and strapped into the left seat. Waved into a hover with hand and arm signals, Schlonger used what little flight deck was available fighting through the translational lift. The plane captain dropped to the deck, his head only feet from the rotors leading edge before the rotors dipped to port to avoid Stingray's superstructure.

Doc and JMan watched the birds evaporate into darkness without a further word spoken.

Except for the hum of Stingray's engine dropping RPM's and wind kicking up JMan's flowing blonde hair, the flight deck was quiet.

"My father," JMan said. "What was he like?"

Doc turned. "Your father was a pretty simple man. I know what the fucker would say if he were standing with us. "Know right from wrong, so do the right thing. Be a good man, a better father, and husband. He would ask no more from you." The blonde-haired blue-eyed ship's cook looked straight ahead and for the first time in his life didn't say a damn word.

"Let's go make ourselves useful," Doc said. In a sudden air of what Doc perceived to be 'purpose' painted across a face that belonged inside a modeling agency, JMan trailed Doc up the steps to Vultures' Row.

49

D-Day

At times called a coral atoll, the ring-shaped geographical feature partially encircling a lagoon or completely encircled initial point "IP Chevy." Hap peeked below his goggles to confirm the land mass 15 miles east-southeast of Isle de San Andres City was the "IP" selected by Roach.

Hollywood's voice passed across the flight's tactical frequency as if speaking to a judge in a bench trial. "Two Killer Eggs at 10 o'clock level Kang, Left-hand turns over IP."

Hap cut his head to the right to bring the IP back into his 40-degree field of view, then said, "Concur." BA had the flight in loose trail flying over the IP in right-hand turns.

The Snakes rocked their snouts in unison to close. Hap roared across Schlonger's rotor disc from the four to ten o'clock at 165 miles per hour, banking hard right, throwing the rotor tips to the heavens to slide into position as Hollywood initiated a wing over maneuver left skid high to dip into position at the Killer Eggs four o'clock.

"Mother, IP inbound," Hap transmitted. A cruise liner skylighted in the distance plowing into their course line. Both Cobra's ammo bays contained 650 rounds of 20mm High Explosive Incendiary, "HEI," a rack of four tows was slung under stations one and four, and two and three had seven-shot rocket pods.

BA initiated a gentle climb shadowed by the remainder of the flight to put air between the cruise liner and four sets of skids. Hap peered underneath the cylinders to escape the lights bunting the Cobra over the floating magnificence racing over, a cluster of antennas extending from a fishing trawler.

"Shit, did you ever see 'em," Hap said. "This fucker had an antenna farm extending from the bridge."

"Sometimes it's better to be lucky than good," Hollywood radioed.

"This guy intentionally masked his vessel from a seaward approach," LD said. "What Captain of a cruise liner would allow such a thing?"

Hap had to think about LD's last statement. He had drinks and played cards with many of the cruise line Captains.

"A Captain who was receiving money below the table."

* * *

"We have choppers overhead," the captain screamed from somewhere on the superstructure. The bearded crewman killed power to the winch dragging in the fishnets, straining his ears for the discernible sound of rotor blades.

Undistinguishable fuselages raced overhead, the Nicaraguan agent posing as a fisherman counted the fourth just as the first two became sky lighted by the lights of Isle de San Andres City. The net hung halfway between winch and water.

He could hear the sounds of boots pounding against metal steps to his rear. "Get the callout, the Yankee invasion has begun."

Turning away from the power box, the agent stooped to reach into a backpack hanging on a nearby cleat pulling out a satellite phone. He punched three on the keypad speed dialing a preprogrammed number. A voice who could have been sitting anywhere came across the link on the first ring.

"Report," the female voice said.

"Four helos inbound to the island," he reported. "It's begun."

* * *

Hap watched members of the assault force begin to move to the edge of the cabin placing both combat boots squarely on the little bird's running boards—the barrels of their weapons were wedged between their legs, barrels down.

"Let's join the fun… you have the controls."

"I have the controls," LD replied.

Hap raised both hands to demonstrate LD had the controls. As if in unison, both gunships lowered their snouts to dash ahead passing on either side of Beaver flight to put eyes on the target and surrounding area.

"Place is kinda dark," LD said.

Hap liked the blackness of the plant to their right as well as the fortress, and its private airfield. Isle de San Andres City, on the other hand, lit up like Christmas.

"Maybe everybody left for Disneyland?" Hap said as their heads moved left and right scanning rooftops and courtyards.

Hollywood crossed just inside the main entrance banking hard to starboard sandwiched between the runway and fortress parking lot. "Clear," he transmitted.

"Press Beaver," Hap communicated banking hard over Isle de San Andres Bay setting up a butterfly pattern to support the assault group's insertion. Both helos flew the pattern of the outline of a butterfly wing. One left, the other on the right to maintain 360 degree coverage for the flight.

LD grimaced. "Whoever stayed back inside the fortress walls, had to be wide awake."

BA and Schlonger approached below the height of the cliff angling to set up a landing to the west. Both pilots used cyclic to trade airspeed for altitude to climb above the cliffs and on past the fortress walls. A quick bank to the left and both birds were in a three-foot air taxi over the Citadel.

Each of the assault group pushed away from the running boards and double-timed to preassigned positions. Simultaneous with the last man's boots touching the ground, each aircraft continued their air taxi, lowered their noses, then bunted over the western wall banking hard right to rendezvous with Stingray.

BA reported back to Mother the first wave was on the ground. "Nina inserted."

Hap nodded his head. "Hollywood, on me. Kang flight will flounder east." Both birds banked to the east to loiter near the refinery.

"Game on, LD," Hap said calmly. "Game on."

50

Arlen Siu

Leaning over the latest embarkation report, Hallesleven sipped from a warm coffee tin engraved with 'Arlen Siu' on one side. He parked the lukewarm swill on the corner of the small desk. He knew that tomorrow afternoon would be the earliest the southern group could put to sea. A tap on his door followed. Hallesleven's dark eyes peered over reading glasses fixed precariously on the end of his bulging nose.

"Colonel Santiago?"

"General, a screening vessel in sector three reported a flight of helicopters passed low and fast with no lights inbound to Isle de San Andres."

Hallesleven cut his eyes over to the situation map. Sector 3 was east of the island. He slowly removed his glasses and began to spin the spectacles by one of the arms. "How old is the intelligence, Colonel?"

"Minutes, General."

Hallesleven spat tobacco to the floor. "You thinking what I'm thinking, Colonel?"

"Will Kellogg has returned to Isle de San Andres," Santiago spoke as if his last comment were a statement of fact versus a question.

Hallesleven retrieved the coffee tin. "Colonel, please close the door on your way out."

Santiago clicked his heals simultaneously with a curt nod and about-face closing the hatch behind him.

Hallesleven reached for the phone to call the President.

* * *

Will Kellogg's neck stretched out past the top of a large condensing unit to scan the Fortress's main structure through a greenish grainy tint. *Any day would be fine.* He could feel his patience growing short waiting for the sound of the leave-taking helos to fade. Moments passed before the wind whipping around the Fortress façade drowned out the distant sounds of Hap's gunships.

"Jackson, proceed to door to our front," he said through the transmitter.

Appearing from behind a stone wall the blackjack dealer leaped over the wall and bound up the stairs three at a time. Two other figures followed close behind. He cinched a loop around an ancient cannon, dropped the rope over the side, and signaled his team to follow him over the wall with two pulses from his lip light.

Jackson was the first down the rope and the entire team vanished over the wall in seconds rappelling the twenty feet into the courtyard settling in next to the front gate. "Jackson in position. Flounder."

Hearing Jackson report he was in position, Will pumped his arm pointing in the direction of the rooftop access door. He approached the door with the stock of his M4 in a shoulder. He stepped left boot over right in a deliberate movement to contact. The two remaining team members provided cover, their barrels scanning left, then right, searching for targets positioned fifteen feet behind. As his left hand dropped from the stock to work the knob, he saw a blast of light from the door he fully expected to blow. Two red dots joined Will's fixed on the figure's tuxedo vest just above the heart. As if by an act of God or as Will Kellogg would say, 'damn good training with solid rules of engagement' not a shot was fired.

Will barked through his headset. "Hold your fire."

One of the dots vanished from the vest as Will lowered his M4.

"Mr. von Bock, what brings you out so late at night?"

With his angular head sky lighted, Franz issued a gentle smile. "I have been waiting for you, Will. Would you and your men join me in my study?"

Will gave a quick tilt to his head and paused. "Jackson, hold your position. Weapons tight."

Switching to UHF, he reached out to Hap. "Kang, can't explain it now. Jackson is in position and will hold. We are weapons tight. Inform mother. Out."

51

Isle de San Andres
Bridge between OP -1 and Knoll

Goggled up, Shaun slowly made his way across the bridge, one combat boot in front the other with the M4 stock wedged into his right shoulder.

"OP 1, Mother SitRep to follow."

He continued across the narrow bridge stalking beneath the overhead metal girders. "Go ahead, Mother," he said.

"Nina is inside the fortress. No shots fired. Continue. Weapons tight."

"Copy, Mother," Shaun responded. "He waved the team forward.

The pavement was similar to the coral-derived aggregates he ambled across flagging down taxis during WestPac tours; he continued forward anticipating the bullet that never came.

As he gained the fortress side of the structure, he allowed the stock to fall to his side. "All clear," he said.

"On our way," Bennie replied.

Shaun heard their boots pounding the pavement from behind. A glance over a shoulder and both teams were double timing across the bridge. He counted heads until reaching eight goggled figures carrying a ruck in one hand and rifles in the other. It had been Bennie's idea to carry Shaun's ruck along with his own in case of incoming fire and two of the men from Black Eddie's team carried the two injured sappers' rucks. Shaun turned and double-timed it down the road carrying his weapon at the port to cover the 400 meters to the low rolling hill between the bridge and Fortress.

He could just make out Kang flight over his left shoulder hovering in front of the refinery to provide overwatch.

* * *

"Hollywood, check out the backside of the hill."

"Roger, Kang." Hollywood lowered the shark-like nose in a sweeping acceleration maneuver crossing Hap's six right to left in a hooking maneuver slide flaring to a 20-foot hover using cyclic and left pedal.

"All clear Kang," Hollywood reported. "Clear to press."

Hap replied with two clicks. "OP One…Kang. Team clear to proceed to Fortress." He watched as Shaun's team and the balance of OP Two mounted the hill while Eddie and one other figure doubled timed down the road towards the fortress.

Shaun issued a long wave of an arm extended above his head. Hap flashed his IR searchlight and Shaun went to work to place the team into a 270-degree perimeter oriented east.

"Join on me," Hap transmitted as he watched Hollywood rock the bird's snout to join in loose cruise as the two snakes clawed into a climbing left-hand turn. Hollywood accelerated forward as Hap crossed his front. Banking into a hard starboard turn, Hollywood jerked the nose into a high perch allowing the nose to fall through the horizon and port, to slide back down to pick up a loose four o'clock. Hap anchored the flight over the refinery in right-hand turns at 200 feet.

"Fuel state?" Hap asked as he eyed his fuel gauge a shade under 800 pounds. Dash-2 would have a little less as they use more power to maintain position.

"Seven twenty-five," Hollywood replied. "Looks like the plant has been idled. Don't see any lights. Somebody knows something?"

BA checked inbound with the second wave. "Beaver IP inbound."

Hap acknowledged with two clicks. "Anchored over refinery 250 feet, right-hand turns. Will push to the fortress coming out of next turn."

"Copy Kang," Beaver said. "Have you in sight." Hap peeled off in a descending turn as the Cobras snout swung towards the fortress. Leveling at 50 feet with Hollywood split out wide to starboard, both Cobras made a slow pass with a snake on either side of the Fortress. Shaun's team was busy digging in pausing long enough to wave an entrenching tool over their heads as the flight roared low overhead.

Hap's goggles cast a halo effect around a speeding vehicle. He toggled his goggles over his brow. "Headlights at 11 o'clock LD. I'm in the bucket." His sweaty brow rested against rubber and he quickly ranged the target. "600 meters and moving away fast."

LD blurted out, "Must be in a hurry!"

Hap watched the single car race down the two-lane connecting the fortress parking lot to the private airfield. His left thumb changed black heat to white heat. The engine compartment switched from a black splotch on the screen to glowing white.

Seated in the front passenger seat of Franz's limo, Will called out over the tactical network. "Check fire. I'm in the limo leaving the parking lot in front of fortress. Emergency lights are flashing. There has been a change of plans. Give me a perimeter at the airport hangar."

"You copy, Beaver?" Hap said.

"Beaver copies. Inbound with pax."

"Safe up weapons Hollywood," Hap said. "Join on me. Inbound to airfield."

Hollywood issued two clicks as LD made a gentle decelerating turn to the left.

"Beaver," Hap barked. "Your section will be hot pumped. Bring us that last stick."

Even as Beaver responded with two clicks, Hap knew the big guy, along with the rest of mission's minds, were racing. *What in the hell just happened?*

*   *   *

Hap's left hand popped the handle and pushed open the front cockpit's bubble canopy as LD locked the rotor brake to the rear. In one fluid motion, Hap's right boot hit the step while his left boot continued to the skid as the rotors nudged to a stop. He unzipped the survival vest sliding it off both shoulders draping it over the three-barrel chain gun in passing. *Thank God, they hadn't fired a shot.* Will leaned over the hood of the vehicle that raced from the Fortress. He held a flashlight above his right ear while studying the map splayed across the hood. A black ebony wood grip dagger and anodized scabbard were on either corner of the map to hold it against the ocean's gentle breeze.

Hap recognized the map of Isle de San Andres. "Can you enlighten me what the hell is going on?"

Will didn't acknowledge Hap's presence and without breaking his train of thought said, "You wouldn't believe me if I told you, Colonel."

Hap didn't give Will a chance to take a breath responding. "Try me."

Will puckered his lips along with a long nod. "I have more questions than answers."

Hap's boot found the front bumper as he leaned in to take in what had Will's undivided attention. "You can do better than that."

As Will's head turned, he pointed to the paperweights. "The old kraut handed me his brothers SS dagger and scabbard. Himmler gave it to the kraut's brother personally for participating in the Night of Long Knives."

Hap took in the history lesson thinking to himself; *Will... where is the meatloaf?*

"Colonel, you're going to call me a liar, but as I was moving to set the explosives to breach the door," his squared head began to swing back and forth. "The door magically opened, and an angular figure clad in black tuxedo, bow tie, and holding a glass of red wine invited the entire team inside. He introduced his house staff, dressed to the nines, all in one straight line inside his study, erect and proud.

Hap's head reeled, "SS daggers, Night of Long Knives, tuxedos, staff, and surrendered. You have got to be shitting me."

Will pointed the flashlight through the windshield outlining a figure with broad shoulders, bushy eyebrows, and crewcut behind the wheel. "Didn't get to the part when your friend entered the study."

Hap laughed as Blad exited the limo. His familiar John Lennon-style glasses dangled precariously from a rounded nose, he didn't bother closing the door and tossed Hap a manila envelope.

By the sharpie marks across the front of the envelope, it was the envelope Blad had given him at the ranch…but then placed into Carla's office safe.

Hap was incredulous and had more questions than answers. "OK Blad, how did you get this?" He paused collecting his thoughts, then said, "Before you answer, how did you get into the limo?"

Blad removed his glasses tucking them inside his leather coat revealing shoulder holstered nickel-plated Colt 1911's under each armpit. "To be blunt, Hap, I have worked for Franz von Bock for five years." He pointed a thumb over his shoulder toward the fortress. "I keep a suite inside the walls."

Hap stepped back to cross-examine the situation. "Will said von Bock is Krueger." Except for the little birds hot pumping with their rotors turning in the distance, it was quiet around the limo.

Blad scratched stubble budding from his chin. "I guess some house cleaning is in order. Short version or long," he asked.

Will motioned with his hand only to Blad cut him off. "Let me handle this one, Will."

Incredulous, Hap stepped away from the bumper beginning to scan the morning horizon emerging to the east. His narrow face exhibited fatigue and rapidly approached irritation.

"He's got the look Blad," Will said as more a statement than a question sliding the M4 off his shoulder. "I know you know the look all too well. It is time to answer his question or duck the infamous left hook."

Adding angst to an already tense situation, Blad waited for the little birds to depart south. "Hap, when you contacted me, Franz had already made the decision after the Border incident to bring your group into the family." He pointed at the envelope.

Out of the corner of his eye, the barrel of Will's M4 elevated slowly followed by a distinct click of the selector switch.

Hap's right hand blocked the barrel from rising as his left hand gripped the pistol's Packard grip, "Let the man speak, Will."

Blad didn't flinch or go for a pistol. "Put the barrel of the piece you're gripping to my temple and pull the damn trigger. The contents in the envelope explain it all."

Hap's fingers slid from the grip. A figure clad in tuxedo and tails exited the back of limo easing next to Blad.

Hap looked to Will. "I guess you forgot to tell me about Fred Astaire?"

The enigmatic man extended his long narrow fingers of his right hand as if a palm leaf.

Hap spoke keeping hands to his side. "Franz Krueger, I presume?"

Franz's hand dangled between the two as if in no man's land. "People know me as Franz von Bock. I have been waiting a long time for this, Mr. Stoner."

52

Lonibelle
D-Day

"In preparing for battle," Hap paused, and then said, "History has shown that plans are useless, but planning is indispensable."

"Head to head, it's why more bad guys die than Marines," Will Kellogg memorialized in a barroom tête-à-tête. "Flexibility is SOP from a unit leader down to the Marine Corps rifleman. Hard to ask questions or receive permission with 7.62 and RPG's zipping by both ears. Better get the job done, and then ask forgiveness."

Hap knew it only took a blink of an eye for a situation to change. For better or worse, the situation adjusting to current events was not sitting well. The instant the Cobra's skids broke away from Lonibelle's flight deck; he carried a mindset to kill the Clint Eastwood looking fella who had just extended his hand in greeting.

As if the boney extremities were nothing more than crab legs needing to be cracked, Hap moved to crush but the German countered with an impressive grip.

"Mr. Stoner, our mutual friends have talked highly of you," he said in a stoic manner. "I wish we would have met years earlier."

Hap let his hand slip from the vice grip latch. "I'm listening, Mr. von Bock."

"Please call me Franz." A smile formed across his narrow lips. "I'm old now, Mr. Stoner, and as you age, you will find witness to God—or maybe it's humanity. I do not dwell on my impending death."

Hap looked up and said nothing. An incredulous feeling balled up in the pit of his stomach.

"You know my history by now. I worked for evil and fortunately, the Nazis lost the war. Regrettably, there are others like them in the world and they must be dealt with." The German opened his arms as if Christ himself and continued in the sentimental discourse. "I don't have a saber to surrender to you, but I do have the Spanish Main Holding Company and everything that comes with it."

Haps arms crossed as the gap between his eyebrows pinched. He pulled his naval aviators from the pen pocket on the flight's suits left shoulder. His gaze bounced between Blad and Will. The ball in his stomach began to break down as he could tell there was no bullshit to this man and he meant every word that passed from his lips.

Will let the M4's barrel go to ground, clutching the pistol grip while scratching his earlobe with his left hand.

"Tried to tell you, Hap," he said looking over towards the Fortress. "Except for Fortress housekeeping and small security force, our new partner flew all employees and their families to Dallas for a Texas Ranger 11-game homestand. To top it off, each took a season pass to Six Flags to get them the hell off the island and out of harm's way."

Hap still had more questions than answers. "So, what's the catch?"

Blad chimed in, "We have to fight off a brigade of Sandinista. It's not if, Hap. They will be here within hours."

Hap nodded and scratched the back of his head taking it all in. "Is this what it's all been about? The bugging of my home? My firing from Vector Data? The Feds? Will being pinched financially?"

"Difficult to explain," Blad replied. "

Hap let out an impatient sneer throwing out expletives under his breath. "You bugged my house, Blad?"

Franz spoke up directing a finger towards Blad. "Let me speak for our mutual friend. We had nothing to do with the bugging of your home, and are currently investigating the matter. Though not confirmed, we believe whoever is responsible tapped your home to get to me."

"That's right Hap," Blad said. "I'm afraid we don't have time to polish off a bottle of scotch discussing the matter as we are about to know how Colonel William Barrett Travis felt at the Alamo. If we can hold out a fraction of time as Colonel Travis's detachment, the Colombians will save all of our asses."

Franz stared Hap down as if the old man was Pop preparing to say something it would take years to understand.

"The criterion for truth Mr. Stoner, is whether it works for the person who holds it. Ask Mao, Stalin, and Hitler, to name a few. To the man, they held on to their truth to the grave costing hundreds of millions lives in the process."

Hap turned to Will speaking through the teeth with forced restraint. "You throwing in?" Laying the M4's stock over a shoulder like on a duck hunt and perfectly relaxed, Will said, "The old man had me citing the word gold."

A perplexed look appeared on Hap's angular face. He gave Blad a pat on his upper shoulder and pointed to the envelope. "What does reading this do for me now?"

Blad's thick lips pursed and he shook his head. "Nothing now."

LD, Hollywood, and Killer closed around the small school circle. "Something we need to know Hap?" Hollywood asked.

Will turned his head looking Hollywood square in the eyes. "You are about to fight the Sandinista army." His edgy eyes moved deliberately to each of the flier's worn faces.

"We already knew that was a possibility," Hollywood answered.

Killer Koch injected his presence. "The more birds and ships the Sandinista launch will give us more targets."

"Who do we have here?" Franz inquired.

Hollywood stared at the figure in the tuxedo, starting at the black Corfam shoes ending seconds later at the German's white widow's peak. "By the looks of it, we missed the party."

Hap gestured with his fingers pinched together as a football referee signaling a first down. "Franz von Bock, let me introduce you to Hollywood Hancock," he said then pointed to LD, and Killer Koch." The two pilots stepped forward each supporting bewildered looks to greet the German with a firm handshake along with a "what the hell" expression across their unshaven façade.

"Franz, I joined this group with the intention of taking what you have but if given the chance, I was going to take pleasure in killing you and your entire ilk."

A broad smile appeared on the old German's face. "Mr. Hancock, if I were you and chasing an old Nazi like me, I would do the same thing. But what's funny is that we are now allies."

Hollywood reeled.

Hap gave out a long yawn, stretching out both arms bent on getting the boys some sleep and catching a couple of winks himself. "Franz, I would like to park our birds in the hangar."

Will interrupted; "we will not wait for Hallesleven. The General and I have a little history. We will attack in depth, beginning in Nicaragua this afternoon and fight them all the way to the Fortress gates."

Hap turned slowly flashing an incredulous look from one side of his face to the other. "Are you nuts? We will be attacking a sovereign country."

"You did that when you deep sixed the trawler," Will uttered.

Hap eyed the tarmac below his feet and gently massaged his temples with the thumb and forefinger of his left hand contemplating possible repercussions. "Latin America is a powder keg worse than the '80s. There wasn't an honest leader in any of the countries. Spanish Main and Nicaragua were destined to meet but today, on their soil, had never been in the cards.

Will let the M4 drop to his side. "If you want to protect the Spanish Main, we need to hit these bastards first."

Franz stepped up gently peeling off his tie. "If I may, let me assist you in this endeavor."

Hollywood standing with his survival vest unzipped, flight suit zipped to the naval splaying a sweaty green tee shirt muttered, "Not sure what you could do unless you have a MEU hidden somewhere in your Fortress."

"You seem to dislike me, Mr. Hollywood. What is it you do in real life?"

Hap chortled, "Bastard wants to go to Hollywood. Johnny is a wannabe writer and one hell of a Cobra pilot."

Franz raised a boney forefinger to his lips. "An artist. Excellent profession Mr. Hollywood, if I might say." Franz turned to Will noticing Hap had walked away with a phone to his ear.

"If you and Mr. Stoner would be so kind as to take relief from your men and join me, I have something to show you. I will let you determine how best to utilize my resources."

Will turned to the befuddled Cobra pilots and pointed to the hangar. "Hangar the birds and grab some shut-eye. You're going to need it."

"Cock the aircraft, LD," Hap said speaking over a shoulder, meaning the pilot has run through the checklist where he only has to turn on the battery and toggle a starter to get the rotors turning. "There has to be a pilot's lounge somewhere inside this magnificent structure. I will have the little birds insert ground personnel and ordnance to give us a shore-based FARP."

"Don't bother with the FARP," Will said. "This will be one of the first targets Hallesleven secures."

Hap rejoined the group. The call to Carla had gone to voicemail. "Concur."

Will slowly turned aiming a stubby finger like a pistol up the two-lane and let his thumb fall to shoot. "Daniel Ortega may be a communist bastard but don't kid yourself, the greedy SOB is one smart hombre. He issued General Hallesleven the order to invade the island for the same reasons we stand on this airfield. Now we have to find a way to hold it."

53

Lonibelle

Roach's lantern-like jaw clenched around the half-chewed cigar as double shots of caffeine and adrenaline trumped the need for sleep. He cut his gaze to the small mission clock located on the bottom right-hand corner of the smart screen. "It's 0600, three hours into the mission, and not a single shot has been fired."

"I can think of worse things," Sluggo replied without looking over his shoulder.

Roach walked up anchoring next to Sluggo to focus on Magellan's feed. "I'm in a fucking place I despise… clueless."

"Stingray is two hours from her assigned position and we are an hour from Isle de San Andres harbor."

Roach's eyes cut over to KB. "Time since last SPOTREP?"

KB glanced down at a tablet laid out on the left side of the console. "Shaun is Johnny on the spot, every 15 minutes—but over an hour since we heard a peep from Hap or Will."

"Nothing from Blad?"

KB shook his head. "Negative."

Magellan's feed showed the Bluefields/El Bluff sector ripe with activity.

"The ruse is up," Roach said plainly as all their attention was on MI 8 Hips lined up along the airfield tarmac. "Each aircraft buttoned up and rotors not tied down telegraphed the birds were on call to launch with their human cargo inside. With armor and infantry scattered along the San Juan, the Sandinista may be preparing to strike with a helo borne operation and the northern force."

A line of three APC's motored into the light surf crawling up the ramp to enter the bowels of Arlen Siu.

Roach patted Sluggo's shoulder, "Get up to Puerto Cabezas."

"Cutting it close on fuel. You sure?"

The side of Roach's mouth twisted south. "Do I stutter? Get on it. I have to know what the northern force is up to."

Magellan banked hard to the North in compliance with Sluggo's control input and spoke in his Boston accent, "I have a TOT of 1 + 15."

Roach turned to KB. "I need comm with Hap or Wil—stat."

Leaning over to catch the last glimpse of Magellan's feed, KB nodded and settled back into his seat. He toggled to Satellite Communications.

54

Isle de San Andres
Von Bock private airfield

Bent at the waist to return to the limo's back seat, Franz froze and backed out. The sun had cleared the eastern horizon reflecting off the hangar roofs and lighting up the back of the limo. The German straightened over the open door to mediate an ongoing conversation. "Sorry to interrupt, Mr. Stoner, my airfield Operations Manager has been instructed to assist in anything you require. I will be flying my housekeeping staff off the island shortly so he is probably in the lounge with the pilots."

Hap turned as one of the hangar doors slowly rolled open revealing a Gulfstream G650. "Has anybody had communications with Lonibelle?"

Will and the Cobra crews shook their heads side to side. "Too quiet for my liking Colonel," Will answered.

"I want comm with Lonibelle. *Now.*"

"Maybe I can be of some assistance. Come with me, Mr. Stoner," Franz said.

Will gestured toward the Fortress.

"Alert status is fifteen minutes," Hap said.

"That shouldn't be a problem, Mr. Stoner," Franz said. "There is a direct line from the pilot's lounge to the Fortress."

"Get some rest," Hap said gesturing toward the aircrews.

LD acknowledged with extended fingers of his right hand just above the eyebrow in haphazard salute and strolled towards the hangar carrying a gait similar to Gary Cooper in High Noon. "I'm going to look for the Operations Manager." He pulled the 9mm from under his left shoulder jacking a round into the chamber. Not impressed with the armed figure sauntering toward the hangar, airport personnel walked each wing while the driver over the tug slumped over the steering wheel as the Gulfstream 650 slowly rolled from the hangar.

Hollywood and Killer sauntered unhurried to their bird to fire up the twin 1900 horse turbojet engines.

Easing behind the wheel Will turned to Hap, fast asleep in the passenger seat.

* * *

Lew tapped the eraser end of the pencil on the vessel's plot. With each turn of her single screw, Lonibelle drew closer as the "sea Gods" offered calm seas and a clear western horizon. Bent over he rested both elbows on the table when the phone by his right hip squawked. Without a glance, he removed the handset from the cradle.

"Bridge."

Roach's voice was on the other end. "There has been a change of plans." Roach had his forefinger resting on checkpoint Ford, a GPS fix of open water 45 miles northwest of Isle de San Andres City. "Need to be on station at 1400 hours. Have Stingray proceed to Bel Aire. I will have the little birds return to Mother and cover them up."

"Is that all," Lew replied.

"Out," Roach barked.

Lew ran his stubby forefinger from Stingray's current plot west of Lonibelle's position to Bel Aire forty-five miles west of Impala. He ran a straight edge to determine distance. He nibbled his narrow lower lip. "Machine Head would have to step on it to arrive on time." He said out loud. What the hell happened? Why would Lonibelle and Stingray be between Isle de San Andres and Nicaragua? He toggled the mixer switch above the handset to VHF and made a point to visit the Ops Center after giving Larson the change of plans.

* * *

Neither KB nor Sluggo fretted over Roach's continual outburst as he purposefully paced one side of the Ops center to the other. With each pass by a screen broadcasting Magellan's feed, he issued a quick glance, walking around Chewie and Love Doctor anchored behind Sluggo's chair. The replacement pilots kept their head in the game where if called, either pilot could strap an aircraft to their back and enter the fight without spending time to gain situation awareness.

"And to think we are now allied with the Colombian regulars stationed at the International Airport," Roach ranted. Cable Networks would be all over this story. He stopped in his tracks and slapped himself on the side of the head. "Shit," he said out loud.

Sluggo spun his Captain's chair around as Love Doctor and Chewie stepped to either side. Roach allowed his squared-off mug to loll to the side and popped a fresh cigar between his lips. He glanced over Sluggo's right shoulder to the drone's screen still sending video of jungle and beach as two Hinds filled the screen.

Sluggo swung the chair. "We have company!"

"Bring Magellan to Mother, Sluggo,"

Sluggo rammed throttle forward and switched off autopilot. Magellan's turbine-driven prop clawed for altitude as the drone entered a hard-climbing turn into the sun. "Fly as if your life depended on it, Magellan." Golf ball sized tracers blew past either side of the camera. He worked the camera to face the Hinds snouts closing in from Magellan's six.

"Break azimuth and plane," Roach called out. "She will never make the cloud bank. You gotta buy some time!"

"Concur," Sluggo replied, quickly dropping the nose to the horizon, and breaking hard left. He swung the camera off Magellan's nose.

KB gripped his seat as if strapped into the drone.

Smoke and veins of fire wicked from the glowing balls before evaporating into a bank of cumulus. Another burst followed passing closer than before.

Roach tapped Sluggo's shoulder. "Break hard right and climb to safety." Another burst passed low and to the left as Magellan's nose elevated and she clawed for the safety of the cumulus cloudbank.

Arlen Siu

Santiago entered Hallesleven's stateroom unannounced to find the general sleeping in the stateroom's lone bunk. Light from the hallway lit up the room, snapping the general's eyelids open. He slowly removed the reading glasses perched on the end his nose and turned on the small lamp hanging over his head. Slowly gathering up the reports resting on his chest, he swung his combat boots to the steel deck. Hallesleven's stomach growled. He hadn't eaten breakfast and it was close to lunchtime.

"Sorry General, it was just reported we shot down a drone snooping around the Northern assault group."

"Any markings?" he asked.

Santiago slowly shook his head. "Negative, General."

"Have our agents been able to find Mr. Kellogg."

"Negative, General."

He looked at the map taped to the steel bulkhead across the desk and scratched the back of his head. *Will Kellogg is a shrewd warrior and with his force on the island, I'm not going to allow them to consolidate their positions. Dislodging his troops would be like prying out a stubborn wisdom tooth. It would be painful through loss of life and worse, give time for the Columbians to enter the fray.*

"Santiago," Hallesleven's head turned slowly to his Chief of Staff. "The northern force will have to go on its own with the heliborne assault."

Santiago nodded, his jawline taut as a drum. Santiago snapped a sharp salute and left the room. Hallesleven reached over the desk to remove the handset. "Operator, get me a secure line to the President."

56

Isle de San Andres
von Bock private airfield

Hap stepped away from the limo to find Black Eddie leaning against the outer wall at the Fortress entrance. A toothpick dangled between his full lips.

"Ops wants you back on the knoll," Hap said. "You look on edge. Something on your mind?"

Eddie removed the toothpick and flicked it to Hap's feet.

"It's good to see you, Hap," Eddie replied. He turned to walk away but stopped. "Hap," he said without turning. He didn't say a thing and motioned for the other sapper to follow.

* * *

Twenty minutes later, Hap, Will, and Blad followed Franz into an elevator and the moment the polished doors closed, the elevator fell out from beneath their feet as the car was sucked several floors into the core of the island in mere seconds. Hap and Will maintained their side arms leaning against the back wall. Hap still carried the bowie knife under his armpit. Will left his M4 and ruck sitting in the old man's study. Blad had settled across from Hap and Will.

As the elevator doors pulled apart Franz held out a long arm to keep the door open to exit. "Gentlemen, I have assets available which can be of assistance. I devoted decades and countless millions countering Ortega, who is no different from the Scorpion. Latin and South America are cesspools. You couldn't fill a phone booth with honest politicians from both regions." Will's gaze met Hap's raised eyebrows as they trailed Blad from the elevator. Hap knew Scorpion's brother died suddenly. Will proffered a crooked smile, and then said, "Did you have Scorpion's brother killed?"

Franz said nothing.

Will then asked, "CIA?"

"Maybe," Franz answered.

Will glanced around uneasily with a look that looked like a question mark. He paused, and then said, "Contras?"

Franz allowed a smile to sneak out of his mouth. "The press and Democrats thought the money came from a few F-14 parts to Iran. Couldn't be farther from the truth."

"Iran Contra," Hap said cutting eyes between the two. He couldn't help but notice the similarity around their eyes. Round and large and both had piercing stares. The old man's face was thin with a sawed-off chin while Will's jawline was square, but both had the dimple in the chin.

"So it was you," Will said.

Franz nodded as he pulled his arm to allow the doors to close. "I was denied much of the exciting life since the war, always allowing my brother to handle such situations. He seemed to have a knack for these types of opportunities and grew our intelligence organization close to CIA. I will contact Major Ramos to prepare to repel a Nicaraguan invasion."

Will's head shook slowly already concluding Ramos would lead his men away from the action without firing a shot. "At least the slob will take the information up the chain of command before he runs into the jungle," Will said. "That being said, the Columbian military presence is better than a stick in the eye." *All too familiar with Ramos, if he died, what would become of the outstanding balance the Major maintained on his Buccaneer personal account?*

Franz smiled. "The turd is a notoriously shitty craps player but seemed to find a way to have a good-looking hooker hanging off either arm."

"Fucker always reminded me of William Holden's nemesis in the Wild Bunch. The swollen midsection and that lower button of his blouse that he couldn't button, to go with a stringy half-filled Fu Manchu and a gold-capped front tooth. Shouldn't have given him so much rope with his account."

As they talked, Hap noticed the soundproof glass. Six rows of workstations divided by two aisles housed at least 50 workstations. Blad had beat them into what appeared to be some sort of operations center shaking hands, yucking it up with controllers and radio technicians manning the consoles. Now he understood why the array of antennas, satellite dishes, and radars atop the fortress Citadel were there. *What kind of organization did Blad belong to?* Hap watched Franz place his thumb on a reader and the steel doors lock tripped.

"Mr. von Bock," a man that appeared to a supervisor said. He wore a headset and moved freely between the aisles stopping occasionally to bend down in front of a console to talk with its operator. Occasionally he would jack the end of his headset into the console and put a finger against the small microphone as he spoke.

"Morning, Motta. Anything I need to know about this morning?"

"You're going to love this one, Mr. von Bock," the supervisor promised. "We received an intercept where the Nicaraguan Air Force is claiming to have shot down a drone."

Franz turned to Will who twisted around hoping Hap could explain the radio intercept. "I'm assuming the craft is part of your operation?" Franz questioned.

Hap held out his Satellite phone. "May I?"

"Here," the supervisor called out handing Hap a phone jack. "Line ties you into the satellite dish topside." After jacking in the cable, Hap rested on the edge of an unoccupied console waiting for Roach to answer his call.

"Well it's about time, dickwad," Roach blurted. "I feel privileged you could finally find time to talk."

"Cut the bullshit, I need a status on Magellan."

"Since you gotta know, a couple of Sandinista Hinds made a run to blow her from the sky."

Hap's head snapped around like an owl in Will's direction. Franz stood on the other side of the room talking presumably to Major Ramos. "You sure?"

"You heard me, go to back up IP and I'll send video feed."

He tapped the supervisor's shoulder, pointing to the Cat 6 connection. "Can you throw my feed on one of the screens?" The supervisor acted disinterested as if the act was small change.

He nodded. "Of course."

"Excellent," Hap replied handing the fellow with a slight German accent the handset.

A group of four 42-inch digital screens in the middle of over fifty 40-inch monitors displaying numerous ports, weather, and news channels from at least eight countries dropped Fox News. Open sky appeared with towering cumulus in the background.

Golf ball-size tracers threw off flickers of flame marking its deadly track. The rounds vanished into the same billowing cumulus Magellan's single prop clawed sky for. Radio operators mesmerized by the firework display grabbed their seats, others their consoles as the horizon on the screen leveled suddenly, then tilted 90 degrees to the left.

Sluggo is maneuvering, Hap thought. *Good Man.*

Will joined Hap to take in the show. Seconds later, the screen rocked 90 degrees to the right leaving the techs clutching armrests and tabletops in a stabilizing gesture. The room had become a flight simulator giving the participants the same sensations as if they were actually in the cockpit, minus the G-forces and engine clatter. The drone's rounded nose rocked up towards the heavens. More flaming balls appeared in their view passing below the fuselage before the screen went into the goo.

As triple canopy conceals a Recon Team, entering the cloud cover concealed Magellan's radar-less aggressors. Without radar and with their prey inside the clouds, the hunters were as blind as Schlonger and his women after a good happy hour excursion. "Can the drone make Mother?

"Barring a change in the winds, I think we are okay," Roach answered. "Engine instruments look fine and controls seem to be fine. We dodged a bullet. *Literally.*"

The video feed verified what Hap's instincts had already told him. He looked towards Will and the old man with raised eyebrows, giving a friendly wink. "Magellan lives."

The German stepped between Hap and Will.

"Delightful to hear your Magellan survived the attack. Gentlemen, Ramos has been notified of the impending attack."

Will let out a chuckle. "I bet that slob is on the phone to Bogota as we speak, searching for a place to hide."

A voice came from the technician where Franz had been standing. "Mr. von Bock, Ramos is on the line to his Headquarters in Bogota. Do you want me to pipe in the audio?"

"Jeez," Hap observed. What else was his new best friend going to pull out of his bag of tricks? Then it donned on him. As far back as the early meetings in Richardson, the son of a bitch had drawn them in as if he had planned *their* operation.

He watched Blad exit through a door different from where they entered. It had to be a long shot that the gold was inside these walls. With the power, this man held, the king's ransom could be anywhere in the world.

Franz looked at Hap and then to Will shrugging. "Shall we?"

Hap's and Will's eyes went wider. No false bravado overwrote the sinking feeling boiling deep down inside. *Should they be surprised of Blad's ties to the German?* Franz Krueger had built a Global Conglomerate, short for empire. The depth and breadth of his tentacles touched all corners of the globe in a myriad of business endeavors. As for this mission, for all practical purposes, the gold was lost. Bashing his head through the glass would feel better than his present condition. Will's M4 might be in the German's study but the 9mm slung low on his right hip and multiple frag grenades hanging from his web gear could be problematic for all in the room.

Franz's fingers snapped and pointed to a technician in the sea of technicians. The tech's fingers danced across the keyboard stopping when Ramos's conversation entered the room.

Hap detected the faces around the room grow long. One of Franz's long fingers gently massaged his upper lip. "What the hell are they saying, Will?" Hap quizzed.

Arms crossed leaning against a console, Will's head nodded slowly taking in the rapid Spanish. He looked over to Hap. "Ramos was just informed by his direct report in Bogota he would be on his own for hours. Ramos has suddenly lost the enthusiasm to be a Commanding Officer. The Major was ordered to hold until the last bullet and last man."

57

Isle de San Andres
The Knoll

Eddie's dark eyes tracked to the direction of Shaun's binoculars. He twisted a toothpick between his front teeth.

"Finally," Lowering the filed glasses Shaun called out in a New York accent, "Glad the tractor trailers are rolling our way. The heavy iron will tunnel through this lava rock like shit through a goose."

Not a word uttered among the team members as they slowly came to their feet. The column with an F350 dually on point carried six souls in back wearing hard hats snaked away from the plant parking lot. Located to the left of the departure end of runway 12, the five-vehicle convoy worked passed the bridge. A second Ford dually towed a trailer carting a front loader with a backhoe attached. Three freightliners followed with a colossal trencher chained to one trailer, a midsize bulldozer to the other, and tail end Charlie's trailer was stacked with prefabricated concrete slabs used as hiway dividers.

Shaun raised the glasses back to his sunburn brow. "Now we will need the two Ma Deuce and recoilless rifles the Roach promised."

Eddie pushed the bush hat back until the sweat covered floppy squatted on the crown of his head. "Seems to be a lot of activity and firepower for a recon position."

"Not going to disagree," Shaun replied allowing the glasses to drop around his neck by its strap. "We will also receive an additional fire team."

Eddie removed the bush hat and slapped against his camo pants. He shook his head slowly looking towards his scarred combat boots. "Somebody is expecting big things from this position."

"I suggest we take special care with the camouflage to be as natural as possible. We can only hope to get the first salvo in before all hell breaks loose on this hill."

Eddie let out a grunt and ran a dirty fingernail along a map he pulled from the cargo pocket of his fatigues. He tapped the area between the Refinery and knoll. "With any luck, the flyboys knock a couple of Hips out of the sky. From the moment we engage this position will become a pretty popular place." Eddie didn't hide the frown spread across his face as worked the map back to the cargo carrier.

"Yeah, air and ground," Shaun said peeking over Black Eddie's hand. "We have to get the initial surprise. It would be a shame for all of us to die in place without firing a shot."

* * *

Hallesleven dropped the phone into its cradle pulsing up smoke rings, preoccupied with President Ortega's last question. "Should there be any concern about Colombia's military capability?" Much larger and formidable, he wanted to say *jack shit* but refrained. Given the time Che Guevara needed to complete their mission, lines of communication of 500 miles would be a backbreaker for the Colombians. The trick is not to allow them to gain a foothold on the archipelago.

Maybe give the Chinese a call to put their submarine into the game. The Chinese were knee-deep into this thing with the loss of its commandos. A submarine from unknown origins in the game would end Colombians resolve in retaking the island short term until they figured out the political landscape. Like the Falklands to the Argentinians, the little archipelago was not worth losing its Navy over.

Rocking out of the chair, Hallesleven casually opened the door and stretched his back. He made a mental note to take a few ibuprofens to help ease his stiffening back. The stress was taking its toll. "Colonel Santiago, can you join me please." Not bothering to close the door, he moved to his right and felt around in his dap kit hanging on a hook to the right side of the sink.

"Yes, General," Santiago said standing at attention.

Hallesleven washed down five pills. "Nicaragua will never win global favor with this expedition."

Santiago shook his head in agreement. "No, Sir. I think we are up against the Americano dogs and should reconsider."

The general's chair creaked as he fell back into the seat. "I'm getting a similar knot in my stomach similar to those years ago going up against Will Kellogg and Commander Zero along the San Juan."

"Somebody propped up that son of a bitch during the revolution?" Santiago replied. "Is Crosscut worth jeopardizing 35 years of the nation's blood and treasure? You have already lost a nephew."

"We have gone too far to call it off, Santiago. When the first Sandinista boot touches Colombian soil, I expect the seas around Isle de San Andres will crawl with Colombian naval assets above and below the surface within 24 to 36 hours. My biggest fear is they move to blockade Nicaragua. Our people already go without enough to eat."

Santiago nodded. "What does the President think, General?"

He pulled a chewed up piece of tobacco and twisted it back and forth between thumb and his pointing finger. "What success brings to Nicaragua, attaches to the President, his wife, and unfortunately blinds them both."

Santiago laughed. "You mean what it puts in his and his first lady's bank accounts."

Hallesleven's dark eyes drifted away from the cigar to Santiago. "I could have you shot for that comment."

Santiago broke his chain of thought, "Yes, General you could."

Hallesleven nodded knowing it was time to issue the order for the hour of the initial landing. "Give the Che Guevara order, Colonel. L Hour is 1500 hours for the Northern Group. The Southern Group can hopefully follow within hours."

"Yes, General, will that be all?"

The general nodded at the same time Santiago turned to issue the order. "Oh, Colonel?"

The Chief of Staff stopped in the doorway, initiating an about face. "Yes, General?"

"Put a little fire in Colonel Torres. We need to be in a position to support the Northern Force as soon as possible." Santiago clicked his heels. "Yes, General."

The chair emitted squeaks as Hallesleven swiveled and tossed down the cup of cold coffee. He faced the map with the realization there was no turning back. They had cast the die.

58

Fortress
Operations Center

Thirty minutes after entering the German's Operation Center, Franz palmed the handprint system energizing a full color integrated scramble keypad. He punched the security code and the gold elevator doors slid closed in a whishing sound.

As the floor fell below their feet, Hap could feel the sleep deprivation and the need for more than the fighter nap he snagged between the airfield and Fortress weigh in. BA and Schlonger were still airborne and would go into a brief for the attack in hours. Not one man within the group reported even one bellyache, or request to reposition. All eyes and thoughts focused on the common goal, to meet an overwhelming air and ground assault. The elevator doors separated, revealing what looked like a scene taken straight from a James Bond movie.

Blue-eyed personnel outfitted in dark jumpsuits and blonde hair slicked back by sweat, crossed in front of the doors rapidly from either direction. Expressions of purpose remained fixed across an obvious European *appearance* and a WWII era German U-Boat served as a backdrop. Moored to a concrete dock as if in Lorient in early 1945 was the world's first true submarine. With the chambers walls and ceiling encased in concrete, the cavernous grotto could easily hold six more submersibles of similar size. Even with the large ventilation shafts moving fresh air throughout the underground dock, the room was warm and humid.

Franz and Will exited the elevator. The instant they cleared the opening, Hap bound out as if a kid in a candy store. His blue eyes darted back and forth in an instrument scan not allowing either eye to lock onto any one object for more than a blink. On the way to the submarine's gangway, his heart seemed to leap from its chest cavity as he stepped around a torpedo nestled in its carrier. A watch officer manned the conning tower with an arm extended towards shirt-less personnel straining to maneuver a 517lb Mk 46 torpedo through the forward torpedo hatch. Cartons of oranges, apples, bread, meats, and other provisions passed between crewmember's hands and up the gangway, vanishing through the boat's galley hatch.

Caught in the moment, a technician on his way to deliver a piece of test gear to a specialist standing over an open torpedo access panel brushed past Hap Stoner. Neither man said a word as an overhead crane's hook swung back and forth precariously close overhead. In line for loading, eight other torpedoes rested safely in carriages on dock going through last minute checks before transporting to the boat.

Hap knew from a voracious reading habit the weapon system went through continual checks of its batteries, propellant, and firing mechanisms before the eventual release to the vessel's torpedo men. Aft, crewmen stripped to their skivvies closely monitored fueled the numerous petrol tanks. Pallets with provisions stacked to eye level continued to enter the human chain up the gangplank, one carton at a time.

He maneuvered through the maze of personnel, weapons, and crates to join Will, who sat on a 55-gallon drum fixed in deep conversation with Franz. Will's rumbling voice reverberated off the walls and ceiling. "So, if I heard you correctly, this boat is going into the fight?"

They were adjacent to a machine shop entrance, the German nodded. "That is correct, Will. I would hope we can take care of most, if not all, of the Sandinista surface assets and if need be, Sandinista allied vessels."

Hap gave a silent *hip hip hooray* hoping to get a ride sooner than later. Will's eyes cut to Hap, who responded with a nod and added, "The Sandinista armor capability would be neutered if the Russian LST's never made landfall. We could deal with the infantry and air elements piecemeal until the Colombian cavalry appeared over the horizon.

Will bit his lower lip, "We will have to blow the fuel farm at both airports, Colonel."

Franz nodded. "Do what you believe needs to be done. Fuel tanks are easy to replace."

Hap said nothing. They had to remove the refueling capability for the Sandinista on Isle de San Andres.

Franz reached into his pocket, fumbling around until retrieving a mobile device. Attentive to what Hap said; he shook his head and returned the phone into the same pocket after offering a curt "thank you." "Gentlemen, the Sandinista have launched helicopters from Puerto Cabezas. Numerous vessels are steaming out of the channel."

Will's stubby fingers worked over his square chin as he felt Hap tapping his shoulder.

"We have to speak Will," Hap said, tugging Will into the machine shop by his vest.

Shoulder to shoulder, Hap leaned in to speak in his ear. "Have you found it odd we have put eyes on everything except what we came for? My guess is the cache is not in the Fortress we plan to defend to the death."

Will peered into Hap's bloodshot eyes. "And your buddy, Blad, saunters around like he owns the place. Is this a set up?"

Hap knew Blad well enough to know stupidity did not fit his panache. If the wise one had used the Borderline incident as a loss leader only to pull a double cross, Hap would beat Will putting a well-placed round between his friend's bushy eyebrows. His thoughts went back to the envelope. "This script was orchestrated and financed by the German." Will nodded and Hap could see he was attempting to work for a time before he spoke. Neither noticed Franz in the entryway.

The German stepped between the two waiting for a chance to speak. He placed both hands firmly over each of their rounded shoulders pulling them close. "It's best we get to work. There is an invasion to repel."

59

Fortress

"If you would please," the German's oversized hand gestured through the elevator doors.

Hap waited for Will to follow Franz onto a 14-foot wide spherical landing. To the right was a wooden door held up by hinges that could have passed as the original. To the left were four polished steel doors.

"Pirates took 13 steps from the dungeon to the torture chamber on the other side of this wall." His hand drifted right then flipped over to the polished doors. "Victims' screams could not be heard by inmates housed in the corridors behind the doors to your left."

Hap and Will remained silent, their eyes fixed on the polished steel protecting something of obvious importance.

* * *

Major Montemayor surveyed an empty sea from an altitude of 100 feet as the lead aircraft making up the northern assault groups air element raced to its objective. In less than an hour, the three elements of four MI-8 Hip aircraft would insert the Company sized force tasked with securing the airport. Rehearsed more times than Montemayor could count, they would remember today as one of the most important days of the Revolution and ensure deep selection to full colonel.

The son of Managua's mayor, Montemayor glanced over to the junior copilot, the twenty-four-year-old Lieutenant sat stiff as a board. "Lieutenant, you have the aircraft." He gestured toward the water with gloved fingers. "Remain on course and go to fifty feet."

The young copilot nodded tautly and slowly lowered the collective. Montemayor pointed at a commercial airliner high overhead at 10 o'clock passing a Gulfstream, trailing spiraling contrails in the opposite direction. "Probably the last jet to be landing at Isle de San Andres for a while." Montemayor chuckled through the ICS in an attempt to loosen up the newbie.

* * *

As the little birds rotor wash smacked his frontside, Shaun clutched the bush hat propped back revealing his receding hairline. After landing between the knoll and road, both crew chiefs stepped away from the skids bent at the waist until clearing the spinning rotor arc. Visors down, both aircrew scanned the landscape.

Eddie screamed over the sound of the spinning rotors, going over last-minute details folded the map, and then waved them towards the waiting helos.

Eddie's lips formed words made up of four-letter words as the team scampered down the knoll. He stopped and took a knee ensuring the sticks boarded the appropriate helos. Turning to look up the knoll, Shaun stood with bush hat in one hand and M4 raised over his head shaking it like a stick. Eddie replied with a salute then ducked beneath the rotors sliding into the lead aircraft.

Once the skids broke ground, both helos pedaled turned into the southeasterly wind. The aircraft slowly air taxied until transitional lift where each aircraft violently shook off earth's gravitational forces, lifting sluggishly into the sky.

"Knoll inbound. Two birds," Big Alabama reported to Lonibelle.

"Roger," Roach replied. "We have a problem."

Both BA and Foxy's heads momentarily looked to the other before BA's brown eyes went forward. "Ready to copy." The little birds initiated a shallow turn to the west. Staying south of the city, he pointed the nose of the aircraft to arrive at the ridgeback north of the dormant volcano.

"Kang's significant other landed at the airport 15 minutes after the hour."

"What's wrong with that," he replied in his Alabama drawl.

Roach stood over Sluggo's shoulder watching the formation of Hips advance from the west. Ducking his head upon hearing the reply, Roach let out a "jeeeeeeez," over the air. Sluggo shook his head throwing Magellan in a hard bank to the west as Roach responded, "It wouldn't be a problem, but it just happens to be the same airport you are about to blow the shit out of and the Sandinista will occupy."

"State intentions," Big Alabama replied, thinking as always Carla with her shapely ass and ample stores topside should have met him instead of Hap. Not sure how many times he told her the same in front of Hap during numerous happy hours. The Nomads went as far as making her an honorary Nomad. Flight Equipment altered a flight suit to include a leather nametag above her left breast and squadron patch with the smoking Camel over her right. Strategically darted to bring out her God-given female qualities, Carla drew the wandering eye of many an aviator throwing back beers in the vicinity of the Nomads. Of course, all of this went away when most of the squadron had to resign after the border incident.

"Shadow Operations assured us she will be at the base of the tower in twenty minutes. Grab her and bring her to Mother."

He looked back to see Eddie listening with a headset nodding. "I got it BA."

Reaching the ridgeback, he banked hard to the north leveling off at treetop level with Schlonger in a loose cruise off to his right.

60

Isle de San Andres International Airport

A quick scan of the manifest bent over the check-in counter, Captain Cruz couldn't help but notice the attractive woman bent over with her shapely features directed his direction as she wrestled her laptop to insert into an overstuffed carry case. The gentleman he was and with a 48-hour layover in front of him, he eased over to offer assistance.

He wasn't surprised to see the American passenger looked as good from the front as she did from that splendid rear view.

"May I help you," he asked in broken English.

She turned her head and smiled. "Thank you, but I think I have it now."

Cruz extended his hand. "Let me get that computer in the bag for you." His hands worked to squeeze a couple of folders closer together and remove tubes of facial makeup stuck midway into the suitcase. "I think I have it."

Carla returned a smile and nodded. "Whatever you say, you're the Captain."

Her deep blue eyes and loose-fitting V-cut blouse was prime real estate with which to spend the next two days.

"Do you do this for *all* your female passengers," she asked quizzically.

He offered a smile and answered quickly. *Conversation was the first step on getting into the door*, he thought. *No pun intended.* "A few. I have to get back to my weight and balance."

When she'd entered the plane, Cruz stood between the cockpit and galley greeting passengers. She smiled the moment their eyes met, and the woman who could be the next Mrs. Cruz made the right turn down the aisle with the bag in tow. By the way the bag banged against seats on either side of the aisle, professionally, Cruz knew this hotty did more than read a few magazines.

Captain Cruz terminated Aero Mexico Flight 775 speaking over the main cabin intercom, "Thank you for flying Aero Mexico and enjoy your stay in Isle de San Andres." With the brake set and shut down checklist verified complete by the First Officer, Captain Cruz removed his headset, released his harness and vacated his seat as if evacuating from a cockpit fire. He situated a shoulder against the open doorway to the cockpit, his dark eyes shifted toward the passenger seated in 3A.

"Excuse me," he said to a newlywed couple as he slid into the line of deplaning passengers and reached out to his new found friend, "May I help?"

Looking over her brow, Carla blew her flowing brown hair from her eyes while issuing a drop-dead smile, "Why thank you, Captain. That is twice you helped me today."

"That's what Captain's do," Cruz replied and politely moved around another couple couple to set her bag in the jetway.

She extended a hand with recently polished fingernails. "Carla McCreery," she said. She vanished down the jetway mingling into the flow of passengers. The lady had her blue jeans on and knew how to swing those curvy hips. He entered the terminal and saw her flag an airport employee holding up a sign "Carla" inside the terminal. She approached the man holding the sign.

Two helos appeared out of the corner of his eye. A quick turn in place and the second aircraft peeled off heading towards two fuel trucks parked to fuel his bird. The lead aircraft presented its underside, turning abruptly away from the terminal scampering in the direction of the fuel farm. Cruz thought it was maybe an exercise by the Colombian Military. Men were dangling out of the jet-black helo's cabin with rifles and combat boots resting on running boards.

* * *

Carla caught a glimpse of the helos, *Was this another Hap Stoner welcome?* Through the years, it was common for him to drop his Cobra down wherever she was. CLE course in San Antonio, or a lecture in Gulf Shores, he would exit the bird with it idled down as the other pilot held the controls. Approaching her with his John Wayne strut, she always broke away from the pack to greet her man. She rapidly approached the friendly man holding the card. "I'm Carla," she said slurring a bit. She gestured her chin over her shoulder towards the helos. The young man's eyes widened and dropped the card to the polished floor. Excitedly he said, "Is there anybody else Ma'am, because we must go *now!*"

She considered how Hap knew of her arrival but wanted to maintain the moment, "Whatever you ask, Señor. Is Señor Hap in the car?" she asked, smearing every word.

The middle aged man's chin shook rapidly side to side. "I know no Hap, Senorita." His round face suddenly appeared flush. As if a ghost stood over her shoulder, his large brown eyes opened ever wider pushing a single brow close to a combed over brow.

Storage tanks on the other side of the airfield erupted into orange and black flame sending dark black plumes of smoke into an otherwise clear Caribbean sky. The report reverberated through the terminal blowing panels of glass and dropping ceiling tile onto the terminal's marble floors. Panic filled passengers screamed, dropped their carry bags in place, and scampered around and over passengers who squatted or laid flat and covered their heads.

Covered in shards of glass, but otherwise unhurt, Captain Cruz came to a knee and turned to glance into the smoke rushing through the hole that used to be a 12' x 12' piece of glass. Two men jumped from a helo parked 30 feet behind his aircraft's tail. Her escort holding the sign 'Carla' dropped her bag and vanished into the jet way.

Cruz put a hand on either shoulder. "Carla," he said in broken English, "the airfield is under terrorist attack. We have to find cover now!"

Armed men exited the helo from either side with their weapons wedged into their shoulder to cover two men racing across the tarmac. Both had satchels slung over a shoulder and shot into the air to send wannbe heroes retreating to cover.

Cruz and Carla moved awkwardly through the terminal complicated by the discarded luggage and carry-on bags. They pulled around a corner into a landing leading to a door propped open by a case of bottled water marked *Employees Only*. Her once well-placed hair frazzled, and makeup streamed down her narrow face. Cruz led Carla down a flight of stairs by her hand. He opened the metal door to see a black helicopter air taxi to the base of the tower.

He tugged her along outside of the terminal until an armed militant with a face darkened by camo paint angled for an intercept.

"Carla!" the man yelled moving his rifle deliberately for hostiles.

She stopped. Her's and Cruz's eyes met. The soldier reached out with his left handballing it into a fist. She had seen this enough in her years with Hap. She froze in place. Armed men began to form a perimeter while another, as if rehearsed, moved down the tail boom past the whirling tail rotor to cover the rear. Cruz looked at the man racing in their direction and broke away as a formation of helicopters as she had never seen roared over the tower.

"He is with me," Carla screamed, pointing to where Cruz had vanished. Eddie moved past a burning truck tire and, without asking permission, scooped her over his left shoulder. He gripped his M4 pistol grip in his right hand to shoot on the move and clutched the back of her knees with his left.

The fighters providing cover collapsed back to the helo as Eddie ran with Carla over his shoulder, then passed under the rotor arc. Big Alabama's rounded cheeks fixed below his dark visor came into view as Eddie turned to the side to flop inside the cabin. For reasons that she couldn't explain, she held her scream as the security detail quickly boarded.

61

Beaver Flight

"Give me a couple," Eddie screamed. BA was looking over his inside shoulder growing antsier by each turn of the rotors as Schlonger passed on the right entering translational lift. Eddie hadn't bothered with the cranial with the radio instead attempted to situate Carla into an already crowded cabin.

"I have tac lead, BA," Schlonger said as the bird shivered past.

"Roger," Big Alabama replied as casual as asking the cute bartender for her telephone number. "I'm heavy. Give me a few knots." He did a quick glance out of the corner of his visor towards the cabin to ensure Eddie had clamped a gunner's belt around her upper body.

The moment Eddie pulled the cranial over his ears he lowered the microphone. "Clear to lift."

BA pulled collective to his armpit and the small turboshaft engine delivered enough torque to the drooping rotor head for the skids to break ground by mere inches. With each forward nudge of the cyclic, BA put concrete between the wavering helicopter and the fuel trucks. He eased in right pedal to give additional power to the rotor head by flattening tail rotor pitch, which conveyed power saved to the rotor head.

Foxie's voice came over the intercom with a sense of urgency. "Hey, BA… one of the pax held up one finger."

BA said nothing but moved the stick slowly to maintain the rounded off nose just above the horizon. Overweight with a slight tailwind was no place to be, but a smile appeared below the darkened visor as the helo vibrated violently sloshing through the transitional lift. BA held on as the helo clawed for airspeed versus gaining altitude.

"Damn," Eddie yelled. The detonators went off on both fuel trucks engulfing the 737 in flames.

BA worked the aircraft to gain position on Schlonger's wing as they passed the beach to open water. "How she doing?"

"Sulking," Eddie replied. "She has her face buried into the palms of both hands but knows we are friends of Hap, which make us her friends.

He felt Foxie tap his left shoulder and point to 10 o'clock. "Flight of Hips, BA."

* * *

As he led the Sandinista air assault crossing the beach, a plume of orange and black smoke in the vicinity of the International Airport startled Montemayor. As the point of the beach was their IP, the flight broke up into four-plane divisions racing to pre-assigned LZ's. On short final, he could see a Hughes 500's flying to the north while another slowly lumbered in pursuit.

As his flight landed in tactical formation to give each door gunner preplanned sectors of fire, the assault troops raced down the ramp. Montemayor's division carried a reinforced platoon tasked to seize the terminal along with the tower. The second division mission was the fuel farm but with the tanks spewing out flames and black smoke, their mission had gone up in smoke.

"Bravo flight, seize any available fuel trucks," Montemayor transmitted. Somebody or something was one step in front of them. Fuel trucks were already burning next to a 737 whose wing tips lay on the ground after each wing root burned through. The third division was to land near the Defense Forces barracks to neutralize the Colombian threat.

They would never know that contrary to orders from higher headquarters, their commanding officer led the island Defense Forces in their retreat to San Andres City..

Montemayor barked into his mike, "Bravo Flight, detach a section and intercept the helo's departing to the north." Seconds passed as he considered the men riding atop the running boards. No doubt, they were the enemy. The next order was easy. "Intercept and destroy."

"Roger," came the reply. Upon the last boot leaving the ramps the twin Klimov engines driving each aircraft delivered the 1950 shaft horsepower required to give chase. Each aircraft's ramps closed while the two aircraft entered a right climbing turn as their troops vanished into the base of the tower.

62

Beaver Flight

The Carribean's humid air whipping through the cabin tossed Carla's long mane about. With her back against the cabin's aft bulkhead, her knees were taut beneath her pointed chin as she scraped at the dried mascara tattooed to her high set cheeks.

Eddie twisted his boots from the running board and rolled back to check on their special passenger. He gently placed a pair of filthy hands on either shoulder and as she raised her head, revealing a pair of bloodshot eyes. He pushed his mike away from his lips and yelled into her ear. "Are you ok?" He waited for a second, and she greeted him with a pleasing smile and thumbs up as a grimy hand pulled him around by his vest.

"Trouble!" Tommy yelled.

Eddie lowered the mike to his lips. "BA, we have two Hips closing rapidly from our four o'clock." Even from a distance, the 12.7mm gun protruding from the rounded nose became more ominous as the void in airspace closed rapidly.

BA torqued his neck right around his shoulder and didn't hesitate on the call. "Beaver flight, bandits 4 o'clock. Break right. I have lead."

Eddie flopped back on the cabin floor and pulled Carla into a spoon position as the bird heaved over on its right side. A burst of 12.7mm tracers streaked wide passed the plane as the helo began a turning climb. BA's call gave the advantage to the good guys, as the Sandinista rotor disc was sandwiched between the little birds and Sandinista door gunners.

"At your four, BA," Schlonger reported. "Bandits have door gunners."

"Tally," Big Alabama replied snap rolling into a hard-left descending turn to gain the Sandinista's six. "Mayday, mayday, mayday," BA announced on the tactical frequency. "Beaver flight has special pax but engaged with two enemy Hips."

"Bandits initiated a split turn," Schlonger reported calmly as the Russian built helos turned away from the other.

"Stay with me Schlonger. Dash-two is ours. Engaging!" Eddie watched over Carla's shoulder as BA lined his eyesight to the X on the windscreen. Simple but effective, the black grease pencil would put rounds on or near the target every time. "Going hot," BA announced.

Before BA could squeeze the trigger, a long burst from Schlonger's guns streaked past the starboard side. Pieces of rotor blade and fuselage flew past either side of the open cabin with some of the smaller airborne shrapnel glancing off the bird's rounded canopy with a deep thud. He raised on an elbow in time to see the Hip's wingman initiate a descending turn. Brass expelled from both cabin doors clanged off the aluminum deck as team members squeezed off three round bursts as fast as their trigger finger could pull.

"Dash-two is bugging out," BA barked in anticipation as dash one rolled wings level, again looking to gain position to engage.

A burst of tracer passed low. "Beaver flight, split turn… go!" Eddie clamped around Carla's waist knowing enough that BA and Shlonger were turning from the other giving the bandit a choice of one aircraft to engage or if smart, withdraw from the fight.

"Now pick your poison," BA called out. "Pick a target or bug out." If he chose a target, the freed-up pilot needed to gain an angle to kill one of Beaver flight before they could place a kill shot on their wingman.

"BA, they are going to fight," Schlonger said. "You have a bandit turning with you."

"Roger," Big Alabama replied as Foxie exited the passenger seat, released the M60 from storage, and attached his gunner's belt to the floor ring next to Carla's ankle.

"Coming around," Schlonger transmitted. "He is coming in for the kill BA. Dash-two is wavering to our 9 o'clock long. No factor."

* * *

"Has Hap diverted?" Roach called out standing over Lew Eglin's dining room table. .

KB answered without turning from the console. "10 minutes ago."

"Magellan has trapped on Stingray and will be turned in 20 minutes," Sluggo announced. He disconnected his headset from the jack on the right side of his armrest pushing away from the Captain's chair.

Roach, still wearing a headset, leaned over the table to place a small ship on the map between Puerto Cabeza and the airfield. "Where in the hell is Hap?" he barked to no one specifically when Hap's voice came across the squawk box.

* * *

"Target in sight. Hollywood, spread right...go." Kang flight raced toward the sound of the guns.

"Range?" LD asked.

Hap kept the crosshairs on target gently gripping the joystick between right thumb and forefinger. "Five thousand meters. We engage at forty-five hundred meters and hopefully get their gunner's attention with the back blast. On the outside edge of the envelope but closure rate will bring us in range."

"Roger that," LD said.

Hap had used this tactic before while engaging a platoon of Iraqi tanks south of Baghdad. He shot the TOW at 5500 meters and out of effective range. Out of nowhere, an H46 on a medevac accompanied by a section of UH -1N's appeared in the scope. Hap instructed LD to press and flew the missile underneath the flight of friendlies to allow the closure rate to bring the tank in range. From the sight picture of the Huey's in his scope as the missile streaked underneath the skids, Hap took away that he could have put the missile in any of the aircraft's cabin doors.

"Go common," Hap announced over the inter-flight frequency. "BA, on my call, break right. Schlonger, go high. Hollywood standby for a shot if our missile goes stupid."

* * *

BA glanced over his shoulder reminiscent of the late nights at the Kadena O'Club when running from the parking lot with a jealous B52 pilot hot on his heels.

"Bandit is jinking with us," Foxie said balancing precariously in the cabin with the M60's stock wedged into a shoulder.

"Schlonger is doing his job," BA said.

Foxie's head continued to look back past the tail rotor. "Persistent son of a bitch."

The Sandinista aircrew continued to work for the kill, but between each of BA's erratic moves and bursts from Schlonger's guns, the Hip's nose gunner couldn't get a good angle for a kill shot.

Sweat rolled freely down BA's forehead burning his blood-shot eyes. He contemplated wiping away the acidic irritant, but both hands remained occupied with buying time, which gave all on board life. The cavalry was just over the hill.

※ ※ ※

Kang Flight

Hap's left forefinger squeezed the trigger switch the moment the digital range display passed forty-five hundred meters. "Missile away," he reported while finessing the joystick to maintain the crosshairs on the right door gunner's window. Even as the Nicaraguan pilot maneuvered to avoid Schlonger's short burst, Hap held the X on the Hip with little difficulty. "Thirteen seconds, BA. Missile tracking nicely."

Hap started counting down over the air. "Beaver, break in five… four… three… two… one. Break right!" BA snap rolled the aircraft and climbed. Skillful to this point, the Nicaraguan pilot followed his prey up the ladder.

"Bandit is dead to right," Hap said to LD. "Three seconds to impact."

Hap followed the missile's exhaust until the nozzles vanished into the hole punched through the HIP's thin skin. A 13l-B warhead detonated behind the cockpit ejecting flame, helicopter parts, and a headless gunner from the gunner's window. Within a blink of the eye, the Hip's transmission ripped away from its mounts sending the rotorcraft tumbling nose over tail awash in flames.

"BA, your six is clear," Hap announced.

"His wingman is bugging out," Schlonger reported.

"Thanks, Kang," BA said. "Now I can wipe the crap out of my flight suit. I owe you one."

"You have an additional passenger, BA?"

"Affirmative, Kang. I still have the bruises she hammered into my back hauling her away at Columbus." A wide grin appears under BA's dark visor. The little lady would get the color back in her face and then put a size six cowboy boot up Hap's narrow ass. The one thing he knew, Hap Stoner wouldn't care, she was safe and if anyone were going to put a boot where the sun didn't shine, he'd want it to be Carla.

"Roger that, BA," Hap replied. "Kang flight, pick up a five and seven on Beaver flight. Mother, mission complete. Checking in with four chicks."

Four helos skirted low across the Caribbean back to Lonibelle with their backs against a western sun. Hap and Hollywood lazily crisscrossed BA's six to ensure there'd be no more Sandinista heroes for the remainder of this sortie.

63

Stingray

A sliver of light extended through Larson's stateroom as Doc slowly opened the door. A familiar voice sounded down the dimly lit passageway.

"Hey, Doc," JMan called out. "Larson called down to the chow hall to tell me to get my ass to his stateroom to lend you a hand."

Doc looked over a shoulder with an extended finger to his lips. He exhaled lightly.

Larson's rack highlighted a shapely figure furrowed in a fetal position. "Xanax is like the Duracell Bunny, just keeps on working. She has been down for four hours and still wore her boots."

JMan ducked his six-foot-five-inch frame into the room as Doc looped her purse over a shoulder then gingerly scooped her into his arms. "What is going on?"

"Hap wants her off the boat," Doc answered heaving her up to get a better hold on her body. "Now stay close and keep her head from banging against the bulkheads."

Without a word of protest, Carla sighed and gracefully wrapped both arms around Doc Perry's neck.

Sweeping her around a couple of corners, with JMan's help he ducked through the head and ankle knockers without issue. The moment his tennis shoes touched Stingray's small flight deck, his face met a blast of salt air.

Both little bird's rotors whipped overhead, ready to lift off upon receiving their human cargo. Doc half spun beneath the rotor arc with JMan now clutching the other side, both bent at the waist cradling their precious cargo. Foxie stood with one foot on a skid in front of the open cabin holding a gunner's belt with a grin as wide as his jawline. The starboard mounted M-60 was stored to allow the shoving of cargo into the cabin. Doc and JMan propped her up on the edge of the cabin and her short legs didn't touch the running boards. Jumping in behind her, straddling a stretcher, Foxie gingerly reached underneath her shoulders to wrap the belt beneath each armpit and clamp it close. Three sets of hands gently laid her back onto a stretcher where she pulled her knees to her chin. As she returned to the fetal position, her head nuzzled Foxie's helmet bag stuffed with grease rags as a pillow.

Foxie settled behind the starboard M-60.

Doc and JMan hustled away from the spinning rotors and turned as the signalman gestured for Big Alabama to come into a hover. He waved his hand to his ear and pointed to starboard as if signaling "first down" at a football game. BA slid the aircraft across the deck and over water and the little bird gingerly climbed out using airspeed over altitude. Nobody's fool, Schlonger used the recently vacated flight deck as a runway before sliding out over the water using the built-up energy to climb in a hard turn to join BA climbing out in a gentle left-hand turn.

* * *

Exhausted from running hard, Will tossed the M4 to Jim Moore, grabbing both knees to suck air.

Jim laid the handgrip across his shoulder taking a step toward his boss.

Will laid out a stop signal with a hand and spoke without raising his head. "Damnit, Jim, I'm fine," he said between gasp. "Just a little winded."

"Just checking, Will. I have seen you in better condition after bedding a couple of female tourists at the same time."

He slowly straightened and arched backward to stretch his spine and didn't bother to respond. How could he forget the four nights Jim was referring to, which he spent with two thirty-something-year-old French ladies?

"Mortars are laid in?" Jim said. .

Will chuckled, took in a deep breath, then coughed up some mucus and spit the wad over the wall and nodded. "Outside wanting a couple of hundred more of us on the walls, that's great news."

Jim gazed east and sighed. "Guess the word is out. No boats, nothing flying. So how many do you think Ortega will bring to the dance?"

Will moved beside Jim gazing across the empty sea and outside of the waves slapping against the fortress wall, there was silence. "You want it straight?"

"Nothing but," Jim replied continuing to gaze out to sea.

He picked up the bino's laying on the wall to cover the ground as Roach's voice came through his earpiece.

"All friendly aircraft launched for intercept. Expect hostiles in 30 minutes. I say again, hostile in 30 minutes. Godspeed."

Jim rolled his head Will's direction. "You ever been in a worse predicament?"

Will thought about the question. A life, for reasons only God knew, evolved around the SAS motto during WWII: *He who dares, wins.*

He allowed the field glasses to drop around his linebacker's neck. "Yes, I have. The leader of this escapade on the other side, General Hallesleven had a 1911 Colt pressed against my forehead once upon a time."

Jim reeled. "Haven't heard this one. So, what happened?"

"He shot me," Will said laughing. He slapped Jim broad shoulder to get one last look at the defensive positions, shake each member's hand and wish them luck. Jim vanished behind the air conditioning casing to join the mortar section. Minutes before the arrival of the initial wave of Sandinista's, Will entered the CP located in a concrete air conditioning casing atop the Citadel. 24-inch concrete walls meant nothing Sandinista had in their arsenal could touch him.

He conducted radio checks to ensure comm utilizing landline, sat phone, followed by FM radio to the Knoll, mortar position, and positions around the Fortress. To occupy time before the fight, he finished with organizing the 7.62, 5.56, and 9mm. Propping the RPG launcher with three additional rounds on the other side of the two-foot wide entrance he placed a Stinger "courtesy of Franz von Bock" against the wall. He ducked underneath the entrance only when he was satisfied that he could find each item in the dark.

Coming into the sunlight, he could see both snipers on either corner of the eastern tower tidy up their manmade sniper's nest. Both used M14 rifles, fitted with a Schmidt and Bender PM II 3 Police Marksman scope. Both men knew if the Hinds gained control of the airspace and began run-ins on their position, to join him inside the CP. Pressing his haunches against the room's back wall, he slowly sank to the ground. He sang softly to himself Marvin Gay's, "What's going on," and slowly drifted into a well-deserved 15-minute fighter nap.

64

Stingray

With her diesel engines at her flank knifing through calm seas, Stingray's bow maintained a south by southwest heading toward a GPS coordinate. Larson leaned over the helmsman's shoulder. "You hungry?"

The former Army Ranger and retired high school wrestling coach's head shook telegraphing a hearty "hell no." Larson issued a pat on the shoulder then dropped both hands to the holstered 1911 Colts he carried on each hip.

Pablo's fingers danced over the 66-inch wooden wheel resembling steerage from the "Pirates of the Caribbean" movie as Larson's jungle boots tapped in melody with the pulsating hull.

"Captain, we have company," Pablo's eyes fixed on the radar screen right of the steering station.

Larson hovered over the scope lit up like a Christmas tree only to shake his angular face slowly. "Another vertical assault."

Similar to geese with multiple formations of four, each division formed an out of balance V. Larson laid a finger on the screen and used the other hand to scratch a head full of jet-black hair. "There are the surface contacts Roach told us about. Nobody told us to expect another wave of helos."

* * *

Graf Spee

"Speed?" Johannes asked calmly. His right elbow rested atop the periscope's right grip. He dropped his hand to the handle and adjusted the scope's optical power. The target came into clear view.

"12 knots," came the reply. "Range 7000 yards, Captain. All tubes loaded."

"Angle off the bow?" Johannes asked.

"90 degrees red, Captain."

He rotated the scope slowly, tracking the crosshairs towards the target and spoke as if placing an order for steak and lobster at the Buccaneer. "Bearing." The crosshairs traversed and stopped at the unlucky recipient's center mass. Now his tone dropped to a softer tone. "Mark, down scope." He stepped away and slapped the handles into their travel position.

The Exec read from the bearing ring. "Zero-four-five degrees red."

A tech quickly punched the data into submersible's Torpedo Data Computer. The exec thumbed through pages of the latest edition of Jane's Ship Recognition Guide. Each officer of the watch had a pocket guide in their back pockets to identify ships currently in service around the world, by type and nation.

In the forward most compartment, torpedo men worked feverishly through open torpedo hatches to hook power cable and wire—guide connections to the nest of six torpedo tubes. As they closed and battened each breech, each torpedo nestled inside each tube initiated a powering up sequence. As the fish warmed, fire control data from the submarine's computer uploaded.

Johannes peered over the Exec's shoulder flipping through his guide. "Go to Russian-built Alligator fleet."

The exec said nothing and flipped quickly to the Russian Alligator fleet. Now he turned the pages at a snail pace. The Captain's finger landed on a silhouette of a "Ropucha (toad), or "Project 775. He tapped it several times.

"That's our boy, Number One. Helm, come right zero four five. All ahead flank. Let's take a peek at our company." Graf Spee's bow angled to the right until straightening on a heading of one-four-five degrees.

"Heading one-four-five…all ahead flank," the exec replied.

The exec marked the open page with his thumb as he closed the book. He tapped down on the periscope switch energizing pressurized hydraulic fluid into the scopes two-hoist rods sending the scope rapidly to the surface. The recognition book was at his side, ready if a quick ID was required for a pop-up target.

"Captain, multiple targets ahead."

Johannes' feet moved slowly with the scope as it skewed to left, with the exec in step on the opposite side of the scope. He stopped moving quickly back to the right one step. "We have company Number One." Pushing the camera button on the left grip, he snapped off two pictures. He moved the scope left, stopped to click off more photos.

"Both targets are turning Captain…" the middle-aged sonar man didn't look up from the scope.

"Downscope," Johannes said evenly. "All ahead, one-third."

The exec picked up the photos off the color printer and joined the Captain bent over the chart table. "Mirage patrol boats, Captain. There was a rumor Russians were going to sell the Nicaraguan Navy hulls."

"Closing fast, Captain."

Johannes looked up from the photos. "Time to intercept."

"Four minutes, Captain."

The exec jumped into the exchange. "They have no anti-submarine capability Captain."

Johannes cut the Exec a look with a question mark. Their eyes met and the exec nodded, giving assurance his words were fact.

"Probably think we are a Colombian submersible, Captain?"

Sonar reported, "Primary target has turned away and picked up speed."

"Flank speed and 150 feet," Johannes said in anticipation of the imminent. Speed of primary target?"

"Fifteen knots," Sonar replied.

"Range," Johannes shot back. Come left to three-zero. Follow in trace."

With a quick sweep across the chart table using a pencil, the exec swept the pictures to the side. He immediately began to plot target position and speed relative to Graf Spee's position and speed. Once assured the MK 46 torpedo would not run out of propellant before impact he looked to the Captain. "Tubes one, two, and three at 3000 yards."

Johannes spoke without hesitation, the adrenaline racing through his body like a hunter before a kill. "Open outer doors."

"Roger, Captain," the Exec replied, then repeated the order.

"Range closing quickly, Captain."

"Captain, we have two targets on top of us."

A grin spread across Johannes' round face as he looked at the sonar man as his breathing picked up slightly. "Too bad we can't charge for the fireworks show."

Chuckles broke out around the Control Room followed by, "3000 meters Captain," from the Sonarman.

"Stand by," the exec said.

"Two nine-zero-zero-meters… two-eight-zero-zero-meters… two-seven-zero-zero-meters… two-six-zero-zero-meters… two-five-meters."

The executive officer eyes cut to the Captain who acknowledged his earlier order with a nod.

"Fire one!" the exec barked. The initial torpedo would take out the stern. "Fire two!" Following in trail the guidance system would conduct a half teardrop maneuver to strike the target underneath the stack at almost 90-degree angle.

"Both fish are running true."

"Hold number three. Reload one and two."

Parroting the order, the exec moved to the chart table palming a stopwatch. "Two-minutes, fifteen-seconds for initial impact, Captain."

Johannes leaned against the periscope counting the seconds looking around the room at the faces of a seasoned crew. Confidence beamed, no fear detected. A reverberating boom passed through the hull, the first fish had found its mark.

"Captain, the torpedo has made its turn and is 500 meters out dead amidships."

With the torpedo running true, there was no need for Graf Spee to send guidance signals through the wire. It was time for the torpedo to finish the last part of its journey on its embedded sonar guidance system. "Go active. Cut the wire,"

Johannes said. "Come right zero-nine-zero, take us to three hundred feet ahead one-third," which was quickly parroted.

"Both targets overhead departing. They appear to be rendering aid Captain."

"Bring us back up to periscope depth." The second torpedo's impact sent the concussion reverberating through the submarine's hull.

"Periscope depth, Captain."

Johannes nodded and tilted the bill of his hat on his forehead. "Up scope." He patiently cleaned the glass with a baby wipe waiting for the scope to break the surface. There was no surprise with the site framed in the scope. Both patrol boats dead in the water to take on survivors. Crew and soldiers from the stricken vessel settling rapidly by the stern jumped overboard into a mix of diesel and salt water.

"Orders, Captain?" the exec chimed.

Johannes didn't want to give the next order. If he dropped the periscope withdrawing to hunt the Southern Naval force, they would only have to engage these same vessels submerged in the Fortress' shadows within hours.

"Captain, the guns on the Mirages will devastate ground personnel and slow-moving aircraft. If roles were reversed, the Sandinista Commander would not hesitate in issuing the fire order."

Johannes slapped the handles with both hands in disgust. "Open outer doors. Bearing, mark."

"Zero-one-zero red, two-thousand meters," the exec countered.

He looked through the scoop in dread. "Fire tubes, one, two, three, and four. Fifteen-second intervals. Down scope."

He pulled away from the scope and met the exec's stare through sad eyes. "The conn is yours, Sir." He stopped by the hatch as the sound of compressed air shoving the torpedoes from the tubes reverberated through the submarine's hull.

"Four torpedoes running hot, straight, and normal, Captain.

"Very well. Number one, verify targets destroyed. Go deep and proceed due south flank speed. Stand down from general quarters and give the crew a rest." He ducked through the hatch and looked across the control room, "Give my appreciation to the crew. Now find Southern force Number One."

The first explosion traveled through the hull as Johannes pulled the curtains to his berthing space together. Before he could settle into the bed, the second explosion rattled the hull. The third dull thud passed through the hull followed by a fourth before he settled into his bunk. He closed his eyes waiting for the 5MC to sound.

"All targets destroyed. Heading of one-niner-zero degrees and submerging to four-hundred feet. Flank speed."

65

Stingray

Larson scanned the starboard quarter as the first dot emerged low ensnaring a cloudless sky in what looked to be a swarm of South Texas killer bees as other dots emerged. "Ummmph," he groaned. His head twisted to Pablo leaving the binoculars fixed around his neck. "Come right two- three-zero Pablo. JMan might get that Stinger shot after all."

Pablo nodded arching his midsection across the wheel sending Stingray heeling to her left side. "Right two three zero, Captain. Let me in on this shit, Captain." Eyes fixed on the magnetic compass fixed to a pedestal in front of the wheel, Pablo repeatedly pulled across the fist-sized handles to maintain Stingray's turn.

Larson raised the glasses to his dark eyes. "I need steady hands at the helm."

Pablo spun the wheel in the opposite direction and stopped. "On course, and flank speed, Captain."

"Understood. Thank you, Pablo," Larson lowered the glasses and removed the leather strap from around his neck. The swarm of dots shifted course to parallel Stingray. "Come left to one four five degrees Pablo. This guy is acting like he knows we have a line of Stinger gunners on our stern." He pulled the handset from the side of his Captain's chair and checked the preset dial Mother in the window. "Mother, Father. SPOTREP over."

Seconds later, KB's voice crackled around the bridge. "Go ahead, Father."

Larson had to be sure he was speaking to Lonibelle and initiated authentication procedures, then said, "Authenticate… Levi Fry." He flipped the bino's onto the chart table.

KB shot back the authentication code. "Dragons."

Larson nodded knowing he was speaking to Mother and eased back into his chair. *This guy was good, but missed an opportunity by turning south.* "Twenty plus Russian-built helicopters fifty miles west of Fortress. Heading east south east."

Roach's voice bounced off the bridge's bulkhead. "Where in the hell did they come from? Standby, Stingray." There was a pause. "At some point, lead will see his mistake and turn northeast."

"Understood, Mother," Larson said with a grim twist to his narrow mouth. "Your move."

Pablo peered over his shoulder. "You talking to me, Captain?"

With their predicted turn, Stingray's Captain judged the hostiles would pass within a half mile well within the kill zone for a Stinger missile. He had held off calling for battle stations in hopes they would pass by the boat. Now he had to give them a reason to make that turn.

"Hard to port, Pablo," ordered Larson which he followed with orders to turn zero-niner-zero. Reaching for the handheld, he keyed the mike and switched to the 5MC. "Man battle stations. Mount weapons. Weapons condition hold, I repeat weapons condition hold."

Stingray's seasoned crew of oilrig resupply professionals from Texas City, Santa Fe and Hitchcock worked in teams to muscle twin M2HB .50 caliber machine guns into Cha Cha's (ships welder) prefabricated pedestals.

"You have the conn, Pablo. I need to inspect the weapon placement. I will be on the handheld." Larson ducked out of the bridge. As a gunner pulled back a fifty's bolt, Larson seemed to be omnipresent looking over a shoulder saying, "Looks good, Mac," or if the gunner ran into a bit of trouble he would have the anxious crewman stand aside allowing him to make a quick adjustment. He would issue a smile and slap the gunner's shoulder muscling the bolt back with his right arm. He flipped his hand back and let the slide ram the bolt into the breech with a clap.

A few minutes later, Larson joined the Stinger teams gathered underneath Vultures' Row. To a man outside of Doc B., there was unnatural stillness, unsmiling and humorless.

"Remember, twenty feet between firing positions," Doc barked out then grabbed JMan's bicep. "Stay close to me." JMan nodded nervously.

Larson stepped onto the flight deck and locked eyes with Doc looking down from Vultures' Row. He stood behind Vultures' Row starboard 50 cal mount. "We will get you relieved in due time, Doc." After the initial salvo of Stingers left the tubes, Doc would release shooters to man pre-assigned heavy weapon's positions.

JMan and Doc B. would be Stingray's last chance standoff armament and would hold the last Stingers before going toe to toe with the Sandinista.

The flight of Sandinista helo began their turn west where Larson calculated they would cross half a mile off Stingray's bow. With Stingray's bow pointed towards Isle de San Andres, Larson settled into his Captain's chair as the lead element of

Hinds arched off the bow as the flight's tail-end Charlie was at Stingray's 3 o'clock.

Reaching up for the transmitter, he barked over the 5MC, "Heavy guns, weapons hold. Go get 'em, Doc." He dropped the handset to its holder and turned to the helm. "Come hard to port forty-five degrees and chop the throttles."

Pablo acknowledged with a nod swinging the helm hard to port keeping a close eye on the twirling compass easing both throttles to idle.

*　*　*

Doc Bennie spaced the gunners across the stern with as much care and attention as a first-grade teacher lining their students for the class's first walk to the school cafeteria. As Stingray heaved to starboard, her turn brought his gunners eye-to-eye with their targets. He moved to the gunner closest to the stern with JMan close behind clutching his Stinger as if holding a newborn.

Number four; take the outside Hind on the starboard side of the lead formation." Pointing at the division of three Hinds on the port side of the formation Ben stepped next to the number three Gunner. "Take the outside Hind." The 19-year-old deckhand nodded, displaying a look of determination. Gunner two looked over Doc B's sausage like pointer finger. "Get the lead Hind on the starboard side as it maneuvers. He turned to JMan as his pointing finger shifted left. Take the lead Hind on the port side." Doc B put a period on his order as the flight initiated a slow turn to follow the lead Hind's turn to the northeast.

"Standby," he barked ensuring his voice carried over the whining diesel and wind whipping across the flight deck. "Let's cut off the head," he said standing by the first gunner who hadn't seen his twentieth birthday. "Good hunting. The Captain will show us their intakes. Got it," he said with a slap across the shoulder. The deckhand nodded nervously as Doc B grabbed JMan away from the back-blast template. "Gunners one and four clear to fire as your target comes to bear."

66

Stingray

"Heavy weapons stay tight!" Larson announced. The Hinds broke left putting all three noses on Stingray. "They took the bait, Pablo. Hard to port, flank speed."

The retired coach and former Army Ranger swung the helm to port and anxious eyes watched locked onto the Sandinista gunships ominous looking snouts. Easing the throttles to the stop, he checked the heading quickly swinging his head over his shoulder.

Larson watched a contrail streak away from Stingray. Seconds later another contrail appeared. He raised the field glasses surprised the Sandinista formation failed to take evasive action. The missiles back blasts were in plain view and he spoke calmly over the 5MC. "Gunners two and three clear to fire." Momentarily, the stern immersed in smoke slid from underneath the cloud. A second flight of Sandinista Hinds turned to join the flight leaving the troop laden choppers vulnerable.

The lead Hind's rotors folded and broke up sending the fuselage tumbling with the flight characteristics of a rock. Similar to the "Charge of the Light Brigade" the Hind's blindly pressed their attack as the Hind closest to lead exploded.

◆ ◆ ◈

The crew of Stingray stood like pillars at the second flight of Hinds. Larson tapped Doc Perry on the shoulder. "I'll take the gun. Get ready to start humping ammo." Doc P stepped back and vanished down the steps as Larson pulled back both charging handles. He reached behind and opened a plastic box housing a handheld. "Weapons free," he announced over the 5MC.

Weapons free is a weapon control order used in anti-aircraft warfare, imposing a status whereby weapons systems may only be fired at targets confirmed as hostile.

Like High School bullies behind the football stadium, the fight was on. Larson elevated both barrels depressing both butterfly triggers. Streaks of tracer spewed from both barrels. He continued to squeeze off short bursts, as Stingray's other guns came to life. As the defenders of the Alamo probably cheered fighting off Santa Ana's initial assaults, Stingray's crew watched in jubilation as the remaining Hinds broke off. Late in breaking with the flight, Dash-3 initiated a climbing right-hand turn in an attempt to break from the first missile but seconds later a missile penetrated the fuselage below the port exhaust. The aircraft shuttered from the explosion as components from both engines exited from the exhaust stacks but its rotor head remained intact leaving the crew no choice except to ditch.

Larson entered the bridge and barked "Hard to starboard. Come to a heading of one six five degrees."

"One-six-five-degrees," Pablo replied watching in horror as two Hinds closed aiming directly at Stingray's bridge. "Sons of bitches are back."

67

Isle de San Andres
Kang Flight D-Day

Seated in the gunner's seat, Hap kissed off BA and Schlonger to harass the Sandinista main effort as the flight crossed the coastline flying out to sea going feet wet. LD pulled collective to his armpit. *So, the main effort to take the fortress would be a heliborne assault. The amphibian ships must be playing a support role. Commander should have launched this flight when he attacked the international airport.*

Instinctively, Hap reacted to the back blast from Stingray's stern. "I'm on it, LD." Hap ranged the smoke peering through the scope. "Thirteen thousand meters to the smoke and a flight of two Hinds closing on Stingray east of the smoke."

"Range to Stingray," LD replied.

Hap slewed the nose turret until Stingray came into view. "7000 meters." Hap ran a quick geometry equation. "The Hinds can shoot on Stingray in less than two minutes." He laid his boot on the floor to transmit to the flight. "Hook 'em to the east, Hollywood."

Hollywood answered before Hap's boot came off the trigger switch. "On it, Kang!" Hollywood's maneuvered the display of the Cobra's belly as he banked hard starboard to gain the target's six.

Hap's helmet growled as the seeker head of the air-to-air missile LD queued growled. The missile seeker head returned immediate tone in his earpiece. LD toggled a missile off the port outboard rail reaching supersonic speed in seconds. The lead Hinds mast separated after the missile exploded inside the port exhaust sending the doomed aircraft tumbling nose first towards the sea. Hollywood's initial AIM-9 shot went stupid, vanishing in an awkward flight pattern toward the setting sun. Without hesitation, Hollywood selected the second missile and, upon immediate tone, fired. The Hind that bugged out to the north never saw LD's AIM-9 dislodge its transmission from its aft mount propelling one of the blades through the aft cockpit moments before the airframe disintegrated.

Hap said nothing. There was nothing that had occurred in this engagement he was proud of; good men were dying, fighting for what they thought was right. As for the hardcore Sandinista, the few that took advantage of their people, ordering the invasion, "Let them rot, but wanted to be the man that sent them to hell."

"Father, Casualty report," Hap queried.

"No casualties, Larson replied.

Hap leaned over the scope cross-armed, letting out a long sigh listening to inter-flight transmissions.

"Father, keep that bow pointed towards the sound of the guns," Roach growled.

"Will do," Larson replied. "Wouldn't miss it for the world."

"Kang flight button two," Hap said as the chatter between Beaver flight picked up. "Beaver flight, break right." Seconds of silence then Schlonger came on the net in urgency. "Bandit two o'clock high. BA, break right—go to the deck." Accompanied with the human chatter, came the discernable sound of 7.62 guns in anger. Hap could picture the weaving, rolling, diving, bugging out from the Hinds only to return like coyotes on the hunt.

"Join on me, Hollywood. Popping flares."

Hap and LD watched Hollywood roll into a wingover maneuver continuing the diving turn until the bird's snout pointed southeast.

"Tally ho," Hollywood said. "Give me a couple of knots and will be on board in a couple of minutes."

"Catch up or burn up," Hap replied. "The boys can't wait." He knew Hollywood expected nothing less from Hap Stoner when friendlies need support and smelled blood. Hollywood's cockpit replied a two-click retort to Haps as a matter of fact rebuttal.

68

Lonibelle D-Day

Twenty-five miles east of Isle de San Andres City, Lonibelle loitered in a box whose sides were outlined by two-mile legs. Seated behind Magellan's controls, Sluggo spoke rapidly behind a quick a low pitch chuckle. "Hey, Roach. You gotta see the furball the Little Birds have stirred before Magellan runs out of altitude."

Against a backdrop of blue sea, the little birds were like mice racing through the blue sky jinking and darting between the Sandinista's formations with a Sandinista helo close on its heels. The Sandinista Mi 24's were faster, but the little birds were more nimble able to break plane or azimuth before the Sandinista gunners could squeeze off a well-aimed burst.

Minutes earlier Roach heard Sluggo announce "off autopilot" to put the drone in a shallow dive to keep the drone's airspeed up to maintain a visual air to air fight resembling something out of a World War I movie. K.B. turned away from the Fox feed carried on his screen to catch the melee.

"Throw the feed to my screen, KB," Roach said. Without looking, KB's hand searched the console and toggled the feed to the Smart TV to their back. He leaned back against the dining room table to admire BA and Schlonger weave their birds in and out of the Sandinista formation with the speedier Hinds hot on their tail. It may have well been Focke Wulf 190's weaving between formations of B-17's chased by sleek P-51 Mustangs in WWII.

"Crap," Roach said clapping his hands together. *Damn lead element of Hinds continues to press and Hips worked to rejoin formation. I could work these Sandinista pilots into squadron shape in six months.*

Sluggo manipulated the joystick maneuvering the drone to get the best angle to take in the air battle. "The good news is that their door gunners suck."

Each man in the room watched misdirected bursts fired from both gunners positions aft of each of the Hip's cockpit and the gunner sprawled between the pilot's seats shooting from the nose couldn't land a hit.

Roach stuffed a fresh cigar into his mouth, knowing maneuver warfare was not mutually exclusive to offensive ops. Learned early in his Marine Corps career, offense, and the defense cannot exist separately. *Even the brightest military minds believed the old strategic offensive war principle that the best defense is a killer offense.* Roach pulled the unlit cigar from his lips, pissed he missed planning for an airborne assault at the fortress. *Just like poker, the poker player bets heavy on a hand to set the tone while the bluffer throws in chips to buy time to be dealt better cards. At the moment, Spanish Main was bluffing.*

The entire room sat glued to a screen and listened as Magellan video and radio chatter validated the action as hot.

Roach turned h his sawed-off jaw toward KB. "KB, get Hap up on Common. I want an ETA and notify all ground elements…20 minutes before the shit hits the fan. Zoom in on those lead Hinds Sluggo."

KB relayed the call about the impending shit storm as Sluggo slewed the camera hanging under Magellans belly. He pressed the red button left of the coolie hat locking onto the lead Hind. His thumb dropped below the coolie hat and he slowly rolled the zoom control forward. "Armed to the teeth, Roach."

Dissappointed but not surprised, Roach chin shook slowly side to side. Under the stubby wings were two pods of 57mm rockets with 32 rockets in each. The outside weapon station on each wing contained a AT –TC wire guided launcher with two missiles each. He knew each of the Hinds nose guns carried thousands of rounds of 12.7mm each. "I have eyes, dickhead. Whoever planned the mission carried enough S/A to press the LZ, then soften the zone with their ordnance in preparation for the transports." He watched a flight of Hinds break away from the formation to fend off the little birds.

KB shifted in his console, then spoke over a shoulder. "Hap's online."

"Got it," The inquisition began the moment Roach switched to Squadron Common. "Where in the hell are you at?" he barked. "The ground element is about to catch hell!"

"We will not be able to stop their initial assault," Hap answered. "Couldn't be in two places at the same time."

"Well no shit, Einstein," Roach replied with full knowledge Hap and Hollywood had been defending Stingray. "Hinds are dashing ahead to deliver hell to our guys."

"Has to be a Russian in the cockpit," Hap said.

"You think?" Roach uttered. "The guy has moxie and is up on tactics."

Hap remained zip lip.

Roach swished the chewed end of the cigar from one side of his wide mouth to the other. He spoke solemnly to KB. "Tell the boys they are about to earn their pay. Semper Fi."

KB parroted the message as a flash on the Fox station displayed on the screen left of his console broke away for a Fox Alert. He tapped the keyboard feverishly sending an email. "What the hell," he said out loud. He punched the send button.

"See current Fox News broadcast. Mother sends."

"Check this out, Roach."

Roach gained a visual over KB's shoulder. An attractive Fox News correspondent with a long dark mane poking from beneath a Houston Astros baseball hat held a microphone in front of a Colombian officer. Sarah was one of the network's top foreign correspondents given free rein to freelance to hot spots all over the world. She had dropped in to report on the dispute between Costa Rica and Nicaragua after returning from reporting along the border between Colombia and Venezuela. A tip from a source inside the Costa Rican Government slipped her a message shortly after the camera cut away from their interview about what was about to happen on Isle de San Andres.

"This is Sarah Salazar with Fox News. I'm standing on top of Isle de San Andres's largest casino, the Buccaneer, with the senior Colombian Military Commander on the island." She turned to a short fat Hispanic wearing a uniform of the Colombian army. "Major Ramos, can you tell our viewers what is occurring on Isle de San Andres today?"

Ramos replied in broken English as three larger helos passed between the smoke at the international airport and casino in hot pursuit of two smaller black helos.

"The Sandinistas have invaded Isle de San Andres ma'am. My orders are to defend this island to the last man." Pushing a bulbous upper lip against a stringy mustache Ramos posed as if he were the Napoleon of the Caribbean for the world to see. He directed a well-manicured finger to the maneuvering helos while his other hand rested atop a holstered pistol.

"Isn't your barracks located at the airport Major?"

"Yes, Senorita. My men shot down many of their helicopters before withdrawing under heavy fire. You can see the smoke of the many enemy helicopters we shot down at the airport." The cameraman panned towards where the Major pointed a well-manicured finger. The airport displayed several columns of dark smoke mucking up a clear sky.

She waited for the camera to pan back to the interview, and then said, "Amazing Major. How many casualties has your Command suffered?"

Ramos shook his head. "Not one scratch to my men. We have killed many enemies," he replied with a broad smile illuminating a gold-capped tooth.

"Will you be launching a counter attack. Major?"

"Soon, Senorita. When the Airforce reports back I will order the attack."

The brunette turned to face the camera, her shoulder length hair tossed by the breeze. "J.C., I will close by letting Eric pan the camera to give our audience an idea the beauty of this marvelous island which, at this moment, is under siege." As the camera panned west, the video framed a swarm of locusts inbound towards the island.

J.C. Dukes spent five years of his career behind the anchor desk in New York City before jumping to Fox where he's spent the last ten, watched the approaching helos descend to just above the waves. "Can we hold from breaking to commercial?" the anchor asked aloud to the producer. "Ladies and gentlemen, we are witnessing a live event none of us are sure of. A large formation of helicopters is approaching the island of Isle de San Andres. According to the senior Colombian military commander on the ground, the Nicaraguan military has lost aircraft and infantry in what appears to be an invasion."

The world watched the helos vanish below the cliffs bordering the eastern beaches. Three lead birds circled lazily over a refinery while the transports reappeared to begin a slow descent into the airfield near the Fortress. Another group of transports landed between a rise in the terrain and the refinery, which was apparently closed.

"J.C., we have two aircraft about to fly over us," Sarah said in a relatively calm voice.

Two black aircraft, completely separate from the activity at the private airfield, skimmed over the casino at a high rate of speed.

Two Cobras came through J.C.'s earpiece from Production. "Ladies and gentlemen, for those of you that do not already know, two American-made Cobra attack gunships just passed over our on-scene reporter's position. This is a Fox News exclusive and we are witnessing an intrusion on Colombian sovereignty."

*　*　*

"Well, no shit," Roach barked. "What a bunch of crap."

"Well, at least we know where Hap is," Sluggo chimed.

"KB, have BA see if he can lure the Hinds from the transports."

KB nodded. "Will do."

"Sluggo, get Magellan to the airport STAT. I have to know if those helos find gas and if the ground forces begin their movement south. Anchor west of the island but keep the legs between Isle de San Andres City and the Airport."

Sluggo nodded but said nothing.

Roach placed a pair of plastic helos on the map east of Isle de San Andres and slowly walked around the table cross-armed, occasionally glancing to one of the TV monitors. "Everything we have prepared for will be decided in the next hour. Button your chin straps, it's about to go down."

* * *

Hap watched BA and Schlonger continue to lure the three Hinds into the hills jinking and darting through the sky south of the dormant volcano. The Hind's huge advantage in airspeed, climb, and firepower, could not overcome a more agile Hughes 500 piloted by skilled airmen.

Hap had planned to shoot a salvo of TOW's somewhere south of the dormant volcano.

As he zoomed over the Buccaneer, Hap couldn't miss the camera aimed from its rooftop and a news truck in the parking lot with its satellite dish reaching into the sky.

Killer Koch could not hold back. "We are making Cable news. The whole world is watching us!"

"Zip it," Hap commanded, as LD stood the snake on its tail to anchor in place. He wanted Hollywood to engage the Sandinista before landing troops. "Hollywood, hook the bogeys over the refinery left around the volcano. I'm anchoring south."

* * *

Fortress Minutes Earlier

Will rested a dirty forehead atop drawn in knees to grab a fighter nap. He felt a nudge to his combat boot and slowly peered over bushy brows to a pair of shiny pistols. With the assailant clutching a 1911 Colt 45 in each hand, Will lashed out with both boots—landing one at the attacker's waist, the other outside the opposite knee. His left boot targeted the attacker's knee while the other boot caught the assailants opposite hip, sending the figure twirling to the ground face-down. Will lunged forward to drive a knee to the back of the neck and press the tip of his K-Bar against the grimacing figure's throat.

"Are you finished, Will?" Blad coughed out in obvious pain.

"Shit," Will said. He twirled the K-Bar between his fingers to return the blade into its leather scabbard located low on his left thigh. He didn't remove the pressure electing to keep the knee firm against the back of Blad's neck. He reached over pushing either 45 to the side. "You're a lucky man." He brought Blad to his feet by the cuff of the leather coat. Taking a knee to retrieve both pistols Blad slowly straightened and returned the pistols to the empty holsters under each armpit. "I wouldn't make a habit of that."

"Gathered that," Blad replied spitting pieces of Fortress roof back from where it originated before he bit off a chunk during his involuntary face dive. He handed Will a flag bearing the markings *Come and Take It* embossed underneath a cannon without the carriage. A Lone Star topped just above the cannon, topped off the Gonzales flag replica. "Hap thought the flag would be fitting to the occasion. If it's any consolation, the Southern air assault broke through. Minutes from being in the shit." Blad reached out in a mocking gesture. "Meet your radio operator."

Will retrieved the M4 and checked it was on safety as Blad retreated towards the cement bunker. Will called out to the snipers sprawled on the deck, "Drop your cocks, and put on your socks. It's show time." Without a word both grabbed rifles and withdrew to their nest of death.

Blad ducked into the bunker to size up the layout and took a moment to wipe the blood from his forehead. He backed out as chopping sounds of helicopter blades clawing air approached from the east.

Will walked over scratching his head. "This guy is good. Fucker is sizing us up while remaining out of man pad range. He pointed south. "Their main assault group remains a mile from the Fortress on a long extended left base to the LZ." Will counted the line of Sandinista helos, "One, two, three, four, five… hell, what does it matter? Hallesleven would throw in everything plus the kitchen sink. Have all units weapons hold until given the order. I want verbal confirmation of the hold fire order." Will's jaw clenched. After 30 years, he was minutes away from going up against the one man he stayed up at nights imagining different scenarios to kill… General Hallesleven.

69

Lonibelle D-Day

The pulsation passing up through Roach's flight boots transitioned through his body to the coffee mug casting small ripples across the cup.

Blad's voice jumped out of the overhead speakers. "Weapons hold." Weapons hold is an order that weapons may be fired at targets only when under attack.

Roach scratched stubble prickling from a square jaw as KB's head traveled back and forth reading email.

"Message," he called out.

"Read it," Roach responded.

To: Lonibelle
From: Fortress Operations
Subject: Sit Rep

Within the past hour, the President of Nicaragua has communicated with the Russian and Chinese Presidents. The President of Nicaragua spoke with President of U.S. since. Colombian Ambassador is waiting in Nicaraguan President's lobby. End of Message.

"Broadcast the message, KB."

KB's fingers danced across the keypad. "Damn, that Kraut is good," Roach said in the form of a statement.

Sluggo twisted in his seat. "I would say the Kraut as you call him, has issued a report or two in his career."

KB reeled in his seat giving the drone pilot a *what in the hell?* look.

"Watch and learn," Sluggo piped.

Roach retreated to place more pieces on the board.

* * *

Moscow, Russia

President Putin bent over his desk scribbling a handwritten message. After snapping the pen's cover back in place, he folded over the letter size paper and handed it to the short man with a shaved head and no facial hair, standing silently across the desk. It had been an hour since their contact, the driver for the Senior Democrat of the Intelligence Committee, notified the Kremlin of an upcoming call between the US and Nicaraguan Presidents.

The Chinese and Russian Presidents had met with the feckless U.S. leader in Australia 96 hours earlier and wanted to ensure President Ortega didn't flinch over hollow boast from the US leader like, "red line." Over breakfast, the US President did most of the talking bloviating about a hollow Global Warming position and made it clear there was no interest involving U.S. in International issues that didn't address the Globe's Number One threat. "Send this to President Ortega," he said handing the message to his Chief of Staff.

"Yes, Sir, immediately." He made a quick exit through a side door and pushed the encrypted message down dedicated circuits terminating in both President's offices. The circuit ran from Moscow to Helsinki, Stockholm, Copenhagen, London, Mexico City, Managua, and another directly to Beijing.

They made the decision for the "hotline" after the Nicaraguan election of 1984 the first time Daniel Ortega gained power.

• • •

President Ortega's eyes jumped from operational reports from the Che Guevara operation to the four TV's pushed into his office on rolling TV stands, which monitored the imperialist Cable News Networks. While three of the networks reporting were in Nicaragua's corner, Fox gave a blow by blow reporting with their reporter on the ground. Anticipating a message from Russia's leader, he quickly reached out for the report as it crossed his desk. "Is this from Putin?"

"Yes, Sir," the middle-aged man with a bulging belly and bushy brown eyebrows said. He leaned over the desk to hand over the message.

Ortega gestured the man with a flick of a hand, quickly peeling back the sticky that held the message folded.

Information reached my desk POTUS will be contacting you over current regional events. Mr. President, stay the course with your intentions. Nicaragua has come too far. Standing down now limits Russia and Chinese options to support the Nicaraguan people. Russia and China currently experience similar border issues. The United States leadership is feeble and their Monroe Doctrine goes against International Law. Russia and China have submarine and bomber assets in theatre. Acknowledge your intentions.

He set the message on top of a stack of opened messages and picked up the handset. After all, the President of the United States had been on hold for 10 minutes. "Yes, Mr.

President. I hope this call finds you doing well."

"Cut the charm, President Ortega. Pull your troops back within Nicaragua's borders-immediately!"

Ortega remained stoic thinking of the Russian message as he listened. "Mr. President, I'm not sure what you are talking about."

He heard a pounding of an open palm into a desk. *"The fucker was probably pissed more about the 18 holes of golf he had to give up in order to make this call."*

The voice of the world's most powerful leader grew stern. "Not withdrawing and landing additional troops Mr. President will cross my red line." Silence followed.

Ortega gingerly picked up the lone cigar butt from the crystal ashtray. Chewy, he thought fat lipping the soggy end, taking a pause from the jaw exercises to firm up the sagging skin beneath his jaws long enough to end the call. "Mr. President, if this is all you have to say I will hang up now. Good day." He called in the Chief of Staff as the phone dropped into its cradle.

The Chief of Staff's head peered around a partially open door, which connected his office to the communications center. "Yes, Mr. President."

"Get a message to General Hallesleven. Che Guevara must continue and send in the Colombian Ambassador."

Shortly after the handset in Managua settled into its cradle bringing a resounding click, POTUS frowned replacing the phone and turned back to the TVs.

Within minutes, the three networks began to report the US President has assured the world Nicaragua will pull back troops inside Nicaragua borders within days. Another crisis diverted.

70

Kang Flight D-Day

Buried in the bucket, Hap watched the Hips assimilate into a tactical formation.

"You seeing what I'm seeing?" LD's voice was calm.

"The next turn they will be making the run in."

Fixed in a hover north of the Fortress oriented south, Hap watched the lead transport point its bulbous nose northwest. As the transports came out of their last turn, a snake-like procession began to form.

"Status, Hollywood?"

Hollywood replied, his east Texas twang-heavy with each word. "Ready to put missiles on the wire."

"Take dash two with your first shot," Hap said beginning the countdown. "Five, four, three,"

With Hollywood off his nine, Hap adjusted his aim slightly right to prevent the wires trailing from the missiles to cross so they didn't short out. "I have the lead," Hap said over ICS. "Two, one, FIRE!" Both Cobra's flashed the telltale back blast signature dispersed by the rotor wash as the missiles ejected from their tubes. The missile's first four wings deployed followed by the four tail control surfaces as the missiles corkscrewed toward the unsuspecting Sandinista transports at six hundred miles per hour. "Missile away," Hollywood replied though the missile came into Hap's view before his call.

"LD, we have a good missile. Tracking lead."

LD held the Cobra's hover just over the treetops. Based on the Hip's flight path, the Sandinista's lead had not caught either of the missiles back blast.

"I got em LD," Hap reported seconds before the missile struck lead where the tail boom connected to the fuselage.

Hollywood's missile exploded aft of the pilot's compartment. The Hip nosed up sixty degrees before rolling slowly onto its back entering an uncontrolled split "S" maneuver. Aircrew and passenger leaped to their deaths as the aircraft nosedived to the ground. Similar to History Channels scenes of aircrew bailing out of spiraling B-17's in WWII, those brave men had no parachutes.

Hollywood broadcast over the inter-flight frequency, "Hollywood has tac lead."

Hap responded with two clicks as Hollywood crossed two hundred meters to their front. LD crossed Hollywood's six and entered a high yo-yo momentarily fixed in space with their snout aimed into the heavens as the rotor tips fell toward the ground nosing down to pick up Hollywood's 7 o'clock.

"Take a TOW shot," LD said as a TOW left Hollywood's starboard stub wing. Their victim, a Hind, waited until mere seconds before impact and entered a sharp climbing right-hand turn and the missile passed harmlessly below the belly of the flying tank.

"He is staying high," Hap barked.

"This son of a bitch is good," Hollywood replied.

Hap called out, "Kang has the lead—break left."

Hollywood's Cobra's snout rose above the setting sun rolling the bird until the rotor tips pointed toward the ground.

Hap came out of his turn as Hollywood nosed down into the trail.

"Go to spread," Hap barked. "It's a turkey shoot. Fuel state?"

"650 pounds," came the reply.

"Bingo at 400 pounds." They still had some airtime, however, when either bird reached 400 pounds of fuel, both would return to Lonibelle to refuel and rearm.

Hollywood responded with two clicks.

"Hoplites at three o'clock," LD called.

A flight of four Russian utility helicopters scattered and hustled south.

"We stay on the transports, Hollywood."

* * *

BA peeked over his right shoulder ensuring Schlonger maintained separation as tracers fizzled between both aircraft.

Foxie knelt behind BA's seat strapped to the helo by his gunner's belt. He left enough slack to allow him to move to guns dangling from bungee cords on either side of the open cabin. He leaned into the wind line to check six as a burst of tracer sent him spinning back into the cabin spewing blood from shoulder wounds.

BA heard rounds striking the aircraft and made a hard-climbing turn to port. He looked between the seats to put eyes on the bandit but instead encountered Foxie writhing on the cabin floor clutching his shoulder.

"How bad you hit, Foxie?" BA asked.

"Flesh wound. Now they've pissed me off, BA," he groaned. "I can still shoot." As if participating in a balancing act, he painfully pushed up on both knees and slid his knees across the blood-soaked floor. He collared the swaying M-60 barrel pointing between his bloodshot eyes, swung the barrel around, and caught the handgrip on its first pass.

"Beaver flight, split turn 90-degrees." BA lifted the nose 45 degrees snap turning to the right. Foxie had the shot he was looking for and let loose with a long burst of 7.62 through the Sandinista rotor disc. Bulletproof glass-sheathed the pilots from Foxie's rounds, which bounced harmlessly away.

BA caught a rotor flash overhead and a Hind anticipated their maneuver and maintained a higher altitude. He rolled the aircraft inverted and pulled 2.5 g in the split S maneuver to keep from thrown Foxie around the cabin. Foxie released the gun and tumbled to the cabin floor then back against the bulkhead crumpling to the floor into a pool of his own blood as BA pulled the helo through the maneuver to level flight.

"Hang on, Foxie," BA said as the Hind overshot low. He snapped rolled the killer egg to gain the advantage, sending Foxie dangling by his gunner's belt. He fought to gain the starboard running board, kicking and reaching out with his good arm as life pumped into the slipstream.

BA screamed into the ICS as the sounds of Foxie's bulldog build banged the fuselage. "Stay with me Foxie!"

Moments later Foxie tried to speak between short gasps for air. "Jimmy…"

Schlonger couldn't help; he was fighting for his own life. BA had to get Foxie into the cabin before the little bird augured itself into the sea or the Hind shot him out of the on its next pass.

"That last… burst… shot me clean through …," He gasped for more air. "Tell… Hap…no hard feelings." He seemed to struggle for more air. "Tell… Hap… thank… you."

BA swung his head around to watch his old friend fumble for the quick release. He pushed the cyclic forward as Foxie's predicament had thrown the aircraft's center of gravity too far aft for maneuverable flight. The aircraft wavered as the bird rapidly lost energy. He watched the Hind through its rotor disk as its pilot banked hard to starboard to gain the kill shot. For sure, he'd had his last drink and then, in the blink of the eye, the center correct weight and balance of gravity shifted forward. The aircraft planed out and a distinct sound of metal hitting metal as the gunner's belt flapped against the tail boom.

"Nooo!" BA's scream raced over the airwaves.

* * *

"Hinds have left the fight, BA," Schlonger said. "Probably out of gas."

BA checked his instrument panel. All gauges green. Apparently, Foxie had taken the bullets, leaving the little bird's critical components unscathed. Big Alabama raised his visor to wipe away tears.

"Fuel state," BA said sniffling.

"600 pounds and way too much ammo," Schlonger reported. "I have had my exhaust pointed at the Sandinista for too long. It's time to show them my guns."

"Let's go get some Sandinista ass," BA replied. "Join on me. Go spread."

Schlonger replied with two clicks

Beaver flight moved south just above the wave tops. East of the island, BA angled to follow the beaches in search of Sandinista targets.

71

Graf Spee

Johannes slumbered to the submarine's gentle rhythm as it pulsed through the boat's frame under battery power. His eyes fluttered, wanting to disregard the feeling something or someone was leaning over the bunk. A fight below sea level was brewing and like the World War II-era sub, the Captain needed recharged batteries to maintain a clear mind. Good men had already died, and more were in the cards. The moment his eyelids snapped open his blurred vision could make an outline of his exec's narrow face.

"I'm up, Number One," he said grabbing Fuchs' hand inches from his outside shoulder. "Did you find them?"

Fuchs nodded "It's the Arlen Siu, Captain."

"Escorts," the Captain asked, swinging his legs to the deck. He stretched his arms above either side of his slept-on hair and spoke in the middle of a yawn. "Did you say how many escorts, Number One?"

"No, Captain. We have another problem."

Johannes said nothing. His dark eyes slowly rolled over his brow to see Fuchs holding the message board in one hand and rubbing the back of his neck with the other.

The exec's eyes narrowed. "Chinese Kilo sub is in the Arlen Siu's wake. Depth, 60 meters." Fuchs reached over to turn on the reading lamp mounted on the bulkhead as Johannes retrieved a pair of readers from the nightstand.

Reading the message, he let out a short grunt followed by a nod. He removed the glasses and handed Fuchs the message board mulling the Baron's words as he moved to his small sink opposite the nightstand. The cold water energized his tired face. "Do the Chinese know we are in the area?"

"The Chinese Captain doesn't know we exist."

A head poked through the drawn curtains. "Sorry Captain," the Graf Spee's Chief said. "The Chinese boat is coming up to periscope depth."

With both sets of eyes on him, Johannes knew there was history with Graf Spee's brain trust. To many sorties and close calls to count, if they ordered an attack on the Chinese submersible, the crew would turn to with nary a complaint.

"Can we gain her baffles?"

The exec's head shook, the muscles around his jawline taut, "No need Captain. The boat will pass south of our position. If they maintain course in less than a half hour the Chinese Captain will do our work for us."

Johannes stroked his wetted hair with a small brush then turned away from the mirror. "Then we will let the Chinaman come to us. We will sink her and as many of the Sandinista flotilla as we can." Johannes turned back to the sink to splash more water to his face. While snuffing out drug runners he never felt guilt. Taking the life of sailors following orders had a way of fraying his nerves.

He shoved down the Captain's top cap over the receding hairline and pushed the privacy curtain to the side. The years had been kind to his father's Kriegsmarine heavy embroider oak leaf wreath and cockade. He stepped over the knee knocker with the hat cocked back. Members of the ready room watch knew somebody or something was about to catch hell. The boat's Chief, a man in his mid-forties with close-cropped hair and broad shoulders stood at the front of the control room. Heinrich Schmidt joined the crew of Graf Spee as a 17-year-old torpedo man. His father was the Chief of the boat on her last voyage to Isle de San Andres as a member of the Kriegsmarine until his son was ready to assume the role as chief.

"Open all outer doors manually, Chief. Let's not give the Chinaman a reason to do anything different from what he's already doing. Up scope."

As Johannes stepped around one of the watches, the Exec spoke up. "Periscope has broken the surface Captain."

Customary peering into the periscope with his cover, he turned the bill to the rear. He adjusted the handle to bring into focus the small helo lifting away from the Arlen Siu's stern. After the machine's rounded nose dipped, the bird's rotors tore into the air and the helo vanished to the northeast. He slowly moved around the scope to search the western horizon. As if the fishermen knew something was amiss in the area, the sea was absent of other seagoing vessels.

"Captain we have fast moving surface targets approaching from the north," the soundman reported over the loudspeakers. "They have to be doing almost 45 knots."

72

Fortress D-Day

Will rested his elbows on the top of the wall as if the two Hinds shot out of the sky had been nothing more than a sporting event. The remaining Hind raced west to outdistance Hap and Hollywood's Cobras. He brought the M4 to his shoulder as the Hind raced south of the Fortress to get a shot at the door gunner. A quick shake of the head followed, and not wanting to waste ammo, he returned the selector switch to safety and placed the weapon on top of the wall.

"Break left," Hap said as LD rolled the Cobra onto her side to take on Sandinista transports turning a lazy base to the east.

Hap sent a TOW spiraling away from the number four station. "Eleven seconds until impact."

"Shit, Hap, they are not maneuvering,"

Hap counted down the time to impact as the tail end Charlie fell out of formation, trailing dark smoke. "Missile away," Hollywood reported.

The instant tracer rounds sizzled overhead, Hap, without hesitation, said, "Kang flight cross turn. Kang will take the outside. Go!" They had to get eyes on the trigger puller. As LD brought the Cobra around Hollywood showed the belly of his Cobra passing inside their turn.

Killer Koch called the target. "Hind at 10 o'clock, Kang."

"Got 'em," LD said.

"Go get 'em," Hap said. The Cobras raced like starved wolves in pursuit of dinner. LD banked hard right and Hollywood continued his turn as LD pointed the bird's snout to target. Hollywood settled in at Hap's 3 o'clock in combat spread. Their prey was now in both Cobra's crosshairs.

The Cobra's 20mm outranged the Hinds 12.7mm main gun by 500 meters. Hap ranged the Hind at 1200 meters, and then said, "Kang flight, cleared hot." Both 20mm's chattered, sending reassuring vibrations through the airframe nose to tail. Before the Hind's pilot pulled the trigger, high explosive rounds ripped through the helo's transmission and engine compartments. Its right exhaust coughed out a dark cloud of smoke as the engine ate itself expelling compressor and turbine blades through the exhaust stack.

The cabin billowed smoke from the ramp as the stricken helo's snout dropped below the horizon and rolled rapidly to starboard trailing a long line of smoke. Both Cobra's continued shooting well-aimed bursts until the Hind passed beneath their skids.

Hap didn't have time to feel sorry for the poor souls on board—there were transports to kill, "Kang flight, split turn go."

Minutes later, Kang flight slashed through the formation of Hips, their cannons sending death into another victim. The stricken aircraft rolled suddenly, until its belly pointed skyward plunging headlong to the sea.

"Hollywood has tac lead, breaking left." Looking straight up through the canopy Hollywood's bird arched over taking aim at a Sandinista Hip lagging behind the formation.

"Hind, 12 o'clock," LD called over the inter-flight frequency. "Aircraft has its vertical tail painted red."

"Stay on your run. Kang has the Hind." LD swung over Hollywood high and to starboard to enter a game of chicken. LD squeezed the trigger, sending a long burst of enfilade fire arching towards Colonel Ivan Ivanovich Smirnoff's flying tank.

Hap lined up the Russian in the HUD throwing a 2.75-inch folding fin rocket off either pod each time his right thumb laid on the firing button.

"Splash one Hip," Hollywood reported.

Another transport laden with troops gone, Hap thought as the Hind rippled rockets from beneath its wings straight at them. LD pulled full collective and aft cyclic to throw the nose above the horizon 45 degrees to a wingover maneuver as the rockets streaked across the sky passing safely below the skids. As LD pulled through the turn, the flying tank raced below. Hap could see Hollywood's tracers streaking past, knowing that within seconds, gravity would pull their Cobra into the projectile's deadly path.

"Check fire," Hap barked as Beaver flight raced into the melee shooting a short burst of 7.62 into the Hinds' tails.

Hollywood climbed to a high yo-yo to gain position on the Hind. Moments later, the little bird's passed losing ground rapidly to the much speedier Hind. Hollywood allowed the Cobra's pointy snout to drop below the horizon and used the energy to give Killer one last burst. "Hollywood is Winchester on the guns. We have rockets and one TOW Bingo fuel. The Hind entered a lazy turn to the east to render support to the transports.

"Bingo fuel," Hap announced knowing it was time to get gas and rearm.

◦ ◦ ◦

Franz laid the 338 Win Mag BAR on top of the wall next to Will, who was taking in the airshow. Wearing a tan shooting jacket as if about to hunt big game in the Eastern Cape of South Africa, Franz pulled slowly on his pipe. He commented, his voice stoic, saying, "Quite the show of airmanship, Will. Your friend's marksmanship is impeccable."

Will stared straight ahead at the swarm of Sandinista transports nibbling on his lower lip. "They didn't get enough of them." The lead Hip passed low over the refinery leading the division towards the airfield. A lone aircraft in second division broke off and set down near the bridges. The remaining two transports seemed adamant on disembarking troops on the fortress parking lot. A lone Hind with a distinct red tail orbited slowly overhead refusing to fire on any of their positions.

Will walked over, reached into concrete bunker reappearing with a rocket propelled grenade (RPG) launcher, and rejoined the Baron with Blad close behind lugging a radio and a carrier with three rocket-propelled grenades.

"Hand me a round and order Shaun to engage their target at their leisure. Have Eddie standby to blow the airfield fuel tanks on my order."

Blad handed Will a round, rolled his ass against the wall, and slid to the ground with the PRC radio resting in his lap.

Will laid the RPG on top of the wall next to the Baron's rifle and propped both elbows on the wall to give him a good platform to observe the Sandinista assault troops disembark at the airfield through binos. Soldiers stormed the hangar while another group kicked in the outside doors to the pilot's lounge. A four-man team dispersed toward the fuel tanks.

Dispensing hand and arm signals, a soldier with another toted a radio and rushed toward the three fuel tanks.

As majestic as a golfer finished reading a putt, Will shouldered the RPG, stood, aimed, and sent a rocket through the closest Hip's cockpit as troops disembarked down the ramp and into the parking lot. "Get down," Will said and all three men ducked behind the wall. He turned and barked out to Blad who had dropped the extra RPG rounds at Will's feet before relocating to the bunker. "Give the order, Blad," he yelled. "All elements commence firing." Ducked beneath the stone wall, he reloaded the RPG as a burst of small arms fire chipped pieces of the wall onto his and the Baron's back.

Blad parroted the order. "All elements commence firing. Repeat, commence firing." Lifting off the moment the last soldier left the ramp, the second Hip closest to the Fortress tucked its nose swinging its tail left towards the safety of the cliff. In total disregard of the crack of rounds passing either side, Will leveled the RPG launcher and pulled the trigger. The missile entered the open hatch and exploded inside the troop compartment. The wounded helo rolled right falling below the cliffs overlooking the beaches. Seconds later a plume of orange and black flames boiled over the cliffs.

Two shots from the knoll's recoilless rifles followed, bracketing the lone helo by the bridge. As Sandinista boots clambered down the aluminum ramp, they charged head-long to secure the bridge as long burst of M-240 from the knoll begin to find its range.

Sandinista within the kill zone fell like wet bags of concrete while the wounded tossed and reeled along the ground. The helo broke ground before the ramp began to raise and the pilot tucked the nose of the helo to begin forward flight as the next salvo of recoilless rifles exploded into the transmission. Like a rhino hit by a slug, the aircraft dropped to the ground with a thud flexing the blades into the ground decapitating one commando and scattering shrapnel across the area as if it were a claymore mine.

Before Will could get the word "incoming" out of his mouth, an AT -2 Swatter missile impacted short of one of the Recoilless rifles firing points spraying the areas in shrapnel in smoke.

"We just lost one of the recoilless tubes," Shaun reported. "No casualties."

"Platoon size elements are mobile departing the international airport," KB said. Blad leaned out of the bunker and called out, "Mounted infantry moving from the International airport south. They're coming our way."

Will dropped to a knee behind the wall, releasing a mag from his M4. He tapped a fresh mag on the concrete seating the rounds, returned the mag, and let the bolt ride home. He rose to his feet and began working on a squad of Sandinista pinned down by the snipers on his right. The distinct sound of outgoing mortar rounds passed overhead. Seconds later both rounds landed in the middle of a squad of Sandinista tossing bodies like rag dolls. The squad dispatched from the other helo remained in the fight placing heavy fire along the fortress rim to cover RPG gunners. A steady stream of incoming RPG explosions raked the wall. Will yelled to Blad at the top of his lungs, "Sappers are moving to blow the front gate! Send it."

Blad radioed over the tactical frequency knowing everyone that had eyes on the fortress's front gate saw the gunmen storm across the bridge.

73

Nicaraguan Trawler

On station, 1500 yards from of the entrance to Isle de San
Andres harbor, a lone sailor stood in what looked to be a
55-gallon drum extending 20 feet above the trawler's superstructure. To the common eye, they used the spotter's nest
to locate schooling fish. The moment the initial attack went
feet dry attacking the International airport, the Captain
ordered the unfurling of a flag carrying a horizontal triband
of blue (top and bottom) and white with Nicaragua's Coat
arms centered on the white band.

They threw the out of place plyboard panels midway
between the bow and bridge overboard revealing a 23mm
twin-barrel gun mount. Manned by a two-man gun crew, the
weapon was capable of 400 rounds per minute carrying an
effective range of two nautical miles.

"Captain," the sailor manning the crow's nest called out
on a small handheld. "Contact off the starboard bow. Closing
fast."

Captain Lacayo grabbed a pair of binoculars hanging on
a hook next to the starboard hatch and raised the goggles.
Slight in build with a thick, jet-black mane, Captain Lacayo's
reputation was as an officer who would never back down from
a fight.

Within seconds, he stuck his head back inside the open

hatch. "The vessel is flying an orange flag with a Black Stingray. She is armed and moving fast. Launch the drone!"

* * *

Larson hovered over the radarscope while Stingray surged forward on a collision course with a contact loitering off the mouth of Isle de San Andres harbor. The little birds had landed a half hour earlier.

"7,000 meters. Maintain course, Pablo."

Pablo's eyes stared straight ahead at the spec on the horizon.

Larson had kept Stingray at General Quarters since shooting it out with the helicopters, calculating that the Stingray would enter a surface engagement outgunned. "Both little birds ready to launch?"

Pablo nodded. "Yes, Captain. Armed, fueled, and ready for launch

BA and Schlonger ducked through the port hatch holding a JMan egg and bacon with cups of steaming joe in either hand. "Anything worthwhile out there?" BA asked, throwing the words out between smacks of his gums.

"Hard to port, Pablo. Steer three five zero." He turned to the pilots and left no doubt, what was to happen next. "Get those birds off the boat now. We have a drone inbound."

Stingray heeled to starboard as her bow swung rapidly to port. BA and Schlonger clambered down the port side ladder to the flight deck throwing dinner overboard for seagulls to fight over. Deck crew removed the chains anchoring the skids to the boat as the rotors spooled to fly.

The initial volley from the vessels forward mount kicked up water starboard and short of the Lonibelle by 50 meters.

Larson reached for the hand mic fixed above the helm and rolled the switch to 5MC. "Doc B, get as many smoke grenades from the forward ammo locker and deploy on the stern." He rushed out of the starboard hatch and moved aft as the Stingray's surgeon and JMan carried sacks of grenades aft to Doc B. Removing a green canister the size of a 12-ounce coke can, Doc B pulled the pins holding the spoon in place, and underhanded the canisters across the steel deck. A popping sound followed, spewing sparks and flame followed by billowing white smoke. Doc B deployed the canisters as fast as he could pull them from the bag and pull their pins.

Larson barked over the 5 MC, "Keep throwing smoke." He rushed forward and leaned into the bridge. "Keep that turn coming Pablo and keep the pedal to the metal."

* * *

Graf Spee

"Captain," the soundman called out. "The Chinaman is changing course. They have made a turn northeast and are accelerating. She will be passing behind us and appears to be going deep."

"Chief," Johannes said calmly. "We will shoot the primary target and go deep. Once we have confirmed the vessel is disabled, my intent is to trail the Chinaman. With any luck, we will gain her baffles. Make ready tubes one and two."

Fuchs leaned against the periscope housing. "You sure the little bastards are not pursuing us?"

* * *

From her perch atop the casino rooftop, Sarah Salazar could make out troop laden vehicles motor south from the airport entrance. She pointed north and spoke loud enough for the cameraman to hear without turning, "Eric, can you get a shot of the vehicles?"

"I got it, Sarah."

In the middle of interviewing a junior South Carolina Senator in the rotunda of the Capital, JC's earpiece erupted.

"JC, we need to break back to Sarah."

Placing a well-manicured hand to his earpiece, JC eyes cut away from the camera. "Senator, I apologize but we need to break away."

"Thank you, JC," the Senator replied with a *go-ahead* head gesture.

JC looked into the camera to his right when told the satellite link to Isle de San Andres was up. "Sarah, can you hear me?"

Sarah turned to the camera with a column of Colombian Humvees, M-35 2.5-ton trucks, and M113 track vehicles appearing over her shoulder.

"Yes, I can, JC. It appears the assault to take Isle de San Andres City has begun. Stay with me as I show our viewers something else." Sarah walked rapidly towards the southeast corner of the building with the cameraman broadcasting video hot on her heels, "JC, in the area of the refinery we have multiple gunshots which you can hear accompanied by large explosions. I believe, JC that Major Ramos' troops are protecting the island in a life and death struggle." She peered down at the street below; Ramos was barking orders waving his arms wildly about urging troops onto civilian vehicles commandeered from the Buccaneer's valet service.

"Below a Colombian contingent led by Major Ramos is leaving the Buccaneer. The Major is a hero, JC."

"Stay safe, Sarah," JC replied. "We will stay with you as long as we can keep the link up."

74

Lonibelle

"Keep the camera on the convoy," Roach barked chewing a fresh cigar watching the video feed from his big screen. "Tell me that stream of shit is our so-called cavalry coming over the hill?"

Sluggo adjusted Magellan's track to orbit over the city. "Wrong direction. That would be called "a retreat," he said. "The Colombian Army is fleeing the city faster than the Iraqi Army fled Kuwait City in 1991. Anybody want to wager if Ramos defends the bridge or runs for the beach to swim out to sea? I'll give odds."

Intrigued with the report, Roach removed the cigar to wash down loose tobacco with lukewarm coffee.

"Stingray and the GCE have this Intel," KB said speaking over a shoulder.

"KB, inform Shaun not to blow the bridge. I want confirmation on this one."

As KB parroted the order, Roach chuckled to himself, considering the irony of maintaining the bridge to give Ramos an opportunity to join the fight. "Members of the watch, in case I miss this, if a Columbian soldier lays a foot on the bridge after crossing, I want it blown. If Ramos has nowhere to run, maybe he will fight." He stepped over to the printer to the left of KB's console and picked up a map hot off the printer noting latest intel pinpointing friendly and

Sandinista positions. He stepped onto Vultures' Row, gnawing the cigar butt working to keep four donuts collared around both thumbs. He moved down the steps graceful as a Kodiak bear with the cigar wedged between clenched jaws and both hands above his shoulders to protect the donuts.

"Keep doing what you're doing," Roach coughed out.

Hap spoke bent over, running his waist straps between his legs. "Not much going on there Roach, for you to be sucking air like you just ran the Boston marathon." Hollywood and LD made a quick check of their 9mm's, then chambered a round and slid their sidearm into their shoulder holster. Out front of the old guys, Killer wiped the lenses of his NVG's in tight circular motions as Plane Captains walked slowly around the Cobras looking for anything loose, or out of place.

"Ramos is pulling out of Isle de San Andres City and appears to be carrying out a movement to contact." He issued two thumbs up, displaying two treats per thumb.

Hollywood chuckled. "Based on what I've heard about the fat bastard, I would call you a liar."

Each of the pilots reached over, grabbed a donut, and wolfed down the morsel, while walking to their birds with helmet bags draped over a shoulder.

Roach retreated up the steps to watch Kang flight turn-up, arm, and depart waving overhead for luck as the Cobras transitioned to forward flight. "Good hunting!" he yelled.

* * *

Kang Flight skimmed over the Caribbean with an ordnance load giving meaning to the phrase, "death from above." Magellan again proved her worth.

Behind the controls, LD struck up the conversation. "So, Sandinista aircrews are draining fuel tanks of anything with JP?"

Hap adjusted his helmet with both hands. "Hoplites, Hips, Corporate Jets—good thing the airliner Carla came in on burned. Even at minimum fuel, a 737 could fuel a flight of Hinds."

"How many are left, Hap?"

"If you are referring to the Hinds, four. Tough fueling five gallons at a time." In the back of his mind, he thought of Foxie. *Good man, and damn good Marine. How many more would have to die?*

"Have you figured out how to block the runway?"

"Not yet," Hap said shaking his head. "Still working that one. But we have to come up with something to prevent the Sandinista from reinforcing and resupplying."

Each member of the Cobra crew listened to BA and Schlonger's chatter back and forth on attacking their target.

"Flushed off Stingray like a covey of quail, they have a lot to consider," Hap said to LD.

Hap eyeballed the vessel through the scope, then pressed the transmit button with his left boot. "Beaver, stay away from this bad boy. Visual on a 23-2-gun mounts forward."

"Enough is enough, Kang," Hollywood said.

"BA is outgunned."

Hap let the whine of the two 1900 shaft horsepower turbines plane out his thoughts. Rearmed and refueled, Kang Flight was looking for trouble. "Beaver, it's suicide. Let's stop it before it starts. Abort and anchor five miles from the target. They may have surface-to-air missiles." For the little birds to engage the boat, they would be inside the boat's defensive weapons envelope. And if the boat had surface-to-air shoulder fired missiles, it was best just to stay away."

BA's voice shot back across the net. "Kang, we got this."

Schlonger stepped on the end of BA's transmission. "Schlonger is a go-to attack."

"Beaver flight, stand down, and anchor. That is an order."

Hollywood banked hard left and crossed Hap's six to set up a shot. "Hollywood has tac lead."

Though he hated to break up the flight, Kang would allow Hollywood to deal with the trawler. He would take a little bird and proceed to the target area. Hap triggered the mike, "Kang will proceed to the primary target," Hap radioed "Schlonger on me. We are passing targets five o'clock."

Making a wide arc southeast, the little birds maintained 6,000 meters from the target. Schlonger anchored then entered a lazy left-hand orbit.

Big Alabama rocked rotors passing Hap on his right flying the opposite direction.

* * *

Hollywood entered a shallow bank left while climbing maintaining a three-mile cushion. "BA, we will keep our attack from the targets 4 to 7 o'clock. Call any back blast and be prepared to dive for deck deploying chaff.

"Killer, keep the scope on the vessel. I don't want our day ruined by a surface to air missile. "

Pulling power Hollywood spooled up the seeker on the Sidewinder and climbed rapidly to 4000 feet. The Sandinista Captain had the vessel in a hard turn to port to get the forward gun into the fight. Both helos adjusted their run-in heading to the northeast.

"Beaver is inbound." Forty-five seconds before Time on Target (TOT) he depressed the firing button. "Rocket down-range," he announced. Seconds later the rocket landed 75 yards short in the trawler's wake.

"Killer, any sign of shoulder-fired weapons?"

Buried inside the bucket, the back of Killer's flight helmet moved back and forth. "Negative."

BA pulled off after firing six rockets. The first landed short and right. The trawler continued its evasive maneuvers and four rockets splashed harmlessly but the fifth and sixth rocket found the stern.

Hollywood selected the outer port station carrying an AIM 9 Sidewinder. Killer lobbed a long burst of 20mm from the nose gun. Hollywood reached his perch at 4,000 feet and, as in training, the seeker's head picked up the exhaust from the stack. The moment tone sounded in both helmets, he toggled the missile off the hard point. "Missile away."

The missile tracked perfectly, striking between the stack and vessel's small bridge at 2.5 the speed of sound. The explosion that followed created fires that burned uncontrollably. Crewmembers not killed by the blast dove head long into the sea or simply jumped, as late afternoon winds whipped the fires across the trawlers wooden hull. Beaver flight, on me," Hollywood said. "Let's go help Kang!"

75

Isle de San Andres
Kang Flight

A quick peek over his right shoulder Hap could see Schlonger's gunner's hair trail from underneath the flight helmet. The gunner's dark visor was pulled down. He radioed over the interflight frequency. "Where is V?"

Schlonger reacted to the question by pushing a stiff upper lip up against his roman nose. "V joined BA for this one."

"So, who jumped in your Gunner's position?"

"JMan," Schlonger answered.

Hap said nothing because, in reality, he couldn't do anything about the decision to put Simmons' youngest boy behind the gun. "Roger that," he replied. He wanted to get a good look at the Sandinista helo deployment and passed west of the airport to put the runway between the flight and high ground to the east.

"The Hinds are at the base of the tower," LD said. "The duty runway is open."

Hap swung his head to the left to see the wing flash of a Sandinista Airliner on a base leg with gear down. "Stay with me, Schlonger. Let him land." Both helos scooted east, diving for the sea to go feet dry between Isle de San Andres City and airfield. Feet dry, the flight ducked into the first significant draw. In unison, both aircraft lifted their noses decelerating and entered a hover using the ridge to their right to mask their position. LD swung the Cobra's tail right, pointing the snout towards the airport. Hap glanced right to see JMan gripping an M60 as he cleared their flanks from uninvited visitors. "Mother, do you have the transport on final?"

"Affirmative," Sluggo said.

"I want to know when the transport is on short final," Hap said.

"I will give you one better," Schlonger replied. "JMan, clear my tail left."

Hap could see Lonibelle's cook nod and step out on a skid as if he had years of aircrew experience.

Schlonger air taxied out of sight, working towards the beach while keeping the rotor head masked below the ridge. The little bird pulled into a hover by the beach. Schlonger edged the nose out until he put a visual on the transport turning final. Hap watched the little bird ease into a back taxi as the first-time crew chief hung his upper body out of the aircraft to look past the tail rotor.

"LD, I'm going to put a missile into the plane as the wheels touch down and, hopefully, block the runway. I can't pass up this gift."

Hap's hand worked the switchology to bring the missile online.

"What about the Hinds?" LD asked.

"First things first," Hap said. "Schlonger, after we flame the transport we go after the Hinds."

Schlonger acknowledged with two clicks

The little bird unmasked to see the Sandinista transport with gear and flaps down on short final. "Unmask Kang. Target is on short final. Schlonger inbound."

Sluggo heard the call and said nothing, prepared to enjoy the show.

Schlonger dropped the nose and glided down the ridge to gain energy and level off just above the white sands of an empty Isle de San Andres beach. Hap lost sight as Schlonger remained masked below the cliff to work to the runway.

LD pulled into a hover. "That's good enough," Hap said, as he bore sighted the crosshairs on the transport crossing the threshold. "Missile away," Hap transmitted over the net. "Tracking true, LD. We have a good missile."

"Roger," LD replied, staying alert for any undeSirables moving his head left then back to the right.

"Got her," Hap said calmly the moment the missile struck above the port side wing root. The subsequent explosion ignited the fuel tanks and sent two pieces of flaming metal tumbling down the runway. The forward section ground looped down and the tail section tumbled, stopping hundred feet short of the fuselage. Both pieces of fuselage remained on the runway expelling geysers of dark smoke and secondary explosions of ammunition into the sky.

Hap watched Sandinista soldiers at the point of their AK 47's urge airfield fire department personnel to mount their fire trucks.

LD adjusted his aim based on the blast from the 2.75-inch rockets and adjusted the nose of the Cobra to walk the remaining rockets towards the Hinds parked at the base of the hanger. Five-gallon cans of precious JP dropped to the tarmac as Sandinista soldiers scrambled for cover. Hap saw a tall fair-skinned man in a Sandinista flight suit draw his pistol and run out in the middle of the mayhem. Thinking the man had to be Russian, he watched as the officer leveled his pistol at six men who were all carrying five-gallon cans in each hand.

The firemen manning the water cannons fixed above the cab foamed the wrecks before the trucks came to a stop. Once stopped, firefighters dismounted.

"I'll take the southernmost truck with a TOW shot." LD dropped a 2.75 rocket in between the trucks attempting to spook the firefighters and guards.

Hap put an exclamation to LD's shot, delivering a long burst of 20mm. The cannon fire ripped up grass and dirt short of the runway. *Message delivered.*

Sandinista weapons clanged off the runway as empty-handed Sandinista soldiers bolted all directions seeking cover. Hap watched the firefighters stare dumbfounded at the retreating guards. After a brief conversation amongst themselves, one of the firemen who probably was the unfortunate shift supervisor began shouting pointing wildly towards the terminal. Firemen holding hoses dropped them where they stood, and each man wearing fire-breathing apparatus's allowed the carrying frames to slip off their backs while sprinting towards the terminal.

Seconds later, a fire truck, under which some of the Sandinista guards sought cover, lifted off the ground and returned to earth in flames, entombing its victims in steel and fire. "You owe me one, Hap," Hollywood said.

"Give me two seconds, LD," Hap said. A heartbeat after he finished the sentence, the northernmost fire truck exploded. LD entered a steep climb and broke right. Schlonger's little bird traveled slowly, level with the control tower. Tracers spit from the starboard door gun shattering the towers glass walls.

LD rolled left and the collective stopped because of his armpit. Hap's head popped out of the scope as the ground approached way too fast. LD pulled cyclic and collective and was able to get another inch of collective to will the shark-like nose through the horizon.

Hap spoke calmly. "You had me for a second, LD." LD positioned to pick up cover for Schlonger as a burst of tracer ripped through the little bird.

The little bird's nose raised and steered right, and the airframe seemed to dance over the tail as it swayed back and forth. Schlonger was clearly wrestling the aircraft attempting to avoid the tower. Hap gritted his teeth. The M-60 had stopped firing. Schlonger gained controlled flight in time swerving away from the shot-up tower.

"Schlonger is out of the fight. Mayday, mayday, mayday, Stingray!" Silence followed. "One aircraft inbound with one Urgent Surgical." Each man hearing the call knew Schlonger had a patient that needed urgent surgical attention within two hours for the preservation of life, limb, or eyesight. "Stingray has been notified," KB answered. "Surgical team standing by."

LD took control of the nose gun. Now where he moved his head, the gun followed. His head on a swivel, he squeezed off a short burst. Looking right, the turrent followed a short burst at a target behind a corner of a vehicle. Chunks of metal, red spray, and flesh flew out in all directions.

"Two o'clock—two armed bandits," Hap said calmly. LD turned his head left and the turret followed and slammed to a stop. He squeezed the trigger in short burst and stopped when there was no visible life left in the assailants.

"I've got your wing, Schlonger. You're trailing smoke," Hap said biting into his lower lip. Just like his Dad, rounds from nowhere struck down JMan. As bad as the day had gone for the Sandinista soldier, one man behind the trigger had experienced a better day than Stingray's cook. It almost seemed unfair a soldier could be having the day of his life, on top of his game and in an instant fall to an unseen shooter.

76

Isle de San Andres
Hallesleven Headquarters ashore

Hallesleven pushed away from the Hoplite's cabin, bent at the waist. Santiago and three soldiers exited from the opposite side clutching radios, antennae, a ruck full of batteries, along with personal weapons. Santiago led what would make up Headquarters table of organization 'T/O' around the helo's rounded off nose. It was easy to pick up the sand trail winding through the native grass leading to the Tiki Bar.

South of the airport, but closer to the western beach than the coast highway Hallesleven trotted up the 30 steps with Santiago's contingent close on his heels. They continued across the 25-foot porch and Hallesleven swung open one of the double screen doors for the headquarters element to enter through.

A Nicaraguan officer clad in green camo fatigues bulging around the waist leaned with his back against the end of the bar smoking a cigarette like a German aristocrat. The weighty officer waved with the lit end of the cigarette pointing towards his pudgy palm. "Damnit," Hallesleven mumbled under his breath. It was none other than LtCol Carlos Chamorro Jr., the son of Nicaragua's first billionaire and member of Ortega's military attaché. "Do you have anything to report, General?"

"How did you get into my headquarters?" Hallesleven demanded, walking quickly along the bar.

"We have our ways, General. The President thought it best he had someone from his military attaché to observe and report back to Managua."

Hallesleven issued a polite smile. "Colonel Chamorro, you're nothing more than a spy." A Major, who had not been aboard the helo, banged through the screen doors with a sniper rifle and scope slung over a shoulder allowing the thicker than normal springs to slam the doors together.

The Radio Operators set up on separate picnic tables as another soldier stapled maps of the island against the bar's plywood wall.

Within a half hour of stepping through the Tiki Bars doors, Hallesleven drove his hammer-like fist into a nicotine-stained palm. "We leave the island either a conqueror or a corpse!" He performed the act in front of his small staff, pointing towards the screen doors. "This stretch of coral road will serve as our expeditionary airfield." He couldn't count the times during the ouster of Somoza he secured roads for resupply.

"But, General…" Santiago began.

Hallesleven cut him off, popping his finger on their position on the map, "Colonel Santiago, this stretch of road is our only lines of communication with the mainland. I have been here before Colonel. So just do it!"

Santiago turned and gave the Major a curt nod who returned a smart salute and exited out the doors with Ortega's spy close on the Major's heels.

* * *

Will stuck his head inside the bunker. "We need air *now!*"

Propped against the back wall, Blad peered over his brow with a handset pressed against each ear. He held his left hand out gripping a handset as if to say, give me a second. "Wait for one second, Will," he said. "Have a message coming through." He plugged a finger in his ear that held the handset. A couple of nods followed then his dimpled chin moved slowly side to side. "Sandinista Headquarters is ashore. Position south of the airport, west of Coast Highway. Ground forces consolidating around the road. Coast highway will be turned into the expeditionary airfield."

Will's gaze dropped to his feet and a boot lightly brushed the deck. "If the Sandinista reinforces the island and has the ability to resupply, it's only a matter of time." He turned and doubled time bent at the waist back to the wall.

Blad slid to the entrance keeping the handsets pressed against both ears. He watched Will expose his upper torso to pump rounds into sappers reported to be moving along the base of the wall. The moment his head dropped below the wall the top of the wall exploded knocking his bush hat to the ground alongside accumulating debris. Will sat with his back against the wall, blood trickling from the prominent scar caused by the bullet ricochet off the Los Americanos roof during Hap Stoner's mission to rescue Warden. Their eyes met as the blood oozed down Will's cheeks and a frightening grin spread across his face. He and Will were not the best of friends and he couldn't explain von Bock's fondness for the tough bastard.

Blad nodded and depressed the transmission button. "Air mission over."

77

Kang Flight D-Day

"Send it," Hap replied, as he began to write the brief on his kneeboard.

"Infantry one-hundred-meters east of Fortress. Attack heading 180-degrees. Pull out to the west. Enemy in the vicinity of airfield hangar and east of knoll. Friendlies on Knoll and within walls. WP."

"Copy," Hap said as he switched over to the inter-flight frequency. "Take care of the boy, Schlonger. We have been diverted." LD broke left, maintaining a half-mile separation from Isle de San Andres's white beaches. The Cobra raced across the water at military power, which by the Manual could pull 30 minutes without interruption.

Roach's voice broke over the tactical frequency. "Hollywood, I want you and BA to divert to the bridge to motivate Ramos and his command to cross the bridge. We have to get that slug into the fight."

"Infantry in the open, north of Airfield. They are moving on the knoll. You just lost your mark."

Hap responded with two clicks. "LD, fly east along the north wall and drop into gorge. When we unmask, let's light them up."

"Will do," LD replied.

The Cobra skimmed between sailboat and yacht masts racing to escape the hostilities enveloping the island.

"You watching this, Hap?

Hap was as amazed by the reactions of the vessels crews as well as the patrons. Some waved with both arms over their hands, some raced below decks, while some stood erect and saluted. LD banked hard into the harbors entrance racing where the gorge emptied into the harbor. He rolled left in a 90-degree bank, and then cranked the nose to the sky. Hap readied himself to drop into the bucket as the Attack Point, or "AP," was the intersection where the northeast corner of the fortress and gorge came together. LD kicked the tail into the wind line and Hap's eyes dropped. "In the bucket."

LD replied with two clicks.

The Cobra unmasked in time for Hap to see the Fortress's main entrance explode. Chunks of wood the size of conference room desks and links of chain bounced across the parking lot. A group of Sandinista rushed forward behind a shroud of smoke.

"Put a wall of steel midway down the bridge," LD said.

Hap squeezed down on the trigger sending a long burst of HEI forming that wall of steel between the Sandinista and the Fortress breach. *Brrrrrrrrrrrrrp.* Hap gave another long squeeze of the trigger, then another. *Brrrrrrrrrrrrrrrrrrrrrrp…* *Brrrrrrrrrrrrrrrrrrrp.*

As the smoke blew south and east toward the airfield, a dozen Sandinista were sprawled between the bridge and parking lot. The moment after the last burst from the Cobra's gun, eight men gained their feet and rushed to enter the breach.

Fire from the knoll, the fortress walls, and Hap's flanking fire melted the Sandinista assault in place.

* * *

Will ordered cohorts to his left and right to join him in the courtyard.

They stumbled across the rubble to exit through the breach and Will led the squad through the parking lot jumping over rubble and bodies in a dead run. He raised a fist to his left ear and belly flopped into the grass to take up a prone firing position. His initial round signaled the others to begin firing into the Sandinista creating the upper jaw of a lethal kill zone.

Will had to get immediate fire support or risk dying in place or retrograding into the walls under enemy fire. He radioed Blad. "Immediate suppression. Grid 456834. Infantry in the open. H E. Adjust fire." Now, he only had to wait for the first mortar round to splash a high explosive (HE) round and then adjust rounds to the target.

He watched the fire from the Knoll maintain a steady rate across the Sandinista line of attack. Enfilade fire from the Fortress telegraphed the unmistakable sound of friendly mortar fire. *Thunk. Thunk.* Two rounds arched high overhead as Will's line continued to weigh in on the Sandinista spread across a two-hundred-meter front.

"The assault force has taken to ground," Will said to Hap as their Cobra anchored short of the road but between two patches of native trees alongside the gorge. Another burst of gunfire followed.

Mortar rounds began to toss both the live and the dead into the air like rag dolls. More mortar rounds followed, throwing up clouds of dust mixed with shrapnel. Will knew

Hap could feel the fear his soldiers had to be experiencing, and knew he truly despised this part of the mission.

'Good men fighting for their country against another party fighting for what they thought was in their best interest.'

Will spotted two heads and an antenna below a ridge and transmitted over the tactical frequency. "Add 50. Left, one-hundred. Fire for effect."

The sound of Wilson's outgoing mortar rounds arched over Will's position raining down on the group beside the radio. Blad broke in, "Have a visual, Will. I will adjust."

"Roger," Will said taking in the scene through a pair of binos. Every time the Cobra fired, or a mortar round exploded, one or two Sandinista's lost their life. Hap's next burst sounded, and Hap reported, "Gun is Winchester."

"Check fire, check fire," Blad called out over the net.

"LD dropped the Cobra's snout to accelerate to the kill zone. Will straightened and waved the team forward to end the fight.

78

Kang Flight

Hap watched Hollywood toss chunks of lava and dirt 100 meters short and wide of Ramos's convoy. LD pulled across Hollywood's tail to anchor at their 3 o'clock with 100 feet of separation. "Winchester," Hollywood radioed.

"We got it," Hap said. "Any recommendations on what we use as a cattle prod?"

Radio chatter for the fight on the Fortress side of the gorge had gone silent. Columns of dark smoke billowed from the Citadel. The fuel tanks at the Baron's private airfield burned uncontrollably.

Hap slowly slewed the optics across the ground from the refinery to the fortress. "The hangar was shot up, but the refinery was unscathed."

"Save the ordnance," LD said, sizing up the convoy situation.

Hap pictured the situation in the eyes of the Colombian soldiers. Two snakes painted black shooting ordnance in their general vicinity would constitute hostile.

LD took his cue and lowered the snout. "On us, Hollywood. Let's herd the cattle," Hap said. "If they engage, we will withdraw."

"Copy, Hap," Hollywood said. "We are at your nine o'clock.

Hap leaned back in his seat to watch the show. Some of the soldiers looked to their NCO's, while others jumped and ran towards the gorge. Like a bandito in a spaghetti western, Ramos waved a pistol wildly above his head to rally his command.

"Hey, Hap, do you think Ramos has figured out that we are on his side."

"Ya think?" From the Cobra's perch, they could see Ramos had the column on the move with the soldiers who had darted away running back to the vehicles. A senior NCO ran down the column waving the drivers forward with one hand waving his other toward the Cobras.

* * *

Ramos held a fist over his head standing in the back of the lead F150 while a column of Sandinista staggered towards the bridge. One Sandinista in the lead had a white tee shirt held over his head.

The Ford came to a stop short of the bridge and Ramos slowly rolled over the side having just enough coordination so that his combat boots touched pavement before his head did. He did a quick once over brushing his blouse with both hands then gestured wildly to the NCO who had been running up and down the column. Ramos pointed his pistol in the direction of the surrendering Sandinistas. The noncom had three soldiers coerced by the barrel of his pistol prodding them to the bridge.

Ramos jumped on the Ford's running board feverishly waving the pistol forward forcing Colombian soldiers to either side. Stepping off the truck, Ramos raised his pistol to stop and approached the Sandinista holding the tee shirt.

* * *

"Mother, this is Kang. We have Sandinistas surrendering at the bridge."

"Copy, Kang. Good to hear," Roach's gruff voice replied. "You have enough gas to fight? We have a situation brewing south of the airport on the island's west side."

"Twenty minutes, Hap," LD said. "And that will be cutting it close."

"Twenty minutes to bingo," Hap replied. "And we land with two low fuel lights."

"Let's join the fight, Hollywood," Hap said.

"Ditto," BA parroted orbiting over the refinery and airfield.

"Roger that," Hollywood said.

LD lowered the Cobra's snout and rolled left. "Join on me."

79

Off the coast of Isle de San Andres

Schlonger spat out a mouthful of salt water with each simultaneous pull of his right arm beneath a leg kick. 45 feet away, JMan's limp body bobbed in the light, face up, eyes directed to the sky. He could see his lower right-hand lobe deflated, probably from the same round that cut through his midsection.

He reached back to flight school training and allowed inertia to move him forward those extra inches before initiating the next stroke. A swim curriculum designed for all future naval aviators and aircrew turned a country boy or girl who grew up wading in ponds or shallow rivers into real swimmers capable of swimming in full flight gear for a mile. Another stroke, leg kick and rest, then spit out another mouthful of salt water.

As he drew closer to Simmons' boy, the Navy swim instructor's water survival gospel bounced through his head. Clad in a Fly Navy t-shirt and tan Navy swim shorts, the Petty Officer lamented, "You will remember this lecture the day you find yourself bobbing with your crew in some far off ocean. It will be your wits versus the elements and you will never be sure how long you will be a cork in the water. Conserve energy and survive."

20 feet of water separated the two with the current sucking them away from Isle de San Andres. Another stroke, coast,

spit out another mouthful of salt water and repeat. At 10 feet, he rolled onto his stomach and began a breaststroke but this time he didn't pause between strokes, just churned water mixed with blood.

He reached out to clasp the collar around JMan's neck, quickly spinning him around. "Talk to me."

With a finger, he probed above the pelvis and his middle finger entered a hole, which brought out a long groan. "Well, at least you're not a corpse."

He put his lips to JMan's ear and whispered, "You keep bleeding and both of us are going to be shark food."

A mouthful of water mixed with blood spewed from JMan's mouth.

"Good to see you still have a sense of humor." Schlonger reached into his vest pouch to remove the medical kit. Using his teeth, he ripped open the package, and then grabbed the bandage. He found the syrette of morphine trapping the flexible tube against the inside of his right cheek. Quickly closing the first aid kit, he stuffed the plastic container between a blood-stained flight suit and vest. He used his tongue to expel the needle end of the syrette and tore off the plastic cover. Without thought, he stabbed through JMan's flight suit into his upper arm and squeezed the painkilling morphine like toothpaste.

"Now let's plug that hole." He spun JMan onto his stomach and shoved the bandage into the exit wound while he searched the horizon. Void of aircraft, plumes of gray, white, and black smoke drifted across the eastern horizon.

First things first, he reached inside his flight suit and retrieved the plastic packaging for the compression bandage. He ripped the plastic packaging open with his mouth. Spitting away the plastic, he quickly looped the bandage around the wound, once, twice and tied it off tight with a square knot. There was another wound where the round ricocheted off the armor and passed across his upper arm.

JMan groaned and a smile appeared as the morphine worked its magic, taking Simmons' boy into nirvana. He latched onto the collar and began to sidestroke towards some wreckage. The meshed aluminum would be easier to spot from the air than two heads bobbing between ocean swells. "You know something JMan," Schlonger said between strokes. "Whoever was behind the controls of the Hind that pulled the trigger was good." Three more strokes. "Never saw him. Now, Sir, we have to find a way to survive."

He tied off JMan to his survival vest and then tied his vest off to the wreckage, an aluminum cross member. Continually kicking away from the wreck's sharded edges, he pulled the radio. "Schlonger on guard," he called out between gulps of salt water. "Schlonger on guard. We are down northwest of the island."

Seconds passed and KB's voice came across the network. "Schlonger, Mother—copy. Casualties?"

Schlonger let out a long sigh of relief. A SAR effort would begin sooner than later. "I'm ok. One Urgent Surgical."

"Copy Schlonger. Give us a long count. Will use our radio and Magellan to DF your position." Schlonger heard the bubbling of air from one of JMAN's lower lobes break the surface. A shard of wreckage beneath the surface punctured the lobe. He kicked away from the wreckage as he spouted into the handheld "Ten, nine, eight, seven, six ...two one."

Within seconds, he was talking to Lonibelle through a link from Magellan.

"We have a fix on your position," KB said.

"JMan is in tough shape," Schlonger said, spitting out another mouthful of salt water. "We are on NW side of the island and current is taking us out to sea. I cannot see land but do see a lot of black smoke. Do you copy?"

80

Off the coast of Isle de San Andres
Graf Spee

Inside Graf Spee's crowded control room, Johannes leaned against the periscope housing as the boat searched the surrounding waters. The crew was at battle stations, and not a sound uttered between them. Sonar reported, "Contact bearing zero-four-zero magnetic seven thousand meters. Target designated Sierra Romeo 1. She's a Russian Foxtrot."

In the middle of a big yawn, Johannes asked. "Speed?"

"Four knots Captain." Johannes bent down to look through the forward hatch. The sonar man leaned his head out from his cramped compartment pressing both hands to the hydrophones. "The boat appears to be angling into the Chinese sub's baffles. Range, seven thousand meters."

Johannes removed his cap and slowly massaged the crown of his head. "All stop. Let's see what Ivan's skipper is up to. Range, seven thousand meters." The Russian's presence was a surprise, but the Captain maneuvering the submarine behind the Chinese was protocol.

"All stop, aye-aye," The executive officer said. "Chief of the watch. All stop."

"Captain," Fuchs said, standing on the other side of the periscope.

"Let the Russian slip in between us and the Chinese boat," Johannes said. "Do it!"

"Bow planes up three-degrees," the chief of the watch said. "All stop."

He knew through conversations with the Baron that the Chinese, along with the Russians, had an interest in Isle de San Andres. "Number one, why is Ivan shadowing a shitty Chinese submarine commander?"

Fuchs hesitated a moment and then said, "Captain, this makes no sense unless Ivan is running a training exercise with or without the knowledge of the Chinese."

"Captain, the Russian contact designated Romeo Foxtrot 1," the sonar man interrupted. "He doesn't see us, Captain."

"Very well," Johannes replied, kicking back the bill of his hat. How he wished to report back to Operations, but the transmission might remove the cloak that Graff Spee's currently enjoyed. It had been hours since receiving any communications. He felt like a boxer fighting inside a darkened room. A fighter pilot attacking with the sun to their back mirrored a submarine stalking another submarine baffles— invisible until it was too late. "600 meters from the screws, Number one. If we have to shoot, I don't want to miss."

45 minutes later, Johannes stood like a sphinx next to the periscope. His eyes gazed over to Fuchs, who was leaning into the forward hatch. "Captain, Ivan has opened their outer doors."

Johannes nodded. "Ivan had cocked the gun in submariner terms and the Foxtrot's Captain only had to order the trigger pulled."

Similar to the two hours Graff Spee dawdled in the Kilo's baffles, the Chinese Captain made no effort to initiate a "crazy Chinaman" maneuver. The maneuver had the bow of the boat turn 90 degrees and like eyes of a fighter pilot, the submarine's sensors reached into the abyss to ensure its 6 o'clock was clear.

Johannes crushed down the dog-eared cap closer to his ears. "Periscope depth."

"Chief of the watch," the exec said coolly, "periscope depth."

Minutes later, the Chief spoke matter of factly, "Periscope depth."

Fuchs toggled the scope up.

Johannes hung both arms over the handles and scanned 360 degrees, walking deliberately around the scope. There was the oilrig supply vessel with a helo on her stern. Stingray no doubt, he said to himself.

"So which one of you sons of bitches will lay cards on the table first?" Johannes said.

Sound barked out, "Captain, the Chinaman is opening outer doors."

"And the Russian?"

"No change, Captain."

"I want the fish active coming out of the tube. Standby tubes one, two, three, and four," Johanne replied.

"Captain, the Russian has put a fish in the water and active seconds after leaving the tube. Two torpedoes in the water."

A stillness in Graf Spee's control room followed. Seconds passed and the soundman turned to speak over his shoulder, "Crazy Ivan, Captain."

The Russian was smart in checking his baffles. "All stop," Johannes said.

"The Chinaman has awakened Captain. Going max turns on the screws and deploying countermeasures. Sir, he is going for the surface in a sharp left-hand turn."

Johannes nodded slowly; Graf Spee had the Russian Captain dead to rights. "Is the Russian going deep?"

"No, Captain, remaining at five-zero meters."

Fuchs leaned into Johannes. "Captain, we need to fire our torpedos."

Johannes looked down at the stopwatch palmed in his left hand. "The torpedoes are not for Stingray." He counted down the seconds. "Fifty Seconds... Forty seconds..."

"How can you be so sure, Captain?" Fuchs asked.

Calm as a church mouse, Johannes' eyes fixed on the watch. "At this point Number One, what difference does it make if we shoot now?"

Off the coast of Isle de San Andres
Stingray

Stingray cut through the calm seas at a leisurely four knots as Larson worked to give the ships surgeon a stable platform to perform surgery. After easing outside the bridge to allow salt air to soothe nerves frayed to its last strands, Larson knew if he was at the end, he could only imagine about the crew's state of mind. As he stopped to talk to the crew, the men asked about the surgery. Each time asked he replied with a shake of the head before saying "Waiting for the word just as you are. He is in good hands." Doing a once over the gun, he would give a reassuring slap on the shoulder and say, "Keep your heads on a swivel."

Pablo barked out over the 5MC, "Captain, I have a sonar contact off the starboard quarter. Whatever it is the bogey is about to breach."

Larson ducked his head into the open hatch. "Hard to port, Flank-speed." Stingray heeled right and the steel beneath his feet became high pitch vibrations. "What was Graf Spee up to," he mumbled. He pulled his head from the open hatch to as a large dark snout broke the surface 300 meters aft.

He reached in for the overhead microphone over the Captain's chair, blaring into the 5MC, "Weapons tight! Weapons tight!" He let the mic fall into the chair bouncing around by the cylindrical cord and vanished down the aft hatch and down another ladder well at the end of the passageway to the makeshift operating room. He cracked open the hatch and stuck his head in. "Doc, I had to put the pedal to the metal."

Half turned; Stingray's surgeon looked through glasses protruding out of the surgical mask. "Need a stable platform Captain. Still probing and the boy is bleeding like a stuck hog. Could lose him."

"It's him or the lives of Stingray and crew. We will be maneuvering."

Doc P and Doc B looked at the other then dropped their eyes into a bloody mess.

Larson bound up the steps three at a time to gain the bridge through the aft hatch, and then ducked out the port side hatch. "Where did the thing go?"

"It went back underwater Captain," Pablo replied. I have him on sonar."

Larson continued to stare where the water churned from where the submarine submerged. Then suddenly the empty sea erupted sending a wall of water and foam into the air beyond the height of Stingray's bridge.

* * *

Doc P looked over to Schlonger standing next to the closed hatch. Both bloodshot eyes jumped from Simmons' boy to the blood pooling around the surgical teams wading boots.

"You going to stand there like tits on a boar hog, or you going to lend a hand?"

Doc B exchanged forceps for a bloody stitch scissor to a suture. "Grab a mop, Schlonger, and start getting the blood off the floor." Doc B moved to a half-filled sink of steaming water to empty a tub of blood-covered surgical instruments. In between in the instrument exchange, he washed down and applied suction to the wounds. The holes in his back were the source for the pooled blood.

Doc P finished the last stitch to Simmons' right shoulder, and then stared down at his handy work art for the abdomen wound. "It would almost be better had he not worn the body armor."

Doc B nodded. "Let's get him on his stomach and close him up."

Schlonger stood leaning over a mop handle as if looking for his lost pup, in a no shit stare.

Doc P dropped two bloody instruments into a tray and looked over to Schlonger. "A little help here."

"Cowboy up and stay in the fight, JMan," Doc B said as three sets of hand gingerly turned him to his side, and then his stomach.

Schlonger returned mopping up blood and ringing the strings into a bucket of soapy water. Doc B checked the I.V. while oxygen continued to flow through a clear plastic mask covering Simmons' nose and mouth.

The alarm on the electronic vital sign monitor let out a long tone. In TV or movies when the device makes noises, doctors and nurses start yelling things like "stat" as they run to the patient. Doc P looked over his glasses and saw three flat lines. "Defibrillator, please. We're losing him."

82

Graf Spee

As Graf Spee surged forward, the soundman's head appeared in the passageway. "Russian torpedo went active after leaving the tube, Captain."

Johannes' brows pinched upward, reflecting a growing concern. "Now Fuchs," he said in the form of a statement versus a question. "We will find out whose side the Russian is on. The Chinese or their own."

Fuchs returned an incredulous look fixed to his face's narrow outline. Everyone inside the control room knew the moment Ivan's torpedo went active, the cat and mouse game between the Russian and Chinaman had concluded.

Johannes' jaws fused together. He had not put a torpedo into the Russian and now there was a torpedo in the water moving towards Stingray. He looked over to Fuchs. "I was going to take the Russian with our first torpedo and wait and see how the Chinese Captain responded." 600 meters aft of the Russian's screws, Graf Spee had the Foxtrot dead to rights. The only question he had at the moment was the number of Stingray crew who would die if he made the wrong decision. He stood cross-armed eyeballing nowhere in particular. Seconds passed would tell which hand Graf Spee would play.

Sonar sounded out again, "Captain, the second torpedo is in the water and active."

He chuckled to himself. The watch was as tense as a poker player going all in on a bluff with one player still in the hand.

"Captain," the sonar's head appeared in the passageway. "Chinese sub began evasive maneuvers the moment the Russian torpedo went active."

Johannes grunted as his light blue eyes focused on the boat's upgraded undersea warfare screen to keep tabs on both subs, "Stay in Ivan's baffles, Number One."

A relic in today's submersible technology, the Graf Spee glided silently while the Chinaman made a hard turn to port along with a rapid rise toward the surface. Throughout the Chinese's dance around death, the Russian maintained course, keeping Johannes decision minimus.

"Captain," the executive officer said, "We have a firing solution on the Russian."

"Very well," Johannes said quietly. "Confirm and standby. I have to be sure the Russian has played his hand."

"Outer doors one through four open, Captain," the exec called out.

Johannes nodded.

"Ivan has turned to port but maintaining depth," the soundman reported.

"Stay with him," Johannes said to the Chief. Johannes wanted Graf Spee to be just a black hole in the Russians baffles. The last thing he wanted to do was give the Russian a chance to take a snapshot at Graf Spee. "Range to target?"

Sound answered. "Maintaining six-hundred-meters, Captain. The Chinaman has breached, Captain."

"Very well," Johannes replied. "Within seconds, the Russian Captain will reveal his intentions."

"The Chinaman is going back down, Captain."

"Do we want to take the Russian while we still have the advantage?" the exec said, his voice thick with concern.

Johannes shot a dagger with his stare. "Stand by, Number One."

"Impact, Captain," the soundman said. "The Chinese submarine is dead in the water and sinking."

Minutes later, the Chinese Kilo's hull imploded, sending reverberations throughout Graf Spee's hull. No shout outs, back-slapping, or high fives between crewmen followed. Each of the men ducked their heads knowing fellow submariner's lives had been lost. They would notify the widows, who would cry out, and then raise children alone. Mothers and fathers would cry over lost sons.

"Thermal layer, Fuchs?" Johannes inquired.

"47 meters, Captain."

Johannes nodded slowly. The ocean's thermals made it difficult for sonar to penetrate with accuracy and provided much-needed protection to submarines operating in stealth mode. "Let's see the Russian's next move. What does it look like on the surface"?

"Stingray is at flank speed heading north by northwest. Ivan is blind to us."

"As much as I want to get a flash report out, I have to wait for the Russian Captain to reveal intentions."

83

Isle de San Andres

Fox New's broadcaster Sarah Salazar stood in the passenger side of the "VW Thing" balancing herself clutching the top of the windshield. She coerced/bribed the driver, a thirty-something-year-old local with no hair for $2,500 cash for the short ride to the combat zone. She showed no visible concern while sweat poured from the driver's exposed scalp from either the sun, or fear. The 1974 convertible slowly weaved through the maze of vehicles, wounded, dead, and dying.

"Keep going, Justo," she said, waving him forward. Out of the corner of her eye, Justo shifted uncomfortably in the torn/sat out seat looking into the terrified eyes of teenage soldiers. With a history of spending 300 days per year traveling the globe following regional conflicts, combatant's stares into an abyss was nothing new for Sarah.

She pointed the microphone as if it were a swagger stick as the cameraman sat in back slewing the camera's lens in wide sweeps to put the carnage into the eyes of Fox viewers. As the sun set to their rear, a Colombian officer was bent over on the Fortress side of the bridge. Sara couldn't make out if he was wounded. "Jump on the possible wounded officer then pan across from the burning helo, then left towards the burning fortress. Give the hill a couple of extra seconds. Looks like something terrible happened there."

Halfway across the bridge, she recognized Major Ramos. She used the microphone as a prod tapping Justo on the shoulder. "Grandma was slow Justo, but she was old. Get a move on."

"Major Ramos," Sara said opening her door to see a pool of bile between his combat boots. "Are you wounded, Major?" The cameraman stood in the back to catch the scene. She looked toward him and received a nod. *They were live.*

"Ladies and gentlemen, Sarah Salazar on the front lines of the fighting on Isle de San Andres Colombia. I'm here with the Colombian senior Military Commander who just received the surrender from the Nicaraguan Senior Officer according to Major Ramos."

She lowered the microphone in front of Ramos's rounded out face as he took in elongated breaths of cordite-laced air.

"Major, are you OK?"

He nodded visibly struggling to catch his breath. "Asthma, ma'am," he lied with full knowledge the scene with him doubled over was not the best to receive the promotion to LtCol.

"Colonel Ramos," she stopped in mid-sentence. "Sorry, Major, due to your leadership Isle de San Andres' outnumbered command just saved the island!"

"Yes ma'am," he said returning a receptive grin straightening for the camera as he palmed the holstered pistol with his right hand. "We still have issues at the International Airport." His rounded chin lolled towards Isle de San Andres City and the airport beyond. "We have to deal with the situation and will mount our counterattack the moment we take in all our prisoners and account for our dead and wounded."

Sarah looked around at the dead sprawled across the field to her front and the herding of the wounded between the road to the Fortress and gorge. "Major Ramos, I don't see any dead or wounded Colombian soldiers."

Framed against a backdrop of lingering smoke, Sandinista prisoners continued to be herded into the holding pen, a piece of ground out in the open with two soldiers holding weapons. A local doctor and his staff from Isle de San Andres City stood at the front in a mock triage center. A lifeflight helo airlifted two more seriously wounded Sandinista to the Hospital Amor de Patria north of the dormant volcano and south of the city. The camera panned towards the knoll and figures framed at the moment of death attempting to take the ground. As if begging God for help, the dead hands were frozen in space reaching into the sky.

84

Isle de San Andres
Tiki Island Bar used for Hallesleven Headquarters ashore

Hallesleven stood in front of the area map tacked to the wall depicting the location of friendly and enemy forces. Intently he studied the display of red and blue markings with his arms crossed clutching an unlit cigar. Red represented enemy combatants while blue noted friendly positions. The map showed more red than blue, which was a growing concern.

Hallesleven rubbed the side of his unshaven face and turned to Santiago, who handed the handset back to the radio operator. The man that could have, and probably should have, been his son wore a sickly expression as he walked over to the map to replace the marking in area south of the bridge, red.

"Status on the southern assault group?" Already knowing the answer, he wasn't sure why anyone would even ask the question.

Santiago shook his head. "There is no southern assault group. Those still alive surrendered, General.

Hallesleven said nothing as he stuffed the cigar between clenched jaws walking slowly through the double screen doors. After lighting it, he took in a deep draw looking past the smoke rising from the International airport. To the east billows of smoke rose appeared beyond the volcano.

The first transport carrying reinforcements can't come soon enough.

With the sun almost below the horizon, a glint from an aircraft wing appeared highlighting an aircraft north of the International airport. Thirty seconds followed and another glint, then another. *Friend or foe*, he wondered, looking over his shoulder toward the screen doors. Santiago would break the news soon enough. *Could the Colombian's reaction forces respond before Managua?* A transport peeled from the circling transports slowly descending over the airport. A smile appeared on Hallesleven's face as the transport set up for final to the Sandinista's makeshift runway.

* * *

With the general on the porch out of earshot, Santiago walked purposefully to the R/O monitoring the aviation frequency. He laid open a palm asking for the handset without snapping a finger. The R/O, who couldn't be more than seventeen-years-old and 115 pounds wet, pushed the handset into Santiago's palm. "Take a break, Private. You have five minutes."

The soldier looked over his thin brow with questioning eyes. "Sir?"

Santiago issued a curt nod. "Did I stutter, son?"

He got up slowly from the table and retreated to the bar and pitchers of water. Santiago propped a boot where the R/O had been sitting and rested the handset over his knee.

"Somebody has to do this," he mumbled under his breath for the future of Nicaragua. He butted the handset to an ear and keyed the mike. "This is the Chief of Staff. I am ancelling Che Guevara. Abort, abort, abort. Return to base. I repeat, Che Guevara is canceled, abort and return to base. Hostiles in the area. Out." As the R/O slid back into place next to

Santiago's dirty boot, the Chief of Staff returned the handset to the wide-eyed R/O who had obviously heard the announcement. "You didn't hear anything, Private. Carry on."

*　*　*

The sight of a Nicaraguan transport on final and the nicotine from his cigar helped calm Hallesleven's nerves. He blew a series of smoke rings in celebration as the transports main mounts threw off puffs of smoke slamming onto the coral pavement.

The doors springs creaked open then slammed shut moments before Santiago slid in beside him. His presence added to his growing confidence the operation's reversed fortunes. Framed in a life and death struggle, he stared by the side of the stairs at a pair of wrestling sand crabs. "You know, Colonel, Che Guevara has been snake-bitten from the start. I could be either of those crabs down there. One will die so the other can live. Will Kellogg has been one step in front as if someone within our staff is working beside him."

Santiago paused said nothing as his head followed the plane down the highway. "Do you really think so, General?" he said incredulously.

Hallesleven nodded slowly. "Since adopting you, I tried to instill in you that failure is the passageway to final success. It's how you handle the obstacles confronting you that ultimately smacks you in the face. I wanted you always to get up after being smacked down and moving forward wanting more for yourself. It's an internal fire Santiago—look up, get up, and never give up. Our lines of communication established now, I believe the worm has turned against Will Kellogg and Nicaragua can salvage this operation."

High pitched revving of the twin turboprops gave cause for both to shift their gaze from the wrestling sand crabs to the transport racing down the highway left to right. As if struck by a bolt of lightning, air came between the plane's nose gear and pavement, and the main mounts sucked back inside the wheel wells. The pilot banked the transport hard over the beach passing right of the Tiki Bar. On short final, dash two throttled up, and rotated its nose sucking in the gear gaining altitude over airspeed. Dash three and four circling north of the International airport came out of their next turn pointing their nose due west.

Hallesleven head jerked to the side throwing the smoldering cigar between the crabs as he retreated back to the radios leaving Santiago on the porch with the wrestling crabs.

* * *

The Knoll

After ten minutes working in terrain for a hastily constructed sand table, Will knelt to a rubber kneepad to slice an outline of a boomerang into the soft ground to map the island's coast highway. Loosely gripping the K Bar's leather handle, he gently brushed the scar he referred to as 'Haps' with the instruments steel butt guard studying his Picasso. He quickly carved an additional line outside the coast highway denoting the island's shoreline and waved the blade above his head looking around at his heroes. "On me…*now.*"

The Knoll defenders increased to 20, and lay stretched out with cross ankles or legs splayed for a fighter nap while others were seated cross-legged cleaning weapons. Eddie and Shaun had acted as sentries as the men worked in a brief but well-deserved rest. Both strolled through the maze of bodies to prod them with a boot followed by a Marine Corps top ten, "Drop your cock and put on your socks. There still a fight going on." Ever so slowly, Will's Buccaneers straightened, stretched their arms over their heads, and slowly formed a school circle around Will's 3 x 3 display.

As the old-timers circled the sand table, Will stuck the tip of the razor-sharp blade into a golf ball-size hole in a plastic canteen resting on its side. "Listen up," Will said. "We are pressed for time so I will be brief. The inboard circle is the coast highway." With the canteen in his left hand, Will ran the blade two foot down the west side and came back around to trace two foot for the north and part of the islands east side stopping at a cantaloupe size chunk of concrete. "Dormant volcano." He placed the canteen between the two lines next to his blood-spattered combat boot. "Tiki Bar," he said tapping the plastic container with the blade. The blade fell onto sticks, which lay lengthwise north and south. "Runway." The blade swept right to an empty ammo can punched through by shrapnel. "Isle de San Andres City. The mound of dirt and rubble piled with a highway etched along its western edge is the high ground at the volcano's base."

"Hey, Will," Shaun said holding out a splintered shovel handle. "Use this. Probably easier on the back."

Will sheathed his knife and straightened, using the splintered handle as a pointer moving it around the high ground overlooking the Coast highway. "We will helo lift a covering force here to provide a base of fire for the main effort convoying from the south around the volcano." He circled the intersection in the dirt where the coast highway and hard surface road running north and south on the west side of the volcano. The stick traveled down the etching in the dirt running to the coast. "Shaun will lead the convoy to push the Sandinista up the highway into the perimeter of the International Airport. The Sandinista Commander will order repairs to the runways. I know the man" He tapped a pile of grass east of the highway on the high ground. "LZ X-Ray. Initial wave to contain crew-served weapons to set local security and covering fire. The second wave will be mortar crews, I want both tubes with 25 rounds per tube. As General Hallesleven repairs his precious runways we will crater them with mortar fire until the Colombian military arrives."

"Excuse me, Will," Billie said raising a hand.

"Not now, it has been arranged the Colombians will use the runway to my right to stage and mass forces. At any time, the Sandinista stand and fight before they make the airfield perimeter, they die in place." He tapped the canteen with the handle. "Secondary objective is the Tiki Bar. You can't miss it. Sits on nine-foot wooden pilings and the exterior walls are painted pink. Sandinista HQ."

Stingray is moving around the north side of the island to be on station to provide heavy weapon support. Call Sign—Stingray. Cobras will be on station. Call sign—Kang."

Heads turned as four F-350's and a civilian Hummer pulled away from the Fortress parking lot. "Let's get back to it, gentleman. Upon the second wave departing, Shaun will kick off the main effort passing north of the volcano," he paused running the handle past the intersection sliced into the dirt then continued speaking.

"Past this intersection to join the Coast highway in a movement to contact," he continued. "I can only hope the

Colombians will show in due time. And X-Ray will provide enfilade covering fire and will be my Headquarters."

Will tapped the canteen, "Secondary objective. All elements at X-Ray will remain in place. Mortar rounds will be controlled by air to crater runways on my command. Be judicious with the mortars…if the Sandinista is able to gain lines of communication with Nicaragua and the Colombian's are late it could be a bad day for the good guys." Will's tired eyes and sunburned face peered slowly to the men situated around his work of art. Dirty faces, bandaged arms, and heads along with bloodshot eyes confidently returned his gaze in kind. "OP's will be placed on these points." Will pointed to two dominant terrain feature offering good views of the airfield. Questions?" he asked. Seconds passed and the only question was the velocity of the wind whipping across the knoll. Will nodded. "Okay then, the helo's are refueling and rearming on our boats and should be on station within 45 minutes."

A lone figure stepped out of a Hummer 2 at the end of the convoy. With the hunting rifle slung behind his neck, the Baron walked as if he was Clint Eastwood, slowly gesturing with his hand for Will to join him. They could hear a lone Little Bird approaching from the south. Will trotted down the hill where the Baron waited slowly puffing a pipe. Will appreciated the aroma; it smelled similar to his father's and took in deep breaths enjoying the tobacco's smoothing effects.

"We have to move now, Will," the Baron declared. "Intelligence has reported Ortega's effort to reinforce Hallesleven have failed."

Will smiled, nodding slowly while looking up into the eyes of the Clint Eastwood looking fella. "It makes logical sense for the general to withdraw inside the Airport perimeter. A military mind would say his remaining forces to include wounded can either be withdrawn by air or by sea."

"Hallesleven would never surrender to me," Will said. "There is history between us."

The Baron removed the pipe and smiled. He pointed the hand-carved stem towards the private airfield. "The Colombian military thinks the same, Will. They will have troops on the ground within the hour and vehicles on the ground within three hours which will then relieve your command."

Will stood scratching the back of his head. "Not sure why we need to proceed with the movement. If the Sandinistas stand and fight, we could lose some people."

Looking stoic the Baron replied, "Hallesleven is at the Tiki Bar. Thought, after all the years, you might want to have words with him. Ramos will follow your main effort. If your team pens the Sandinista, he sees a promotion to Lieutenant Colonel, but I have been told by Colombia's President the little fat man will be deep selected to full bird Colonel."

Will bent over and swept up a long piece of grass. He slipped it between his teeth and began to chew, intrigued if he came face-to-face with Hallesleven, who would be the better man.

Minutes later Will stepped to the side and reached into BA's window. He clutched the Big Alabaman's broad shoulder then began to assist the two machine gun teams of three men. Each had linked ammo draped over their rucks falling forward over each of their shoulders. The gunner carried a 240 by its handle forward of the breach and tripod. The A gunner and ammo bearer carried two cans of ammo and an M4.

Will raced beneath the spinning rotors, bent at the waist to join the mortar crews formed to the side of the road.

85

Kang Flight

Head down in the bucket, Hap slewed his scope up and down the highway, then back to the Tiki Bar. Full of gas and rearmed, he anchored Kang Flight, masked behind the hill and trees labeled "X-Ray" on his map.

"The intel about the reinforcements appears to be true," he said.

"Sounds too good to be true," LD replied maintaining the Cobra snout just above the tree line for Hap to keep eyes on the target.

"No massing of troops so the Roach finally said something worth a shit," Hap replied in a jesting tone. "But the explosion near Stingray minutes after a submarine breached is intriguing."

"Let me drop and slide to the left to get the palms off our nose out of the way." LD masked the Cobra behind a stand of palms to their front and slid left. The helo rocked back right as he anchored, stabilized the airframe before slowly raising the helo to peek above the trees. "Makes you wonder if this was the sub we saw in Magellan's feed the night we attacked the trawler."

"BA lifting," came across the radio.

Roach's gruff voice followed. "Proceed, BA. Magellan will be on station in five minutes. Give me one turn around the Fortress before pushing to LZ X-Ray."

"Roger," BA replied.

Minutes passed as Hap and Hollywood's birds popped up, then masked to reposition with one bird always keeping eyes on the hiway passing in front of the Tiki bar. "BA push. Good luck, gentlemen."

Moments later Hollywood cut in, "Tally one little bird inbound, Kang."

"Kang flight," Roach said. "Magellan just caught a section of Hinds clawing sky. You will have company about time BA inserts."

Heads on a swivel," Hap barked across the inter-flight freq.

"Tally two bandits at 2 o'clock," Hollywood reported.

Hap popped out of the bucket and the Hinds bore down between the two highways padlocked on BA's little bird, and then broke away to the Coast highway.

Hollywood verbalized Hap's suggestive thought, "Let's go get em, Hap."

"Negative. Slide left and pop."

Hollywood's rotors dropped ever so slightly below the tree line, slid back, and left past Hap's six.

"Anchor Hap," Sluggo called. "If I didn't know—"

"The Sandinista are shooting their own," Roach said in a guttural tone.

"Unbelievable," Sluggo answered, his voice immersed in disgust.

"Russians," Hap replied.

"Well, no shit Kang. Who else would paint their vertical tail red?" Roach guttered. "Hap, the red tail bird has broken off for X-Ray. Keep your head down and will call your pop. You and Hollywood are about to have to do some of that pilot shit. It will be sundown in three minutes."

Hap and Hollywood replied with two clicks each. "You have rockets LD. I will take the gun," Hap said.

"Hollywood. If the Bear makes it through our ambush, you take Dash-2. I want to get a TOW shot on the red tail."

Two clicks followed.

"Stand by," Roach reported. Seconds passed. "When you pop, the Bear will be at your 1:30," he said, before counting down from five.

When he hit zero, both snouts popped like a pair of agitated King Cobras, their dark eyes fixed in death. Both guns spit 20mm tracers into the cabin of their prey. Strapped safe inside titanium wrapped cockpit tubs, the Russian broke hard right allowing the helo's armored belly take the punishment. "Let's get a missile on the red tail," Hap ordered.

LD pedaled, turned slight left, and rocked the Cobra's nose between a gap of trees in pursuit of the Hind racing to the coast.

"Come left a bit," Hap said, working to put the "X" on the Hind. He slowly eased his left trigger finger and the TOW corkscrewed from the port outside rail. Within seconds, he said calmly, "Good missile." He only had to keep the X on the maneuvering Russian and the missile would fly to the target.

"Come left and keep it coming. The Russian is going to try to get over the water staying low," Hap blurted. "One smart Ivan. Stay on him."

LD pulled military power arching the Cobra skyward putting air between the helo and the ground as the optical wire reeled out from the back of the missile at 300 feet per second. Made from two sub-millimeter wires, the strong sewing thread signal would short out the instant it came into contact with water rendering the munition 'stupid'.

"The additional altitude might give us that added second to smoke this turd," LD replied. "Hollywood is on Dash-2 like a chicken chasing a lizard.

"Turning into your flight path, Kang," Hollywood said calmly.

"Hollywood will be entering your field of view, Hap—right to left," LD said. "Ivan made a turn to the southwest. I think he is working back to the airport perimeter, even after killing all the Sandinista soldiers."

As LD reported, Hollywood's bird entered the scopes field of view. Hap slammed his left boot on the transmission switch. "Hollywood, do not maneuver. I need five seconds."

Hollywood replied his understanding with two clicks.

Hollywood's bird blocked the red-tailed Hind from Hap's view. Whether luck or good piloting, the Russian's left turn stayed in line with Hollywood's flight path. "Give me a wingover to the north Hollywood."

The nose of Hollywood's Cobra pitched skyward as the missile passed only feet below the skids. "Hello dolly," Hollywood called out. "Our target is inside the perimeter. We will join on your four o'clock in spread."

* * *

Santiago un-holstered the Makarov and emptied the magazine in the general direction of the murdering Hinds. As he navigated down the steps, the empty magazine clanged off the Tiki bar's bottom step. As the fresh magazine was inserted, that sixth sense kicked in and slowly turned to look down the barrel aimed from the porch.

"You have betrayed yourself, Charro?" Hallesleven replied.

"I would have never thought it would be the man I raised as my own."

The bags under Hallesleven's eyes seemed to sag more as a Hind streaked along the road toward the airport perimeter.

"So, is this your revolution, General?" Santiago stood with the pistol hanging by his side jerking his head towards the Hind, and then toward the sound of a line of Ford duellies motoring deliberately up the coast highway. Out in front a Hummer 3 sped ahead of the main group while the Hinds with the red painted tail raced low and fast between the convoy and the Tiki bar. Trailed by two Cobras, a smaller helo raced toward their position with the volcano as its backdrop. As the bubble-shaped helo flared to land between the highway and Tiki Bar parking lot, a commercial airliner arched over the volcano's crest. "Colombian soldiers, General." Other airliners appeared lit by exterior lighting and stacked against a darkening eastern horizon waiting their turn to land. "It's over, General!"

Santiago slowly holstered the Makarov as if waiting for the bullet to fire. "Che Guevara has failed, General. Your President will have to find other means to feed the Nicaraguan people then have them killed in senseless war for the benefit of the Chinese."

Hallesleven took a series of short breaths in an attempt to regain control. "You will never know, Charro." He looked down the sites of his Makarov as a figure jumped from the helo's running board. The helicopter's skid never touched ground, continuing its forward motion, and rotating around its rotor tip to make a sharp left turn. As if a marvel cartoon character, the lone figure that had leaped from the bird's running board raced toward the bar with his weapon at the port.

Santiago half turned back to the general. "By the looks of things, General, if you don't clear your head, the same goes—"

Hallesleven didn't let him finish the sentence, squeezing off a round. The man he raised as his own son spun around falling facedown in the sand.

"Hallesleven, you son of a bitch!" The approaching figure continued to advance yelling out, "Drop the weapon."

An insincere smile flashed across the General's drawn facial features. *"You may have won the day, Will Kellogg, I will win the moment."* He looked away from Santiago's lifeless body to see Will Kellogg spun around like a rag doll crumpling to the sand.

Hallesleven turned to the direction of where the shot had come from. One of the screen doors had a single hole shot through it. Trained by Russian Spetznatz, the Sandinista Major who pulled the trigger shouldered through the screen door.

"Are you ok, General?" Two steps later, he was lifted off the wooden deck and banged into the wall ending up in a fetal position. A gaping wound poured blood from his forehead. Franz von Bock peered through the scope, placing the crosshairs on the lone figure standing alone atop the steps of the Tiki bar. Prone on the top of the Hummer 3's hardtop, he ejected the shell casing while lowering the scope to Will's motionless body. A quick swipe past his right eye wiped away tears. He repositioned the scope back to the steps only to find the target gone. He dropped the scope back to Will to find the barrel of his M4 buried to the stock in the sand.

. . .

Colonel Ivan Ivanovich Smirnoff raced the Hind 10 feet over the water flying from the flying tank's rear cockpit.

"The missile has us, Colonel. Four o'clock," the crew chief reported, leaning over the 12.7mm machine gun and sticking his upper torso into the windstream.

Smirnoff banked left waiting for either the missile's optical wire to short out, or explode against the Hind sending the helo tumbling into the water at 195 miles per hour.

"Colonel, the missile has gone high and is racing to our nine o'clock."

A smile appeared below Smirnoff's clear visor as his head slowly rotated past his left shoulder to see the missile climb into a darkening Caribbean evening, go left, and back to the right before the nose dropped and exploded into the sea. He reported to the crew, "Pilot cut the wire the moment he lost control of the weapon. We outran the missile where its guidance wire touched water shorting out the system." He steered the Hind north with a gentle right turn, attempting to put space between the two aircraft. His attempt to stop the pullout of troops from their positions covering the coast highway had failed.

True, some of the peasant soldiers had died in the effort, but firing on the defenseless Sandinista soldiers was just a Colonel following marching orders from Moscow.

86

Kang Flight

Hap and LD watched helplessly as the Russian escaped. "What I wouldn't give for a Sidewinder," Hap said.

"Not a damn thing we can do about it now, Hap. How far you taking this chase?"

Hap said nothing, thinking as he nibbled his lower lip.

Hollywood transmitted, "Give me a couple of knots."

"He is turning right, Hap," LD reported.

Hap shook his head. The Russian slowly swung his nose around as if leading the charge of the light brigade.

"Hollywood, hook em left. The son of a bitch is coming back at us."

Hollywood stood the bird onto its rotor disk banking the Cobra to port into a shadowy horizon. "On it, Kang,"

"Going hot on the rockets," LD said, rippling 2.75-inch rockets arching toward the onrushing Russian. In kind, the red tail Hind responded with 2.2-inch rockets and 12.7 mm rounds from the nose gun slewed beneath the gunner's cockpit.

Ping pong-size tracers and rockets raced towards Hap's prominent nose. "Break plane!" he said.

LD pulled aft cyclic and the collective went beneath his armpit propelling the Cobra to climb the ladder allowing the ordnance to streak beneath the skids.

LD had already raised the snout before Hap finished the order bringing the collective into his armpit allowing a streaking line of tracer and rockets to pass beneath the skids. Hollywood continued his climbing turn before laying the bird onto its right side and pulling the nose through the horizon with aft cyclic. Killer engaged immediately, firing down through the Russian's rotor disk from the three o'clock position. The Russian plane, clawing for altitude, broke right seconds later. Hollywood pitched nose-up, giving Killer a few additional degrees to elevate the chain gun. Hap watched Killer's tracers strike pay dirt, scoring multiple hits behind the aft cockpit.

"He's going underneath us," Hap called as the red tail Hind's rotor disc passed below their skids. "Don't lose him!"

"Got it," LD said snap rolling the aircraft onto its side like a whale breaching then pulled the nose through the horizon giving Hollywood room to streak overhead.

"Dropping in the bucket," Hap announced. He didn't have to slew the gun far to get a bead on the red tail Russian; he had him in his sights just seconds after his forehead brushed up against the rubber padding. "Going hot." He squeezed the trigger sending 20mm High Explosive Incendiary down range finding the mark aft of the Hind's transmission punching into the cabin until the twirling barrels expelled smoke. The ammo can half the size of a human casket nestled underneath Hap's armored seat was empty. Smoke trailed from the Hind's number two engine cowling area.

"He's making for the airport, Hap."

"Smart thing to do," Hap replied.

Hollywood settled in on the Russian's red tail to give the coup de grace.

"Let's escort him to the airfield Hollywood," Hap radioed. "There has been enough killing today."

* * *

"Listen up," Hallesleven said standing by the bar. He needed to buy time. "You have done all a soldier can do. Your mission is over." He slowly raised a hand to point at the screen doors. "Leave your weapons and walk through those doors with your hands over your head. Move it!"

Hallesleven sidestepped toward the double screen doors on the back veranda overlooking pristine beaches and beautiful dunes. Nicaragua's senior military commander high stepped down the beachside steps toward the dunes and safety. After dark, it was only a matter of evading and escaping to the airport perimeter using darkness as his cloak

As his left boot touched the bottom step, he went sprawling face-first into the sand. He looked back and, even in the darkening surroundings, recognized the familiar face.

* * *

With the sun below the western horizon and barely able to keep eyelids open Will Kellogg leaned against the rail draped in his own blood. Knowing unconsciousness could be a half a blink away; he attempted to draw his pistol but couldn't feel his fingertips and the 9mm dropped to the sand after clearing the holster. Instinctively, he patted himself with the other hand, attempting to locate a grenade, which would kill both of them.

Hallesleven reached for his pistol as Will fell face-first into unconsciousness. He crawled over on all fours and raised Wills head by the scalp, then whispered in his ear, "The last time we met, you told me something I have never forgotten.

You stated the barrel that fired the bullet into your forehead was so close, the round would splatter the assassin's face." Firmly pressing the barrel against Will's forehead—covered in sand, blood, and sweat—his finger eased to the trigger.

Without firing a shot, Hallesleven dropped back onto his haunches dropping Will's head in the sand. Dazed, Hallesleven slowly reached up to wipe away moisture from his forehead. In the blink of an eye, both eyelids suddenly grew heavy and he had to strain to keep them from sliding shut. Painfully he slowly turned to find Colonel Santiago looking over a smoking barrel. His chin slowly dropped to see blood pouring from the hole in his right breast. Slowly shaking his head, he mumbled, "Why, Charro?" The next round spun him face down next to Will Kellogg.

Nicaragua's Chief of Staff continued pulling the trigger until he felt a hand on his shoulder. The pistol slid from his grip as he slipped into unconsciousness. Franz grabbed the blouse with one hand, placing the other behind his head. He managed the Shadow agent's fall laying Santiago's head gently to the wooden deck. The sound of a helicopter landing on the highway side of the bar was loud. Will Kellogg's commandos appeared around the corner of the bar just as mortar rounds sounded in the distance cratering the runway.

87

Over the skies of Isle de Isle de San Andres

Would the coup de grace come from a burst of 20mm from the Cobra crawling up the Hinds tail or the grinding inside the transmission come apart freezing the four-bladed rotor system?

To Colonel Ivan Ivanovich Smirnoff, either way, it would be a brutal death for him and his crew. As the Hind limped along with no radios leaving trailing a long trail of dark smoke, a kilometer separated the crew from the airport perimeter and friendly troops to provide ground fire.

Smirnoff gritted his teeth with full knowledge the perimeter may as well been 100 kilometers when the wounded crew chief called out, "Yankee aircraft has broken off the attack. Coward waved off to the southeast, Sir."

The aircraft and crew were far from being out of harm's way. "Understood," he said. "Keep eyes on the Yankee bastard." He reached over and dropped the landing gear handle. Absent was the familiar sound of the motor dropping the gear. A quick glance at the breaker panel showed the breaker for the motor on the third row far left had not popped. He quickly reset the breaker and cycled the handle again. No joy, he said to himself. "We lost our landing gear. Strap in and hold on, I'm going to have to use a running landing."

The aircraft began to vibrate as if it would come apart in the air, and Smirnoff could see the runway cleared of the debris from the commuter plane. The runway and taxiways now pocked with holes from well-aimed mortar fire. Shot-up Hoplites, Hips, and Hinds littered the tarmac. The fuel farms three storage tanks continued to throw off clouds of black smoke into a night sky while small fires could be easily seen burning inside the terminal.

Che Guevara's air force was no more.

Surprisingly, none of the Russian crewmen who had manned the aircraft appeared. The heat behind his head intensified, as Smirnoff smacked the aircraft onto the grass in a level attitude. The instant the armored belly touched grass, the gun turret ripped from the airframe, flipping off to the side, and transmission seized. The rotors overhead froze and, amazingly, the aircraft came to a stop rocking up on its nose 15-degrees and then falling back to the ground with a crunching sound.

They exited with flames leaping from both engine compartments helping the wounded crew chief with one of the crew chief's arms around each of the pilot's necks. Smirnoff pointed toward the base of the tower. Palates parched, Smirnoff gestured with his free hand to a group of Sandinistas gathered outside the terminal for water. A figure approached holding out a canteen. Close behind, a half dozen Sandinista soldiers followed. The canteen fell to the tarmac and Smirnoff's pistol cleared the holster as the Sandinista officer screamed "Halt!" and held an arm out like a traffic cop. The soldiers behind him swung AKs into their shoulders.

Smirnoff's copilot drew his Makarov from his right hip allowing the moaning crew chief to fall face first into the concrete. Drawing beads on their target, both Russian's fired sending the Sandinista Captain's to the tarmac from the chest wounds.

The soldier on the right of the line pirouetted in his dance of death spinning crumpling to the concrete. Not quite the firing sequence they had conducted on the other Russians, the Sandinista firing squad dropped to a knee. Five 30-round magazines were emptied into the last of the Russian contingent still alive inside the airfield perimeter.

* * *

Stingray

Doc Perry moved beneath Vultures' Row through his makeshift triage unit, stepping over an empty body bag into a pool of blood dammed up against Will Kellogg's vest and body armor. He knelt next to the operations senior fellow to find the lifeless figure's face pale, skin cool to the touch. His breaths came in short, shallow gasps. "Little help here," Doc P called out.

Doc Bennie slid in beside and the two and pushed Will onto his side to allowing the medical team to unwrap bandages to check entry and exit wounds.

"More wounded inbound," Doc B said, sticking Will with a syrette of morphine.

"That's unfortunate," Doc Perry replied as he rolled Will gently to his back using a stack of grease rags stuffed into a green helmet bag as a pillow. Bennie attached the empty syrette to Will's collar.

"Let's get an IV started and get him inside."

Doc B nodded. "I'm on it." He gestured with a hand over his head. "Need a stretcher—STAT!"

The medic that rode in with BA unfolded a stretcher next to Will's unmoving figure.

Doc P pivoted to the next man, a Sandinista officer with a blood-soaked blouse. A Stingray crewman worked feverishly to cut away the bloodied material.

"This man has a sucking chest wound, get him into surgery."

Larson appeared from around the corner. "Doc, we will be traveling to join Lonibelle in Isle de San Andres Bay. How dicey is the surgery?"

"It's a frigging Sandinista prisoner," he answered in a composed tone. Travel as fast as you want. Why should I care?"

Larson scratched the back of his head. "I just received news this Sandinista is on our side. I'm having him transferred to the hospital in Isle de San Andres City. Somebody has been courteous enough to have surgeons standing by. BA will act as medevac." Larson raised the bill of the baseball cap with an orange Stingray balanced on its tail above his brow.

Doc P gestured with two fingers in a mocking salute.

Buccaneer Casino and Resort

Quiet as a church mouse, Hap eased the door closed to one of Doc Perry's recovery rooms—a Buccaneer penthouse suite. He veered towards the business desk skirting around the 65-inch flat screen fixed above the dresser towing the high back chair through the suite's French doors leaving it next to the king size bed. To the right of the bed's nightstand was a narrow break where the partially open high-end leaked enough sunlight to outline Carla's slender face enjoying a peaceful sleep. Hap tugged the curtain to blot out the light and settled into the chair inches from the bed. After a half hour passed, neither had moved an inch. Hap straightened and leaned over to kiss her forehead and quietly left the room

Hap entered Will's suite through an open door making the left turn into a scene he pictured as General Stonewall Jackson's deathbed. Instead of doctors and generals surrounding the bed, the German clad in his shooting jacket palmed the smoldering bowl of his hand-carved pipe as his cupped hand slid away from Will's white-as-a-ghost cheek. Hap stepped to the foot of the king size bed as Doc Perry leaned past Franz slowly pulling down the sheet, dotted with blood droplets, to his abdomen.

Hap couldn't help but notice the scars from multiple skirmishes, received in all corners of the globe. Doc P placed the stethoscope over Will's heart, cocking his head to the side while listening. He paused, nodded, and then dropped the earpieces around his neck. "This guy has lived an interesting life."

Through the years, Hap had never noticed the scars. Now, there were two new wounds—both bandaged. Franz let out a short grunt but said nothing. Doc's head rolled up to Franz, paused, and then turned down towards Hap. A smile appeared beneath Hap's prominent nose followed by a chuckle.

"Will's chest is a journal," Hap said.

"Each wound its own story," Franz replied.

Hap and Doc shared a quick look, almost asking each other, what does this man know?

"So, you know Will?" Hap asked as Franz stepped to the side and tapped the pipe bowl against the side of a polished metal trash can. After straightening, he nodded. "Met Will for the first time days after he closed on the Buccaneer. His grandfather on his father's side and I were like clones of the other."

Hap's lips pursed. "Funny, Will never mentioned it. "

Doc P stepped back to peruse Will's medical chart.

"He never knew," Franz replied in the form of a statement, tone confident.

"German?" Hap said.

The old German sighed while tucking the pipe inside the lower right pocket of the shooting jacket. Will moaned but continued to lay in morphine laced sleep.

"He was," Franz said nodding slowly. "He died in Vietnam at a small outpost called Dein Bien Phu fighting with the French Foreign Legion. He parachuted in after they surrounded the outpost. Hell of a man."

Doc stepped between the two and softly clamped Will's wrist between thumb and forefinger to check his pulse. Satisfied, he stepped back. "Touch and go but suspect this tough son of a bitch is too ornery to die. If you would excuse me, need to continue with my rounds." He dropped the stethoscope assembly into the side pocket of his blood-stained lab coat. Hap reached out and grabbed his arm.

"JMan?"

Doc looked at Hap and smiled. "He is young, Hap. Thought we lost him, but Doc B brought him back." He turned to Franz. "We should have Colonel Santiago fit to leave the island in a couple of days." Doc wacked Hap's shoulder in passing and acknowledged the German with a curt nod exiting the room.

Silence followed for what seemed to be an eternity but no more than thirty seconds when Hap looked up at the Baron, "We saved a lot of lives today."

The German nodded slowly as a wily smile appeared across his pointed face. "The world needs good deeds, Mr. Stoner."

Hap paused. "Isn't that what the UN is for?"

The Baron continued to smile casually stuffing the bowel of his pipe with tobacco holding it up like it were a peace pipe. "Brazilian, would you like a bowl?"

Hap shook his head as the German flipped open a Zippo lighter and drew the flame into the bowl. Satisfied, he exhaled and returned the lighter to a coat pocket.

"The UN is man's endeavor to feel good doing little to stop all the wrong in this world. On the other hand, my brother and I were on the wrong side in an earlier life. He is dead, but while I still walk on this life it's time to right as many wrongs of man as possible."

"Is that why you brought Colonel Santiago into Shadow Operations?"

Franz narrow lips pursed. "Mr. Stoner. General Hallesleven executed his family. Santiago was a mere child when he watched the rape and murder of his parents and siblings. How we met is not important. What is important is the information he passed to the organization."

The entire scene became clear. Hap was standing next to the puppeteer who orchestrated the defense of Isle de San Andres. "Why didn't you reach out to the Columbians when you knew the Sandinista was going to invade? I'm sure Ortega would have backed down to remain in power."

A glint of a smile appeared on the German's face. "That would have been too easy Mr. Stoner. The Columbian government is not capable of providing what I need."

Hap shook his head back and forth as both eyebrows arched to the ceiling. "I don't get it."

"Neither did Will."

"Then why go through the trouble?" Hap was realizing he and Will were part of a greater plan.

"You will know when it's time for you to know Mr. Stoner. Even Blad does not know the full detail of my plan."

Hap's eyes narrowed, his jaw drew taut. "A man could die doing what I think you want to do."

"Why do you think I brought you and Will Kellogg here?"

Hap's eyes cut back to the German.

"Would you doubt me, Mr. Stoner?" Franz said as his face reddened. "Never...ever doubt me, Mr. Stoner. You don't know me, but rest assured I know you and Will Kellogg."

Hap followed up his shrug with a nod. "So, why us?"

"For me, it's simple, Will Kellogg came to your assistance when you needed him and, in return, you did the same. Both of you put your life on the line for the other."

"You didn't answer my question."

Franz pressed his lips together as he leaned into Hap. "With so much need in this world and so many politicians that can't look beyond the end of their nose, humanity needs a white knight."

"You mean a white knight like the former U.S. President lining his pockets with monies earmarked to avert human misery."

Franz smiled. "President Williams and his wife Jessica are part of the problem, not the solution. I have so much to make up for, but I am an old man now. On the other hand, you, Blad, and Will Kellogg have the energy and the wherewithal to right my wrongs made earlier in life."

Hap nibbled his lower lip thinking of his and Carla's argument when she stormed out of their living room. Women's intuition. With an empty feeling in his stomach, he looked back into the German's piercing gaze.

The Baron nodded and returned a polite smile. "The question in your eyes will be answered over the next several months. As I look ahead and the end draws closer, there is something I can't do without, the likes of Will Kellogg and people like you. Blad recommended you three years earlier."

Will gingerly rolled to his good side, a smile spread from one cheek to the other, still out cold.

"I will be Chairman until death or declared mentally incompetent. That would be, as you Marines would call, rules of engagement. Spanish Main Holdings, Shadow Operations, and von Bock industries are the vehicles for a little bit a peace in this world."

Hap's eyebrows could have raised all the way to the ceiling of the suite, but one thing was certain, he had more questions than answers. The former German agent had plans for them, but what would these plans lead to? *Will I tell Carla? Should I tell her?* "This would take cash!"

"You mean my net worth?' the Baron said with a slight chuckle. " My boy, individually I will have more wealth at my fingertips than the top-five families in the United States... combined."

Will's eyes fluttered to life and he did something rarely seen—he laughed aloud. As soon as he finished, he gave out a long yawn and fell back to sleep.

The Baron's demeanor remained stoic. "Let me suggest you get things straight with the young lady."

Hap allowed a crooked grin to materialize.

"And what is with the grin, Mr. Stoner?"

Hap swept a boot across the tile floor and eyes went to ground. He shook his head and walked slowly to the door. *And to think my fingers were crossed behind my back when I promised her this mission would be my last.*

It was as if the Baron had the ability to read minds. His face didn't flinch as he asked the million dollar question. "And what did it get you?"

Hap had opened the door to leave, stopped, turned while pushing his shoulders back. "It gave me a friend's life back while costing another friend his." Franz von Bock (The Baron) said nothing, only nodded. The fate of Hap Stoner and Will Kellogg were already sealed.

Semper Fi!

About the Author

Hugh Simpson has worked for over 25 years in the Telecommunications Industry and Family Law Firm. Prior to entering the Telecommunications Industry, he served in the U.S. Marine Corps retiring as a LtCol serving in 3 overseas deployments including Operation Desert Shield/Storm. He lives in Richardson, Texas.

After 33 years of writing stories in the closet, *Borderline Decision* was the first in the Hap Stoner series to be published and now, *Caribbean Cabal* is the second.

To learn more about 3Span Publication and Hugh's writing career, visit his website at 3SpanPublications.com.

Made in the USA
Coppell, TX
04 December 2019

12343672R00273